Murder at Sea

Gregor barely knew the difference between an Uzi and a Colt .45, but he did know poisons. Strychnine wasn't even a very difficult poison to detect. The convulsions, the rigor, the look of shock on the face, the strange, leaping St. Vitus' dance of agony—there was nothing in the world like it. He had probably been dead before Gregor or Tony ever saw him. In a more superstitious age, the assembled company would have taken one look at what was happening in the bow and started looking around for a witch.

Gregor held on ever more tightly. The one thing he had no intention of doing was letting this corpse out of his custody until he got it safely into a cabin.

"Let's get him out of the rain," Gregor said. "Then I think we'd better all sit somewhere and talk."

Feast
of Murder

Jane Haddam

BANTAM BOOKS
NEW YORK · TORONTO · LONDON · SYDNEY · AUCKLAND

FEAST OF MURDER

A Bantam Book / November 1992

ISBN 0-553-29389-3

Published simultaneously in the United States and Canada

Bantam Books are published by Bantam Books, a division of Bantam Doubleday
Dell Publishing Group, Inc. Its trademark, consisting of the words "Bantam
Books" and the portrayal of a rooster, is Registered in U.S. Patent and Trademark
Office and in other countries. Marca Registrada. Bantam Books, 1540 Broadway,
New York, New York 10036.

PRINTED IN THE UNITED STATES OF AMERICA

RAD   0 9 8 7 6 5 4

Feast of Murder

Prologue

The Death of Donald McAdam

1

It was twilight of a day at the end of August, one of those times when light and dark wrap themselves around each other like tresses in a braid. For Donald McAdam, standing on the corner of Fiftieth and Park, waiting for the light to change so he could go uptown, it was—oddly enough—the best hour of the best day of the best year he had ever had. The oddness came from the kind of year it had been, full of judges and grand juries, subpoenas and district attorneys. Not much more than a year ago, Donald McAdam had been nothing but another Wall Street suit. He'd had an office downtown and this apartment uptown and small branches in Philadelphia and Boston. He'd had a closet full of J. Press suits and a shoe rack full of custom productions from John Lobb and five Rolex watches. When he got his name in the papers it was always in Liz Smith's column, as the faceless escort of some aging society queen who had just underwritten the Peppermint and Wintergreen Ball for the American Multiple Cancer Homeless Advocacy Association.

The light changed and McAdam crossed the street, moving carefully, catering to his only real fear. That his fear was real was evidenced by how much it made him forget.

Here he was moving into the intersection, and for the first time since he had run into Fritzie Baird downtown, he could not feel the heavy weight of the mason jar in his pocket. The mason jar was full of something called melon rind marmalade, made by Fritzie herself with her precious postdebutante hands. McAdam hadn't known what to do with it when she thrust it into his hands, so he'd simply stuffed it into his jacket, not bothering to worry about the bulge. Now he didn't worry about it because he'd forgotten it. From the day he had first come to New York City, forty years ago, he had been secretly convinced that he was going to die by being struck by a car. In the years since, he'd developed a positive genius for arriving at intersections seconds after they became accident scenes. He couldn't count the number of times he'd put his feet into puddles of blood. He couldn't count the number of times he'd gone home to be sick about it, either. Today nothing like that seemed to be happening. There was no danger. He thought he could relax. He didn't even have anyone else on the street to worry about. The street was empty.

Getting to the opposite curb, he began to move quickly, swinging his arms a little as he went. He was, he knew, the perfect picture of Park Avenue, a silver-haired man in expensive clothes exuding an air of confidence and command. He had been just the same thing a year ago, but then, if someone had spotted him, he wouldn't have been recognized. Now he still wouldn't have been recognized, most places—tract house mothers in Levittown and black boys with ghetto blasters in Central Park didn't read the financial news—but on this street and among the people who lived here, he was famous. He was Donald McAdam, the man who had paid the Feds a $400 million fine and still been left with enough money to live the life. He was Donald Mc-Adam, the man who had gone wired into clandestine business meetings in three states. He was Donald McAdam, who might not have been the most successful man of his generation or the most socially prominent one—but who was going to be the one who sent the rest of them to jail.

He had managed to cross Fifty-first Street without incident. He had only two more blocks to go before he reached his apartment. He picked up his pace, bouncing a little on the balls of his feet. It had been a bad August, hot and still and thick with humidity, but over the last few days it had been getting better. Now there was a breeze coming in from the river. Every time McAdam got to an intersection, he could feel it pressing against the trousers of his suit. Above him, what he could see of the sky was pink and black. Around him, the streetlights had just begun to glow.

He got to Fifty-second Street just as the walk light went green. He crossed and made his way to Fifty-third. On Park Avenue, it was easy to imagine that New York was a normal city. There were trees in the divider in the middle of the street and flowers in the boxes next to the front doors of the apartment buildings. The doormen were all in uniform and about as alert as sleeping puppies. While McAdam waited for the last of his lights, he saw a woman coming out of the apartment house directly across the avenue from his own. She was an older woman in a longish dress and pearl earrings, much too unfashionable to be one of the older women he knew. Still, McAdam thought, she might be someone who would recognize him. She might turn toward him and look up and start, as if she'd heard a shot. She might even come up to him and try to start a conversation, the way so very many of them wanted to do. Instead, she turned in the opposite direction and began to go swiftly uptown, a woman with a mission.

The light changed and McAdam crossed, looking both ways twice, trying to understand the mentality of people who left work at noon on Fridays in the summer. McAdam had always been a man obsessed with work and obsessed with image, the only two things that seemed to him to have any real effect on a life. To leave work to take Mrs. Halstead Vandergriff to a benefit—or to spend the weekend at Mrs. Charles Inglesman's country place in Cornwell Bridge— that was one thing. To leave work to have a few extra hours to spend in a hovel of a beach house out on Long Island Sound was beyond him. And yet people did do it. They did it all the time. That was why the city was so deserted at times like this.

McAdam walked the half block up to his apartment building, waited patiently—and with a smile on his face— while a doorman he didn't know opened up for him, and headed for the elevators. He would never have admitted it to anyone, even to himself, but deserted places always made him terrified. Even his apartment, devoid of any humanity besides himself, was intolerable to him. He called for an elevator, watched a set of doors bounce open in front of him with no delay at all, and stepped inside the car. The car had thick pile carpeting on the floor and walls inlaid with colored glass. He ought to calm down now, he told himself. He ought to get his mind organized and concentrate on the future, in spite of the fact that the future held a lot more trials and a lot more depositions. It also held a lot more money, and money was something he and everybody else he knew always seemed to need.

The elevator got to the penthouse floor. McAdam took out the tiny key that would make the elevators open here and used it. The elevator doors opened directly into his foyer and he stepped out. Quiet, quiet, he thought. Then he reached into his inside jacket pocket and came out with a small manila envelope. He felt the hard side of the mason jar bumping against his hip and took that out, too, putting it down on the occasional table. Then he picked the mason jar up again. Maybe he would eat some of this melon rind marmalade. Maybe it would be interesting. He felt himself start to giggle and suppressed it. Quiet, he thought again. Quiet, quiet, quiet. He turned and sent the elevator back downstairs, to all the ordinary mortals who had to get to their apartments through empty corridors and endless halls.

"Quiet, quiet, quiet," McAdam said aloud, and then started to laugh.

A year and a half ago, when the Feds had first approached him with their deal, Donald McAdam had done a few quick calculations. If he played it wrong, he would lose everything. If he played it right, he could save a little or a lot, depending. What he could not do was save it all. If nothing else, the business would have to go. McAdam Investments— a public company by then, with stock quoted on the American Exchange—would have to crash and disintegrate in the glare of scandals and revelations, like Drexel Burnham Lambert before it.

Except it hadn't.

It hadn't.

And now—

The manila envelope was still in his hand. McAdam put it down on his occasional table and turned it over and turned it over again. He picked it up and put it down again. Finally, he picked it up and carried it with him into his living room with the wall of windows looking uptown.

Quiet, he told himself again.

And then he started to laugh for real, hard and gasping, because it was so funny.

2

For Jonathan Edgewick Baird, the real problem with being in prison was not the stigma—in his case, there wasn't much of that—but the casual assumptions of half of everybody he knew that because he was in prison, he couldn't also be in the office. Of course, in some ways that was true.

Sixteen months ago, he had pleaded guilty in federal court to three counts of insider trading. Fourteen months ago, he had been remanded to the Federal Correctional Institution at Danbury. Since then, his official residence had been a small square room with bars making up one wall and a peculiar hard-plastic covering on the floor. Even so, he was neither down nor out. He had founded Baird Financial Services thirty-two years ago. He had run it ever since. He was running it now, in spite of the fact that his partners—his younger brother Calvin and good old Charlie Shay—were down there in Manhattan on the scene, supposedly making decisions. Like a Mafia don with the unfortunate luck to have landed in Sing Sing, he was ruling his empire from inside.

Actually, there was nothing Sing Sing–like about it. Danbury wasn't the poshest of country club prisons— Allenwood was that—but it came close. The inmates were all financial types, with a couple of spies thrown in. Newspapers and magazines were delivered to the mailroom every morning. In the evenings, the cell blocks looked like enforced reading rooms for Yuppies. Behind the bars, men in prison uniforms pored through the fine print of *Barron's* and *Forbes*, the *New York Times* and the *Wall Street Journal*. They did deals, too. Almost everybody here had phone and library privileges. Almost everybody here was operating a business or doing a deal or running a scam. Sometimes, listening to the hum that rose and fell around him, day and night without surcease, Jon thought he had not been sent to prison as much as to a form of Business Purgatory. That was one of the reasons why he had been so diligent at his shipbuilding from the day he got here. Shipbuilding was what Jon Baird did for a hobby—building ships in bottles, to be precise. He'd done two since coming to Danbury, including the one he had finished today, sitting proudly on top of his filing cabinet. It was not as good as it could have been, because the bottle he had used was made out of shatter-proof glass, the only kind of bottle the prison authorities would allow him to have. It didn't matter. It was better than contemplating his sins.

Tonight, Jon was contemplating his roommate, a too-youngish man in his forties named Bobby Hannaford. It had been a long and stressful day, just as long and stressful as any he had ever spent in the Baird Financial offices in the World Trade Center. Like many of the prisoners here, he had almost unlimited visiting privileges. He had seen a stream of people, each and every one of whom had seemed dedicated to giving him a headache. Calvin, Donald Mc-Adam, Courtney his temporary secretary, Charlie Shay: coming on top of yesterday, when Jon had seen his ex-wife Fritzie, it had almost been too much. He was beginning to get on in life now. He was sixty-two.

He lay on his bunk, a barrel-chested, bandy-legged little man who looked vaguely like a cross between Hemingway and Benjamin Franklin, and considered Bobby's greying head. Bobby's greying head was bobbing up and down, back and forth as he paced from one end of the cell to the other. It wasn't much of a stretch, but Jon knew from experience that it suited remarkably well. Bobby kept running his hands through his hair and swiping the backs of them across his lips. Jon thought he must have looked much the same way, when he'd first been caught doing whatever he had done with Donald McAdam.

"I've thought about it and thought about it," he was saying, "and the only way I can justify what you've done is to think you've got some kind of plan in mind. Some kind of trick. You're supposed to be a financial genius. You could have something up your sleeve."

"I could," Jon said. Then he stared at the ceiling and sighed. His meeting with Donald McAdam had been held behind closed doors, in the secluded room provided for matters of "confidentiality." So had all his other meetings, both today and yesterday. Word had gotten out all the same. It always did.

Bobby was standing just above him now, looming. "You could," he repeated. "Does that mean you *do*?"

"No."

"But how could you? How could you? This is Donald McAdam we're talking about. The man who put me in here. The man who put you in here. The man who put half of Danbury in Danbury and half of Allenwood in Allenwood. And he's sitting in that damned apartment in New York, ordering out for caviar."

Could you order out for caviar? Jon supposed you could. He'd never tried. He sat up and sighed again.

"Bobby, listen to me," he said, "I don't like Donald McAdam any more than you do—although it isn't true, you know, he isn't responsible for putting me here—but the thing is, I have no choice. Baird Financial owns McAdam Investments. McAdam Investments is sitting on a pile of assets no one will touch as long as McAdam has anything to do with them—"

"I heard that," Bobby said. "I hope it's true."

"Oh, it's true enough," Jon said drily. "Even the middle management drones at the banks don't want anything to do with our Donald. I don't suppose I blame them."

"I want to applaud them," Bobby said.

"If you're going to applaud them, you can hardly castigate me." Jon swung his legs over to the side of the bunk. "I have to get rid of him. The only way I can get rid of him is to buy out his contract. I'm buying out his contract."

"If this was a different kind of prison, you could get rid of him in better ways than that. And it would cost you less money."

"With my luck at crime, it would cost me twenty to life in Attica and Attica is not like here. Hand me my tooth mug, will you? I broke another bridge last night and my gums ache."

"*Another* bridge?"

"The same bridge," Jon admitted. "And that was my spare, of course, Charlie brought it in for me yesterday, we talked about that. Now I'll have to wait until my dentist makes up another."

"Twice in one week," Bobby said. "You couldn't do better if you were cracking them with hammers."

Jon took the mug Bobby handed him, swirled the salted water in it through his mouth, and put the mug down on the floor. Bobby had stopped pacing, but he hadn't stopped moving. He fidgeted and bopped like an overexcited four-year-old. Jon wondered what kind of man Bobby had been to do business with—all that bobbing and weaving, all that childishness and neurosis. Jon had made it a point in his life to deal only with grown-ups, but other people didn't. From everything he'd heard, Bobby had been a successful man. Jon just couldn't imagine at what.

He got up, took his tooth mug back to the sink, and left it on the rim. He didn't want to rinse it out, because it would take the devil's own time to get a replacement for the warm salt water. He made sure it was steady on the porcelain and went back to his bunk, wandering in and around Bobby on the way. Bobby had gone back to pacing.

"Listen," he said, to Bobby's jiggling back, "let's talk about something more pleasant. You know I'm getting out on October first?"

"I'd heard that, yes. Is it certain? The parole people have agreed?"

"It's not parole. It's the end of my sentence. Anyway, I have this boat, replica of the *Mayflower*. I don't know if you've read about it in the magazines—"

"I have read about it. Everybody's read about it."

"Yes, well. I'm giving a combined Thanksgiving-dinner,

welcome-home-to-myself party there. I mean at sea. I've had Courtney out here half the afternoon, working out the details—"

"I thought you were working out the details of the McAdam thing."

Jon waved it away. "There are no details to the McAdam thing. Write a check. Sign a paper. It's over. Getting to sea in a replica of the *Mayflower* is a lot more complicated. I've always wanted to do it. Journey around for a while. Land someplace. Use all the original cooking methods and the authentic utensils. It's what I dream about when other men dream about girls."

Bobby had finally stopped moving. "If you're inviting me along for the ride," he said, "I'll have to decline. I don't get out of here for another five years."

"I'm asking you for a favor, Bobby. I need an introduction to someone you know."

"Who could I possibly know that you don't know?"

Jon thought he could list a host of such people, including wheeler-dealers and con men and financial smoke artists of every description. Jon liked Bobby, but Bobby was naturally bent, and like all the rest of the naturally bent he attracted members of his tribe to his side. Jon didn't want to hurt Bobby's feelings, so he didn't say any of that. He also really needed a favor.

"If I've got my facts straight," he said slowly, "and I might not. I got them from *People* magazine. Anyway, if I've got my facts straight, you have a sister named Bennis Day Hannaford."

"That's right. She writes fantasy novels. You know, knights and ladies and unicorns and magic trolls. They do really well, I think. Do you want her to go in on some kind of deal?" Bobby looked confused.

"No, no," Jon reassured him. "It's just that I think she might be the means for you to help me with something, if you want to help. I want to get in contact with a man named Gregor Demarkian."

"What?" This time Bobby really stopped still, stopped dead. Then he started to grin. "You do have something up your sleeve. You are pulling some kind of trick. You're going to get Donald McAdam."

Jonathan Edgewick Baird was emphatic. "I'm going to do nothing of the kind."

3

Sheila Callahan Baird had worked long and hard to become a trophy wife, but when that job turned out to have unexpected difficulties, she decided to put up with them. God only knew, there were other things she could do. She had a degree in history from Smith. She had her own interior decorating business with offices and showrooms on Madison Avenue. She even had her own private interest income, just like a real tycoon. Of course, the degree from Smith was twelve years old and hadn't been much use to her even when she'd first gotten it. The interior decorating business wasn't doing very well, either. If Jon hadn't been bankrolling it, it would have been bankrupt months ago. As for the private interest income—Sheila didn't like thinking about the private interest income at all. It was, in fact, the income on a sum of money in trust, and that trust was "revocable." The word had confused her at first, but she'd figured it out soon enough. It meant that if Jon wanted to, he could take it back.

Now it was seven o'clock on the last day of August, and she was sitting in front of the mirror in her dressing room, trying to decide if Desert Pink foundation would be too light for a ball at the Metropolitan Museum. Behind her, a hall lined with walk-in closets held the endless parade of dresses, shirts, shoes, slacks, ball gowns, caftans, sweaters, and whatever else that sometimes seemed to her to be the theme of her marriage. Imelda Marcos collected shoes, and Sheila collected the rest of the wardrobe. She collected everything else, too. The chair she was sitting on was a French vanity seat that had once belonged to Marie Antoinette. It had cost $30,000 at auction at Sotheby's. The table she had spread her makeup across was a Viennese occasional that had once belonged to a Hapsburg. She had picked it up for $42,000 on the Avenue Foch. The dress she was wearing was a custom Dior, strapless and backless, satin and velvet, $12,568. The diamond earrings in her ears were six carats each and flawless. Jon had bought them for her, but she had made sure to check them out. They had literally cost millions. If a trophy wife was a wife to hang trophies on, Sheila Callahan had definitely reached her goal.

She decided against Desert Pink foundation and picked up the Night Blush instead. She applied a little to her right cheek, squinted at it, and frowned. Then she turned to the pale-faced woman sitting on the ottoman next to her and said: "The problem with all this nonsense about business is that nobody minds their own. I mean, this thing with Donald McAdam. It only happened today. I only heard about it because Calvin came by to talk to me last night—to warn me, he said, and he was right. Everybody knows about it already. Everybody calls me about it. I don't know what it is they think I'm supposed to do."

The pale woman on the ottoman was named Lydia Boynton, and as far as Sheila knew, she wasn't anyone in particular. She was, in fact, a *first* wife, the daughter of one rich man and the divorced wife of another. In her grass widowhood, Lydia had set up shop as a "social image adviser," meaning as one of those women who sell their connections to the inner circles of debutante balls and benefit committees to the climbers coming up. Sheila had hired her because she was bored. With Jon away for over a year, getting social seemed to be the only thing left in the universe to do.

Lydia was dressed in a long satin gown that looked exactly like a shirtwaist. Sheila wondered how long it would be before she could fire the woman and go it on her own. As long as it took Jon to get out, she supposed. With Jon back in circulation, Sheila would get invited to everything as a matter of course.

"What makes it all worse," she went on, abandoning the foundation for the mascara. For a ball this big, she should have hired a makeup artist. They charged $3,000 to do your face, but it was worth it. "What makes it worse," she repeated, "is that I'm in the middle of all this mess. I mean, Jon's getting out on the first of October. I have to plan for that. Then there's this party he wants to throw. Did I tell you about this party he wants to throw?"

"I don't know," Lydia said doubtfully. "You told me about Thanksgiving dinner. On his boat."

"It's not just a boat," Sheila said impatiently. She glared at the mascara, looking fake in the hard lights that surrounded her mirror. "It's an exact replica of the *Mayflower*. No motor. No bathroom in the ordinary sense. He wants to get the whole family on it—including Fritzie, by the way, and Charlie Shay—and sail it up to Massachusetts someplace and land on this island. I think he may own the island."

"Isn't Fritzie his first wife?" Lydia asked. "Could he get her to agree to that? Could he get you to agree to it?"

"He could get us both to agree to anything," Sheila said. "All those trusts he set up are reversible any time he wants to reverse them. And Fritzie's got an old family name, but she's stone broke on her own and she's much too old for anyone to want to marry her. I mean, she must be forty-five."

Lydia Boynton coughed.

"Anyway," Sheila said, "I'm having the headache of my life setting up for Thanksgiving, and then this thing comes along with Donald McAdam. Could you please tell me what I'm supposed to know about Donald McAdam? Except that he's a crook, of course. That was in all the papers."

"Well," Lydia said, "the fact is, he is a crook, but he tattletold on all the other crooks, and the other crooks went to jail and he didn't. I'm sorry to sound like a kindergarten teacher, dear, but it's really that simple. The people who have been calling you have probably been—hurt by Mr. McAdam. As you have too, of course."

"I have? Why?"

"Because it was Donald McAdam who put your husband in prison," Lydia said. "At least, that's who I understood it was. Without Mr. McAdam's testimony, your husband wouldn't be in jail."

There were twenty-two shades of eye shadow in the makeup tray at her elbow, six with glitter in them. Sheila passed over the glittery ones and settled on a deep rose, thinking all the time. What Lydia said didn't sound right, although she couldn't put her finger on why not. There was something about there not being a trial, and something else about some securities in a safe deposit box—the particulars of Jon's case always confused her. In the end, he had simply pleaded guilty, or guilty to a lesser charge, and that had been that. She couldn't remember anything at all about Donald McAdam.

"I still don't get the point," she said to Lydia. "So Donald McAdam belongs in jail and he isn't there. Go complain to the district attorney."

"Mr. McAdam has immunity," Lydia said. "There's nothing you can do about that. And it's not the same thing as paying him twelve and a half million dollars."

"Is that what the company is paying him? Twelve and a half million dollars?"

"That's what I heard, yes. That's what it takes to buy out his contract. Some people do feel that paying him that money is—rewarding him for being a traitor."

"Twelve and a half million dollars," Sheila said again. "That really is remarkable. But you're wrong, you know, Lydia. He couldn't have been responsible for Jon's going to jail. If he had been, Jon would have done anything before he paid him any money. He'd have killed him first."

"A lot of people wish they had," Lydia said.

"If they really wanted to they would have," Sheila said confidently. "Isn't he one of those people who takes strychnine? I heard he was."

"What do you mean, one of those people who takes strychnine? How can you 'take' strychnine? It's a poison."

"I know. But it's gotten to be a big thing the last two or three years. People mix a very little bit of it with their drug of choice—you know, cocaine, or downers or whatever—or else they do it with baking soda. Then they snort it up in lines. I think the danger is half the point. If you make a mistake, you end up dead. But they do it."

"Dear God," Lydia said.

"All you'd have to do is slip him a little extra at a party or something," Sheila said. "Make him a present of some cocaine if he takes that and have the cocaine stuffed full. I mean, everybody knows his habits. The police would just think it was his own damn fault."

"Mmm," Lydia said, and looked pale.

Sheila decided that her face looked just fine and that she would have to live with it. Since she had excellent genes for both bone structure and wrinkling, it would have looked fine without any makeup at all. She picked up her gold-link minaudière—$72,500 at Tiffany's—checked to make sure it held a lipstick, a fold-up comb, and a hundred-dollar bill, and stood up. The Dior ball gown was perfect for her, obviously expensive but not at all conservative. Her arm needed a bracelet and she got the one that matched the earrings. Then she let herself feel just a little guilty that she had all this real jewelry in her apartment. She knew she wasn't supposed to wear real jewelry. She was supposed to have it copied and wear the fakes. Sheila had never been able to see the point.

"Well," she said, "I'll tell you what I think. I think it would be a good thing if somebody did slip Mr. McAdam a little something. He's ruining my life. Missy Berringer was so upset, she disinvited me to her birthday party."

"I thought you'd decided not to go to Missy Berringer's birthday party."

"I had. But I hadn't told her that. I was waiting until the last minute. Now she gets the points and I get the shaft. It isn't fair. Are you coming, Lydia?"

"Of course I'm coming," Lydia said.

"Good," Sheila told her. "Eight o'clock is incredibly hick for a dinner party, but it is the Metropolitan Museum, and there's nothing we can do. Maybe Mr. McAdam will be there and I can kill him."

"Mmmm," Lydia Boynton said.

Sheila swept out past her, never looking back. Really, with Jon coming home, it would be all to the good to get rid of Lydia. It would be so damn nice not to have to cater to a woman who was shocked by everything she said. As for Mr. McAdam, she decided to add him to the list of people she prayed hard for the deaths of, the list that included her mother, her stepfather, and the boy who had thrown her over for Monica Jess in the third grade.

At the top of that list was her husband, Jon Baird.

4

Anthony Derwent Baird was usually known as Tony, and he didn't want Donald McAdam to die as much as he wanted him to disappear. *Disappear* was probably the wrong word for it, too. Cease to exist. Never have existed. Become real only on an existential plane. Tony kept thinking there had to be something that would cover it. He just couldn't seem to find it. He kept thinking there had to be some way to fix it, too. In his saner moments, he knew that was impossible.

It was now seven o'clock on the last day of August and not one of his saner moments. Tony was sitting in a back booth at the Grubb Clubb, under a tangle of wires and pipes and raw insulation in a corner just far enough away from the noise to make conversation feasible. The noise was coming from a rap-and-thunder group called Heckler Dick, which was as local as you could get in Manhattan and also very bad. The conversation was coming from Mickey Kendrick, who had been Tony's roommate at St. Paul's and suitemate at Yale and who was wearing a suit. Tony himself was stretched out along the bench shoved up against the back wall, a tall lanky man in jeans and a black chambray work shirt. Tony took after his mother's family, and people often said he looked nothing at all like his father. It wasn't true. He had Jon Baird's eyes, right down to the glint at the center of them that told anyone with any sense at all that this was not a man to mess with.

"So," Mickey was saying, "why don't we go about this rationally? Why don't we start from the beginning and go through the middle and get to the end. Maybe that way I'll understand what you're talking about."

Tony Baird took a sip of his beer and sighed. Mickey was such a straightforward person, such a natural straight. He always did exactly the right thing at exactly the right time for exactly the right people, never even considering the possibility that the wrong thing might be more interesting. Even Mickey's rebellions had been straight. He'd known he was supposed to have them. He had therefore had them, getting dutifully drunk in Concord and stoned in New Haven and laid enough times to catch crabs in New York. Now he was making his way cheerfully up the ladder at Kidder, Peabody and looking for a girl who had come out at the Grosvenor. He was only twenty-two years old, but in Tony's estimation he might as well have been dead.

Tony had run his life in a very different fashion. He had been reasonably circumspect in prep school—although less circumspect than Mickey; a rabbit could have been that— but once he'd gotten to New Haven he'd started making a serious run at getting a little broadened experience. Now he was twenty-five years old, the owner of the most outrageous performance art gallery in Soho, and the next best thing to a celebrity in the world of New York art. He had spoken at a rally organized to defend the National Endowment for the Arts from Jesse Helms. He had been interviewed in *Interview* magazine. He had gone to bed with women without number, all of whom seemed to be named some variation of "Viveca." He was also bored out of his skull and thinking of chucking it all right after Christmas, but that was beside the point.

He took another sip on his beer, considered Mickey's proposal, and said, "I can't do it that way, because it won't work that way. I mean, if it wasn't for the twelve and a half million dollars, it wouldn't be anything at all."

"Well," Mickey told him, "I'll agree that twelve and a half million dollars does tend to make something out of nothing if it wants to, but that's not your end of it, is it? I mean, you have nothing to do with the twelve and a half million dollars, do you? Assuming the twelve and a half million dollars exists."

"Oh, it exists all right. Dad told me about it last time I was up to see him at Danbury. Two weeks ago. I thought it was going to happen right away."

"Maybe your Dad had second thoughts," Mickey said. "Paying off Donald McAdam. Yuck."

"Yuck on every possible level," Tony said. "The guy's a sleaze, let me tell you. I mean, not a sleaze sleaze. Not like one of those Arabian bankers that turned out to be running the BCCI scam and I kept telling Dad about and he wouldn't listen to me—"

"Did he ever?" Mickey was curious. "I mean, when BCCI broke did you go to him and say I told you so and did he admit—"

"Yeah," Tony said. "Dad's good with that. No ego in the ordinary sense and credit where credit's due. But McAdam." Tony shrugged. "You can feel it. Bent."

"Bent," Mickey repeated. "But he was a friend of your father's, so—"

"I thought he was a friend of my father's," Tony said, "at the time, which was about a year and a half ago, maybe a little more. Before anyone knew he was talking to the Feds. He was still commuting back and forth to Philadelphia, or at least he said he was, and that was why he needed the stuff."

"Strychnine," Mickey said solemnly.

"Cocaine with strychnine in it," Tony said. "Do you remember when people used to do that? You don't hang around here very much. Maybe you don't. Cissy Esterhaven bought it right in the middle of the dance floor at The Hang Out. Just started jerking around like she'd been electrocuted and ended up dead on the floor. It wasn't a fad that lasted long, do you know what I mean? Too many people ended up dead."

"I took cocaine once," Mickey said. "It gave me a headache."

"I took cocaine once, too. Exactly once. I took everything exactly once. I thought I was being smart. Then Len Bias died." Tony shrugged again and looked back up into the tangle of pipes. The problem with going out to cram your life full of experiences was that it was like going out to cram your mouth full of chocolate. After a while it began to seem pointless. It didn't even taste good. He held his bottle of beer up to the light and saw that it was empty. He thought about ordering another one and decided against it. Maybe after Mickey was finished nursing his whiskey sour they could go uptown and find a bar that was lighter and airier and full of more expensive people.

"Anyway," Tony said, "he shows up at my apartment door one morning at eight o'clock, Thursday morning, I had Cheka Lee doing nude art with tempera and poster board in the gallery the night before and I was washed. He comes in, he explains who he is, he says he wants to ask me a favor. I tell him I have to hit the john. I get up, lock myself in there and make a phone call. You know I've got a phone in the bathroom?"

"You've got a phone in the pantry. Who did you call?"

"Uncle Calvin. Under more normal circumstances I would have called Dad, but like I said, this was about eighteen, twenty months ago. Just around the time the indictments came down. Dad was in Washington or somewhere with the lawyers. I should have waited until I could get in touch with him. Uncle Calvin. For God's sake."

"I dated one of your uncle Calvin's stepdaughters once. Delia Ransom. You know her?"

"She's a fish. Back to the subject. You can imagine what Uncle Calvin was like. All he wanted to do was give me a lecture about whether Dad had or hadn't committed the violations in the indictment, and I didn't want to talk about that. Dad and I had already talked about that. So when I finally got Uncle Calvin to the subject of Donald McAdam, he was pissed at me. He came off like one of those guys who's afraid to write a job recommendation because anything they say they can be sued for. If you know what I mean."

"Yeah."

"Yeah. What McAdam wanted was, like I told you, cocaine with strychnine in it. The fad for that was over, really, but the stuff could be had, except that I didn't have it. You know how I feel. Do all the drugs you want, just keep the damned stuff out of my life. And especially real nuthouse shit like that strychnine business. There's a limit even to my tolerance. But there he was, and I wanted to get rid of him, so I gave him a name, an address, and a telephone number."

"The name, address, and telephone number of a place where he could get what he wanted," Mickey said helpfully.

Tony laughed. "I sent him to Ashaki Madumbra. You've heard about good old Ash. He can get you cocaine. He can get you women. He can get you a Stealth Bomber and someone to fly it."

"So did McAdam go?"

"He must have," Tony said, "because of what happened today. At the time, I had no idea. He left my apartment. I went back to my life. Dad decided to plead guilty. I drank too much for three weeks because it was so totally unnecessary and I was so totally pissed off. And that was that."

"Until today," Mickey said solemnly.

"Until today," Tony agreed. "Today, there I am again, asleep on my couch again, except I'm recovering from the performance of a woman who shoots Ping-Pong balls out of her vagina and wouldn't be considered anything but a burlesque queen except she's suing the Endowment for not giving her a grant because she says she was denied on political grounds. Which, hell, maybe she was. How should I know? All I know is, there goes the door, and on the other side of it is good old Ash."

"Uh-oh."

"You bet, uh-oh. This is eight o'clock in the morning, remember. The deal hasn't even been done yet. And Ash has heard about it. And he's upset."

"Upset that he's got a customer with a cocaine habit who's going to have twelve and a half million dollars?"

"Upset that everybody's going to be so royally pissed off that McAdam got paid that there's going to be another investigation, maybe a state investigation this time, and state investigations aren't like federal ones. With Morgenthau's office, they check everything."

"Including possible drug use," Mickey said.

"Right," Tony answered him.

"Including possible drug connections," Mickey said.

Tony pushed his empty beer bottle halfway across the table. "What Ash wants," he said carefully, "is for me to run a buffer. I should take delivery of McAdam's stuff. I should deliver it to McAdam. I should pass the money back and forth. I sent McAdam to Ash, now I should protect Ash from McAdam."

"Is this a matter of principle?" Mickey asked him. "Is it that you don't approve of drug use or what?"

There was a smear of something on the opposite wall, a dark place where the flies clustered and glinted green in the fitful pulsing backshadows of the neon lights. Tony let himself imagine for a moment it was blood—in the Grubb Clubb it was more likely to be vomit—and then checked the wall at the back of his head before he let himself rest against it. There were people who wondered why Tony kept Mickey around, but Tony didn't wonder at all. Mickey was the only person on earth who knew him well who could understand what he was about to say next.

"What's it's a matter of," he explained carefully, "is foresight. Next year I don't want to be here. I want to be at Baird Financial. Dad and I have talked about it. He's throwing one of his patented Thanksgiving parties this November and we're supposed to seal the deal there. This is a tough regulatory atmosphere. We can't seal the deal if I've been arrested for dealing dope. Or even having dope."

"And you think if Morgenthau's office does investigate McAdam, they're going to find dope?"

"Hell," Tony said, "I don't even think you need Morgenthau's office. McAdam is a jerk. He's one of those idiots just asking to get caught. At everything. Look at the man."

"Oh," Mickey said.

"Right," Tony said, "but you know Ash. Ash is going to insist. I've been hanging out all day trying to think of some way out of this mess, and all I can come up with is that I wish Donald McAdam were dead."

"Maybe he is dead," Mickey laughed. "Cocaine and strychnine, cocaine and strychnine. Maybe he's writhing around on his bathroom floor right this minute."

"Maybe he is," Tony said, but he didn't believe it. He didn't have that kind of luck. With the kind of luck he did have, McAdam would go on taking tiny doses of strychnine with his cocaine until he was a hundred and six, and never feel the ill effects at all.

Unless, of course, something other than luck came along to change the prescription.

5

"Let's start this all over again at the beginning," Julie Anderwahl said, stopping dead in the middle of her husband Mark's wall-to-wall carpeted office floor, throwing out her arms in a wide sweep meant to indicate a willingness to capitulate she did not feel. "We're talking about twelve and a half million dollars. Not serious money in this market, granted, but still. Twelve and a half million dollars. And

Baird Financial is giving this twelve and a half million dollars to a man who pleaded guilty to one hundred and forty counts of securities fraud. A man who shopped half his friends to the Feds. A man who told Geraldo Rivera, on the air, in an upper-class accent so phony it could have made a three-dollar bill look like gold bullion, that the rich can't be *expected* to follow the same rules as other people. Baird Financial is going to give twelve and a half million dollars to this man, and I'm supposed to *make it look good*?"

On the other side of the room, sitting on a black leather swivel chair behind a polished mahogany desk the size of a table tennis table Mark Anderwahl closed his eyes, dredged up an image of the Almighty from his very misty memories of Episcopalian sunday school, and prayed. What he prayed was that his wife was not about to go on one of her certified rampages, reducing his chair, his desk, and his tie to rubble in the process. He prayed harder than he otherwise might have, because this time he knew she had a point. Julie was an excellent PR woman—probably the best one on the Street—but making the McAdam payoff look good to the Great American Public was an impossibility, and even Jon Baird had to realize that. Even making the McAdam payoff look neutral was probably out of the question. There had been just too much insider sleaze, too many cosy back-room deals, too much fraud. Sometimes it made Mark's head ache. Passing the racks of magazines in the Pan Am station with their headlines full of Dennis Levine and Ivan Boesky and Michael Milken and Donald McAdam made him physically ill. On the other hand, he had perfect trust in the judgment of his wife. What there was to be done she would do. What could be thought of to be done she would think of to do.

Actually, Mark had always had perfect trust in Julie, from the very first time he saw her, standing in the middle of Harvard Yard at four o'clock on a Saturday afternoon and letting snow fall on her head while she searched through her bookbag for he didn't know what. He never found out, either. He was too busy accidentally-on-purpose bumping into her, helping her pick up what she had dropped, getting acquainted. He was too busy thinking how absolutely perfect she was. And she was perfect. Mark Anderwahl had been brought up in very thin air. He was the only son of Susannah Baird Anderwahl, only sister of Jon and Calvin Baird, widow of Stephen K. Anderwahl, once president of the largest commercial bank in The Netherlands. Brought back to the States after his father's death, Mark had been carefully shepherded through all the schools his family considered "right" for him, including Collegiate in Manhattan and the obligatory trip through Groton to Harvard. He had always envied his cousin Tony, who was willing and able to put his foot down and demand a change, even if the change was as minor as accepting a place at Yale. Mark had never been good about putting his foot down about anything. He had never been good at asserting himself in any way. Left to himself, he would quickly have become one of those perpetual boys living on a trust fund, wandering through the expensive restaurants and charity balls of New York City like the Ghost of Achievement Past.

Julie was one of those girls who was at Harvard less on scholarship than on determination. Her education was being financed by a jury-rigged hodgepodge of student loans, summer jobs, financial aid, and moonlighting. She knew what she wanted to do because she had to. She did what she had to do because she wanted to. She had it all mapped out as early as freshman year. First, Harvard. Then a job with a bank. Then a Harvard MBA. Then—everything. Julie told Mark this in a tone of conviction so strong, she might have been Moses come down from Sinai with the tablets. And Mark believed her. Mark always believed her. And he always let her carry him. If there was one thing Julie understood it was that a woman who wanted "everything" could only get it as part of a partnership, as one half of a "dual-career couple" whose "dual careers" were really one big amalgamated one. She latched on to him as fiercely as he latched on to her, although for different reasons. Whatever the reasons, they were off.

Now she was standing in the middle of his office, ready to brain him, and he couldn't blame her. In the years since they had first come together, things had gotten a little complicated. He had made the suggestion, in their senior year, that they both apply to work at Baird Financial. With his connections, their assignments would be more interesting and their chances of getting recommendations for business school would be better. As it turned out, that wasn't all that had been better. Their promotions and their bonuses had both been unbelievable, Julie's more so than his own, so that now, when they were both only thirty-two, they were worth at least $5 million apiece and far higher up the ladder than most of the people they had graduated with. They were also just a little bit stuck. Julie had never gone back for her MBA. Without it, the fact that she was the youngest head of PR at any firm on the Street might be more of a liability than an asset. Mark suffered from what he thought of as Family Syndrome. Without the MBA, nobody out there knew if he could really do a job, or if he'd been being carried all these years by the fact that he was a Baird. For better or for worse, both he and Julie were now intricately concerned with the fate of Baird Financial.

Julie had stopped pacing and stopped posing. She was now standing stock-still in the middle of that great expanse of nothing, looking smaller and blonder than she did when she was throwing a tantrum. Mark cleared his throat.

"Julie," he said, "it was necessary. Trust me."

"Why?"

Mark was about to ask "why what?" but he didn't. It was

silly. "We bought the firm," he said patiently, "don't you remember that? There was a stock market crash, and then another stock market crash, and on the heels of the second one McAdam was about to go under."

"And McAdam Investments was famous," Julie recited dutifully, "with all these ads on the air with movie stars in them, and the public was very jittery with two big crashes coming so close together like that, and everybody was afraid that if someone as big and well-known as McAdam went bankrupt there'd be a run on the bank, figuratively speaking—"

"There'd be a run on all the banks," Mark said, "and maybe not so figuratively. That was the problem."

"No," Julie said. "That was not the problem. We were heroes when we bought McAdam Investments. We had every right to be. How could Jon have been so stupid as to not check on McAdam's personal employment contract? How could he do that? Jon never makes that kind of mistake."

"Maybe he didn't."

"Meaning what?"

"Meaning," Mark said slowly, "maybe he thought, at the time, that it didn't matter. This was before McAdam turned state's evidence on everybody in creation. Maybe he just thought we could go on carrying McAdam indefinitely, until he was sixty-five, and so what?"

"Why can't we?"

"Junk bonds," Mark said reverently.

Julie looked confused.

Mark sat forward a little and put his hands on his desk. "Junk bonds," he said again. "There's been all this moaning and groaning in the media about how junk bonds are going bad and losing value and blah, blah, blah, and some of it's true, of course, but you know what? Milken was right. A diversified junk bond portfolio outperforms the market by twenty-five percent and then some. McAdam Investments is sitting on a gold mine of junk bonds that didn't go bad and paid off big—or would pay off big, if we could sell them, or even if we could sell the stock we could convert some of them to, except we can't."

"Because of McAdam?" Julie asked.

Mark nodded. "People are *angry*," he said. "They're worse than angry. They're out for blood. Any time any of that stuff gets sold, as long as McAdam is still on the payroll he gets a bonus. A big bonus. And everybody knows it. And nobody wants to touch the stuff on those terms."

"But it won't last," Julie said reasonably. "If we wait it out for a year there'll be plenty of bidders. We wouldn't have to pay off McAdam. He was in my office half the morning, Mark. I hated him on sight."

"A lot of people love him," Mark said. "But think. What's going on in this place in just three months' time, if we're lucky?"

Julie thought. "The takeover thing," she said. "We're set to buy the holding company that owns some bank. I have a file on it I'm supposed to get to over Labor Day."

"We're set to buy the holding company that owns a whole string of banks from one end of Asia to the other, and a few other things besides. We could use a little cash under the circumstances, don't you think?"

"The terms of that deal are all set up already," Julie said stiffly. "We don't need—"

"I didn't say need. I said use."

"What we can't use is a lot negative publicity right before Jon gets out of jail," Julie said. "I made him look like a persecuted innocent going in, but with this McAdam thing he's going to look like spoiled meat coming out. How am I going to face him? How am I going to spend a week and a half on a boat with him after I've failed—"

"You think too much about failing," Mark said sharply.

Then he caught his breath, and sat back, and made himself calm down. He really hadn't been himself lately. He'd been under too much pressure. And as for the boat . . . "Don't worry about the Thanksgiving thing," he told Julie. "He's been doing that since I was a kid, on and off. Not with the replica. That's new. But with one boat or another. Jon likes boats. Jon likes you. It'll be fine."

"This is the first time we've ever been invited to anything like this with your family. It makes me nervous."

"Everything makes you nervous," Mark said, and caught his breath again. It was crazy. Maybe he was sick.

The one thing he couldn't be, of course, was out of love with Julie.

6

Frieda Derwent Baird kept a notebook in her purse—one of the palm-size ones with the little pencils attached, made especially for Tiffany's—and at the end of every meal she took it out and wrote down what she had eaten. This was something she had been doing for over thirty years now, and in her mind it was "a strategy that worked." "A strategy that worked" was the kind of thing she said to magazines like *Vogue* and *Queen* and *Harper's Bazaar* when they interviewed her, which they did about once or twice a year. She was, after all, the almost-famous "Fritzie" Derwent, only daughter of one of the oldest and most distinguished families on the Philadelphia Main Line, most popular debutante of her year, longtime wife of the spectacularly successful Jonathan Edgewick Baird, chairwoman of committees for everything from benefit galas to club memberships. Even now, after her divorce, she was a force in the city of New York, as long as you defined "the city of New York" as that part of the island of Manhattan below seventieth Street on the East Side and Eightieth on the West and above Forty-second all the way across. She also looked just the way she was supposed to look when photographed in Calvin Klein flannel skirts and Laura Ashley shawls, because she was very, very thin. She was so thin, in fact, that she looked skeletal, and people passing her on the street sometimes wondered if she was dying of AIDS. If this had been anyplace else but New York, they probably would have asked.

Cassey Hockner never asked Fritzie anything. In spite of the fact that they had known each other forever—they had been roommates years ago at Madeira and then again at Smith—Fritzie sometimes wondered if that was because Cassey didn't like her very much. Maybe that should have been: didn't respect her very much. Fritzie wasn't sure if there was a difference. She wasn't sure of very many things, because her head seemed to be fuzzy all the time, and she had the attention span of a gnat. These things were definitely not true of Cassey. Cassey had grown up and come out and gotten married like all the rest of them, but then she had done what Fritzie thought of as a very strange thing. When her fourth and youngest child was safely in the fourth grade, Cassey had applied and been accepted to the graduate program in archaeology at Columbia. Now she had not one doctorate but two—in archaeology and Semitic languages—and a shelf full of books she had published on the dig she was overseeing, off and on, in the Sinai Peninsula. She also had what Fritzie delicately referred to as "a weight problem." Fritzie began to feel fat as soon as she put on a pound above 110, and she was five feet eight inches tall. Cassey never seemed to feel fat at all. She sat in the middle of Fritzie's living room, her enormous bulk spread across Fritzie's white satin couch like an amoeba in a muumuu, picking happily away at a plate of chocolate chip cookies.

"I can't diet," Cassey had told Fritzie once. "Every time

I start I get crazy. I can't concentrate. All I can think about is food. I never get anything done."

Fritzie was carrying a plate of cookies covered in powdered sugar in from the pantry. She put it down on the coffee table in front of Cassey and retreated. She was tempted to give Cassey another lecture about her weight—it had been a while—but since the divorce her heart had gone out of it. There was Cassey, 200 pounds if she weighed an ounce, with her husband who adored her and a pack of children who worshiped her in spite of it. Fritzie was sure it must be "in spite of it," because for Fritzie weight was something that could never be neutral, or positive. Whatever it was, here was Fritzie, on her own again at the age of fifty-odd, with a son who barely seemed to tolerate her. Here was Fritzie, with her hold on the only kind of life she had ever wanted to live beginning to slip—the magazines weren't calling as often; she wasn't being chosen as automatically to head the committees or serve on the governing boards. Here was Fritzie, thin as a rail and just as pure. It didn't seem right somehow.

Cassey looked over the plate of powdered-sugar cookies, took one, and said, "So from what I can see, you don't have any obligation in this thing at all. You are divorced from the man. That does mean you don't have to do what he wants you to do. What I'd do if I were you is just tell him to stuff it."

"I can't tell him to stuff it," Fritzie said. "He's got control of my income. That trust he settled on me can be reversed at any time."

"Maybe. But it won't be. That was part of the court settlement, remember? I'd think the last thing Jon wants to do now is land in court again."

"It's the last thing I want to do now."

"Just don't let him know that. Really, Fritzie, you're all grown up. You've got to learn how to operate with these things. Jon Baird has got no right to expect you to drop everything and spend a week or more on a leaky old boat in the middle of the Atlantic Ocean in the company of his much younger wife."

And that, Fritzie thought, was certainly absolutely true. It was also certainly absolutely beside the point. She picked up the cup of tea she had left on the coffee table when she went out to get the second plate of cookies and sipped it gingerly. Sometimes her friends did very odd things to sabotage her diet, like putting sugar in her tea when she was was away from the table. She'd never been able to understand what they were afraid of. Even after she got down to her ideal weight, she would still love all the people she loved now. She would still cherish them. This tea was unadulterated. She took an immense gulp to fill the hard painful hollowness of her stomach and put the cup down.

"The thing is," she said, "it's more than Thanksgiving or the boat or—or Sheila. It's all this other business, too. I had a call from Margaret Denton today. Do you remember Margaret Denton?"

"Peggy Devereaux?"

"That's right. She was all upset, because Jon's company has decided to pay this man Donald McAdam—you met Donald McAdam here once, I don't know if you remember—"

"Oh, I remember all right, Fritzie. For goodness' sake. It's not every day you sit down to dinner with a man who shows up in the paper two days later indicted for everything."

"I suppose you're right. Well, Jon's company is going to pay Mr. McAdam a very large sum of money to get him to quit his job, which doesn't make sense to me but seems to be necessary because for some reason they can't fire him. It was supposed to be a great big secret, but somebody told somebody, and Peggy heard about it and she called me. It was a terrible phone call, Cassey, it really was. She shouted."

"About what?"

"About how awful it was that anybody would pay Mr. McAdam—oh, I don't understand it all. I really don't. When we were growing up, women didn't have to pay any attention to business and I don't want to pay attention to it now. And it shouldn't be my problem, should it? Jon and I are divorced."

"Right," Cassey said.

"But anyway," Fritzie said, "Peggy is a friend of mine and she was so upset and everything that I decided to see what I could do. I decided I'd go over there and talk to him."

"What?"

"Well," Fritzie said defensively, "why not? He's been part of our—my—circle for years, hasn't he? He's been to dinner in this house. He contributes to the Cancer Society and the Metropolitan League. He's supposed to be one of us in spite of all these things he seems to have done. So I thought I could talk to him."

"Talk to him about what?" Cassey marveled. "About giving up this money you say Jon is going to pay him? Is it a lot of money?"

"I brought him a jar of my melon rind marmalade," Fritzie insisted. "You know how I'm always making marmalade. I brought him some of that. I only bring it to very important people in my life."

"I know," Cassey said drily, just drily enough so that Fritzie began to wonder about her tone of voice. "But it's hardly worth—what? How much money?"

"Peggy said it was more than twelve million dollars." Fritzie looked away, toward the kitchen, where she had more melon rind marmalade. She had thirty jars of it, in fact, because last week had been one of those very bad times when only cooking could keep her from eating. Cassey was

staring at her. She plunged on. "I wasn't going to talk him
out of taking the money, Cassey," she said, "I'm not that
naive. I'm old enough to know that anybody will do anything
for the money. No, I was just going to talk to him about
keeping quiet about it."

"But what good would that do?" Cassey said. "If it really
is that much money we're talking about, Baird Financial
would find it necessary to issue a statement."

"They will now," Fritzie said, "but that wasn't the way it
was supposed to be. It was supposed to be an absolute
secret. After Peggy called I called Calvin, just to check; I
didn't want to go off half-cocked on the strength of a rumor.
And Calvin hit the roof. That was this morning. The agreement hadn't even been delivered yet. Mr. McAdam was
supposed to pick it up from Jon at the jail—"

"At the *jail*?"

Fritzie waved it away. "They all do it. All those men in
Danbury. You'd be surprised. The point is, nobody was
supposed to know about it. It was supposed to be an absolute secret. And of course Calvin knew there was only one
way the news could have gotten out."

"What way was that?"

"Why, Donald McAdam must have been spreading it, of
course. Calvin said that was the kind of man he was. That he
liked publicity. So I decided to go over there to talk to him."
Fritzie looked into her teacup, empty now, and reached for
the sterling silver pot in its nest of sterling silver filigree. She
had to be careful with the tea in the pot, too. There was
nothing to say that sugar could only be added to the cup. "I
thought," she explained slowly, "that under the circumstances I might be able to bribe him. Not with money—"

"Not on the heels of twelve million dollars," Cassey said
drily, "no."

"But there are other things. There are. Especially with
someone like Mr. McAdam. He's a terrible social climber,

Cassey, he really is. He's always trying to get himself invited to things and on the boards of things. He hasn't been having a good time of it lately, either. With all these indictments, he's been really out in the cold. So I thought, I'm chairing the Anniversary Gala for the Hayes-Dawson Museum of Contemporary Art. I still have open places on the committee. If he was willing to stop talking to people about this deal of his, I could give him a place. It would be a small price to pay. I don't like being hounded by people."

"Mmm," Cassey said again, and Fritzie got the uncomfortable feeling that she had just said something very stupid. Maybe she had. This whole thing had made her feel very confused and bumbling, and the deeper she got into it the worse it seemed to get. She gulped at her tea again and scalded her throat.

"Well," she said, "I didn't see him when I went to his apartment because he wasn't there, but I ran into him later, around five o'clock, outside the Cosmopolitan Club downtown. I don't know what he was doing there. It's a woman's club."

"Maybe he was just passing in the street."

"Maybe he was. I did talk to him about it then. In a way."

"I take it he didn't bite?"

Fritzie frowned. "I don't know if he understood what I was talking about. I was trying to be very discreet about it, trying to go at it by indirection, but maybe I was being much too subtle. He interrupted me right in the middle of everything and then he said the oddest thing. The oddest thing in context, I mean. Considering what I was talking about."

"What did he say?"

"He said, 'Greed is the drug of choice for otherwise sober people.' Just like that."

"Did you ask him what he meant?"

"Of course I asked him what he meant," Fritzie said. "All he would tell me was that he'd been trying to figure something out for weeks and he finally had, and then he said he had a stock tip for me. 'Go out and buy Europabanc Limited,' he said, 'and watch very, very carefully what it does.' Then he started laughing, right there on the street."

"And that was it?"

"That was it. He said good-bye and walked away. He didn't even offer to see me home." Fritzie sighed. "Peggy's going to call me back again today and she's not going to be the only one. And I won't even be able to say I'm divorced from Jon and it's none of my business, because with this Thanksgiving dinner party it's going to look like a very different kind of divorce than the one it is. Or at least, than the one it is when Sheila's around. Do you think that's a nice name for a woman? Sheila?"

Cassey Hockner was eating her way through a powdered sugar cookie. Fritzie stared at her and almost leapt. It got that way with food sometimes, she got so hungry she wanted to tear it out of people's hands. But that was neurosis. Real hunger wasn't like that at all. Real hunger didn't hit you when you'd already eaten your 800 calories for the day. Fritzie poured herself another cup of tea.

"Calvin said the oddest thing when I called," she told Cassey. "Do you know what it was? He said the way Mr. McAdam was behaving, he knew half a dozen people who if they had a chance to kill him, probably would."

7

Ever since Charlie Shay's wife had left him and gone to Vermont—to find herself, to find a tree, just to get away from him—he had been feeling rootless and upset, as if he were a helium balloon without a string, attached to nothing, floating. The floating feeling was exacerbated by the subtle change that had come over his status in the office since Jon had gone to jail. It was a change that had as much to do with how he saw himself as with how the others saw him, but it bothered him that he couldn't pin down when it had started or why. Lately, he had been having a difficult time pinning down much of anything. Charlie Shay had always been one of those people adept at moving on. Leaving high school, he had abandoned his high-school friends for new ones at college. Leaving college, he had abandoned his college friends for new ones in business. Leaving one business, he had abandoned his work friends for new friends at his new place of work. People had always drifted into Charlie's life and then out again, barely noticed, until he met Jon Baird. Now, after over thirty years, it was Jon who was drifting out.

Except that he wasn't, not exactly. Jon was still in Danbury, expecting a visit from Charlie Shay once every other week. The office was still where it had always been. Calvin and Julie and Mark and all the other people Charlie had gotten used to during the past few years were still taking up space in the hallways of Baird Financial. Even the holiday schedule was still the same. Charlie's life had emptied out to the point where he had to spend Christmas at his club and his birthday buying himself a drink, but this year, as for every year but one since he had first met Jon, Thanksgiving was taken care of. The exception had been last year, while Jon was in jail and Sheila was so distraught she'd had to go on a cruise to Bermuda to quiet her nerves. Now Jon was getting out and the Thanksgiving party was on and Charlie was invited. That this invitation seemed to have nothing to do with him—that it had been extended to everyone with a significant emotional investment in fortunes of the business—bothered Charlie Shay not at all.

What did bother Charlie Shay was that it was seven o'clock on a Friday night and he was still in the office. Years ago, that wouldn't have been very unusual. As a young man he had been very ambitious. What he had been ambitious for was no longer completely clear and he couldn't have said if he'd achieved it—but that was the way life went, after all, and he didn't feel entitled to complain. You worked and worked and worked and worked and then one day you looked up and decided you were tired. That was what had happened to him. He was tired. The only time he perked up was when he had an errand to do for Jon, like bringing the McAdam papers and the spare bridge out to the prison so that Jon could review the deal and not have to chew with his gums while he did it.

Charlie Shay was at the office at this late hour because he had gotten lost in a book of crossword puzzles. Crossword puzzles were what he did with himself most of the time these days. Over time, he had developed a mild compulsion—always buy the *Times*, always do the crossword puzzle, first thing—into an elaborate mania, so that he knew the names and styles of most of the puzzle constructors and the weaknesses of each. He'd even entered the *Games* magazine national crossword championships this year and come in third. Today, coming back from lunch with a new collection and a determination to have nothing more to do with Donald McAdam or his deal, Charlie had shut himself into his office and let himself go mentally missing. He would have been mentally missing for hours yet, except that Julie Anderwahl was having an argument with Mark in the office next door and she had thrown something. The something had bounced against the wall Charlie shared with Mark, bringing Charlie to. Charlie had wondered for what must have been the millionth time if the two of them behaved the same way in bed, complete with screams and curses and sharp-edged flying objects. Charlie had never had anything but the most conventional forms of sex, and the idea of variations with a little violence (on the part of the woman) intrigued him.

Julie called Mark a son of a bitch in a voice loud enough

to be heard across the river in New Jersey, and Charlie stood up, went to his door, and looked into the hall. This was the hall where most of the really important offices were, the offices of the senior executives and the one or two lower-level people expected to make it all the way up, and as Charlie would have suspected, most of those offices were still inhabited. Calvin Baird's office was certainly inhabited, sitting down there at the end of the hall next to Jon's illuminated shrine like a dog at its master's feet. At Baird Financial, there had never been any ambiguity about who ran the company or from where. Jon had pleaded guilty to a count or two of insider trading, not to major fraud. He hadn't been barred from the securities industry or made ineligible to own or run a bank. What he'd been jailed for wasn't even illegal in Europe and Japan. He was the founder, chairman, chief executive officer, and patron saint of Baird Financial—and if he'd been sent to jail for ten years instead of just over one, it would still have been his company.

Charlie edged out into the hall, past Mark Anderwahl's door—passing strangers in the halls had sometimes been pulled in to Mark and Julie's fights; Charlie didn't want any part of that—and then started making time toward Calvin's door. Mark and Julie seemed to be arguing about the McAdam thing, which figured. To Charlie's mind, there was a lot to argue about in the McAdam thing. On the other hand, it had been Jon Baird's personal decision, and that really ought to settle it. Charlie got to Calvin's open door, looked in at Calvin bent over a spread of papers on his desk, and knocked.

"Cal?" he said. "Don't you think you ought to go home?"

Calvin Baird wasn't much like his brother Jon. Instead of being barrel chested and bandy legged, he was tall and thin. Instead of having eyes full of humor and a mouth that crinkled up at the edges, he had the face of a Puritan preacher. He was angled and sharp, self-righteous and cold, impossible to deal with—at least on the surface. Charlie had known Cal for what felt like forever and not been able to figure him out yet.

Charlie knocked a second time, and coughed, and said, "Don't pretend you don't hear me. I know it's been a long day. That's my point."

Calvin Baird looked up from his papers and sighed. It was mostly in profile that he looked intransigent. Full-face, he simply looked exhausted.

"Charlie," he said. "Hello. It has been a long day."

"Is that more on Mr. Donald McAdam? I'd think you'd be sick of him by now."

"I am sick of him. You don't know how it annoys me that Jon couldn't wait to get out of jail to do this thing. If he had waited, at least it would have been his problem and not mine. But, no. This isn't Mr. McAdam. This is Europabanc."

"Everything going smoothly?"

"As smoothly as it can when you deal with the French."

"Ah," Charlie said. He came fully into Calvin's office then and sat down in the single chair kept for visitors. Calvin was one of those people who preferred to keep his appointments in public places, like restaurants. "I heard Mark and Julie having a fight just now. About McAdam. About selling McAdam."

"There's no way to sell McAdam," Calvin said. "I tried to tell her that. She's too much of a perfectionist. In the meantime I've got this Europabanc thing, and there's been a leak. In the middle of all this McAdam business nobody seems to have noticed, but someone will."

"Noticed what?"

"Noticed this." Calvin reached into the bottom drawer of his desk and pulled out a copy of the *Wall Street Journal*, folded carefully back to a center page. Calvin passed it across the desk to Charlie and said, "Column three. Halfway down what you're holding."

Charlie looked at column three, halfway down what he was holding, and found:

"Rumors on the street suggest that the long-anonymous 'significant bidder' in the Europabanc buyout may be none other than Baird Financial Services—"

Charlie put the paper down. "Well," he said.

"Well," Calvin echoed. He looked down at the papers on his desk and rubbed his eyes. "I've been going over it and over it," he said. "All the people who were privy to the information. All the people who might have had reason to sell the information, or give it away, for that matter. It's an impossible job."

"It ought to be," Charlie pointed out. "The secretaries must know. And if one secretary knows—"

"—all of them know, unless a matter's been stamped confidential. And this one hasn't. I don't even know if it matters if anyone knows. Jon said to keep it tight, but he wasn't fanatical about it. You know how he can get. It wasn't like that. I don't even suppose he'll really mind. But I really mind. I keep thinking I have to know. Especially now with this thing with McAdam."

"It was probably McAdam who leaked the news about McAdam," Charlie said. "How long have we known Donald?"

"Too long," Calvin said. "You're right, of course. He leaked the news himself. He would."

"Do we at least have the deal signed, sealed, and delivered?"

Calvin shook his head. "Jon wouldn't hear of it. He gave

McAdam the copies of the agreement and a stamped, self-addressed envelope—self-addressed to the firm, that is—and told him to go home and think it over very carefully. McAdam thought he was nuts and so did I, but Jon is Jon. But I thought you knew all this. I thought you brought all that stuff out to Jon when you went to Danbury."

"I went to Danbury yesterday," Charlie said, "but the papers were in an envelope. I didn't open it. I was too busy trying to find a way to carry Jon's bridge in that flimsy little box without breaking it myself."

Calvin laughed. "Jon broke it. The same day you brought it to him. We got there this morning and one of his cheeks was sucking in like an old man's. God. All the time we were there, I was wondering. Whether the rumors are true, if you know what I mean. Whether it was McAdam who shopped Jon to the Feds."

Charlie was startled. "I don't think so," he said. "If that had been the case, I don't think McAdam would have gotten his deal. Do you?"

"I don't know."

"I know," Charlie said with conviction. "If that had been the case, Jon would have hired a hit man if he'd had to, but McAdam would be dead. I think it's just more of those rumors you've been worried about. And the fact that Mc-Adam has shopped everybody else to the Feds."

"Maybe you're right."

"Of course I'm right," Charlie said. He got up off Calvin's visitor's chair and shook out his pants until the pleats were hanging straight. Calvin kept the air-conditioning in the offices up so high, Charlie always felt like wearing a sweater, no matter how hot it was outside. He checked his back pocket to make sure he had his wallet—he had been losing weight lately and things had been falling out of his clothes, often in the most awkward places—and began to drift toward Calvin's door.

"So," he said, "I guess I'll be heading on home. Are you sure you don't want to come with me?"

"I'm due up at the club to play bridge," Calvin said, "and I have to clean up here. We're getting old, Charlie."

"Oh, I already got old," Charlie said. "I've been enjoying my golden years with scarcely a break for months now."

"Do you mind it, Charlie?"

Charlie didn't answer. He was already out in the hall, for one thing. For another, it was a complicated question to answer. It was far more complicated, for instance, than the possibility that Donald McAdam might have turned Jon Baird in to the federal authorities for insider trading.

That, Charlie was sure, wasn't possible at all.

If it had happened at all, Jon Baird wouldn't have needed a hit man. He'd have found a way to kill Donald McAdam with his bare hands.

Since Donald McAdam was alive and well and soon to be in possession of twelve and one half million of Jon Baird's dollars, Charlie dismissed the allegation out of hand.

He found it far more pleasant to plan what he would wear for all those days on Jon's little boat, a modern-day Pilgrim to an upmarket Plymouth Rock.

8

In the end, Donald McAdam decided not to wait. The envelope was lying there on his occasional table, and his mind kept going back to it, worrying at it, gloating over it, no matter what. He had waited a long time for his twelve and a half million dollars. Now that he had it he wanted to have it, all wrapped up, beyond the possibility of anything going wrong. Exactly what could go wrong, he didn't know. The papers were there and Jon had signed them. As soon as McAdam signed them himself, the money would belong to him. It was just that he had been around long enough not to trust Jon Baird.

He laid out five short lines of cocaine on the marble surface of the small table he kept pushed against the wall of windows that looked out across Manhattan. Now he stopped in the middle of reaching for his silver straw and changed his mind about how his day would end. He got up and got the envelope from the occasional table, looked curiously at the mason jar full of marmalade, and brought them both back.

It was all in there, just the way it was supposed to be, three copies of the agreement (each signed by Jon acting for Baird Financial) and a stamped, self-addressed envelope. It was all on Baird Financial stationary and neatly typed. He had already read through it three times today, but he decided to read through it again, very carefully, just to be sure nothing was wrong. It took him half an hour of what was really hard work, but he knew for certain that what he had was what he was supposed to have. He looked up and out the windows. While he had been concentrating on other things, the city had moved closer to night. The lights lit in the windows in the distance looked like thousands of candles held up to the dark.

The melon rind marmalade looked like the jar with the pulsating brain in it from some Z-grade 1950s horror movie. McAdam got up, went to the kitchen, and came back with a spoon. He pulled the cotton cover off the top of the jar and dug through the clear wax underneath. The marmalade was greenish black and oddly mobile, as if it were alive. McAdam got a small quivering blob of it on the end of the spoon and licked at it experimentally. It was outrageously sweet, a distillation of pure sugar. It made him feel sick on contact.

The copies of the agreement were still lying on the table. McAdam signed all three, put one copy aside, and folded the other two. He put the two folded copies into the stamped, self-addressed envelope and sealed it. Then he turned the letter over, stared for a moment at the address, and stood up. He was being paranoid and he knew it, but he couldn't help himself. Someone could break into the apartment during the night and steal all three copies of the agreement. There could be a fire. He could have a heart attack. He went back to the elevator, punched himself in, and rode down to the lobby.

Three minutes later, he was back home, feeling proud of himself and a little relieved. The agreements had been mailed. The doorman had been greeted and dismissed. The fat woman in the elevator who had seen his picture on the cover of *Forbes* had been fended off and forced to depart on her own floor. Now he had the weekend in front of him, and he knew exactly what he wanted to do with it.

He sat down at the marble table, picked up the silver straw, and smiled. The first line went up his nose feeling as cold as menthol. The second went up feeling like nothing at all. By the time he'd gotten to the fifth he was not only high but happy, jumping, perfect, clear. He felt like dancing and singing and shouting at once, but most of all he felt like being out in the open air. He went to the French doors and let himself out onto the roof garden, high above the city. It all looked so wonderful out there, so perfect, exactly the way he had always expected it to be. It all looked so clean and he was going so fast, so fast, he was jumping and—

—and then it began to hit him, the pain, and the jerking convulsions he could not stop. In one awful moment he felt his body snap and grab and trip and jerk, whipping back and forth as if he were a flag being shaken out in a gale-force wind. He was out of control and the pain was getting worse. He was dipping and riding and jumping back and forth and back and forth in no known pattern and making no known sense and then he saw it—

—the railing—

—the end of the roof and the air, the air, the railing was nothing but two thin lines and not nearly high enough, not nearly high enough—

He felt himself slam into the railing, and jerk upward and push out. He felt himself in the air, still snapping and still in pain. He thought of the cocaine and the time and then he couldn't think at all.

It was twenty-two minutes before eight o'clock at night on the last day of August and he was floating high above the city, in the air and free, and any minute now he was going to start falling down.

Part One

November 16–November 17

One

1

On the day the very young man from the Federal Bureau of Investigation came to Cavanaugh Street, Gregor Demarkian found a picture of the *Pilgrimage Green* in the morning mail. Actually, the morning mail was the only mail he had—and from what he'd heard from friends who lived in other parts of Philadelphia, he was damned lucky to get it in the morning. His problem with the mail was the same as his problem with half of the rest of his life lately. Gregor had spent twenty years in the FBI himself, ten of those years as founder and head of Behavioral Sciences, the department that coordinated interstate manhunts for serial killers. Like any other high Washington official—like senators, congressmen, presidents, cabinet secretaries, and heads of major departments—he had lived a life free of bureaucratic bungling, management inefficiency, and general bad service. The Bureau made it a point not to bungle with the sort of people who could influence its next appropriation. For the ten long years of his reign at BSD, Gregor had had tax refunds that showed up in his mailbox two weeks after he'd filed his return, phone equipment that got fixed within an hour or two of his making a complaint, and mail that arrived

at his office at least twice a day. The Social Security Administration never botched his name or got his number confused with that of a retired miner from Bozeman, Montana.
The Post Office never delivered his Visa payment to the
Vi-Sal Hair Salon in downtown L.A. He lived, in fact, in a
kind of paradise, except for two little problems. In the first
place, his wife was dying, painfully and slowly (but much too
fast for Gregor) of cancer. For another, long before she
started dying, he had begun to hate his job. Sometimes, in
his sleep, he saw the cases he had handled strung out before
him like beads of blood: the young man who had roamed
through Alabama, Mississippi, and northern Florida, killing
small girls and taking their right hands for souvenirs; the old
woman in Texas, Oklahoma, New Mexico, and Arizona who
had gone from one live-in elderly help job to another, offing
each of her charges as she went; the sweet engaged couple
from western Virginia who had first murdered all of her
living relatives and then all of his. Back at the beginning,
when there was no Behavioral Sciences Department, and
getting one started had been a holy crusade, Gregor had
kept a picture in his office that was meant to remind him
how important his work was and why he had to keep going
no matter how much pain they made him take. The picture
was of a twelve-year-old girl named Kimberly Ann Leach,
the last of the countless victims of a man named Theodore
Robert Bundy. In the end, not even Kimberly Ann Leach
could motivate him. It was one thing to pick up a serial
murder case here and there, over the years. It was another
thing to live for nothing else. He tried to sleep and the crime
scenes played back on the inside of his skull, crime scenes
made more vivid and more lurid because he had not actually been at them. For some reason, those badly lit five-by-
eight color prints were as potent as lime rickeys made with
151-proof rum.

On the day the picture of the *Pilgrimage Green* came in

the mail—and the FBI reentered Gregor's life with a typically two-left-footed crash—all that was at least three years in the past. Gregor's wife was dead. Gregor's career with the Bureau had ended with his polite letter to the director two years before the old mandatory retirement age. His life in the District of Columbia—if he'd ever had a life in the District of Columbia, which was doubtful—was something he preferred not to remember. He lived on Cavanaugh Street in Philadelphia now, the very same Cavanaugh Street on which he'd been born. It had transmuted itself from an immigrant Armenian ghetto to an upscale urban enclave, but Gregor had owned his third-floor floor-through apartment across the street from Lida Arkmanian's townhouse long enough to be used to that. There was no reason at all why he shouldn't be completely adjusted to life as he expected it to be for many years to come. There was no reason why he should keep flashing back to life as he had gratefully left it in the past. There were and weren't reasons, but none of them mattered, because here he was.

Where he was, precisely, was standing at his living room window, looking down on as much of Cavanaugh Street as he could see. It was ten o'clock on the morning of Friday, the sixteenth of November, less than a week before Thanksgiving. On the other side of the street, the facade of Lida's modest stone palace was hung with brown and yellow cardboard cornucopias and sprightly turkeys made of quilted crepe paper fans. If he had been able to see his own building, Gregor knew, he would have found the same sort of thing. Down on the street, the store windows were plastered with Thanksgiving decorations, too. An hour ago, he had watched as the children of Holy Trinity Armenian Christian School marched from their classroom building (at the north end) to the church basement, decked out as Pilgrims and Indians for their parts in the school play. It was business as usual for Cavanaugh Street. Give these people the slightest excuse for a holiday and they would run with it. Gregor was used to it. What he wasn't used to was—the other thing.

At the moment, "the other thing" was represented by a crudely colored, and oddly tentative, paper flag, drawn on the inside of a carefully cut up grocery bag and hung from Lida's third-floor guest-bedroom window. It was crudely colored because Lida had drawn it herself. Donna Moradanyan, Gregor's upstairs neighbor and the street's only real artist, had been out on the Main Line visiting her parents overnight. The flag was tentative because it had to be. The Republic of Armenia had declared its independence from the Soviet Union on September twenty-fourth. Since then, a positive rain of Armenian flags had descended on Cavanaugh Street. So had a positive rain of Armenians.

Gregor pressed his face to the glass, and looked down on the street again, and sighed. There was a little knot of them sitting on the steps of the church, young men in jeans so new and pressed the legs had creases, young women in brightly colored sweaters bought in the last week or so at K mart and Sears. If Gregor had had to guess what they were doing, he would have said reading the paper, although reading didn't quite cover it. They puzzled it out, with the help of dictionaries and passersby. They were terribly proud of themselves when they were done, and asked questions about municipal elections and the state lottery. Every last one of them bought at least one lottery ticket a week, just in case.

"Why not?" Gregor asked himself now. "Old George Tekemanian buys half a dozen lottery tickets a week."

Then he backed away from the window, rubbed his hands against his face, and told himself he had to get going. He had promised more people than he could count that he would do more things than he could count today, and he had to pack and be ready to leave tomorrow morning on top of it. Bennis had probably had her suitcases ready and waiting in her hall closet for a week.

At the thought of Bennis, Gregor Demarkian stopped, crossed his fingers, and listened. He was disappointed. No clatter of fitful typing came from the heating grate at his feet. No clang and clash of pots and pans rose up from the second-floor apartment's kitchen. Bennis had to be taking the day off—and that meant, of course, that Bennis had to be resting. When he went downstairs, he'd find the standard sign on her door: ASLEEP UNTIL FURTHER NOTICE.

"I wish I was asleep until further notice," Gregor said to no one in particular, but that sort of a thing wasn't even a hope to him. Bennis Day Hannaford was one thing. Gregor was another. The people on Cavanaugh Street allowed him to get away with much less.

"Snobs," Gregor said.

Then he grabbed his jacket and headed for his front door.

2

The picture of the *Pilgrimage Green*—sealed into a brown envelope with the logo of Baird Financial in the upper left-hand corner—was sitting on the hall table with the rest of the mail when Gregor came downstairs, meaning that someone (probably old George) had picked it up off the floor and sorted it out. Gregor got the envelope open just as old George got the door to his first-floor apartment open and began to peer out. Old George was eighty-something and had to have a first-floor apartment because he hated elevators and couldn't take stairs. At least, according to old George's grandson Martin's wife, old George couldn't take stairs. Old George's grandson Martin's wife was a bit of a terror. Old George's grandson Martin was a bit of a nut. He bought his grandfather all the gadgets his wife wouldn't let him have himself, so that old George's apartment was filled with things like sterling-silver liquor decanters in the shape of National Football League helmets and egg timers that sprouted crowing roosters instead of ringing bells when their cycles were done.

Eighty-something or not, there was nothing wrong with old George's eyes. He spotted the photograph in Gregor's hand and bobbed his head, excited. Old George was always excited about something. That was what made his grandson Martin's wife so crazy.

"Is that the boat, Krekor?" old George asked. "It doesn't look like much of a boat, to spend a week on with so many people."

"It's supposed to be a replica of the *Mayflower*," Gregor said. He turned the photograph over and read, "Pier 36. Berth 102. Saturday, November seventeenth. Nine o'clock."

"That sounds right," old George said.

"It's going to be ten days, not a week," Gregor told him. Then Gregor pawed through the rest of the mail, searching until he found an identical envelope with Bennis's name on it, feeling satisfied when he found it was there. Gregor didn't pride himself on knowing much about people. He was a facts and logic man, not a psychologist. Still, everything he had ever heard about Jon Baird—and every impression he had gotten the one time they'd met—said that here was a man who did everything through his office. A wife would have known that Gregor and Bennis were coming together and sent only one reminder. A secretary would send reminders to everyone on her list. Unless, of course, she was a very confidential secretary—and Jon Baird hadn't struck him as the kind of man to have one of those. Gregor pushed Bennis's envelope back into the stack.

"I remember reading about it five or six years ago, when it was built," Gregor said. "Baird went to an extraordinary amount of trouble. Finding people who could duplicate the methods of construction. Having fabrics made that no one had produced for a hundred and fifty years. It was quite a project."

"All so that this man could sail the boat from Virginia to Massachusetts to have his Thanksgiving?"

"I don't think he's ever used it for Thanksgiving before," Gregor said. "Mostly it's used for schoolchildren. They come on field trips and visit it. I think Baird even offers an overnight sail for parents and children. Or Baird Financial does. Jon Baird is the kind of man who makes it difficult to work out where the person ends and the company begins."

"How much of a replica is it?" old George asked. "Does it have plumbing? Does it have gas to cook with?"

"I don't know."

"Does Bennis know?"

"I don't think so."

Old George peered over Gregor's shoulder at the picture and shook his head. "I don't know," he said. "There's too much you don't know, Krekor, and none of it sounds promising. I think you should stay home and have your dinner with Lida the way everybody expected you to."

"I had last Thanksgiving dinner with Lida. I had Christmas dinner with Lida. I had Easter dinner with Lida."

"You would be welcome to have every dinner with Lida."

"That's not the point."

"What is the point?"

Gregor stuffed the photograph into the breast pocket of his sweater. "We're late, that's the point," he said. "We promised Tibor we'd meet him at the church at ten o'clock and it's already ten past. Get your jacket and get going."

Old George gave him a long, steady, and slightly reproving look—but it didn't have any effect, and Gregor knew old George hadn't expected it to. He watched the older man return to his apartment for his latest jacket—something new Martin had bought him, made of leather and covered with zippers and chains—and was impressed again at how quickly the old man moved. Old George's gait was vigorous and shaky at the same time, like the progress of a car whose engine is capable of anything but whose chassis is held together with spit and chewing gum.

"Even so, Krekor," he said, as he came back out into the hall and pulled his door shut behind him, "I think you are being foolish. I think Bennis is also being foolish. If the two of you feel so badly that you are taking too much of our hospitality, you should make a Thanksgiving dinner and invite us yourself."

"You mean we should do it together?" Gregor asked.

Old George shot him a look. "Don't joke, Krekor. We're all very worried about you. We're all very worried about Bennis, too. She's old enough to be married. You're too old not to be married again."

"If we were married to each other, we'd provide Cavanaugh Street with its first known homicide. And I don't know who would kill who first."

"I think I will kill you both and put the neighborhood out of its misery," old George said. "Besides, with all the refugees we could use the apartments. Next week I will have four people staying with me. How many people will you have staying with you?"

Actually, Gregor had no idea how many people he would have staying with him, because he had no intention of being there to meet them. He had given Lida a copy of his key so that she could use his living room as "a temporary hotel," as she put it. He supposed she would fill his modest one-bedroom place with stranded Armenians of various shapes and sizes—and Bennis's, too. He also supposed those stranded Armenians would be long gone before he returned. Lida and her cohorts at the newly formed Society for the Support of an Independent Armenia were supposed to have a regular real estate service going. They seemed to have better luck finding rental space than Donald Trump.

Old George stepped through the main front door to the stoop and waited. Gregor followed him, trying not to look back at old George's apartment door. Gregor locked his apartment religiously, as all policemen, ex-policemen, and burglars do. Bennis locked hers because she had lived so much of her life in places where it paid to be cautious. The rest of Cavanaugh Street thought it was living in the nineteenth century. Doors were for going in and out of, not for locking up. When they locked up, they just lost their keys anyway. Besides, what could possibly happen to them in a neighborhood like this?

Gregor had tried many times to explain to them that their precious "neighborhood like this" was surrounded by neighborhoods like *that*, but it hadn't done any good. Hannah Krekorian was still enamored of the theory that there are no bad boys, and Lida Arkmanian thought a crack house was one of those little metal chalets you bought from Hammacher Schlemmer to break the shells of nuts in. It was enough to make a grown man weep.

"Krekor," old George called from the bottom of the stairs. "Come on now. I'm halfway there and it's you who are daydreaming."

Gregor wasn't daydreaming. He never daydreamed. He fell asleep when he tried.

He climbed down the steep concrete stairs without holding to the railing, joined old George on the pavement, and turned his head toward Holy Trinity Armenian Christian Church.

3

Two hours and ten minutes later, long arrived at his destination for the morning and long made miserable by the stiff mid-November chill, Gregor sat on top of a pile of brown packing boxes and wondered just what it was he had allowed himself to get talked into. Then he wondered which of the various things he had allowed himself to get talked into he meant. There was the trip with Bennis and the collected luminaries of the Baird family and Baird Financial on the *Pilgrimage Green*, of course—but for a number of reasons, if that trip hadn't materialized on its own, he and Bennis would have had to invent it. Then there was the project of the moment, which consisted of reading the numbers off packing boxes while old George Tekemanian and Father Tibor Kasparian fussed around the base of the pyramid, clucking at each other in Armenian. Every once in a while, one or two of the new people would come up and offer to help. Tibor and old George always turned them down, as if it wouldn't have been just as easy for both of them to take down numbers called out in Armenian—which was, after all, their native language—as in English. Every once in a while a child came by and asked what was going on. When that happened, Tibor stopped and tried to explain it all, starting with the Crucifixion, moving through the establishment of the Armenian state church, coming to a climax with the Turkish invasion, and rounding off on a note of triumph with the expulsion of the Soviets. The tale was riveting and the children were fascinated, as they were fascinated with anything this bent little man had to tell them. They had all heard stories about Tibor's life in the Gulags and daring escape into freedom, and most of them didn't care that the stories were not true. Over the past three years, Tibor had become the closest male friend Gregor had ever had, and Gregor normally approved of anything that made the man happy, as telling the history of Armenia this way certainly made Tibor happy. The problem for Gregor was that the speech took half an hour to make, and all during that time Gregor would be sitting on his box, rubbing his hands together in a vain attempt to keep them warm. Old George Tekemanian was really only here for show, and to give Tibor someone to mutter to in Armenian. The temperature was dropping steadily if not rapidly, making Gregor less comfortable by the minute.

Tibor moved away from the base of the pyramid, pointed at boxes as he counted them under his breath, and shook his head.

"Two short," he said fretfully. "Two short. Where could the two boxes be?"

"Have you tried looking in the back room in the basement?" Gregor asked. He asked in English, because he spoke almost no Armenian. He did understand quite a bit.

Tibor climbed carefully up a pile of boxes to where he could speak to Gregor more naturally and said, "There is nothing in the back room in the basement, Krekor, I know because I have checked. I will tell you what this is. This is Mrs. Krekorian."

"Hannah?"

"Fussing," Tibor said solemnly. "I have told her over and over again. These are packages for people who are starving, not gifts to send to your mother-in-law. They do not need to be pretty, only generous."

"Hannah's certainly generous," Gregor said.

"Generous," old George said from the street. "Hannah stuffs people the way she stuffs turkeys."

"Mrs. Krekorian," Tibor said, "makes everything pretty with ribbons. I have seen her, Krekor. I have gone to her house and there are her boxes next to the kitchen table and in the bottom of the boxes are the blankets and each of the blankets is tied up with little bows. You understand, Krekor, there is nothing wrong with bows. I myself very much like bows. Now, however, we do not have very much time, we have people who need food and warm things because the winter is coming and they have nothing. And Mrs. Krekorian gives me bows."

"What he's trying to say," old George said, "is that she fussed so much with the bows, she didn't get done on time."

"And I have people to pick up the boxes and take them to the airport at four o'clock," Tibor said. "Bennis and Donna will drive them and then at the airport there is the plane from the Red Cross that will take these boxes and the Red Cross boxes and the vaccinations we have paid for, and if Mrs. Krekorian's boxes are not there she might as well give them to her mother-in-law, except I think her mother-in-law is dead."

"Her mother-in-law is most definitely dead," Gregor said. "Hannah's a year older than I am. She was in Lida's class at school."

"My son David was in Lida's class at school," old George said. "I'm not dead."

Gregor stretched his long legs and began to climb carefully down from the packing boxes. The packing boxes were made of wooden slats and reinforced with steel corner guards, but although Tibor climbed up and down with impunity, Gregor didn't dare. Tibor was a small man, short and wiry and fragile of bone. Gregor was over six two and heavy in that solid, Rock of Gibraltar way some Armenian men get in middle age. Bennis always said Gregor reminded her of Harrison Ford with an extra twenty pounds on him, but the description made Gregor uncomfortable. For one thing, he didn't like to think he was carrying an extra twenty pounds. If he was careful not to look too often into mirrors, he felt good enough to convince himself he was in near perfect shape. For another thing, he could never remember just who Harrison Ford was.

"I take it you want me to go talk to Hannah Krekorian," Gregor told Tibor. "You should get Lida to do it, you know. Lida would have more effect."

"I've already had Lida do it," Tibor said. "Maybe a man will be better. For that generation, a man had authority."

"For Hannah Krekorian, the only human being on earth with authority is Ann Landers. That beats Sheila Kashinian, though. For Sheila Kashinian, the only human being on earth with authority is Shirley MacLaine. Why don't you go yourself?"

"She will try to feed me, Krekor."

"She will try to feed me, too. You've got to get down if I'm going to go any farther. You're directly in my way."

Tibor hopped off his crate into the street, earning an admiring glance from old George and a look of exasperation from Gregor. Old George might not have noticed it—and nobody else might have, either—but Gregor could see that the little priest was something beyond exhausted. The rosy red of his cheeks was fever, not good health, and while Tibor had been close to Gregor on the pyramid of packing boxes Gregor had seen his hands shake. Now Tibor was standing on the pavement, but not standing still. He was hopping back and forth, doing a little shuffle-step pace. Anyone who didn't know him well might have thought he was getting rid of nervous energy. Gregor thought he was trying to disguise the fact that his legs were shaking, too.

"Hey," Gregor said, as he got to the pavement himself. "Go home and rest. Get Lida to take over here. You can't save the entire Republic of Armenia on your own."

"I am not trying to save the entire Republic of Armenia on my own, Krekor. I am merely trying to commit an act of corporal charity. I am all right, really. Trust me."

"I don't."

"I know."

"Who do you figure that is up at our house?" old George

Tekemanian said. "I had thought he was one of the men Bennis knows, but now that I look at him I don't think so. He is too—pressed."

"Pressed?"

Gregor and Tibor had been standing on the side of the box pyramid away from the brownstone where Gregor and old George had their apartments. Now they came around the corner and looked up the street at the young man old George had noticed there. He was a very young man, and also—as old George had said—much too pressed to be a friend of Bennis Hannaford's. In fact, Gregor didn't think he'd ever seen anyone so pressed in his life. The very young man was wearing a navy blue suit with the trousers pressed into knife-edged creases and the end of his regulation rep tie tucked into his vest. He had very blond hair cut too short and a collar that rode just a little too high on the back of his neck.

"No, no," Tibor said when he saw him. "Not Bennis's. Bennis does not know nice young men like that."

"How do you know the young man is nice?" old George Tekemanian said. "Just because he's wearing a suit?"

"It is better than a torn sweatshirt and a nose ring," Tibor said, "which is the young man she introduces me to at the Armenian festival last year. The young man who sings somewhere with a band nobody has ever heard of."

"Everybody's heard of him," old George said. "Even I've heard of him."

"I don't care who's heard of him," Gregor said. "I've got to go."

The two other men turned to look at him, curious, but Gregor was already on his way. He had done his share of speculating about Bennis Hannaford's love life—since she had moved onto Cavanaugh Street after Gregor had met her on the first of what he thought of as his "extracurricular excursions into murder," he had speculated on that sort of thing a great deal—but old George and Tibor were right. There was no way this young man fit the general description of "one of Bennis's friends."

What he did fit the description of was Rookie Agent, Federal Bureau of Investigation.

Gregor had trained too many of the damned idiots in his time to mistake the breed for something normal on the street.

Two

1

Gregor Demarkian had never been much of a Cold Warrior. While the Cold War was still going on, he'd had other things on his mind—kidnapping detail, when he'd first joined the Bureau, and then serial murderers, and then Elizabeth dying. He wasn't political and he wasn't much upset by change, as long as it was someone else's change. He hadn't minded beatniks and he hadn't minded hippies and when college students took over administration buildings just to declare their solidarity with revolution in Nicaragua, he wondered why they expended the energy. Once the Cold War was over, he couldn't make himself get any more involved. What struck him were always the confusions, not the confrontations. Father Tibor stayed up night after night, watching governments fall in Sofia and Prague. Gregor bought a paper and stared at the headline for hours, not sure what he was supposed to do with it: "COMMUNIST PARTY BANNED IN SOVIET UNION." Lida and Donna and Bennis and Hannah hung on the television set, listening to Gorbachev and Yeltsin and gunfire in the background. Gregor sat deep in his club chair and listened to the head of the KGB get interviewed on *60 Minutes*. Even the independence of Armenia hadn't broken through to him, in spite of the fact that the whole neighborhood had been up and about for that one. There were a pair of speakers over the door to Ohanian's Middle Eastern Food Store. Little Donnie Ohanian managed to get them hooked into the television set in his parents' apartment on the building's second floor, and the speakers had blasted out regular doses of CNN all that long morning while they were waiting for the news to be confirmed. While that was going on, Gregor had been sitting in the Ararat restaurant, reading over and over again a tiny article on the back page of the front section of the *Philadelphia Inquirer*, about how the tiny Republic of Elekteria had replaced its capital city statue of Lenin with a picture of Ronald Reagan. The story turned out to be apocryphal—and the Republic of Elekteria to be nonexistent—but those things only made the story seem that much more important to Gregor. That was the way things had been since everything had started to go seriously nuts. Gregor had a feeling that that was the way things were going to go for a while now.

Gregor also had a feeling that some people wouldn't accept the change, no matter how radical. He had that feeling because the very young man from the FBI who was standing on his stoop was a throwback—but not really, because he was much too young to be thrown back to anything. The Bureau had always had a reputation for treating the citizens of its country as if they were an alien invading force. It was a reputation it had earned, even though most Bureau agents had no more tolerance for red baiting, domestic spying, and "counterrevolutionary" campaigns than anyone else. The truth of the matter was, as long as old J. Edgar Hoover was alive, the Bureau had been two organizations, not one. Even after his death, the Bureau had continued as two organizations to one degree or another, at least as long as Gregor had been a member of it. To this side was the great majority of Bureau agents, "real policemen" as they liked to think of themselves, who handled all those nasty interstate crimes the Bureau had been founded to combat in the first place. Kidnapping, interstate bank robbery and international bank fraud, mob-connected trucking and union activities, smuggling, the bribery and extortion of national political figures—as long as you stayed away from drugs, real police work in the FBI could be much more interesting and much more exciting than the real police work in Dallas or New York. It had to be much more exciting than what those people over there did, which no one on this side ever quite figured out. "Infiltrating" the Yippies hardly seemed worth the bother. The organization accepted anyone who walked through the door and left its records lying around on desks for anyone at all to read. "Monitoring" the peace movement was worse, especially after 1973. For one thing, there wasn't much left of it. For another, it did its business at rallies in public parks. Gregor was only sure of two things about what was going on over in that part of the Bureau's ranks. One was that the regular agents were right, and that the whole domestic spying enterprise was Looney Tunes. The other was that all the Looney Tunes agents were Looney Tunes themselves.

The problem with the agent standing on Gregor's doorstep was that he was a Looney Tune par excellance. If Gregor had had to reinvent from memory the epitome of a very dedicated domestic spy agent, he would have come up with this young man. The pale hair. The overneat clothes. The air of nervousness that just wouldn't quit—the man was so tense, he was generating electricity. He was also about twenty-six, and that couldn't be. Gregor had had a conversation just last week with a friend of his who was still in the Bureau. The big news over there now was that the Looney Tunes boys were being trimmed. "Not eliminated," his friend had told him, "but there's a hiring freeze and they're not training any more and we all keep crossing our fingers and praying to God that we're going to get rid of the nuts entirely."

Gregor wrapped his arms around his body and marched up Cavanaugh Street away from the church, watching the young man on his stoop and the jumpy way he kept seesawing from one foot to the other. That the young man looked out of place in this neighborhood went without saying. He was the wrong body type and had the wrong coloring. That he would also be out of place in the Bureau was Gregor's to ponder alone, but it presented an interesting chain of reasoning. If you're paring back on Looney Tunes but you can't really fire them all, what do you do with them? What sort of work would a Looney Tune be qualified for, once he could no longer spend his time tapping the phones at the Organization for the Vegetarian Solution to World War?

Gregor crossed the street, dodged a little to avoid a standing display of Indian corn that had been wound around a lamppost as if the lamppost had been a maypole, and noticed in passing that the paper flag on Lida's third floor had been changed. This new one was much more neatly and professionally done, meaning Donna Moradanyan was back from the Main Line. It was also three entirely different colors. It made Gregor wonder where the confusion lay, here or on the other side.

Gregor got to his stoop, went up the concrete steps without touching the rail so he wouldn't disturb the brown and amber ribbons someone had braided there, and then wondered when the braiding had been done. Donna Moradanyan was not only back, she was back with a vengeance. He stopped at the top of the stoop where the young man was standing and watched for a moment while the young man looked around himself, making wide arcs with his head like an electric eye scanning a security field. Then the young man turned back to the door, picked out the buzzer button next to "Apartment 3, Demarkian," and pressed.

Gregor leaned forward, tapped the young man on the shoulder and said, "Excuse me. I'm Gregor Demarkian."

"Gregor Demarkian," the young man said blankly, and then seemed to snap to. "Oh. Yes. Oh. Excuse *me*. My name is Jeremy Bayles. I'm from the Federal Bureau of Investigation. Steve Hartigan sent me." He plunged his hand into his hip pocket, pulled out a small square sealed envelope, and handed it to Gregor. Then he tried to smile.

Gregor held the envelope for a moment and wondered if he were really old enough for people named Jeremy to be old enough to be agents at the Bureau. He supposed he'd run into an agent named Tiffany next. He opened the envelope, pulled out a square of what was closer to cardboard than paper, and read:

> *Gregor. I know, I know. I couldn't help it. I was swamped and I didn't have any other choice. Be nice to the boy. I need the information. Steve.*

Gregor folded the card and put it in his pocket.

"Well," he said.

"What are all the flags?" Jeremy Bayles asked. "I mean, everywhere I look, there are flags."

"Armenian flags," Gregor said. "This is an Armenian neighborhood. Armenian-American, at any rate."

"But they're not all the same flags," Jeremy Bayles said reasonably. "Which one is the Armenian flag? What are the others? Why is everybody in the street? Is there some kind of international festival going on here or what?"

In a way, there was some kind of international festival going on every day on Cavanaugh Street, but Gregor didn't think it was something Jeremy Bayles would understand. Gregor wasn't even sure it was something he could explain.

He got his key out and opened the front door instead, thanking God once again that this door, at least, was on automatic lock. He'd had the automatic lock installed himself, after his first Christmas in the neighborhood, when the old lock had never been on unless he put it on. The rest of them might want to court burglary like maidens at a dance, but he wasn't that stupid.

He stepped back, let Jeremy Bayles enter the foyer before him, and brought up the rear.

"Armenia only declared its independence this past September twenty-fourth," he explained. "I'm not sure anyone really knows what the flag will be like in the long run. Every time a new version comes out over there, a new version goes up over here."

"What about the people in the street?"

"There are always people in the street."

"Oh."

"To be fair, we're playing host to a lot of new immigrants these days. They like to be out and around. When they're not, things get to be a little crowded."

"I didn't think cities were like this any more," Jeremy Bayles said. "I thought they were all like Washington. Armed camps."

"Even all of Washington isn't an armed camp."

"It isn't?"

"Haven't you ever been to Georgetown? Or Foggy Bottom?"

"Oh." Jeremy Bayles looked confused. "But those aren't really Washington," he said. "They couldn't be. Rich people live there."

If Steve Hartigan had been forced to take this idiot on staff, he was more than swamped and the hiring freeze extended much farther into the Bureau than the Looney Tunes camp. Gregor took another look through the mail— you never knew when you might miss something—and then gestured to the stairs. Jeremy Bayles nodded, but he wasn't really paying attention. He was looking at the enormous cardboard turkey that covered old George Tekemanian's door, and the papier mâché Pilgrim's hat that sat on the newel post at the bottom of the stair rail. The papier mâché Pilgrim's hat was big enough to fit the Jolly Green Giant and had been made by Bennis, who had revised her latest sword and sorcery novel by making papier mâché copies of everything in the book. For weeks, Gregor's apartment had been a mine field of papier mâché trolls, papier mâché dragons, papier mâché knights and papier mâché castles. It was only when the papier mâché unicorn stabbed him in the rear end that he finally put his foot down. Jeremy Bayles picked up the Pilgrim's hat, admired it, and put it down again. Then he began following Gregor to the stairs.

"You people sure do like to celebrate Thanksgiving," Jeremy said.

"Mmm," Gregor said. They reached the second floor landing and Gregor saw that the ASLEEP UNTIL FURTHER NOTICE sign had been taken down from Bennis Hannaford's door. In its place was a cardboard turkey even bigger than old George Tekemanian's, but with a fan of (possible) Armenian flags for tail feathers. Donna Moradanyan was back and on the warpath.

"So," Gregor said. "How is Steve? Is he still doing fugitive work?"

"Oh, no." Jeremy Bayles sounded shocked. "I didn't even know he'd ever done that. He's with the banking and fraud division now. He's been heading up our investigation of the savings and loan mess and possible criminal fraud involved in that. It's very important work."

"I'm sure it is. He used to like more excitement than that, though, when I knew him."

"But it is exciting work. It's fascinating."

"It doesn't have any high-speed car chases in it." They

had reached the third floor and the landing outside Gregor's door. When Gregor had left that morning, his door had had a nice, polite spray of Indian corn hanging under the bell. Now it had another of those enormous cardboard turkeys. This one had a pair of wirerim glasses on its nose and a copy of *Criminal Procedures and Practices* in its beak. Gregor tried his door, found it was unlocked—neither Bennis nor Donna ever remembered to lock up again after they'd been inside—and ushered Jeremy Bayles into his apartment. There was a life-size rag doll in Pilgrim goodwife clothes standing in his foyer, but he ignored that.

"So," he said. "What could Steve possibly want me for? The only thing I know about the savings and loan mess is that my own went bankrupt and got merged with something I can barely pronounce."

"It isn't about the mess," Jeremy Bayles explained. "It's about a man. Or two men, actually. One of them's dead."

"Dead?"

"Donald McAdam. He's dead. Then there's the other one, and Steve said you'd know, because it was in the paper you were going to see him. It was in *W*, I mean."

"What was in *W*?"

Jeremy Bayles blinked his pale, lashless eyes ingenuously. The worst of that ingenuousness was that it was undoubtedly sincere.

"It was in *W* that you were going to spend Thanksgiving with this guy Steve is so worked up about," he said. "You know. Jonathan Edgewick Baird."

2

There are men who retire to desert islands and Caribbean beaches and ski chalets in Vermont, glad to abandon the work they've spent their lives doing and dedicate the rest of their days on earth to wasting time. There are others who are haunted forever by their titles and their offices and their commercial selves, doomed to wander for eternity among the forever lost. For Gregor Demarkian, retirement had been more like trading paid employment for unpaid and forced assignments with chosen ones. Less than two years after he had left the Bureau for good, he had accidently become involved in the Main Line murder of Bennis Hannaford's father. That was how he had met Bennis, and how he had acquired the title the *Inquirer* and all its sister publications had become so enamored of: the Armenian-American Hercule Poirot. The title might have stuck in any case, but it was reinforced by what came next—Gregor's involvement in one of the most sensational cases of the decade, backed by the Archdiocese of Colchester, New York, and served up to the media like a flaming desert. Other cases had followed, if you could call them cases— Gregor resisted—and by now his dogged insistence that since he didn't have a private detective's license he couldn't be a private detective felt weak even to him. For one thing, it was an easy distinction to get around. John Cardinal O'Bannion had merely called him a "consultant" and gone right on treating him like a detective. For another, it was obvious that Gregor wasn't going to stop involving himself in extracurricular murder and didn't even want to. The kinds of murders he dealt with these days were far more interesting than the ones he'd dealt with at BSD, and far more soothing to the soul, too. It was comforting to realize that the world still operated on logic, even if it pretended not to. Under other circumstances, Gregor would have been almost pleased to hear about a suspicious death that someone wanted him to look into. It had been a long dry stretch since the last one, and he'd been getting bored. Under these circumstances, he wasn't so happy. The death of Donald McAdam had made all the papers and all the magazines, but it had seemed fairly cut and dried to him. Donald McAdam had been a damned fool and died the way damned fools often do, by pushing his luck once too often. Then there was the question of Jonathan Edgewick Baird, whom he knew as Jon Baird, a friend of Bennis Hannaford and her brother Bobby. Gregor had nothing at all against investigating Bennis Hannaford's friends, but if he was going to do it he wanted Bennis Hannaford's permission. He at least didn't want to accept an invitation she had given him in good faith and then use it to spy on people she might care about.

Of course, knowing Bennis, the mere suggestion that there might be a murder out there to investigate would leave her thrilled, and she wouldn't care if the chief suspect were her own grandmother.

Gregor moved into his kitchen, put the kettle on to boil, and rifled through his cabinets for his jar of instant coffee. He and Tibor had both given up trying to make coffee from grounds. They were afraid they were going to poison themselves. Gregor put the jar on the kitchen table and got out two mugs and two small silver spoons. Then he sat down and waited for Jeremy Bayles to do the same.

"It's not that I don't want to help," he said, "it's just that I can't see what I can help with. I've read the newspaper accounts of the way McAdam died—"

"It's all much stranger than that," Jeremy Bayles said quickly.

"—and I can't see that there was any way for his death to be suspicious. And as for Jon Baird, I've been thinking about it ever since you mentioned his name. He couldn't have had anything to do with McAdam's death. He was in jail at the time."

"Oh, I know," Jeremy Bayles said. "We don't think Baird murdered McAdam. It's not like that at all."

"What is it like?"

Jeremy Bayles coughed. The kettle was already spewing steam. Gregor had an awful feeling that he hadn't put enough water in it. He'd ruined two other kettles that way in the past six months. He got up and poured water into the mugs anyway, and came up with just enough.

"Donald McAdam," Jeremy said, "was under investigation by our unit because of his possible involvement in a green mail fraud at the Farmers and Mechanics Savings and Loan in Bimalli, Florida. We thought there might be a connection because he had the same sort of deal with a man named Robert Hannaford here in Philadelphia. Steve said he thought you were acquainted with Robert Hannaford's sister?"

"I'm acquainted with Robert Hannaford's sister."

"Yes. Well. The deal went like this. McAdam would find a stock with a nice low price, call it Consolidated Widgets. He'd go out and buy a tremendous amount of this stock on margin, and then his confederate—in Philadelphia it was Robert Hannaford; in Bimalli it would be a man named Chester Evans who works for Tamm-Norwick Investments—anyway, his confederate, always a broker or an investment banker, would float a rumor that there was going to be a takeover attempt of Consolidated Widgets. Takeover attempts mean rising stock prices. Buyers would flood the market bidding up Consolidated Widgets. McAdam would sell out at the inflated price. And then the rumor, of course, would turn out to have been untrue. McAdam would have made a killing. His confederate would have received about fifty thousand dollars in cash for services rendered. And the ordinary buyers in the market would have been bilked."

"Including a few savings and loans," Gregor said.

"Including savings and loans, including insurance companies, including pension funds." Jeremy Bayles waved his hands in the air, took a sip of his coffee, and grimaced. "Yes. Well. McAdam and his confederate would do well and the brokers would do well because they'd still make all those commissions, but what we're talking about here is major fraud and McAdam did a lot of it. They had him testifying in more than three dozen cases at the time he died."

"Good Lord," Gregor said. "The man really did get around. You say you don't think Jon Baird murdered him. Would he have reason to, by the way?"

"No," Jeremy admitted. "No opportunity and no motive from what we can see. Baird's company owned McAdam's and McAdam had one of those impossible golden parachutes where it's not worth it to fire the guy, but the day McAdam died, he signed an agreement with Baird clearing all that up."

"From jail?"

"If you mean Baird, yeah," Jeremy said. He tried his coffee again. He grimaced again. Gregor didn't know what he was complaining about. Compared with Gregor's usual coffee, this stuff was ambrosia. "I know it's not supposed to be legal for federal prisoners to operate businesses from prison," Jeremy went on, "but the fact is that we can't deny them access to the phones as long as they've got anything going on appeal, and these guys are great at figuring out how to keep going at appeals until the day they're released. I'm not kidding. Baird was running Baird Financial from his cell and there was this other guy who did a computer fraud on a bank out in Iowa and got out of prison with twenty-five million dollars waiting for him that we could never find."

"He must have been a better con man than most."

"Oh, he was. Anyway, as for McAdam, that was in terms of Jon Baird and the people at Baird Financial, and to tell you the truth, even if the agreement hadn't been signed the McAdam thing would have been pretty small potatoes over there anyway. Just before Jon Baird went to prison, Baird Financial started negotiations to merge with Europabanc. Just about the time McAdam died, the negotiations paid off. Baird Financial and Europabanc are set to merge next month, and it's going to be the biggest thing in international finance since the birth of the first Rothschild. Next to that, McAdam's twelve and a half million dollars isn't much."

"No," Gregor said, "I can see it isn't. But then what is? What is going on with the McAdam investigation that makes you want to ask me about Jon Baird? Or about the death of Donald McAdam at all."

"It's not just Jon Baird we're looking at," Jeremy said, "it's all of them, because they were the people we know McAdam spoke to on the day he died. You see what I mean?"

"Not exactly. You just said McAdam wasn't murdered."

"I said we didn't think McAdam was murdered."

"Has Steve gotten this convoluted in his old age? Does he talk in circles about this thing, too?"

"Yeah," Jeremy Bayles sighed. He looked into his coffee cup, pushed it away from him, and said, "Could I have a glass of milk? I've got an ulcer and coffee sort of gets to me sometimes."

Gregor got up, went to his refrigerator, and hunted around for milk. He found an aluminum-foil covered pan with a pile of *yaprak sarma* inside it that hadn't been there when he'd left for old George's in the morning. He got the milk from the door shelf, smelled it to make sure it hadn't died, and handed it over.

"Donald McAdam," Gregor urged Bayles, reaching into the cabinet for a clean glass.

"Donald McAdam," Jeremy agreed. "You know what happened to him? He was this guy liked to mix a little strychnine in his cocaine—if you ask me, all druggies are nuts—and so he came home after signing this agreement with Baird Financial and decided to toot up in celebration except the celebration got out of hand and he got poisoned—"

"You don't get poisoned by strychnine," Gregor said. "It's not that kind of a substance. It's a drug that magnifies your body's response to external stimuli. If you could lie absolutely quietly in a room without light or sound—and I mean without, some kind of scientifically engineered environment—if you could do that, you could swallow all the strychnine you want and not die from it. What you die from with strychnine is convulsions caused by stimulus overload."

"Wonderful," Jeremy said, "that must be why the druggies took a shine to the stuff. Let me tell you, though, whatever you die from, you definitely do die. When we were doing the paperwork on this, I got the NYPD stats on deaths of this sort and they're incredible."

"Donald McAdam."

"Donald McAdam," Jeremy said. "Right. Well. He goes home, he takes this stuff all stoked with strychnine, he's out on his balcony, he has a series of convulsions and goes flipping over the rail and falls splat, all because of the strychnine in the cocaine, right?"

"Right," Gregor said.

"Wrong," Jeremy Bayles said.

"Wrong?"

Jeremy Bayles took a swig of milk as if it were liquor and tapped the bottom of his glass against the kitchen table. The glass hitting the wooden table made a hollow bell-like sound that was oddly pleasant.

"Wrong," Jeremy Bayles said, "because there were

traces of the coke lines he'd done on the table where he'd set them out and there wasn't any strychnine in them. There wasn't any strychnine in the food in the refrigerator, either, or in any of the bottles in the medicine cabinet or in any of the rest of the cocaine in his stash. There wasn't a single grain of strychnine anywhere in that apartment."

Three

1

Julie Anderwahl got seasick for the first time standing on the corner of Willow and Wall, five blocks north of the World Trade Center, at four o'clock on the afternoon of Friday, November sixteenth. It was one of those bright-cold days in New York. The air was as thin and brittle as glass, and the thick waves of exhaust that rose from the buses and cars that were trying to maneuver through the twisting streets were self-contained, as if they'd been born in bubbles. In spite of the lateness of the hour, Julie had just eaten lunch. She'd gone through a long day of work on the public relations campaign for the Europabanc merger thinking of nothing but shrimp with lobster sauce, and then, when the calls from Brussels and Geneva had all come in and her secretary had retired to the ladies' room in a storm of tension tears, she'd taken off for Chinatown. It had even felt like a good idea, in the beginning. The walk up had cleared her head. Julie always found it hard to sit for hour after hour in canned air. The food had been good, too. Like a lot of people who worked on Wall Street and in the Trade Center, Julie had a little list of perfect Chinatown restaurants in her head. She knew where to go for Szechuan and Hunan and

Cantonese, and which places were "authentic" because they promised pickled chicken feet in Chinese characters on strips of paper hung along the walls. Today, she hadn't been prepared for chicken feet. She'd gone to Madame Lu's, which was decked out for Westerners in fake black leather upholstery and paper satin wallpaper of gold. Madame Lu's served shrimp with lobster sauce on lo mein noodles instead of rice. Julie had eaten a ton of it, so much she began to feel like a balloon blown up to the bursting point, ready to pop.

Later, going back downtown, Julie began to wonder if she should have left the office at all. This was an important day. There were a million things to get done, and she was dealing with a lot of Europeans, who still thought a woman's place was in the typing pool. Every last one of them was looking for an excuse to complain about her to Calvin. She could already hear them in her head, their voices drawling and low in the way only speaking French could make them, saying, "Of course, she has no concentration. Women never do."

At the corner of Willow and Wall, Julie stopped, put her hand against the street signpost, and closed her eyes. People swirled past her, paying no attention. She was an expensive-looking young woman in a red suit with a very short skirt. There were hundreds like her spread through the law firms and brokerage houses and consulting companies that filled this part of town. She opened her eyes and closed them again and opened them again and closed them, wondering why she was so dizzy. It took hours for food poisoning to work, but food poisoning was just what she felt like she had. Underneath her feet, the pavement seemed to be rippling. The air around her had begun to feel too cold at just the same instant when her skin began to feel too hot. Even her suit felt wrong, and it was one of her best, raw silk, imported from France, made by Dior. She gripped the signpost tightly and began to heave. Her ribs expanded and contracted against the rough thread knobs that held the buttons on her blouse. Nothing's coming up, she thought. That's good. And then, of course, something did come up. Everything came up. Great gobs of undigested Chinese food. Thin streams of brown that were probably cups of coffee. The hard-edged remnants of fortune cookies. Julie leaned as far into the street as she could and let it happen. Her body felt possessed by demons and her mouth felt full of fire.

Less than a minute later, it was over. Julie straightened up and looked around. There was a puddle of goo in the street she couldn't bear to look at. There were people passing back and forth as if she weren't there. Only one woman had stopped to watch. She was thin and black and standing better than an arm's length away, as if Julie might turn out to be crazy or angry or full of drugs and not worth bothering with.

"Are you all right?" the black woman said.

"Fine," Julie told her, looking down at her suit. The suit was clean. At least she hadn't thrown up on that.

"You ought to have that taken care of," the black woman said. "Whatever it is."

"I will," Julie said. "I will."

"I just hope it's not that AIDS," the black woman said. "If it's that AIDS, you're as good as dead."

"It's not AIDS," Julie said.

"If it's not AIDS, you're probably pregnant," the black woman said. "That's why I stopped to ask. You look pregnant."

"What?" Julie said.

The black woman was gone, vanished, as thoroughly disappeared as if she had been a shade or a telepathic premonition in a novel by Stephen King. Julie looked into the crowd to see where she might have gone, but it was useless. That was when the light changed to "Walk" in front of her, and Julie decided it was time to go. The puddle was still there in the gutter at her feet, but there was nothing to connect her to it. The people around her now had not been around her then. They had no idea she had anything to do with the mess. They probably never imagined she could. Julie crossed the street and began to pick her way carefully along the cracked and curving sidewalks that led to the Trade Center, picking up speed as she went.

Ten minutes later, she came out of the elevator on the 101st floor of the World Trade Center, leaned against the metal ashtray sticking out of the wall there, and closed her eyes again. The elevator from the 45th floor was an express. It traveled so fast and went so high it made your ears pop, and at right about that point Julie had thought she was going to be sick again. She hadn't been, miracle of miracles, and if she just stood here for a moment longer she wouldn't be now.

The second miracle of miracles came to pass. Her head cleared. Her stomach settled. She straightened up and brushed herself off and marched through the hall to the glass doors that led to the reception desk. Since Baird Financial rented this entire floor, it could have had its reception desk directly in front of the elevator doors—and it had, in the beginning. Then there had been a bomb threat and a client so angry he threatened to use a gun, and the firm had decided that the 1980s were roaring a little too loudly to do without security.

Julie went through the glass doors and around the corner and found Lindsay at the desk. Lindsay was a pleasant-faced straight-haired blond with bones so fragile she looked like she'd have osteoporosis by the time she was twenty-three.

"Hi," Julie said. "I'm back in for the day. Any messages for me?"

"You look really awful," Lindsay told her, ignoring the part about the messages. Julie had a private secretary to take her messages. "Are you sure you want to go back to work? You look like you ought to lie down."

"I'm fine. I'm just a little tired. Is Mark in?"

"He's been in the main conference room drawing up subsidiary employment contracts for the past hour. Are you *sure* you're all right?"

"I'm fine. And I'm going on vacation tomorrow. What about Europabanc? Any wild-eyed Europeans calling up to say how I did everything they wanted me to do wrong?"

"No wild-eyed Europeans at all. No Europeans. Just bankers."

"Bankers?"

"To see Mr. C and Mr. J. About the loans and the cash and the stock and the rest of it so we can close after Thanksgiving. I think I'm going to hate it when we close."

"Everybody will."

"Sukie in accounting says there's going to be wads and wads of actual cash lying around the morning of."

"There won't be. It's two hundred million dollars we're talking about here. It'll be done by computer."

"That's too bad," Lindsay sighed.

Julie was about to say it wasn't too bad at all, having that much cash around the office would just be inviting a robbery, but instead she backed away from Lindsay's desk and began to retreat down the hallway that led to the offices. Her stomach had begun to roll again and her vision had begun to blur. It was much worse than it had been in the elevator. It was almost as bad as it had been at Willow and Wall.

"Damn," Julie said, not quite to herself, not quite under her breath, so that a typist passing her in the hall looked up, stepped back, and stared. "Damn, damn, damn."

There was a communal washroom that the secretaries

used right around the corner from where Julie now stood, but she knew she couldn't use it. She had to get to the back hall and the private lavatories she had the keys to. Then she had to throw up again, and then she had to think. At the moment, that list of chores looked long enough to take up the rest of her life.

She was moving as quickly as she could without running, pumping along the thick carpet in her fashionably high and wretchedly uncomfortable heels, when the feeling passed. She came to a full stop, surprised and a little suspicious. She took a deep breath and found she didn't feel dizzy any more. She looked around and found that she was standing with the Divisions Comptroller's office on her left and one of the doors to the main conference room on her right. Since the main conference room was in the center of the block and had doors that opened into every perimeter hallway, this was not surprising.

"Mark," Julie said to herself.

She opened the door to the main conference room and looked inside. Her husband was at the far end of the conference table, surrounded by three assistants and entranced by a stack of papers. Other stacks of papers were laid out along the table in front of the seats that would be occupied on the day they closed. They were laying out the documents the principals would need to have and making sure they had enough copies. At least, if Lindsay was right, they were doing that for the subsidiary employment contracts.

Julie came in, shut the door behind her, and said, "Mark?"

Mark looked up, nodded to the young women around him, and hurried to Julie. "Are you all right?" he asked her, as soon as he was close enough to whisper. "I just had a call from Lindsay at reception. She said you were white as a ghost."

It was really a cold day, one of the coldest so far this year. Julie could feel that even standing in the center of the building like this, where no wall of the room bordered on the outside. She wrapped her arms around her body and tried not to shiver. She'd always thought there was something unprofessional about showing the effects of temperature. She'd always thought there was something inherently wrong with being unprofessional. She looked over at the table and the piles of papers on subsidiary contracts and almost came over ill for a whole new set of reasons altogether.

"Jesus Christ," she told her husband. "What would you say if I told you I was going to quit work?"

2

Calvin Baird had always been one of those people who believed in details. Even as a child, his difference from his brother Jon was clear. Jon would climb trees and plan grand strategies for the conquering of neighborhoods. Calvin would calculate the exact number of foot soldiers they would need to successfully storm the Ackmartins' back lawn. It was that way in life, too, on every front but the emotional one. Calvin was of a generation, and a temperament, that didn't think men were required to have emotions. What this led to was a kind of superficial schizophrenia, professional perfection and personal chaos. Calvin's business life was full of neatly drawn lines and exactly totaled sums, while his home life was a roiling mass of confusion and resentment. He had had two wives so far and six children, and they all hated him. He wouldn't have cared except that they kept dropping into the real part of his life and forcing disruptions. His first wife wanted more money. His second wife wanted him to spend more time with their children. His oldest son from his first marriage was in drug rehab and threatening to escape. His oldest daughter from his second marriage was plain and dumpy and cried every time she had to go to dancing class. It was enough to make any sane man crazy.

It had been a bad fall for personal problems, culminating in his second wife's demand for a divorce, but by the time Calvin reached five o'clock on the sixteenth of November, he thought he was just getting a break. There was nothing like real work to take your mind off things. He'd had real work all day, combined with the nagging last-minute details of getting ready for the ride on the *Pilgrimage Green*. Calvin had found the combination irresistible. Even the typists' feeble attempts to "celebrate" the holiday on office time gave him an emotional jolt, pathetic though they were. Calvin thought if he had to see another hollow chocolate turkey wrapped in badly colored tinfoil, he'd pop a blood vessel. He wanted to pop a blood vessel on general principles. On one side of his desk he had long sheets of computer printout full of columns of numbers, showing every possible permutation of the deal they were doing with Europabanc. There was a column for the stock Baird Financial would hand over to Europabanc's officers and another column for the stock Europabanc would hand over to Baird. There was a column of figures representing cash on hand in the various accounts Baird Financial kept in various banks all over the world. There was even a column of figures representing office supplies, right down to boxes of pencils and cases of typewriter ribbons. These last figures were not necessarily accurate—they wouldn't do a complete inventory of the two companies until the merger was finished and the two were one—but they made Calvin deliriously happy nonetheless. When they also made him tired, he turned his attention to the other side of his desk, where he had the list of things his secretary had packed for him to take on the

Thanksgiving break. Jon's Thanksgiving parties were the only exception Calvin had ever found to his distaste for out-of-office life. In spite of Jon's fevered reveling in their status as descendents of men who had sailed on the *Mayflower*—which Calvin thought was silly—Jon's parties were always better than tolerable. They sometimes even made Calvin think he was having a good time.

The discrepancy came in a cross-reference between the column of figures indicating cash on hand and the column of figures representing the cash infusion from the sale of the McAdam Investments junk bonds. The junk bond sale had gone off a little more than a week ago, and they had just this morning received word from the bank that the checks from the various participants had cleared. Calvin wouldn't even have noticed the discrepancy except for the fact that he had been bored. As the day wound to a close and the vacation loomed, he seemed to be slowing down. He punched the cash-on-hand numbers into his hand calculator, added the junk bond infusion numbers, and checked the total against the number on his sheet marked "total available liquid funds." And came up short.

It *was* five o'clock on a Friday night. Calvin Baird knew that. He could hear his secretary packing up to go home on time for once, and he knew that if he stuck his head out his outer office door he would see the place nearly deserted. Calvin even accepted, in principle, the idea that his employees had a right to desert him. The rights and responsibilities of employees were set out in detail in a brochure the firm had printed to give to all new hires, *Working at Baird*. Even so, it nagged at him. It worse than nagged at him. The discrepancy was probably nothing. It could certainly be corrected during the ten long days he was away. There was absolutely no reason why he should insist on having it corrected now. He just couldn't help himself.

If he'd been entirely honest, he'd have admitted he

didn't want to help himself. Yes, the mistake could be corrected while he was away, but he didn't think it would be. He truly believed that all his employees started frolicking as soon as his back was turned. They threw spitballs and did crossword puzzles and made personal phone calls whenever he was out of the office. The fact that there was never any evidence of any of this didn't faze him. He was sure it was being done in secret, and that the secrecy was part of the point.

In the outer office, Sidney Stack was putting on her lipstick. Calvin knew that because he had heard her compact snap open and a sharp metallic ting as something—the lipstick tube's upper half, undoubtedly—went down on the desk. Calvin thought of her going home on the subway to Queens, with the discrepancy uncorrected. He thought of Alexandra Haye, his special assistant, spending her night in whatever disco the single young of Manhattan were frequenting now. He thought of everyone in the office, off work and free of responsibility, leaving him with this mess.

There was another snap and another ting, Sidney packing up and ready to go. Calvin hurried to his office door and stuck his head out. He caught Sidney bending over to pick something up off the floor, presenting her ass to him like a beach ball. Any other man would have felt a faint stirring of desire or a spurt of adolescent appreciation. Calvin Baird didn't even notice.

"Miss Stack?" he said.

Sidney Stack straightened up and turned around, suspicious. She was a pretty woman nearing thirty, who lived with her parents in Queens and was saving up to get married. Calvin had the uncomfortable feeling that she'd heard this tone in his voice before and didn't like it.

"I'm giving a birthday party for my father tonight," Sidney said. "I've got people coming at seven o'clock. I really can't stay late."

"Of course," Calvin said. He did his best to smile, but he was angry as hell. That was why Sidney was a secretary, why so many people were secretaries, why women would never get ahead. They always had something else to do that was more important than staying late at the office. He saw Julie Anderwahl come out into the hall from Mark's office and corrected himself. Julie was an exception.

"We've got a major problem," he told Sidney. "We've got a discrepancy in the Europabanc figures."

"I can't do anything about a discrepancy in the Europabanc figures," Sidney said. "I'm really going to have to insist, Mr. Baird. I can't stay late tonight. I've had this party planned for months."

"If the Europabanc thing falls through, you won't have to plan anything ever again. You won't have a job to interfere with your personal life. This is an emergency."

"My father's birthday party is an emergency," Sidney said.

"What's really the emergency?" Julie Anderwahl asked them. She had drifted in from the hall, attracted by the sound of their raised voices. Calvin thought she looked pale and pasty and just a little ill. "Is there something I can help you with?"

Although Calvin Baird respected Julie Anderwahl's work habits, he didn't respect her mind. He didn't respect the mind of anyone who worked in PR, and he respected the minds of women even less. He thought feminism had been inevitable once women realized how stupid their lives were without real work in the real work force, but he didn't think women should have been allowed in. They were just so much fluff.

At the moment, they were also his only audience, so he gave it a try. "The Europabanc figures," he said. "I've just been going over them. They're wrong."

"Wrong?"

"They don't add up. I add up the column with our cash on hand, and then I add up the column with the junk bond sales, and then I add the two together, and I don't get as much as I'm supposed to get."

"Did you talk to Mark about this? Aren't those Mark's numbers?"

"Mark," Calvin Baird said.

Sidney Stack grabbed her coat from the rack and picked up her pocketbook. "I have to get out of here. You two may want to sit around all night figuring out what numbers belong to who, but I have a birthday party to give. For my father. Like I told you."

"You'll never get ahead if you take that kind of attitude," Calvin told her prissily. "It's counterproductive."

"As soon as Joey passes his sergeant's exam, I'm going to get married," Sidney Stack said, "and as soon as I get married I'm going to get pregnant, and as soon as I get pregnant I'm going to stop working for good. I've had the life of the New York career girl. I just can't take it. Good night, Mrs. Anderwahl."

"Good night," Julie said.

"Silly little ass," Calvin said. "She's condemning herself to a life of mediocrity, that's what she doesn't understand. She's just asking to spend the rest of her life in Queens."

Sidney Stack was out in the hall and really pumping, headed for the reception desk at full speed in spite of her four-inch heels. Calvin sniffed after her and then turned to Julie, who was still standing by his desk, cool and professional.

"Now what do I do?" he asked. "I can't just let this go. It could bring the whole project down."

Julie Anderwahl shook her head, stepped back, and said, "Do you have any specific information we can work with? Are these Mark's numbers? Do you know which set are coming up short?"

"They're not Mark's numbers, they're Jon's. And I know which set. It's the cash on hand."

"Does your assistant know how to operate a computer? It's Alexa Haye, isn't it?"

"It's Alexandra Haye, yes, but I don't know if she knows how to operate a computer. I suppose she does. They all do coming out of business school these days."

"We'll call Mark in anyway," Julie Anderwahl said. "He definitely knows how to operate a computer, so we won't have to worry about that. And I'll get Alexa from the copy room. She was down there making sure we had enough protocol sheets not five minutes ago."

Julie put her hand to her forehead and rubbed. For a split second, Calvin noticed that she did not look well, that she looked almost green, and the terrible thought came to him that she was going to back out on him too. Then she murmured something about being right back and walked out of the office, and he realized she was going to get the others and come back.

Back in his own office, Calvin sat down in front of the computer printouts and smiled. He'd been behaving like a prima donna out there, of course, and like a weak and petulant man. He was none of those things, but he didn't mind being perceived that way. There were men who set great store by their dignity and others who wanted to believe in their own integrity, but Calvin had only ever cared about one thing. You went into a fight to win it any way you could. The outcome was the only thing that mattered.

Calvin just wished Jon could have been here, to see how he had turned them all around, and made them do what he wanted.

3

Five hundred and fifty miles away, lying in a high-sided bunk in the captain's cabin on the *Pilgrimage Green*, Jon Baird put down the file he had been reading and closed his eyes. It was early yet, and he was alone. The crew had gone into town for dinner and Sheila had gone off with some friends from MacLean. He had hours yet to do the things he wanted to do, without being bothered by anyone. Then, tomorrow, the whole pack of them would arrive together and he would be on stage all the time. Sheila would try to crawl into bed with him and when she found out that would be impossible she would cry.

There was a cold stiff wind blowing out on the water, rocking the *Pilgrimage Green* in its berth. To Jon Baird the motion was like the swaying of a cradle and made him feel he had to go to sleep. Instead, he opened his eyes again, sat up a little straighter, and turned his attention one more time to the file. It was a file he had no business being in possession of, or even reading. His access to it was prohibited by law. For Jon Baird, that was the best of what it meant to be himself, a man with more than a billion dollars, a man with power and connections from one end of the globe to the other, a man who couldn't be turned down. The deals were fun and the toys were nice and being able to order a dozen suits custom made at Brooks any time he got the urge was a definite kick, especially after a childhood spent wondering if he'd ever be able to buy anything at all. None of that compared with the simple access he had, and the being privy to secrets.

He wore glasses when he read, with real glass in them, so they lay heavily against his nose. He took them off now and rubbed his forehead a little. There was no electricity on the *Pilgrimage Green*. He had been reading by candlelight, and he had given himself a fair case of eyestrain.

He also had no reason to go on with what he was doing. He had read this file fifteen times since he had first gotten it, and it always said the same things, it always made the same points. He kept rereading it because it gave him comfort. It convinced him he was doing the right thing.

He put it down on the table next to his bed, thought better of that—he could doze off and Sheila could come in—and opened the cabinet under his bunk to put it in there. Just before he let it go he looked at the cover of it one more time, and smiled.

AGENT REPORT: FEDERAL BUREAU OF INVESTIGATION,
BACKGROUND.

it said, and under that, the name of the agent whose background had been checked:

GREGOR DEMARKIAN.

Jonathan Edgewick Baird had never in his life allowed himself to depend on anyone relying on reputation alone. He required facts and he required proof and one way or the other he always got both.

Four

Gregor Demarkian had told everyone on Cavanaugh Street that he was traveling on the *Pilgrimage Green* because Bennis Hannaford had asked him to—and, in a way, it was even true. It had certainly been Bennis Hannaford who had first brought Jon Baird to Gregor's attention, first by relaying his message through her brother Bobby and then by digging through Lida Arkmanian's near-complete set of *People* magazines to find the articles on Baird's indictment and the rise of Baird Financial. Since Bennis had been born and brought up on the Main Line, middle daughter of one of its most socially prominent families, her take on Baird and the people he represented was invaluable. Bennis always seemed to know someone's aunt's second cousin's husband or to have gone to camp with somebody else's first wife's sister. Gregor sometimes thought she had come out with the entire female population of the Greater Philadelphia Metropolitan Area. However tenuous the connection, Bennis would be able to find it. She would also know enough gossip to fill in the gaps.

"Everybody was surprised as hell when Jon Baird went to jail," she had told him, "because he was the wrong Baird to have gone to jail. Tony, now, that's his son—my sister Emma knew him when she was living in New York. Sex, drugs, rock and roll, and really strange art. You'd have expected him to go to jail."

"What about the charges?" Gregor had asked her. "Do they sound like the sort of thing Baird would have been involved in?"

Bennis shrugged, her great black storm cloud of hair hovering in the air around her face, her wide blue eyes looking almost navy. "If you're asking do I think Jon Baird does things that are against the law, the answer's yes. And awful lot of things are against the law these days even I don't think ought to be. If you're asking do you think he did the things he was accused of doing, I'd have to say he must have. I mean, he pleaded guilty. Some of these guys plead guilty because they get threatened with RICO, but I never heard of that coming up in this case. And it was such a small case. It's not like he doesn't have good lawyers."

"But you find it strange," Gregor said.

Bennis got out a cigarette, lit it, and blew smoke at the ceiling. "It was a couple, three counts on insider trading and not very serious insider trading. It was nothing, really. Why would he want to bother?"

"Some people are just naturally bent."

"Well, Gregor, that's fine, but naturally bent or not, Jon Baird isn't stupid. These were straightforward insider trading charges, not the fraud charges that get called insider trading because they come under the same law. What Jon Baird went to jail for isn't even illegal in Switzerland or France. If he wanted to do that kind of thing, why didn't he just get on a plane and go talk to his brokers over there?"

"Maybe he was keeping his traveling down to pacify the IRS. They get very nervous about people who take too many trips outside the country."

"If they do, they're getting ulcers from Jon Baird. I think

he owns his Concorde. I *know* he owns his own 747. No, if you ask me, it's that second wife of his. All flounce and flooze and forty-thousand-dollar ball gowns from Carolina Herrera."

Gregor decided not to make an issue of the $40,000 ball gowns from Carolina Herrera. "It's his second wife what?" he asked Bennis. "Who put him up to insider trading? Who committed the insider trading herself?"

"Who ought to be in jail," Bennis said. "She was at that American Heart Association thing I went to back in June—although why she bothered is beyond me, because Baird's first wife was on the committee and she had to know she wasn't going to get a decent table—but anyway she was there, bopping around like a high-school freshman on marijuana at a Guns and Roses concert. Maybe what I'm trying to say is that I thought Jon Baird ought to have been arrested, for marrying her when he was old enough to know better."

"How much older?"

"I don't know. But look at it this way, Gregor. Baird has at least twenty years on me if not more, and I'm thirty-six. And I'll bet I have at least some time on Sheila Baird. Which makes it a minimum of twenty-two or so years, and Baird's no movie star. He doesn't work out ten hours a week and have his face lifted in Los Angeles. He's this grizzled old man with sags under his eyes."

"I'm this grizzled old guy with sags under my eyes."

"You're not dating a representative of the Smith College Bulimia Squad. Of course, you might be a lot older than I think. I don't know. I haven't been able to nail down your birthday, because you won't tell me and Lida and the rest of them don't remember. I think you were very deprived, you know, growing up in a culture where people didn't make a fuss over children's birthdays."

"They made a fuss over my name day."

"That's not the same. Tibor suggested I look up your baptismal certificate in the parish records, and I did, but it was a funny thing. The date of birth had been smudged right out with black gunk. It looked like ink from a typewriter ribbon."

"Did it?"

"It's no use not telling me, Gregor. I'll just go on giving you presents whenever I think it might fit. Donna and I have even discussed giving you two or three surprise parties a year. Besides, we have a clue."

"What clue?"

"You were born on Friday the thirteenth. Hannah Krekorian says she remembers your mother talking about it to the other women, saying what an unlucky day that usually is but it was lucky for her because she got you."

"I'm glad she thought so," Gregor had said, and then he had deflected the subject. The last thing he had wanted to think about was the campaign—subtle at first; now approaching full-scale war—that Bennis and Donna Moradanyan were running to discover his birthday and give him a party. The only good luck he'd had in that was in the fact that none of the other people on Cavanaugh Street were interested in joining in. Armenian culture really was traditionally Christian, in the most venerable definition of the term. It was entirely uninterested in the physical birth of anything. It cast its vote on the spiritual side.

Gregor himself had cast his vote on the prudent side. The conversation he had had with Bennis about Jon Baird had taken place in the living room of her apartment, among the papier mâché models of trolls and dragons and unicorns she had made to help her revise her latest fantasy novel. That was what Bennis did for a living, and a very good living it was, too. Main Line or no Main Line, she had no family money. Her father, a misogynist of the first water, had seen to that. All the things she did have, and the list was consid-

erable, came out of the series of books on knights and
damsels and leprechauns in distress she'd been writing for
almost five years now, the good old dependable regularly
produced volumes of the *Chronicles of Zed and Zedalia* that
showed up year after year on the *New York Times* hardcover fiction best-seller list. When Gregor had first met
Bennis, he had thought that Zed and Zedalia must be
people. As it turned out, they were places. Zed was a place
ruled by men. Zedalia was a place ruled by women.

"It all works out," Bennis had told him, "because none
of it is supposed to be real, just taking place in real time."

Gregor sometimes wondered if Bennis's life took place
in real time, but he let that pass. He understood her mood.
He'd gone downstairs in the hope that Bennis would help
him decide whether to take Jon Baird up on his proposition.
As propositions went, it wasn't very interesting.

"He says he's got a link and it has to be in his inner
circle," Gregor had told Bennis, "and I told him that for that
he needed a tape recorder and a little old lady with a nasty
mind. The whole thing smacks of rich man's paranoia."

"The whole thing smacks of an escape hatch," Bennis
had told him solemnly. "Do you really want to spend another holiday on Cavanaugh Street, with Lida trying to
shove us together in closets and Hannah Krekorian taking
you aside for little chats about all the widowed men she's
known who've just keeled over in their prime because they
lacked companionship?"

"No."

"Well, then."

"From the way you've described them, they sound like a
thoroughly nasty group of people."

"They are. They'll make me feel right at home. Like
being back around good old Daddy's table, except it'll be
somebody else taking the abuse."

"Maybe there'll be an eligible bachelor on board and

you can come back to Cavanaugh Street with an engage-
ment ring on your finger. That would set Hannah Krekorian
on her ear."

"Maybe I'll have discovered the solution to the great
mystery of the Baird family relationships: why would Jon
Baird even want both of his wives on the same little boat.
Maybe he'll even kill one of them, and then you'll have a
murder to investigate."

"God forbid."

"God hasn't forbidden it up to now, Gregor. I think it's
a perfectly reasonable request on my part."

Whether it had been a perfectly reasonable request on
her part or not, Gregor did not, to this day, know. He only
knew that Bennis had been right—he really couldn't have
stood another holiday dinner on Cavanaugh Street, not
right this minute, although he had no intention of giving all
that up for good—and he'd been feeling the need to get
away for months. From that moment it had been decided,
almost without him, and he was on his way to this foggy
street in coastal Virginia.

Foggy was a very weak word for it. It was now eight
o'clock on Saturday morning, an hour before they were
formally expected. They were sitting in the car they had
hired—a nondescript Ford, this time, instead of the pale
pink Rolls Bennis had almost insisted on; the nondescript
Ford came with a driver anyway—parked at the curb in
front of the boardwalk that led to Pier 36. They could see
the sign that said "Pier 36." They could see the sign underneath it that was supposed to list the boats parked in its
berths. The line for Berth 102 had a notation beside it that
said *"Pilgrimage Green,"* but the rest of the lines were
empty. The fog was too thick for Gregor to tell if that meant
the rest of the berths were empty, or that the harbormaster
didn't really care whether his charges were listed on his
signs or not.

Their driver was sitting impassively behind the steering wheel, making no move to get out to open the doors for them or see to their luggage. Bennis shot an exasperated look at the back of his head and opened her door herself.

"I'm sure we can't actually sail in weather like this," she said. "I wonder what we're going to do if it doesn't let up."

"Fog like this always lets up," Gregor told her.

Bennis climbed out of the car and made her way around its nose to the boardwalk. In her jeans and turtleneck and flannel shirt, she looked like a college student who had streaked her dark hair with random polka dot spots of grey. Then she took a step into the fog and disappeared altogether.

"Don't do that," Gregor called after her. "If you get lost, we'll never find you."

"I'm not lost," Bennis called back, "I'm holding onto some kind of post. I was going to go look for the boat but I've changed my mind. I'd end up falling into the water."

"You can't fall into the water," a voice said. "There are guard ropes all up and down the pier. Give me a minute and I'll get this light on."

If there was one thing Gregor didn't want to hear coming out of a thick fog, it was a voice he wasn't ready for coming from a place he couldn't determine attached to no visible body at all. When the sound reached him, he almost jumped out of his skin. Then he opened the car door next to him, stepped carefully out onto the curb, and said, "Who is that?"

"Where is everybody?" Bennis called back. "I feel like I'm floating in mutagen ooze."

"Just a minute," the voice said. There was the sound of something metallic being scraped back and forth and then of something plastic hitting the boardwalk. The voice said *"Damn"* much too loudly and made the fog near Gregor's ears seem to quiver. The sound of something metallic being scraped back and forth resumed in staccato. "Damn, damn," the voice said again, and then a light came on, strong and round and well-defined, cutting through the fog. "There we go," the voice said again, except that this time it was attached to a young man with high cheekbones and long lines and a shock of straight dark hair. He was leaning over to pick up something from the boardwalk. It looked to Gregor like one half of a child's walkie-talkie toy. The young man got it into the palm of his hand, shoved it into his pocket, and straightened up. Then he turned slowly until he caught Bennis hanging onto her post and smiled. "You must be Bennis Hannaford," he said. "I'm Tony Baird."

"I know," Bennis said. "I think we've met."

"You think we ought to have met," Tony corrected her. He turned to Gregor and held out his hand. "If this is Bennis Hannaford, you must be Gregor Demarkian," he said. "I'm very glad to see you. My father's never hired himself his own private expert on murder before."

2

If Gregor had wanted to, he could have spent an hour correcting all the misimpressions Tony Baird had gotten about his stay on the *Pilgrimage Green*. For one thing, Gregor had never once allowed himself to be "hired" by anybody to be an expert in murder, or in anything else. For twenty long years, he had been an employee of the U.S. government as an agent of the Federal Bureau of Investigation. Since that time, he had been an employee of no one and nothing at all, and he intended to keep it that way. It was true that Jon Baird had offered him money to sail on the *Pilgrimage Green*. People did offer him money when they wanted him to do something for them. Gregor never took it. He wasn't rich, but he had more than enough to live on as long as he didn't develop Bennis Hannaford's tastes in personal amusement. He liked his independence more than he wanted to buy anything he couldn't already afford. The furthest he would go, at the end of a successful investigation, was to suggest that Father Tibor's Armenian Relief Fund was running a little low—which it always was, because Tibor could spend money even faster than Bennis could. Such a suggestion had prompted John Cardinal O'Bannion and the Archdiocese of Colchester, New York, to find an official way of providing the fund with two healthy infusions of cash, for which Tibor and Gregor had both been suitably grateful. It was not the same thing as "hiring" Gregor Demarkian.

The other place Tony Baird had got it wrong, of course, was in the assumption that what his father wanted was an expert on murder. Gregor could have corrected this impression very easily, but he decided not to. There were sometimes advantages to being considered an expert on murder in a situation where no such expert seemed to be required. It put people off balance. It even attracted a few of them, so that they came and told him things he had no right to hear. This was a tactic he had heretofore confined to much more serious investigations, investigations that really were investigations. In spite of the strange visit he had had from Steve Hartigan's young man from the FBI, Gregor had no reason to think that Jon Baird's little problem would be anything but inconsequential. He let the misimpression stand because, for some reason he couldn't pin down, he didn't like this young man. He didn't like him at all. As soon as he'd gotten a good look at his face, all the hairs on the back of his head had stood on end.

Bennis was having none of the same problems. She was walking up ahead at Tony Baird's side, and as the three of them moved toward Berth 102, Gregor found it easy to eavesdrop on their conversation.

"Nobody was supposed to be here before nine," Tony was saying, "but you know how these things are. Dad and Sheila were here last night and so everybody got antsy that they'd be late or miss out on something or they wanted to get Dad's attention, so they came. And my mother—have you met my mother?"

"I might have," Bennis said.

"Well, my mother is a flake. Not that I don't like her. I like her. I just don't know what to do with her. I mean, what woman in her right mind would have come along for this weekend?"

"Does your father control her money?"

"Of course he controls it. So what? He couldn't really take it away from her. She'd make a stink in the press and he'd end up having to give it back just to keep himself from being picketed."

"I see what you mean."

"She got here at seven thirty, if you can believe it, dragging me along behind her, and the next thing I knew she was in a cat fight with Sheila. She always gets into cat fights with Sheila. She always goes totally ballistic when she sees the glitter on Sheila's nails."

"I take it she didn't storm off the boat," Bennis said.

Tony Baird laughed. "Nobody's stormed off the boat, and I think they all ought to. They're the ones who're going to have to put up with all the fighting. I shouldn't make it sound like that. It's not really that bad. Except for Mother and Sheila, the rest of them get along pretty well."

"Who are the rest of them?" Gregor puffed mightily and managed to catch up, putting his head between Tony's and Bennis's so that they had to part to let him in. Before he'd come up, they had been walking so close together, their shoulders touched. "I got a guest list with my invitation," he said, "and little descriptions of everybody from your father when we talked, but I still don't have any flesh to go along with the names."

"What kind of flesh do you want?" Tony asked. They had reached Berth 102, and he shone his light directly on the plank going up to the *Pilgrimage Green*. Gregor found himself nonplussed. He knew the boat was a replica of the *Mayflower*, of course, and he knew that the boats of that time were smaller than the ones that sailed now. He'd visited the whaling ship at Mystic Seaport and found vessels that would have been considered small by most of the operators of modern day cabin cruisers. Still, he had expected something a little larger than this, and a little more sturdy looking, too. The *Mayflower* had sailed across the Atlantic. If it had been this small, how had it managed not to sink?

"The fog's lifting," Bennis said. "Maybe the driver will deign to bring up our things once it's gone. I told you we should have hired the other car, Gregor, we would have gotten better service."

"I'll get one of the crew to get your things," Tony said. "My father's not totally crazy. We are traveling with a full crew and a cook and a waitress besides. He had to pay them an arm and a leg to get them to sail on this thing, but he's got an arm and a leg to pay them, so I suppose that's his business. Be careful when you get to the top of the plank. There's a nail sticking up I've been tripping over all day."

"You were going to tell me about the other people on the trip," Gregor said, being very careful of the nail, even though he couldn't see it. He climbed off the plank onto the deck and looked around. Seen from here, the boat looked even smaller than it had from the pier. It also looked . . . richer. The original *Mayflower* had been a poor man's boat, built with good but no luxurious materials. The *Pilgrimage Green* was all teak and polish, thickly applied wax, and four coats of paint.

Tony led them to a formal hatch door that looked like a little tree house perched inexplicably on the deck. Inside it were a single set of steep and narrow stairs leading to the deck just below.

"All the guests' cabins are on this level," Tony told them, "with the crew cabins on the deck below. You two are on the port side toward the center. Not too bad."

"Is it port out and starboard back or the other way around?" Bennis whispered in Gregor's ear.

Gregor shrugged.

"My father's got the entire bow on this deck," Tony was going on, "and my mother's got the cabin in the stern. That's the one she liked best when the boat was being built, meaning it was one of the two or three things she didn't hate without limit. Sheila hates the boat, too, but we don't know if that's because she'd rather have luxury or because she gets seasick sitting in port and then throws up without stop until she gets back on dry land. My cousin Mark's wife Julie gets seasick, too. She's got the cabin next to yours. She does PR for Baird Financial. Then there's Charlie Shay. He's got the cabin on the other side of you. He's one of the three partners in Baird along with Dad and Uncle Calvin—am I giving it enough flesh for you?"

"No," Gregor said.

"I didn't think I was. But you really can't blame me, can you, Mr. Demarkian? I don't even know what you're here for."

"*I'm* here to get away from my apartment," Bennis said firmly. "Where are these cabins you've been talking about? And where's the bathroom? I've had a long ride out from Philadelphia and I feel like grunge."

"I wasn't trying to get you to implicate your entire family in a spy ring," Gregor said. "As far as I know, there isn't any spy ring. There isn't any murder, either. I was just mildly curious about the people I was going to be traveling with."

Tony Baird stopped before a door, turned the knob, and looked in. "Here it is," he said. "And there isn't any bathroom. This is a replica. If you want to use the john you have to," he shot Bennis a look and grinned, "you've been on sailboats. You must know what to do."

"For ten days?"

"Whose cabin is this?" Gregor said, sticking his head through the door and looking at the two berths, deep coffin-shaped things that had been built into the wall with thin foam mattresses at the bottom of them. The berths looked short, the way this whole deck felt. Gregor was well over six feet, and the average height of the full-grown Puritan male had been five four. The difference showed. Maybe this was the cabin that was supposed to belong to Bennis and his own would be something different, built to accommodate someone of his size and bulk.

Bennis Hannaford cleared her throat. "Gregor," she said, "I think this is it."

"What do you mean, this is it?"

"This is our cabin," Bennis said. "Both of ours. You know. Together."

"Together," Gregor repeated.

"I'll leave you two to get settled in," Tony Baird said. "I'll have your luggage brought up. I hope you didn't bring too much. Sheila's already got practically all the storage space on the boat stuffed with clothes. There's breakfast being laid out on the upper deck right this minute. Normally we eat in the mess, but Dad thought you'd all like to be standing there watching when we got tugged out to sea. That ought to be at nine thirty, fog permitting. Everybody else is here except Uncle Calvin and he's on his way. We shouldn't get held up. Anything else you want to know?"

"Together," Gregor repeated in stupefaction.

Tony Baird didn't notice. He looked around the cabin one last time—there wasn't much to look at; it was tiny and low-ceilinged and cramped—and then withdrew into the hall, ducking his head as he went. Gregor hadn't noticed it before, but Tony had to be close to six two himself. On this deck he kept himself always carefully stooped, so he didn't bump his head.

Gregor was keeping himself carefully stooped, too. It was giving him a sharp stabbing pain in the side of his neck.

"I can't believe this," he said. "We come all the way from Cavanaugh Street to get away from being match made to each other for a little while and they give us a cabin together?"

"It's worse than that," Bennis said, "look at the bunks."

"What about the bunks?"

"Well, I don't know about you, Gregor, but I couldn't get into the top one. The space between the side of it and the ceiling is too narrow. I'd scrape my skin into shreds if I tried. That means we've only got one operative bunk."

"One operative bunk," Gregor repeated.

"Don't get upset," Bennis said. "We'll work something out."

Gregor didn't know if they were going to work something out or not. He didn't know what they could work out. He only wanted to get off this deck and up into the air, where he could stand upright.

He started to stomp back down the hall to the narrow staircase, forgot where he was and what he was doing, and smacked his head on a beam.

Five

1

Gregor Demarkian had never been to a family reunion of his own. His father had died when he was very young. His one, much older brother had been killed in France at the end of World War II. His mother and his single maiden aunt had moved in together soon after Gregor had gone into the army and stayed together until his aunt had decided to visit distant relatives in Alexandria. His aunt had died in Egypt. His mother had died six months later at home. From that time to this, except for Elizabeth, Gregor had been alone. Thinking back on it and on all its peripheral oddnesses—strange to think that he'd been drafted right out of college, in peacetime, and thought nothing of it—Gregor would have said he had the best sort of deal. He was close to what family he had and enjoyed visiting with them. He was spared the hosts of great-aunts-by-marriage and third-cousins-twice-removed that plagued so many of the people he'd grown up with. Of course, he knew happy extended families. Lida's was one. It had enough people in it to qualify for a small country and they all got along beautifully. They were definitely the exception. In Gregor's experience, large and extended families were usually involved in war games if not in actual war—and that became truer the larger and more extended and richer the family got. When the family got so large and so extended and so rich it began to include people who were not really family at all, there was almost always trouble. The longtime business partner, the best friend from the old days at Alpha Chi Alpha, the family doctor who had assisted at the births of every family member now over the age of forty-five: these people were buffers or lightning rods, drawing out all the nastiness and attracting it to themselves. As soon as Gregor had seen the guest list for this excursion, he had had his suspicions. As soon as he had heard Tony Baird assuring him that most of the people on this boat got on very well together, he had been convinced. He thought back to the cases he'd had—the Hannaford case in particular, with Bennis and her parents and her six brothers and sisters all stuffed together in a house that would have been too small to contain them if it were the palace at Versailles—and almost decided to go straight back home.

Untangling himself from the low beam that had caught him and the narrow passageway that passed for a hall on the deck where his cabin was, Gregor climbed ponderously and carefully into the light on the upper deck and looked around. The fog was nearly gone now. Wisps of it trailed just above the water a little farther out into the bay, but they were like fairy dust. They lent enchantment without having the power to threaten. Gregor looked up and down Pier 36 and then up and down the piers on either side. The *Pilgrimage Green* was one of very few boats in dock, and the only one of any size. There was a jaunty little yellow single-masted sailboat at Pier 35 and a pair of fiberglass-hulled motorboats at Pier 37. The presence of even a moderate-size modern vessel, like a two master or a cabin cruiser, would have reminded Gregor how small the *Pilgrimage Green* was, but there was nothing like that and Gregor began to feel better. He looked into the rigging and saw men working there. Then he looked into the stern and saw men working there, too. Gregor had no idea what it took to sail a boat. He'd only traveled on boats once or twice in his life—to take Elizabeth on a cruise to Bermuda; as part of an FBI instructional tour on a submarine parked in Chesapeake Bay—and his basic opinion was that they were pleasant but not particularly necessary adjuncts to modern life. He was glad, though, that the men around him seemed so competent.

He wandered forward, toward the bow, looking around him as he went. There were a great many ropes, which Bennis had already told him to call "lines." There were a great many pieces of metal, too, including heavy iron rings that seemed to hold the lines together and sharp-edged hooklike things that reminded him of harpoons, but couldn't have been. There were even a few self-conscious Thanksgiving decorations. Ever since he'd come aboard, Gregor had been half-assuming there wouldn't be any decorations. Decorations for a holiday like Thanksgiving didn't seem to be the sort of thing people like these would do. The passion for decorating must have been more widespread than he realized. Somebody had put up a tall thick pole with Indian corn attached to the top of it. Underneath the corn was a small wood plaque with words written across its shiny surface in old-fashioned script:

> *God bring us safely to the shore*
> *or safely home to Thee.*

In spite of the script, the pole looked lethal enough to kill somebody. The whole deck looked like it would have been a wonderful place for a murderer intent on crushing his victim's skull with something heavy, or smothering his victim with material guaranteed to cut off all air in thirty seconds flat. The deck was littered with large pieces of heavy, dark, closely woven cloth. Gregor had no idea what the cloth was for, but he was sure it had something to do with authenticity. On a modern boat, the cloth would probably have been replaced by plastic.

He passed a small hutlike structure that he assumed to be the place from which the steering was done—he'd have to ask Bennis what to call it—and came out well to the front, in the space like a triangle that led to the bow. In that space, a table had been set up and half a dozen chairs set out. The table was a rough-wood replica. The chairs weren't authentic at all. They had been made out of canvas and machine-planed wooden slats and could be bought for less than fifty dollars from the "Home and Camp Specialties" catalog from L.L. Bean. Gregor wondered where everyone was. The table was full of food: great plates of Danish pastry; long racks of toast; huge bowls of fresh fruit. there were even little orange and yellow and brown ribbons strung along the edges of the serving plates, looking limp but trying bravely to be festive. The food that needed to be kept hot had sterling silver warmers under it—battery operated, and no more "authentic" than the chairs. There were two big urns of what Gregor assumed were coffee and water for tea, and they were the battery-operated kind, too. Was that a Coast Guard regulation? Did the Coast Guard make regulations of that kind? He went toward the coffee. There was steam rising from the sides of both urns. Gregor could see his breath. He understood the idea that some people might want to watch while they were set firmly and finally out to sea, but it *was* November. Somebody should have considered the possibility that at least some of the guests on this boat would rather not catch pneumonia doing it.

Gregor got a cup from the stack of cups on the table—they were secured by a plastic holder that wasn't authentic either—and sniffed at the urns until he determined which was actually coffee. Then he turned on the spigot and filled up. Then, because he was still alone, he went to the side of the boat and looked out across the piers. At this point the side came just up to his knees and made him feel unbalanced.

"Dangerous," he murmured to himself.

"Get away from there," Tony Baird said from behind him. "We've already had a sailor go over the side this morning. We don't need you going into the drink, too."

2

It was the second time in less than an hour that Tony had surprised him, and Gregor wanted to say that the young man was something of a sneak. The truth of it was that Tony was probably nothing of the kind. Earlier this morning, the fog had hidden him. That had hardly been his doing. This time, nothing had hidden him at all. He wasn't even alone. Gregor just hadn't been paying enough attention. Gregor looked beyond the young man's shoulder and saw a small, pretty woman with too much eye makeup. Then he moved away from the side and shook his head.

"Why is it so low?" Gregor asked. "I'm not surprised somebody fell overboard. I want to know how you're going to keep that from happening over and over again all through the trip."

Tony Baird shrugged. "I'm not going to keep anything from happening. It's not my boat. And it's low like that because the sides were low on the original *Mayflower*. Or at least I assume they were. Do you know my stepmother, Sheila Callahan?"

"Sheila Callahan Baird," Sheila said, stepping out from behind Tony. She held out a single long-fingered hand and smiled that bright and overwattaged smile women develop when they spend too long paying court to famous men. Gregor had just taken the hand when they were joined by two more people, a young man and a young woman, both dressed impeccably in outfits for sailing from Abercrombie & Fitch. Tony saw them, nodded a little, and said, "Mr. Demarkian, this is my cousin Mark Anderwahl, and his wife Julie."

"Fritzie was just behind us," Julie said, and then darted a nervous glance at Sheila. "She looked so pale I thought it would be a good idea, getting her out in the air."

"She won't want to get around all this food," Sheila said. "Did any of you see Calvin come on board? I was supposed to be notified as soon as he got here so I could check him off on my list, but I haven't heard a word."

"I saw him come on," Mark Anderwahl said. "He stopped to talk to Charlie Shay. I think they had business to discuss."

"Charlie never has business to discuss," Sheila said dismissively, "but at least if Calvin's here we're all here and I can stop worrying about it. Jon has been fretting so much about getting off on time. Do you all like the breakfast spread? Jon is so picky about everything being authentic, but this time I just put my foot down. You can't have a lot of people on deck like this in the middle of November and serve them cold food. And you can't light fires under things, either, not docked the way we are. There are regulations. I suppose once we set off, Jon will insist, but as long as we're docked I can carry the point. Don't you think it would have been a much better idea if Jon had done what builders do, and made this a replica on the outside with modern plumbing in?"

If Sheila had been talking to anyone in particular, that person might have answered her. Instead, she had been talking to the air, for general consumption and background noise. That was something else women did when they had spent too long paying court to famous men. Gregor had to assume it had some salutory effect on the famous men. For everybody else, it was an embarrassment. They looked at their shoes. They looked at the water. They looked at everybody and everything except Sheila, and then they began to edge together, drawing into a circle for protection.

"Sheila's always so definite," Julie Anderwahl murmured, sidling up next to Gregor and coming to a halt. "Tony said you were Mr. Demarkian. You must be our detective."

"This week I'm just a guest," Gregor said politely.

"Are you? They're all convinced you've got something going with Jon. I've heard them talking about it all week."

"Have you?"

"Sheila was insisting just last night that you'd been hired to run some kind of murder game. Charlie Shay believed her, I think. Nobody tells poor Charlie anything any more. Have you been hired to run a murder game?"

"No."

"I didn't think so. I take it you aren't here to investigate the death of Donald McAdam, either."

"What?"

"Never mind." Julie Anderwahl shook her head. Her hair was fine and blond and perfectly cut. Because of that, she looked much better and younger than Sheila did, even though she was probably older. She ran a hand through her bangs, took it down and frowned at it. The air was thick with moisture and her hand had come out wet.

"I get seasick," Julie Anderwahl said suddenly. "I get seasick all the time. Even just sitting in port like this."

"Why did you come?" Gregor asked her.

"They're my husband's family," Julie said, "and my bosses on top of it. I had to come. Did you know I worked at Baird Financial?"

"I'd heard it, yes."

"My husband works there, too. It's a very odd situation. Mark is the son of Jon and Calvin's only sister. The sister wasn't part of the partnership, of course, so Mark doesn't have any direct stake in the business, at least not yet. Tony does, of course, and so do Calvin's daughters. He has a pack of them and they're each more mindless than the rest. They'll probably inherit anyway. It makes me very nervous. Mark has never worked for anyone else and neither have I."

"If they're as mindless as you say they are, I don't see that they'd fire you or your husband once they did inherit—which wouldn't be for some time yet, would it? I haven't met Calvin Baird, but I have met Jon Baird and he seems to be in perfect health."

"He is in perfect health. He's going to bring Tony into the business right after the first of the year."

"Ah."

"And he doesn't have his mind on his work any more," Julie said. "Sheila. Everything that goes along with Sheila. She takes him to parties. And if you want to know the truth, I don't think he'd have gone to jail if it wasn't for Sheila."

Gregor considered this. "Do you mean he did something for her he wouldn't have done for anybody else? Or are you trying to suggest that she turned him in to the Feds?"

"Neither." Julie tapped her foot in agitation. "I just think he didn't have his mind in gear, that's all. She—unfocuses him. When she's around him, he can't think."

"Somehow, I can't picture that," Gregor said.

"I know," Julie admitted. "I can't picture it either. But it's the only explanation I can think of. That conviction made absolutely no sense, you know. His pleading guilty. His going to jail. People like Jon don't go to jail for insider trading."

"What about Michael Milken?"

Julie waved it away. "Milken was a maverick, taking on the establishment. From what I hear, his conviction will probably be overturned anyway. Jon Baird is the establishment and he always was, even though he was from a run-down branch of it. And besides—"

"What?"

"Well, it was dumb, wasn't it, and Jon isn't dumb. He didn't admit to doing a single thing here that wouldn't have been legal half a dozen other places, including Paris, where he keeps a huge apartment and spends three months a year. I suppose people have told you that before?"

"Constantly," Gregor said solemnly.

She turned away from him, resentful at his tone. "Well, it's true. It's more than true. I know you're supposed to be here to investigate all this. I know you've probably been told to be fair and impartial. I don't really care. If you've got any sense, you won't look any farther than Sheila Callahan Baird."

"Any farther for what?" Gregor asked, a little desperately. When this conversation had started, he had thought he was being treated to a simple recital of information—too freely given, perhaps, but then Julie Anderwahl was, if he remembered rightly, in public relations. Those people did give information too freely. Now Julie Anderwahl was anything but free. She was screwed up tighter than a vacuum-sealed jar and biting her lower lip so hard she was making it bleed.

"I'm not going to tell you what to do," she said. "I'm not going to interfere in your investigation. I have no interest in any of this except the kind of interest any sane person would have in seeing justice done. I'm just telling you, I know what Jon wants and I know he's used to getting what he wants, but this time he's just out of luck. That little bitch is as crooked as they come."

Gregor was about to protest once again—what had

happened here? what was going on?—but two things happened at once to shut him up. First, new people began to stream into the area, including a frail man in a three-piece suit, Jon Baird, and an older man who looked more like Jon's son Tony than Jon ever could. Gregor was just about to decide that this was the mysterious and as yet unmet Calvin, when the men parted to let a pair of women through. One of them was an older lady in regulation boating gear, right down to the canvas shoes, but so unsteady on her legs Gregor's first thought was that she belonged in a hospital. The other was Bennis Hannaford.

Gregor shot a quick look at Julie Anderwahl—still fuming, but no longer paying attention to him—and edged quickly behind the food table until he got to Bennis's side. He looked back at Julie Anderwahl and saw that her rage had dissipated in a wave of seasickness. She was green and bleary-eyed and rocking back and forth on her heels. Gregor looked past Bennis at the unsteady older lady and blinked. She was staring at the food table in a peculiarly intense way, her eyes so wild they might have belonged to a starving cat.

"This is even worse than I expected," Gregor whispered, leaning over to get close to Bennis's ear. He was so used to her now, he sometimes forgot how very short she was. "There's a woman over there, being seasick, and I just spent five minutes listening to her accuse me of—I don't know what."

"The woman on the other side of me is Jon Baird's first wife," Bennis whispered back. "She got me up near the stern about two minutes ago and accused me of being here just to sabotage her. I asked her what she was doing I was supposed to sabotage, and she said she knew all about you and she didn't trust you an inch, and after that I couldn't get anything out of her. Does this make any sense to you?"

"No."

"It doesn't make any sense to me, either. The world has changed, Gregor. When I was growing up, you never discussed private matters with strangers, never mind going right up to someone you'd never met and—what's that?"

"That" was a tremor under their feet, growing stronger by the second. Gregor looked up and saw there was a man all the way forward in the bow now, pushing off against the pier with a long pole. It startled him, even though it made sense. They had no motor. They had to get out to sea somehow or other. He bent a little closer to Bennis's ear and said, "He can't pole like that all the way into the Atlantic Ocean. How do we get under way?"

"We've got a wind," Bennis said. "As soon as we get out to reasonably open water, we'll hoist the sails. This is a sailboat, Gregor."

"I know."

"How did you think a sailboat worked?"

Gregor was about to tell her that he hadn't thought about how a sailboat worked—why should he have?—when the third thing happened. They had moved rapidly away from the pier and were now turned around, headed in the right direction. Men were yelling at each other and running back and forth, doing Gregor knew not what. High in the rigging, a sail opened and then another. Tony Baird, standing almost exactly midway between the bow and the food table, was raising his cup of coffee in the air.

"I took care of this boat the whole time Dad was— unavailable," he was saying, "and you know what the hard part is? Getting the sails. I'm not making this up. Getting the sails made just the right size and just the way they used to be. Getting the sails will make you absolutely nuts."

"Dealing with this boat in any way whatsoever makes me absolutely nuts," Sheila Baird said. "I still don't understand why we can't just have an ordinary little yacht like everyone else."

"I think I'll buy an ordinary little yacht," Bennis whispered in Gregor's ear. "You know, something like the *Cristina*."

"Don't do it," Gregor whispered back. "Tibor will have it filled with refugees before you ever get it out of dry dock."

"We're pitching," Tony Baird said. "I can't believe this. We're not even out of the harbor and we're rolling around like a marble."

"Watch your step," the man Gregor thought must be Calvin Baird said. "We're always having accidents on this boat. It's a damned menace."

"I never have accidents on boats," Tony Baird said. He put his coffee cup back on the table, watched it slide along the cloth for a moment, and then picked it up again. Then he shook his head and laughed. "I'll bet they didn't let passengers up near the bow when the original *Mayflower* sailed to Massachusetts. If they had, they'd have lost half the company to the sharks."

"Watch *out*," Calvin Baird said again.

Tony put the cup back in the plastic holder it had come out of and stepped back, grinning. Gregor had a sudden vision of him as a child, high in a tree and threatening to dive off, half-convinced he could really fly. Of course, the inevitable would have happened then, just as it happened now. It didn't even constitute a crisis. The *Pilgrimage Green* swung around just another fraction of an arc. The ocean opened up ahead of them, untamed and unlimited. Tony Baird stretched his arms, shuddered, looked surprised, and hopped. A second later, his legs were bumping against the low side of the boat and buckling beneath him.

"Damn," he said, as he proceeded to go over.

"Damn yourself," Jon Baird laughed after him. "Watch your head. We don't want you to drown."

"He is going to drown," Fritzie Baird said, almost squealing. "He is, he is. Do something about it."

"For God's sake, Fritzie," Calvin Baird said, "the boy swims better than Mark Spitz."

Then there was a secondary splash, caused by only God knew what, and Fritzie Baird started screaming.

3

Ten minutes later, it was all over except for Fritzie's hysterics. Since no one was paying attention to Fritzie, Gregor assumed that hysterics were something she engaged in often. Swimming was something Tony Baird obviously engaged in often. Gregor didn't think he was really better than Mark Spitz, but he was good, and he kept his head. When he got back on board they could see he'd chucked the heavy boots he'd been wearing so he wouldn't be dragged down. Gregor had no doubt he would have chucked his sweater and his turtleneck if he'd been stuck in the water long enough to make it necessary. This was definitely a young man who could think.

"Damn boots cost me three hundred dollars," Tony said to his father, holding up his sock feet. "Eddie Bauer. I hope you're ready to replace them."

"Of course I'm ready to replace them," Jon Baird said. "Go get out of those clothes. You're going to get hypothermia."

"Go calm down your mother," Sheila Baird said. "Now I know what people mean when they talk about a high-pitched whine."

"Don't get started," Calvin Baird said. "That's all we need on this trip, the wives quarreling."

In Gregor Demarkian's opinion, the only way Calvin could have escaped the wives quarreling was to be on some other boat—but this was so obvious, it hardly needed expressing. Instead, he bent even closer to Bennis's ear and began to whisper again.

"Did you notice anything funny?" he asked her.

Bennis shot him a look that clearly said she'd noticed a host of things funny. Everything on this boat was funny. Then she went back to watching Tony Baird, who was methodically stripping to the waist and throwing his water-sogged clothes in a heap at his feet. Gregor felt himself wince slightly and then shook it off. Tony Baird was definitely a very good-looking young man and right up Bennis's alley in the psychological department. Bennis had always liked men who could have conceivably starred in a movie version of "Leader of the Pack." Tony Baird was also at least ten years younger than Bennis, and Bennis had never had any use for younger men. At least, Gregor didn't think she had. Gregor put it all firmly out of his mind and said, "Were you watching him when he went over?"

"I was watching that woman you were talking to with the blond hair," Bennis told him. "How much you want to bet that she's pregnant."

"She's seasick."

"That explains the green. It doesn't explain the waist."

"I was looking straight at Tony Baird," Gregor said. "Do you know what I saw?"

"No."

"He was leaning forward, not backward. He was leaning in toward the table, not out toward the sea."

Bennis looked at him curiously. "I don't get it," she said. "Are you saying he should have fallen forward instead of back?"

"If he had fallen, he would have fallen forward instead of back."

"What's that supposed to mean?"

Gregor sighed. "That's supposed to mean," he said, "that I not only saw him fall, I also saw Jon Baird push him. Good Lord, Bennis, it wasn't even subtle. He might as well have picked the boy up at the knees and pitched him overboard."

Six

1

Fritzie Derwent Baird had been brought up to preside at parties with organization. Her own coming-out party had featured not only a receiving line but three different bands playing three different kinds of music in three different places on her parents' broad property in Radnor, a fully equipped diner serving hot dogs and hamburgers and cotton candy to anyone who asked, and a session of water games held at midnight in the indoor pool. It was the kind of coming-out party that had been popular at the time, meaning before Jackie Kennedy had brought coming-out parties to national attention and made everybody too embarrassed to spend so much money. It was also one of the reasons why Fritzie had been left nearly destitute when her parents died—except, of course, for what she had as Jon Baird's wife. Fritzie had never made the connection, any more than she had made the connection between Ronald Reagan and the rise of the religious right or Gorbachev and perestroika. All that sort of thing took place on a different planet, or in another time warp, and had nothing to do with her. Besides, she felt so drowsy and fuzzy and weak, it was hard to think in an orderly way about anything at all. When she did try to think, what she thought about was Sheila, and it came down to this: if that young woman had had any kind of upbringing at all, she would have been up and around and leading the guests in deck games. She would at least have done what Fritzie herself had done, which was to bring something special and important for the holiday, to make her guests feel special and important themselves. Fritzie had brought thirty jars of her Thanksgiving pumpkin rind marmalade, made over the course of two days she could have used for packing or going to the theater or seeing friends. The mason jars were capped with harvest-pattern cotton and sitting patiently in rows at the bottom of her footlocker, waiting to be handed out. Sheila seemed not to have thought about her guests at all, at least not as far as the holiday was concerned.

Actually, Fritzie was more than a little relieved to find that Sheila really hadn't been well brought up. For one thing, that solidified Sheila's image in Fritzie's mind. It would have been terrible to have been going around for the last she didn't know how long, thinking of Jon as married to someone no better than a chorus girl, only to find out that the new wife had gone to Spence and been presented at the Junior Assemblies. For another, Fritzie was very tired, and a little panicked. Usually, food served outside didn't bother her too much. The wind carried the smells away and flies came, which always made her feel faintly sick. Today, for some reason, the mere sight of Danish pastry had been enough to make her ravenous—and that was very odd, because she hadn't eaten Danish pastry in years. Maybe it was because of the saving up. A few years ago, Fritzie had taken the advice of one of her favorite women's magazines and started "saving up" calories for holiday parties. For three or four weeks before she was supposed to eat some-body else's fattening but lavishly proffered food, she would allow herself only 400 calories a day instead of her usual

800. Those 400 uneaten calories would be her "calorie bank," which she could spend on Alida Halstead's chicken lasagna or Muffy Stegner's full-cream tea from Martha Stewart. It was a very good system, really. It let her eat like a horse when she was out and inflamed the envy of all her friends, who stood around at parties nibbling on celery stalks and wondering out loud how she managed to eat like she did and never gain any weight. The only problem with it was that it made her feel as if she wanted to spend her life in bed, and not with a companion. Fritzie never wanted to spend her life in bed with a companion. Being naked in the presence of other people made her much too self-conscious about her thighs.

After the breakfast party had broken up and everyone had gone below—especially Tony, who hadn't spoken to her but who had needed her, Fritzie was sure of it—Fritzie had gone below herself, crawled into her bunk, and closed her eyes. In no time at all, she had been in one of those floating states that always reminded her of the man who had had himself suspended in water. She had been awash on a sea of projection, rocked by the real sea and half-asleep and busy making plans all at once. She worked out what she would do about lunch—not go—and about dinner and schemed pleasantly through the ways she might make contact with Tony. In the middle of all that, she must have fallen asleep for real, because when she came to with a start in the middle of a dream about executing Sheila in an electric chair made of maraschino cherries, her watch said two o'clock.

Two o'clock, Fritzie thought, sitting up carefully so that she didn't hit her head on the beam. She ought to feel good about it's being two o'clock. That meant lunch was over and she had missed it, without ever having had to go through an elaborate charade to pretend that was not what she was doing. At home with her own friends, she wouldn't have had to pretend at all. They all skipped lunch all the time, too, because it was the only sensible way to live on a night when you had to go out to dinner. Here, though, Tony and Jon would stare and disapprove, and she didn't like to put herself through that.

There was a basin and a jug of water secured into the top of the cupboard that was built into the cabin's other long wall. Fritzie got up and went to it, poured water out, found soap, and started to wash her face. When she was done she got her makeup out and applied it very carefully, until she looked, as she thought of it, "like herself." Then she put the makeup away and went to the door to look out into the hall.

"*I* don't know what these figures are supposed to mean," Calvin's voice said, floating down to her from somewhere out of sight. "They're not *my* figures."

"If you're going to use unicorns, you're going to have to be careful not to fall into clichés," a woman's voice said. "Everybody thinks they know everything there is to know about unicorns, and it's enough to drive you crazy."

Fritzie analyzed the woman's voice and came up with the picture of the small black-haired one who had come with Jon's friend Mr. Demarkian. She analyzed the laugh that followed the little lecture on unicorns and came up with Tony. Then she bit her lip and shook her head. The woman was very familiar, but she couldn't quite work out why. The idea of Tony falling in love with anybody made her sicker than the sight of flies on food.

She came out of her cabin, closed the door behind her, and made her way carefully to the staircase-ladder that would take her up on deck. She passed the room where Tony and the woman who had come with Mr. Demarkian sat and stuck her head in the door, noting with relief that they weren't anything at all like sitting close together. Tony was stretched out on the floor, and the woman had taken a perch on Tony's water cabinet.

"Well," Fritzie said. "I heard you talking about unicorns. I didn't think anybody talked about unicorns any more."

"Bennis writes about unicorns," Tony said, leaving Fritzie to wonder what that meant. "This is Bennis Hannaford. And this is my mother, Frieda Baird."

"How do you do?" Bennis Hannaford said.

"Are you related to the Bryn Mawr Hannafords?" Fritzie said. "I did quite a lot of volunteer work with a woman named Cordelia Hannaford, before I moved to New York."

"Cordelia Hannaford is my mother," Bennis said.

"Ah," Fritzie said.

"Are you all right?" Tony asked. "You look a little unsteady on your feet."

Fritzie felt a little unsteady on her feet, unsteadier by the minute, in fact. The motion of the boat seemed to be getting to her, even though she'd never been seasick a day in her life. She wondered how far out to sea they were. She'd grown up with sailboats. She knew how fast they could move. How fast they could move when they were built like this was beyond her, but—

But her mind was wandering again, the way her mind always did these days. If she gave it a chance, it would be planning the holiday again, the holiday that was really Sheila's to plan. It was just too bad that Sheila didn't seem to understand what was really involved. The island. The cooking. Was Sheila taking care of any of that? Fritzie retreated into the hall and stretched her smile wider, unable to decide whether she was happy this woman was a Bryn Mawr Hannaford or not. Surely she had to be much too old to be interested in Tony.

"I'm going up on deck now," she said cheerfully. "I'll see you both later."

"We missed you at lunch," Tony said.

"I slept through lunch. I've been very tired lately."

"Mother?"

Fritzie didn't answer. She went quickly to the staircase and climbed up, making the best time she could in spite of the fact that her legs felt like sand. With her head stuck up into the wind she felt cold. Once she got her shoulders through, she felt frozen. There was a stiff wind blowing in off the water, filling the sails over her head and chilling her body. She was wearing a turtleneck and a wool sweater and a jacket as well, but she could have been naked. She'd become very sensitive to cold over these last few years, anyway. Tony and Jon and Calvin and Julie would all be sitting around pouring sweat, and she'd be ready to get under a good wool blanket.

She got herself all the way up on deck and looked around. There were men in the rigging, but no one she knew. She knew the man at the helm, but he was just the captain Jon had been hiring since he bought his first boat more than twenty years ago. She moved carefully up the deck and looked into the bow. It had been cleared of all the things that filled it that morning and now looked like nothing more than the front part of a boat, well-polished but littered with lines. She retreated again, feeling stopped.

In the beginning, she had wanted to find Tony and talk to him. She had found Tony, but she hadn't been able to talk.

After that, she had decided to find Jon, and she was still looking for him. She had thought he would be standing on deck, the way he often did for hour after hour on the first day of a sail. Instead, he was nowhere to be seen, and that left her with two possibilities. Either Jon was relieving himself, sitting on one of those terrible forklike things and hanging off the back of the boat like the bait for a whale. If that was the case, she only had to sit still and she would find him soon enough. If he wasn't there, though, the situation was hopeless, because it meant he was down in his cabin. Jon never spent daylight in his cabin unless he had something serious and secret going on. When he had something serious and secret going on, he didn't want to talk to her.

He never wanted to talk to her.

She started to think it all through again, working out the options one by one, in case she'd missed anything, and then she heard a noise. She looked up, half-hopeful she would find either Jon or Tony, and was surprised to be confronted by a wooly mammoth version of Mr. Demarkian instead. Wooly mammoth was really the only description of it. He had on a thick coat and a scarf wound three or four times around his neck and even a hat, although that only seemed to be half on. Fritzie backed up a little and tried her smile again. It was silly to be so disturbed by this. Mr. Demarkian was a guest on this boat. She was likely to stumble across him more than once in the next ten days. It was entirely natural.

"Oh," she said. "Well, It's Mr. Demarkian, isn't it?"

"That's right," Gregor Demarkian said. "I was just going to do something very foolish. I was going to ask if I could help you with anything. But you must know this boat much better than I do."

"Know the boat?" Fritzie was blank for a minute. Then she brightened up. "Oh, I don't *know* the boat," she said. "It was never a family thing with Jon, not until this time, anyway. It was more like his private hobby. I've been on it before, of course."

"Of course," Gregor said. "Can I help you with anything?"

"I don't have anything I need help with. I should have worn a heavier coat. There's that. I was looking for Jon, that's all."

"Mr. Baird is in his cabin," Gregor said solemnly. "With

the other Mr. Baird. I left them there not more than five minutes ago."

"Oh, dear."

"You had something private you wanted to discuss?"

What Gregor Demarkian had just said was an impertinence. Fritzie knew that. She also knew that in the old days, she would have frozen him out or left him standing where he was. Now all that seemed like much too much effort.

"It hasn't been a very cozy divorce," she said suddenly. "I don't go to dinner with Jon and Sheila. There's been nothing like that."

"I hope not." Demarkian sounded faintly shocked.

"It has been an amicable divorce, though. I think that woman tricked him, if you want to know the truth. I really think she did. Jon didn't want to leave me. He hasn't completely and absolutely left me yet."

"Oh?"

"He pretends he needs my help," Fritzie said. "You know how that is. You're a man. An ordinary man would have lost a button and needed me to sew it on or shown me his refrigerator when it had nothing in it but moldy Chinese food, but of course Jon has a valet for his buttons and a cook. Jon did the most obvious thing he could do, just to let me know."

"What was that?"

"He came to me and borrowed money," Fritzie said triumphantly. "Just this past August. Can you imagine that? Jon Baird needing money?"

"This past August," Demarkian said slowly, "Jon Baird was in the Federal Correctional Institution at Danbury."

"I know where he was, Mr. Demarkian. I went there to see him. He called me up and asked me to come."

"And then he asked to borrow money?"

"Three million dollars from the trust he set up for me. He's got control of it anyway. He didn't have to ask my permission. He was just trying to let me know, if you see what I mean."

"Not exactly," Gregor Demarkian said.

"I've got to go," Fritzie said, suddenly feeling confused.

And she *was* confused. In fact, she was more than a little horrified. She tried to remember what she had said over the last minute or so of conversation, but all she could retrieve was a vague feeling of: *this will get him.* She had no doubt whatsoever who the "him" was, it was who the "him" always was except that she would have said, not ten minutes ago, that she didn't feel that way about Jon at all. And yet, she was not surprised. It was as if the emotion had been there all along, and this man Demarkian had only brought it to the surface. She backed away from him and swallowed, hard.

"You're nothing at all like a great detective," she said. "I don't even like you."

"Mrs. Baird?" Gregor Demarkian said.

But by now she was almost all the way back to the staircase, ladder, whatever you called it, almost all the way back to her escape route. She'd decided to throw that woman out of Tony's room and make him talk to her. She'd decided to do something definite, at any rate. It wasn't true that she felt about Tony just the way she felt about Jon. It wasn't true that she wanted to kill both of them.

What she really wanted was a Roquefort cheeseburger from Hamburger Heaven and a plate of deep-fried onion rings in batter.

2

"Damn," Jon Baird was saying, almost two hours later. "There goes another one."

"Another bridge?" Charlie Shay called back. "The same one?"

"I only have one," Jon Baird said. Then he stuck his

head into the main room of his two-room suite and smiled so that Charlie could see the gap in his gums, a long line of unrelieved pink that ran along the bottom on the right side. Then Jon stuck his hand out and showed off the broken bridge, lying cut in half across his palm. Charlie shook his head, and on the other side of the cabin Calvin Baird wagged a finger in the air.

"That dentist of yours ought to be sued for the work he does," Calvin said. "Nobody should get away with producing shoddy workmanship of that kind."

Jon Baird shot Charlie Shay a look, and Charlie found himself smiling, just slightly enough to go undetected by Calvin. Charlie wouldn't have liked to have had to admit it, but that look had made him feel good, almost physically warm. In the old days, he and Jon had been that way together often, sharing secrets, knowing what each other thought. Theirs had been a college friendship, and like all college friendships it had had elements of small-boyishness in it. They hadn't cut their fingers and sworn to be blood brothers, but if they had it wouldn't have been out of place. Then the years had gone by and all Charlie's inadequacies had been put on display. Charlie didn't even bother to deny that they were his own inadequacies. There were men who were geniuses at business and men who could get along in it without too much trouble. Charlie would have done himself better service if he'd gone into teaching or art. Jon, being a genius, hadn't had much patience with that. Charlie didn't see why he should have. Now, however, Calvin's prissiness had drawn them together again, temporary though that might be, and Charlie was glad.

"It's not bad workmanship," he told Calvin. "It's the shape the bridge has to be to fit into Jon's mouth. Jon was warned it was going to be a lot of trouble."

"I was warned not to eat pistaschio nuts, too, but I haven't stopped." Jon came in from the back room, fitting the new bridge in place. "These things are put together just like airplane models, I swear. It's just that they use porcelain instead of plastic. Maybe there are airplane models that use porcelain instead of plastic."

"Don't look at me," Calvin said. "You're the one who always liked airplane models."

"I didn't always like them," Jon said. "I just put together a few when we didn't have the money to do much of anything else. Did you two come up with any answers while I was off breaking apart my mouth?"

Charlie looked down at the pile of papers in his lap and sighed. For most of the afternoon, he and Calvin and Jon had been poring over Calvin's figures on Europabanc, trying to see where something had gone wrong—and coming up with nothing, of course, because (Charlie was convinced) there was nothing to come up with but a computer error. Calvin's bad luck with computers was notorious. He couldn't even send his letters to word processing without causing a breakdown in the main system. If he hadn't been so intent on making himself look important, they wouldn't have been here all these hours fussing at something that didn't matter any more anyway. If the discrepancy had shown up back in August, when they were making the final moves in their offer for Europabanc, then there would have been a problem. They'd had to have a certain amount of cash on hand to make the deal fly, and that cash had had to be verified. But the discrepancy hadn't shown up then. To satisfy Calvin, they'd just gone through the old reports and found everything to be just as it should be. Whatever this was was recent and therefore minor, something the accountants could have straightened out when it came time for the year-end report. At least, that's what this should have been. It wasn't, because Calvin was Calvin.

Jon dropped into a chair, stretched out his legs, and said, "We're not going to straighten this out. Nobody's going to straighten this out. It's going to turn out to have been a glitch in the computer, and when we run the program again it will be gone."

"We ran the program four times last night," Calvin said coldly. "We were at the office until four o'clock in the morning."

"Too tired to see straight, probably, and making mistakes because of it." Jon yawned. "I really don't want to spend this whole trip talking business, Calvin. I was looking forward to a chance to relax."

"You don't have any right to relax," Calvin said. "You're about to be the head of the largest financial services combine in history."

"It sounds more impressive if you just say I'm going to be head of a bank. What about you, Charlie? Are you as sick of all these numbers as I am?"

"I was sick of them before we ever got started," Charlie said truthfully. "I'm afraid I'm not very good at dealing with the Europabanc thing. I can't even think about it without feeling a little dizzy."

"I can't think about it without feeling tired." Jon pulled his legs back in, stretched his arms this time, and shook his head. Charlie had seen him get like this in the past, innumerable times, because Jon Baird was the sort of man who couldn't sit still for long. These days, if he'd been a child, some teacher would probably have wanted to put him on Ritalin. Now he got up and paced around the cabin. It was a much larger cabin than any of the others had—and not really authentic, either, since the captain's cabin on the original *Mayflower* hadn't had two rooms—but it was still tiny and the ceiling was still low. Jon had to stoop slightly while he paced, in spite of the fact that he was a very short man.

"The thing is," he said finally, "I've got more trouble than I want on this trip anyway, and I don't need business around to complicate things. Did I tell you I got the private detective's report in on Sheila?"

"Was that Mr. Demarkian who did the private detective's report?" Charlie asked. "I didn't think that was his field, somehow."

"It isn't. I hired a perfectly ordinary private detective to check up on Sheila, the same one I used to check up on Fritzie. I got the same answer, too. What is it about me, my wives aren't unfaithful with other men, they're unfaithful with credit cards and diet programs."

"The kind of woman who marries you isn't really interested in sex," Calvin said stiffly, "she's interested in money."

"Sheila spent six thousand dollars in the month of August on cosmetics alone," Jon said, with a kind of wonder. "That takes talent, if you want my opinion. That takes dedication."

"I take it you want to divorce her," Calvin said.

"Of course I do." Jon sat down on his bunk, stretched out, thought better of it, and stood up again. He was a little too fast, and bumped his head against the beam. He rubbed his hand against the spot—sore, Charlie supposed, although he himself was always so careful on the *Pilgrimage Green*, he never got conked—and went to the porthole, to look out on God knew what. There wasn't anything to see any more. They were well out on the water now and headed north. They wouldn't spot land again until they reached the coast of Massachusetts and the passage to Candle Island.

"The thing about women like Sheila," Jon said, "is that you're supposed to divorce them. The other thing about women like Sheila is that they don't like you for it. I was wondering whether the two of you would like to do me a favor."

"No," Calvin said.

"Of course," Charlie insisted.

Jon smiled slightly. "I just want you two to talk to her, keep her out of my hair, keep her out of Demarkian's hair especially, if you know what I mean. His presence here bothers the hell out of her. I think she's convinced he's the—other private detective."

"If he had been, you'd have got more on her," Calvin said.

"Maybe so. Right now, she's really not the person I'm principally interested in getting something on. Women like Sheila are always very reasonable in divorce courts. They have to be if they want to get their settlements. It's the people who aren't very reasonable who worry me. Aren't they the people who worry you?"

"I don't know," Charlie said, feeling confused again. "I suppose people aren't unreasonable very often around me. Maybe it's because I'm not a strong enough personality."

"Maybe it's because you barely remember what's going on in the business from one day to the next," Calvin said. Then he flushed and apologized, in his way. "I'm a little on edge," he told them. "This discrepancy. Sheila. Mr. Gregor Demarkian."

"You leave Mr. Demarkian to me," Jon said. "Charlie doesn't ask me about Demarkian."

"That doesn't mean he doesn't worry me," Charlie said. "What is he here for, anyway? I thought he went around investigating murders."

"I thought he went around meddling in other people's business," Calvin said. "If you want my opinion, Jon, what you'll do about Demarkian is—"

"But I don't want your opinion," Jon said. This time, instead of pacing, he went straight to the door and opened it. Outside, the hallway was lit. Since there was no electricity on the boat, there was nothing to light it except the candles they might carry, and neither Charlie nor Calvin had candles. Seeing their predicament, Jon rummaged around in his table until he found a pair of tallows and lit them off his own lamp.

"Go," he said. "It's not all that long until dinner and I have a lot I want to do. We'll talk about numbers some more in the morning."

"But—" Calvin said.

Jon shooed him away. "Even if I didn't have anything else on my mind, I'd have this damned Thanksgiving dinner. Do I want yams or do I want sweet potatoes? Should the onions be cooked in lard? You should see the damn fool note I got from the cook this afternoon. Four pages long and requiring an answer faster than FDR expected answers from Harry Truman. Go."

"But," Calvin said again.

"*Go*," Jon insisted.

Charlie stepped into the hall, holding one of the candles, lit now, in his right hand. It provided very little light in the long, narrow, low-ceilinged place, and the one Calvin was carrying didn't make much of a difference.

"If you ask me," Calvin said, as Jon shut the door firmly in their faces, "it's a kind of jinx. You're just asking for trouble."

"I don't know what you mean," Charlie said.

"Of course you do. Asking a murder expert to go along for the ride. You do that, you're likely to land yourself with a murder for your expert to be expert about. That's what I think."

Then he stomped off down the hall, apparently sure of where he was going, apparently undaunted by the cramped space or the lack of light.

Charlie rocked back and forth on his heels, feeling more nervous than he had even a few hours ago, when the numbers had been whizzing around his head and he'd been afraid that one of them would find him out. He didn't know anything about numbers, but he didn't want them to know he didn't know anything about numbers. But as for this—

Charlie Shay was what he thought of as an ordinarily superstitious man. He checked his horoscope in the *Daily News* and was careful not to walk under ladders. He didn't believe in ghosts and goblins and predestination by sidewalk crack. And yet . . .

If you ask a murder expert along for the ride . . . you're likely to land yourself with a murder for your expert to be expert about.

It was the sort of silly thing Calvin said when he got his temper up, the sort of thing that Charlie never paid much attention to, and it was, of course, ridiculous.

What bothered Charlie Shay was the fact that he couldn't shake the feeling it was true.

Seven

1

Jon Baird had asked Gregor Demarkian aboard the *Pilgrimage Green* in order to investigate the press leaks that had plagued Baird Financial for most of the last two years—at least, that was what Jon Baird had told Gregor Demarkian, and Gregor Demarkian had accepted, during their one long luncheon meeting in New York. In some measure, Gregor had actually believed this story. He had known a great many rich men in his time, and most of them had been in the grip of what he privately thought of as "affluent paranoia." Affluent paranoia came in numerous forms, often familial. Rich men always seemed to suspect either that they were about to be murdered (by their wives and children, by their business partners or their business enemies or the latest auditor sent out by the IRS) or that they were the targets of elaborate plots to embarrass them. All in all, they feared embarrassment more than death. Certainly all this nonsense about leaks fit right into Gregor's theory. He had tried to tell Jon Baird what any good policeman would have told him about leaks, and Jon Baird had refused to listen. Jon Baird hadn't wanted to make a series of differing, clandestine, and wholly false statements to a series of different and individually accosted employees. He hadn't wanted to tap the phones at the World Trade Center offices of Baird Financial. He hadn't wanted a grey-faced private investigator from one of Manhattan's more discreet firms going through the office mail. He hadn't wanted anything, in fact, that might get him what he did want, and from this Gregor concluded that either one of two things must be true. Either Jon Baird had a true case of affluent paranoia, pitched so high by now that it gave him a thrill he didn't want to give up. Or Jon Baird was lying about both the leaks and the reason he had invited Gregor Demarkian on this trip, and Gregor Demarkian would have to wait and see.

As it turned out, Gregor Demarkian spent most of that first day on the *Pilgrimage Green* waiting and seeing—except that he didn't see much and waiting was almost intolerable. His run in with Fritzie Baird was interesting, but not diverting. She was obviously a severely disturbed woman. There was no way to know what he could and could not take at face value of what she had presented to him. He wanted to say "nothing," but he knew that was unlikely. Even certifiable schizophrenics weren't that seamlessly wrapped into fantasy. It was Fritzie's interpretations he really had to distrust—what Jon felt, what Jon thought, what Jon wanted—and they were too textbook to hold his attention for long. After all, he was the man who had hunted down the Stick Pin Killer, via telephone and computer printout. A standard case of delusional projection hardly fazed him.

The only other diverting thing that happened during his day was a chance meeting with Calvin Baird, who had come barreling out of Jon Baird's cabin while Gregor was on his way up to the main deck, caused a collision that knocked Gregor's head into a beam and his back into a ladderlike grid of supports near one of the doors. Then he had scowled his very best Calvin scowl and declared it was all Gregor's fault.

"I know what you're really doing here," he said, trying to brush Gregor aside. "You're getting in the way and gumming up the works and making it impossible for anyone to get anything done."

Gregor tried to move aside so that Calvin could pass, and so that Calvin would stop reflexively hitting at his shoulder with the back of his hand. He couldn't do it, because the passage was too narrow. The best he could manage was to move a little closer to the stairs, where there would be slightly more open space and a chance to maneuver.

"I'm glad that you know what I'm doing here," he'd said pleasantly. "I've been a little confused about it myself."

"I think Jon's out of his mind," Calvin said. "It's prison that's changed him, if you want my opinion. He doesn't care about numbers. He does care about you. You know what he said to me just a little while ago?"

"No."

"He said going to prison was a wonderful thing, if you knew how to go about it the right way. Isn't that crazy?"

"Maybe."

"I think it's crazy," Calvin said. "I think he came back addled, to tell you the truth. Before he went to jail, he would never have been so—so cavalier about these numbers. Even if they weren't going to have any effect on anything we did. It's the principle of the thing."

"Mmmm."

They were nearly at the stairs, a circumstance that made Calvin fussier and more prissily furious than ever. He, after all, wanted to go in the other direction. Gregor wedged himself into the stairwell and sucked in his stomach. Calvin squeezed by him, sniffed, and ran a hand through his hair.

"In the old days we never had strangers along for family

holidays," he said. "In the old days, we never had leaks, either."

"Good for you, Gregor said.

Calvin sniffed again, loudly enough, this time, to have qualified for a television commercial for an antihistamine. "Silly ass," he said, presumably meaning Jon Baird. "If he goes along the way he's been going, the whole company is going to fall into the sea."

Gregor didn't know about the company, but he did know about Calvin Baird. The man was a first-rate little prig, and if Gregor were Jon Baird he'd have done a good deal more to tweak his ears than suggesting that there might be some good in going to jail. He watched Calvin stomp down the narrow hall to a door that presumably opened on Calvin's own cabin. Calvin opened it, stepped past it, and then closed it behind him. Gregor stared at the closed door and wondered if he ought to do what he really felt like doing—what he'd actually wanted to do since he first came out of his own cabin and headed upstairs—and that was to knock on the door just beyond Calvin's now closed one and find out what Bennis and Tony Baird were *up* to. It was driving him crazy, just the way it had been driving him crazy all morning and all afternoon. It was going to go on driving him crazy until he dragged Bennis back to Cavanaugh Street or did something to confront the situation directly. He couldn't drag Bennis back to Cavanaugh Street any time in the next few days. Even after they'd landed on Candle Island, he would be at the mercy of Tony Baird's father's boat for any trip he might want to take to the mainland. As for confronting the situation directly—Gregor had spent a great deal of his life in direct confrontation, not only with serial killers but with chairmen of Senate subcommittees and presidents of the United States. He had no idea how to proceed with a direct confrontation here. After all, what would he say? He wasn't her father, her brother, her husband, her lover, or her son. She was a young woman who knew her own mind—or who said she did. He could hardly rise up righteous in the guise of a Victorian paterfamilias and tell her her present interest was much too young.

Much too young for what?

Gregor stomped his way up to the main deck, down to the stern, and up to the high rail there that was meant for observation. Then he leaned over it and contemplated the mobile black glass sea. He was still leaning over it, nearly two hours later, when the bell for dinner rang.

If he had come to any conclusions at all, about anything, he would have thought the time well spent. Instead, all he had really gotten out of it was a pair of frostbitten ears.

2

Like every other American who had been educated in public schools in the years just before and just after World War II, Gregor Demarkian had had a fairly elaborate introduction to the myth of the *Mayflower*. He had learned about rough seas and calm winds, cramped quarters and women screaming their way through labor into the howling winds of storms. He hadn't learned anything at all about the mundane details of day-to-day life. What details he did know about living on a ship came from late-night flashlight reading of the sea novels that had enthralled him when he was ten. In those, stiff-spined officers with starched white shirts were served dried beef and venison on china plates by mess boys in pristine uniforms decorated with gold braid.

On the *Pilgrimage Green,* dinner was held in the officer's mess, because on the original *Mayflower* there really hadn't been a mess, properly speaking, for passengers. In this as in everything else except religion, the Puritans had been stiflingly conventional. First-class passengers had a room to themselves, tiny because there were so few of them to accommodate, that they used as both a lounge and a dining room. The rest of the passengers ate on their bunks or in the open air when weather permitted. The officer's mess, however, was nothing at all like the ones in Gregor's old books. For one thing, it was much smaller, meaning that the passengers on the *Pilgrimage Green* had to crowd in next to each other much closer than was comfortable. For another thing, the table and the sideboards and all the other furniture except the chairs were bolted to the floor. Maybe the furniture had been bolted to the floor in Gregor's old books, too, but if it had, Gregor had never noticed it. There was something about this enforced immobility that made the cramped quarters feel even more claustrophobic than they really were. Then there was the large ship in a bottle tucked into the niche in the wall at the table's rear. Surely that couldn't be authentic to the Puritan experience. The Puritans had been Calvinists and distrustful of decoration.

As for what was authentic to the Puritan experience, Gregor decided he wouldn't have blamed these people if they'd decided to hold a Thanksgiving as soon as they hit land, to thank God just for letting them off their boat. The sheer misery of this existence shed a whole new light on Thanksgiving dinners full of chestnut stuffing and candied yams. Gregor had always thought that rich American WASPS failed to celebrate Thanksgiving (or anything else) with enthusiasm because they were too damned polite to have enthusiasms. Now he wondered if it was some kind of race memory. In their bones they remembered their ancestors' voyage from England. In their heads, they didn't think they had anything to celebrate.

Coming down from the upper deck, Gregor had worked out a plan to make sure he would end up seated next to Bennis Hannaford, but when it came time to put the plan in action, he was foiled. Bennis had gotten to the mess much earlier than he had expected her to. When Gregor reached the door, she was already inside, pushed up against the back wall with Tony on her side and Calvin across from her. She was even on the wrong side of the table. The side where Calvin Baird was sitting left a good bit of space behind the chairs, so that it wouldn't be difficult for someone to get up and go out of the room during dinner. The side where Bennis was sitting had the chairs much closer to the wall. Sheila Baird and Julie Anderwahl had taken chairs on that side now. Gregor wondered if they thought the tight fit would keep them from falling over if the boat pitched. Then Charlie Shay sat down next to Julie, and Gregor gave up speculating altogether. Fritzie Baird had taken a seat next to Calvin and Mark Anderwahl had taken one next to Fritzie. There were now only two seats left, both on the Calvin Baird side of the table. Since Jon Baird was obviously waiting for Gregor to seat himself, Gregor decided to do it. He pulled out the chair next to Mark Anderwahl's, tried and failed to catch Bennis's eye, and sat down.

His move seemed to break a conversational barrier. Calvin Baird coughed. Sheila Baird giggled.

"Look," Sheila said, picking up a mason jar from a row of mason jars in the middle of the table. "Pumpkin rind marmalade. Fritzie has been making preserves again."

"I like to do something special for the holidays," Fritzie said stiffly. "If you don't do something special for a holiday, it isn't a holiday at all."

Julie Anderwahl jumped in. "Oh, Lord," she said. "I've been smelling cooking all afternoon and it's just been terrible. I hope you're not serving us roast buffalo meat."

"The Puritans didn't have buffalo meat," Jon Baird said. "They'd never seen a buffalo. I don't even know if they ever did see a buffalo. Wasn't it a western animal?"

"There's Buffalo, New York," Charlie Shay said.

"Would they have named it Buffalo if there hadn't been any buffalos there?"

"Jon likes everybody to think he knows so much about the original *Mayflower*," Sheila said, "but he really doesn't."

There was a knock on the door. Jon Baird called, "Come in," and a white-jacketed young man entered with a large covered tray in his hands. It was the kind of thing that in movies is always opened to reveal a stuffed goose, and Gregor half-suspected that a goose was what he was going to be presented with. Jon Baird, however, was even less stringently insistent on the "authentic" than his second wife had accused him of being. He waited until the young man had put the tray down in the middle of the table, jumped up, and said, "Here we go. Salad. Hand me your plates, ladies and gentlemen, and I'll dish out."

"Did they have salad on the original *Mayflower*?" Julie Anderwahl wondered out loud. "I didn't think they had salad at all until the twentieth century."

"Oh, they had to have had salad a long time before that," Fritzie said. "The French, you know. The French have always been interested in salads."

"I don't think they had tossed salads much before that," Tony Baird said. He stood up and handed his plate to his father, took it back, then took Bennis's and handed over hers. "I don't really care what the Puritans ate. From what I've heard, it had a lot of lard in it."

"From what I've heard, it had a lot of sugar in it." Julie Anderwahl took her filled salad plate from Jon and immediately began to munch on a sliver of cucumber. "I think about what it would be like sometimes, to live in a world where everybody was just expected to get fat as they got older. That way you could eat what you wanted and never have to think about diets."

"I never do think about diets," Sheila Baird said.

"You will," Fritzie Baird told her. "Trust me, my dear, you will."

"You forgot me," Charlie Shay handed his plate across the table. "You got everybody else but—"

"Got you now." Jon Baird stood up again—he had only just sat down—and piled salad on Charlie Shay's plate. Then he handed the plate over, sat down again, and surveyed the table. For the first time since Gregor had met him, he actually looked pleased. "Well," he said. "Here we are. You don't know how I've been looking forward to this trip."

"He must have been looking forward to this trip," Mark Anderwahl murmured at Gregor's side. "If he hadn't been, he'd never have gotten the rest of us to go along with it."

There was a clear cruet of salad dressing traveling around the table, family style in the best middle-class tradition, and Gregor caught it as it came by and doused his lettuce vigorously. Then he turned his attention fully to the young man at his side. He had, of course, been in contact with Mark Anderwahl before, although they hadn't exactly been introduced. Mark had been present in the bow when they had gathered to watch the boat set sail that morning. Unlike the rest of the Bairds, however, Mark had not done any talking. He had simply stood back and watched his wife with fierce and restless eyes. Now he was paying no attention to her at all. Gregor picked up his fork, tried the salad, decided the salad dressing was abnormally bitter, and put his fork down again.

"You're Mark Anderwahl," Gregor said. "I don't think we've ever been properly introduced."

"No, we haven't." Mark picked up his fork, took a taste of his salad, put down his fork, and winced. "Oh, God," he said, "here we go again. One of Jon's salad dressings. They get worse every year."

"If you knew it was gong to be bad, why did you use it?"

Mark Anderwahl blinked. "I work for Baird Financial. I had to use it. Jon gets very huffy if you don't eat his salad dressing."

"Is it just salad dressing, or are there other things he cooks and makes you eat?"

"He tried a pie once, but it didn't work out. And he grills steaks, of course. All the men of that generation grill steaks. The steaks are all right."

"Oh."

"Look at old Charlie," Mark Anderwahl said. "Practically gagging and stuffing it down all the same. That's how he got to be a partner. Uncle Calvin, now, he got to be a partner because Uncle Jon knew it was either make him one or be nagged to death. You don't know what kind of trouble it causes, having so many partners who don't know the first thing about business."

Gregor was surprised. "Calvin Baird and Charlie Shay don't know the first thing about business?" In his experience, really successful enterprises—and Baird Financial certainly was that—didn't carry a lot of deadwood.

Mark Anderwahl chewed slowly on a lettuce leaf, considering. "Well," he said, "it's like this. Charlie doesn't know anything about business—and I mean anything at all. If you're not going to go for the salad dressing, the only way to explain him is that he's one of Uncle Jon's really old friends. With Uncle Calvin it's different. He's a businessman, all right, he's just the wrong kind of businessman."

"What do you mean, the wrong kind?"

Mark waved his fork in the air. "Small-minded," he declared. "He'd be really good with a McDonald's franchise somewhere or running a five-and-dime store, but at Baird Financial he just doesn't do any good."

"Do you mean because of these numbers he's worried about?" Gregor asked, thinking about the meeting in the hall before dinner. "He was talking to me about some sort of discrepancy in some sort of record."

"In the cash-on-hand reports in the back-up research for the Europabanc deal." Mark shook his head. "That's silly, but at least it's understandable. You don't want discrepancies even if they don't matter. No, I mean when we first decided to buy Europabanc, a couple of years ago. Uncle Calvin didn't want us to."

"I thought the Europabanc deal was a good one."

"It is a good one. It's a spectacularly good one. It's not just the chance of a lifetime, it's the chance of a millennium. There hasn't been an opportunity like it before and there probably won't be one again. I mean, for God's sake. We're going to do in one fell swoop what it took the Rothschilds generations to put together."

"Then why was your uncle Calvin opposed to it?"

"He got hung up on details. It bothered him because we didn't have any money."

"What?"

"I have to go topside for a moment," Charlie Shay said, standing up at his place and looking a little green. "I may be up there for quite some time. I don't think you ought to wait for me."

"Oh, for Heaven's sake," Sheila Baird said.

"If you're going to throw up, go to the bow," Jon Baird said. "The rail's low there. You won't splatter all over the polished teak."

"What an awful thing to say," Fritzie Baird said. "You ought to have proper toilets on this boat. That way you wouldn't be forced to worry about your teak."

"I've got to go," Charlie said again.

He lurched painfully toward the door, stopped still to get it open, then had to jump back a little as the young man came through again, this time carry a gigantic tureen. There was a ladle sticking out of the tureen at one end, through a small round notch that also let out the smell of nutmeg and pumpkin and thyme. Charlie Shay stared at it for a moment, got even greener, and then lunged into the hall outside.

"Oh, dear," Sheila Baird said. "That's just what we needed, isn't it? Someone going right off their feed and doing it in full view of the rest of the company. Isn't it just like Charlie Shay to be rude?"

Gregor didn't think Charlie Shay had been the least bit rude—and he didn't think anyone else did either—but Sheila Baird was one of those women nobody argued with. It was too much trouble and it wouldn't do any good. She wouldn't listen to reason and she had no common sense.

"Excuse me," he said, standing up. "I think I'll go topside and make sure Mr. Shay doesn't fall overboard."

Jon Baird flushed red. "I'm the one who should go," he said. "After all, I'm the one who invited Charlie here. Sit down, Mr. Demarkian. I'll take care of this."

"I'm already up," Gregor pointed out, "and besides, I could use the air. I'm not a much better sailor than Mr. Shay is himself. Leave it to me."

"But—"

"Leave it to me," Gregor said firmly, propelling himself to the door quickly enough so that he could not be overtaken by a man who was still sitting down. He got the door open, looked out into the hall, and was a little disturbed to see that it was already empty. He hadn't thought Charlie Shay would have been able to move that fast in his condition.

"Leave it to me," he said again.

Then he went out into the hall himself, shut the mess hall door behind him, and headed for the stairs to the upper deck.

3

Sitting at the mess hall table, Gregor had thought it was a little strange that Charlie Shay had been taken so ill so fast. Once in the hall, he changed his mind. What he hadn't noticed in the mess, maybe because of where he was sitting, was how much the weather had changed since they'd first sat down to eat. There had been a stiff, steady wind coming out of the south all day, pushing them forward evenly and relentlessly, allowing them to make much more progress than they had had any right to expect. Now, however, the steady wind had evolved into a gusting one. Instead of a steady push, there was a fretful power jerking them forward and sideways, up and back. Instead of a gentle roll there was a kind of roller-coaster pulse. Gregor made his way along the passage carefully, but no matter how careful he was he couldn't help bumping into the walls around him or the ceiling above his head. Just when he thought he understood how the boat was going to move, it changed its mind and he was thrown against a beam or into a latch on a door. Making his way to the upper deck was worse. He got hold of the rails on either side of the staircase and hauled himself upward, tensing himself against the motion of the sea, but his shoes slipped on the slick wood of the risers. By the time he got his head up out of the hatch, he had hit it at least half a dozen times, and not lightly, either. He was well on his way to having a roaring headache. The sea seemed to be getting more violent by the minute. He had to drag himself upward onto the deck, pulling himself forward with his arms. When he was finally standing in the wind he lasted only moments upright before he was pitched sideways into a pile of lines. There was rain in the air now and a wind that whistled. If Gregor had to make a prediction, he would have said they were about to be visited by a very serious storm.

He sat up against the lines, stretched his arms, and

looked around. There was no sign of Charlie Shay and no sound of him either. Charlie must have taken Jon Baird's advice and gone forward to be sick. Gregor hauled himself carefully to his feet, holding onto lines and rails and anything else he could find as he stood. Then he began to move very carefully forward, toward the bow, where he supposed Charlie Shay was. He had just made it to the wheelhouse wall when he turned back and saw a head pop out of the hatch behind him. He turned back and waited while Tony Baird came out.

"Loosen up," Tony Baird told him. "Don't think about it. If you think about it, you fall over."

There had been an exercise like this for new recruits at Quantico, at least since the 1970s. Gregor had never had to go through it himself, but he had heard about it. He let go of the wall he was holding onto and willed his body to relax. He didn't quite make it, but he did get close enough so that he could feel his body begin to move with the boat and not against it. For the first time since he had left the mess hall, he was in no danger of falling over.

"Thanks," he said. "The way I was going, it would have taken me a year just to find Mr. Shay."

"Charlie is probably as far forward as he can get, trying to do exactly what Dad told him to do."

"Maybe we ought to go stop him."

Tony nodded slightly and came forward, moving easily past Gregor and on toward the bow. Gregor followed him patiently. He could walk now, but not really well. Tony moved as easily as he did on dry land.

"What's that?" he called back.

Gregor strained to hear something besides the ever-increasing wail of the wind and failed.

"What does it sound like?" he asked.

"It sounds like—Jesus H. Christ," Tony said.

"What?" Gregor asked him.

Tony was in that narrow place that was the only open passageway between the main part of the upper deck and the bow. The other side was still clogged with tables and chairs from this morning's breakfast. The place was like the hall downstairs, too small to take two people at once. Gregor had to push Tony forward to get into the bow and see. His task was made that much harder because Tony seemed glued to the deck beneath his feet.

"Jesus H. Christ," Tony said again, as Gregor pushed on through.

And then Gregor saw it—or him, to be precise.

It was Charlie Shay, jerking and jumping and shuddering in convulsions, coming closer and closer to the low bow rail every time he moved.

Part Two

November 17–November 18

One

1

Later, Gregor Demarkian would wonder what on earth possessed him to go for Charlie Shay's feet. Certainly it wasn't anything he'd learned about fighting at Quantico, because he hadn't learned about fighting at Quantico. Of course, even in the days when he had joined the Bureau, agents had been expected to know how to protect themselves. They'd been put through a short training sequence that had seemed to Gregor like a cross between boot camp and a National Rifle Association Expert Eye Gun Club. The thing was, in those days almost everybody who joined the Bureau was male and almost every male had been in the army. They were all assumed to be in good shape or capable of getting that way. That was good, because as a matter of fact Gregor Demarkian had never exactly been in good shape. He was not a physical man. He was not comfortable with guns, either. The Bureau had wanted him to learn how to shoot a machine gun—what had been going on in the minds of the people who set up training for the Bureau in those days, Gregor would never know—and so he had spent the requisite amount of time duly aiming one of the silly things at a target. He got muscle spasms in his right shoulder and a crick in his neck and a pass up at the insistence of an officer on kidnapping detail, who wanted him available for an assignment out in Palo Verde, California. After that, he'd been allowed to do what he was good at doing, meaning use his head. He'd used his head carefully and methodically for ten steady years of promotions and then been handed Theodore Robert Bundy. Never in all that time had he had to shoot anybody, or fight anybody, or even much raise his voice. In the higher echelons of the Federal Bureau of Investigation, crime—even the habitual pursuit of murder—was a very civilized way of life.

On the *Pilgrimage Green*, the death of Charlie Shay was anything but civilized. That he was dying, Gregor had no doubt. Gregor barely knew the difference between an Uzi and a Colt .45, but he did know poisons. Strychnine wasn't even a very difficult poison to detect. The convulsions, the rigor, the look of shock on the face, that strange leaping St. Vitus' dance of agony—there was nothing in the world like it. There was no question that Charlie Shay might live. He had probably been dead before Gregor or Tony ever saw him. The only mystery here was whether or not Charlie Shay would end up in the sea. The storm had built up around them now. The boat was pitching and yawing under their feet. The motion exaggerated Charlie Shay's dance beyond the merely grotesque. In a more superstitious age, the assembled company would have taken one look at what was happening in the bow and started looking around for a witch.

Gregor's only thought was that, no matter what else happened, Charlie Shay must not disappear. He might be able to spot strychnine poisoning just by looking at it, but no district attorney would prosecute—and no court would convict—on just his word. If Charlie Shay's body fell into the sea, whatever investigation there might have been would be dead before it started. Gregor kept staring at

Charlie Shay and what he saw was Charlie Shay leaping. Charlie Shay's feet came up off the deck and did little tap steps in the air. Charlie Shay's body arched back over the sea and snapped forward again, almost making the dive.

Gregor couldn't stand it any longer. The boat dropped with the water beneath it. Charlie Shay went into the air one more time. Gregor held his breath and launched himself forward, sliding across the wet deck toward the low bow side. As he was skidding, the water and the boat rose again and Charlie Shay came down. Gregor got a single fistful of grey flannel trouser and felt it tear away from the trouser itself as Charlie once again began to rise in the air. Up and down, up and down. If Gregor had had a chance to think about it, he would have been seasick. All he had a chance to think about were Charlie Shay's ankles. The boat began to rise again. Charlie Shay's body began to fall again. Gregor put out his hands and grabbed. One of those hands got hold of something solid, dead flesh and brittle bone. The other got smashed. Charlie Shay was wearing thick-soled canvas deck shoes, the tie-up kind people order from catalogs like J. Crew and Land's End. One of those deck shoes hit Gregor's hand like a hammer hitting a nail. Its full force was blunted by the fact that Gregor had hold of the other leg and was pulling it in the other direction. The result was paralyzing and painful, but nothing worse. Gregor got his hand out from under as soon as he could and put it up near his chest.

"For God's sake, help me," he called out in the general direction of where he thought Tony Baird must be. He felt as if he'd been fighting the sea and the wind and the corpse of Charlie Shay for hours, even though he knew it must only have been seconds. "Help me," he said again, with a strength born of exasperation in his voice. "What in God's name are you doing over there?"

What Tony Baird was doing over there was nothing,

because he hadn't been over there for most of Gregor's struggle with the body. As soon as he'd seen what was going on, Tony had headed for the mess, running and shouting at the top of his lungs. His report had been impossible to understand, but also impossible to ignore. Now he was back on deck, with the rest of the company behind him, craning over his shoulder to see anything they could.

"For Heaven's sake, help him," Bennis Hannaford screamed. "You can't just leave him out there like that in the rain."

"Tony, you're blocking up the passage," Jon Baird said.

"Right," Tony said, suddenly leaping forward into the wet.

Gregor felt him land beside him just a moment before he was about to let the body go. Tony got hold of Charlie's other leg and then seemed to be trying to push Gregor aside. Gregor held on ever more tightly. The one thing he had no intention of doing was letting this corpse out of his custody until he got it safely into a cabin. Tony shoved again. Gregor held on. Then Gregor got hold of a coiled line and began to use it to haul himself upward.

"I can do this," Tony shouted in his ear.

The shout seemed abnormally loud, because it was no longer really necessary. The wind had begun to die down. Gregor secured his hold on the lines and pushed himself almost to a standing position. He was still holding on to one of Charlie Shay's ankles with his right hand.

"All right," he said to Tony Baird. "Forget about the legs. Take the hands."

"I can carry him myself."

"No you can't."

Tony shot him a black look, but this time he obeyed. He dropped the leg he'd been holding, making it necessary for Gregor to bend over again to pick it up. Then Tony moved around until he was standing over Charlie Shay's head and reached for the corpse's hands.

"Let's get him out of the rain," Gregor said. "Then I think we'd better all sit somewhere and talk."

2

Getting the corpse of Charlie Shay out of the rain was a project easier planned than executed. Gregor had always thought of the halls and passageways belowdecks as "tight." Now they made him feel as if he were being squeezed through the neck of a tube of toothpaste. In order to keep Charlie Shay's body off the floor, both Gregor and Tony had to keep their elbows cocked slightly outward. They were both too big to do that comfortably on this boat. Elbows smashed into doors. Elbows smashed into beams. Elbows smashed into the smooth-planed wood of the walls. Their heads took a beating, too. Gregor was getting used to what was happening to his. Getting knocked on the head was practically a definition of his life on this boat. Tony seemed more surprised by just how much of a beating he was expected to take. Every time his forehead smashed into a beam, he swore.

The maneuver wasn't aided much by Jon Baird's taking charge of it—but Jon Baird had taken charge of it, and there was nothing the rest of them could do. Gregor supposed Jon Baird took charge of everything. That was the kind of man he was. Gregor also supposed Jon Baird created a fair amount of resentment in his employees. Now what Jon Baird wanted was Charlie Shay's body on the lower passenger deck, one flight down from the deck where they were all staying for the holiday. That required the navigation of a second flight of ladderlike stairs and the negotiation of a second set of even tighter passageways. What was worse, the rest of the company insisted on coming along with them, en masse. Gregor had refused to let go of the body. Now they were refusing to let go of it, too. They were refusing to let go of anything.

Going down to this deck, Jon Baird had taken the lead. Now he stopped in front of a narrow door and waited for Gregor and Tony to catch up. Behind Gregor and Tony, the rest of the party was murmuring and coughing and nervous. They had every right to be nervous. Nobody had thought to bring a torch or a tallow candle. It wasn't absolutely dark down here—nothing outside a scientifically engineered black box, or a deep-earth cavern, is that—but it was close. The darkness made the air seem wetter and clammier and more alive than it was.

"Here we are," Jon Baird said. "We can put him in here. This is the crew's deck. They'll look after him."

"I don't want the crew to look after him," Gregor said. "I want the room locked up."

"We should have buried him at sea," Tony Baird said. "That's what you do in cases like this. It's going to be days before we reach land."

"We'll radio the Coast Guard for help," Gregor told him.

Tony Baird snorted. "We can't radio the Coast Guard for help. We don't have a radio. We don't have a motor. We don't have anything. We should have buried him at sea."

Jon Baird opened the door behind him and peered inside. Then he rummaged around in his pockets and came up with a box of wooden matches. "Just a minute," he said, "I'll get things going here. There's the candle. There we are."

The candle wasn't much help, but it was some. Jon Baird placed it in the holder just inside the door he had opened and then edged back out into the passageway to let Gregor and Tony and the body pass. Gregor and Tony edged the body inside and then headed for the only thing they could head for, the small built-in bunk on the far wall. The bunk was even smaller than the ones on the deck above. Gregor didn't think they were going to be able to get Charlie Shay to lie down flat in it.

They came up to the bunk's open side, sidled around until they were holding the body with its head where its head was supposed to be, and then began to lower it carefully into position. The legs were stiff, although not as stiff as they would be later, with rigor. Gregor winced a little as they resisted his attempts to bend them. He managed to get them cocked just enough so that the body would fit into the bunk. As soon as he did, he stepped quickly away from the corpse and back toward the center of the cabin.

"Dear God," Tony said. "He's stiff as a board. I thought it took hours for rigor mortis to set in."

"It does," Gregor told him. "That's not rigor mortis. That's a side effect of strychnine poisoning. It's not a hundred percent sure—"

"Strychnine poisoning?"

"—the stiffening doesn't occur in all cases and it's rarely as pronounced as this, although I have seen it this pronounced before. I shouldn't call it strychnine poisoning, though. I just gave a young man a lecture about that yesterday. Technically, no one gets poisoned with strychnine."

"Wait a minute," Tony Baird said, "what are you trying to tell me here? Do you want me to think somebody murdered Charlie Shay?"

"You've either got to think that, or you've got to think he took strychnine in cocaine like your father's friend Donald McAdam—"

"Donald McAdam was no friend of anyone on this boat."

"—and my guess would be that Charlie Shay wasn't the cocaine type." Gregor nodded. "Quite frankly, the way he appeared to me was as someone who wasn't even the cocktail type. A nice, steady, middle-of-the-road gentleman."

"He was a cipher," Tony Baird said positively. "Why would anyone want to murder Charlie Shay?"

"I don't know."

"If you're thinking it's business, you might as well know right up front you're wrong. Charlie Shay didn't know shit about the business. I knew more about what went on at Baird Financial, and I didn't even work there. Charlie's been a nonperforming partner for years."

"So I've been told."

"So you're probably wrong," Tony insisted. "It wasn't strychnine poisoning. It was some kind of fit."

Gregor looked back at the bunk. His own bulk was blocking most of the weak light of the candle from reaching Charlie Shay's face, but it wouldn't have mattered if he'd been able to look at the body under a Kliegl light. Strychnine poisoning wasn't like some other things, like arsenic or lye, that left telltale traces long after death. There would be no blue tinge along the jawline or burned patches of skin. A forensic pathologist would be able to find traces in the blood, but all the outward manifestations were limited to the time when the victim was in the process of dying. If you didn't see those, you had to wait for a coroner's report. If you did, though, there was nothing else like them on earth.

Gregor retreated to the door, took the candle out of its holder, and gestured to Tony to follow. "I'm not wrong," he said, "because I saw Charlie Shay die—or immediately after he died—and I know what someone looks like when they're dying of strychnine. I'm also not wrong because murder is the only thing that makes sense in this case. Don't you think so?"

"No," Tony Baird said.

"You're lying," Gregor told him. "And you don't do it very well."

"You're obsessed with murder," Tony said. "You've spent so much of your life dealing with it, you've started to see it under every bush."

"Do you really think you're going to help anyone with this attitude of yours?"

"Do you really think you're going to help anyone with this attitude of yours?" Tony shot back, and then he moved toward the door, furious and cold, the fine-boned lines of his back almost as rigid as Charlie Shay's had been in death. "I told my father it was a mistake to invite you here. I told him he'd regret it. I was right."

Gregor moved away from the door. Tony had it all the way open now. He was presented with a bouquet of faces, looking in expectantly, waiting for something to happen. He turned his shoulder toward them and started to edge through.

"Wait," Gregor said. "I want to talk to your father. Do you think you could ask him to come in here for me?"

"Do it yourself."

"I want all these people to get back up into the mess hall as soon as they can," Gregor went on. "It isn't good for them to be crowded up out there like that. A couple of them have been sick as dogs since we started out anyway. Tell them I'll come up and explain the whole thing in a minute or two."

"You tell them," Tony said. Then he whirled around, stared at Charlie Shay's body in the shadows, and whirled back. His face was white. His eyes were red. His jaw was so taut, Gregor thought it was going to snap in two all on its own volition.

"You damned interfering son of a bitch," he said.

Then he shoved his shoulder into Sheila Callahan Baird's throat, pushed her aside, and plunged into the passageway, not caring in the least who he had to rearrange to get where he was going.

That, Gregor thought as he watched him leave, is one very ruthless young man.

3

Five minutes later, with the (expected) help of Bennis Hannaford and the (somewhat surprising) help of Fritzie Baird, Gregor had what he'd asked Tony Baird to help him get. The spectators had retreated to the deck above the one where he now stood, probably to crowd together in the mess hall and speculate. Gregor had been present at a number of these mob scenes over the last five years, and in his experience the witnesses liked to talk—to each other. Once the police started to ask questions, some of them inevitably clammed up, but Gregor had never known an innocent witness not to want to talk to other witnesses as long as he thought he wasn't being overheard. Gregor's instinct was to let this sort of thing take its course, without interference. Every once in a while there was a case where individual impressions, unfiltered by group consensus, were important. Then you had to divide the witnesses up. The rest of the time, it only helped their memories, and their moods, to let them talk.

The other thing Gregor had wanted, and got, was a private meeting with Jonathan Edgewick Baird. He would have preferred to have had that meeting someplace else besides this small room with Charlie Shay's body in it, but every time he'd tried to figure out where, the logistics had been too rough. Going to the deck above only invited interruption. At the least, he'd have had Tony Baird hanging over their shoulders, making threatening rumbles in the back of his throat. Going to the main deck wasn't the answer, either. The storm was dying down by the second, but it was still cold up there, and wet, and every enclosed place had a crew member in it. Gregor supposed there were other empty cabins on this deck, but he didn't know where they were. It was easier just to stay where he was.

The one thing he did do was to light another candle. It was sitting in the holder on the opposite side of the doorway where the already lit candle was, and he lit the new one off the old, grateful for even this small sliver of extra light. Then he sat down on the low plank that had been built into the open side of the bunk to serve as a stair for someone climbing into bed and as a bench for someone who needed to sit. Jon Baird stood in the doorway, his back in the passage, waiting.

"Well," Gregor told him, "I take it you heard what I said to Tony, or somebody heard it and told you."

"About Charlie dying from strychnine? Yes, I heard it. I wasn't very far from the door. Nobody was very far from the door. They all heard it."

"You realize it must have happened at dinner?"

"I don't realize it was strychnine, Mr. Demarkian. I think I'm with Tony on this. I know you're supposed to be an expert, but you're not a medical doctor and you haven't run the tests a coroner would run to determine cause of death. You're just speculating."

"Am I?"

"Tony was right about something else, too," Jon Baird said. "Nobody would want to kill Charlie Shay. Even his wife only wanted to divorce him, and she's off in California or Tibet or something anyway. Charlie Shay wasn't the kind of man who made enemies. He wasn't even the kind of man who made good friends."

"Mmm," Gregor said. "Of course, we're in a better position than I thought we were going to be. I thought we were going to lose the body. Now we have the body, and we can give it to the proper authorities as soon as we can contact them. Can we contact them?"

"Eventually."

"There is no radio on this boat?"

"No."

"What about emergency signaling equipment? What about flares?"

"There's not a single thing on this boat that couldn't have been here in the seventeenth century."

"But that isn't true, is it?" Gregor insisted. "There were the chairs this morning, for one thing. There was the salad tonight. Your commitment to authenticity isn't anywhere near monolithic."

"Oh, it's monolithic all right," Jon Baird said with feeling. "All those things you're talking about—and there are more—all those things were Sheila's idea. Sheila's always got ideas. It doesn't do to thwart them."

"So you're saying that everything on this boat that is anachronistic to the seventeenth century was brought on board by your wife."

"Exactly."

"All right." It wasn't all right at all. Gregor didn't believe this nonsense for a minute. After all, even if the salad had been Sheila Baird's idea, the salad dressing had been a Jon Baird specialty. Mark Anderwahl had said so. Still, for the moment it was better to let it drop. "Let's go about it this way," Gregor said. "What about making land. We have a dead body on board. Something happened to make it dead. It seems to me we ought to make contact with a police force as soon as physically possible."

"I agree."

"Then you'll order the crew to head back to land."

"Well, I could," Jon Baird said, "but it wouldn't do any good."

"Why not?"

Jon Baird rocked back on his heels, smiling slightly. "Do you know why the Puritans landed in Massachusetts? They were on their way to Virginia. They got blown off course."

"What's that supposed to mean?"

"It's supposed to mean we don't have a modern compass on this ship. We don't have navigating instruments. We don't have radar or sonar or any of the rest of that. We don't even have a motor. All we do have is the sun and the moon and the stars. Which right this minute happen to be covered by clouds."

"Does that mean you're not going to do anything at all about finding us a way to contact the authorities?"

"Not at all. I'm going to do everything I can. I'm just trying to tell you it's not going to be much."

"Do you expect that to look good when we finally do get to talk to the police?"

"I'm not sure it's going to matter what it looks like. You know, Mr. Demarkian, there's one thing you haven't considered."

"What's that?"

"This ship was headed straight out to sea from the Virginia shore. It wasn't supposed to have gone out past the twelve-mile limit, but it might have. And even if it didn't, how is anybody going to be able to tell? Who is going to have jurisdiction here? I still say this wasn't a murder. It's absurd to even think Charlie Shay might have been murdered. There wouldn't be a sane motive on earth. But as for the police—" Jon Baird shrugged. "I've never had much use for the police," he admitted. "I've never understood how any man could take a job that was so unlikely to make him any money. I'm going up now. Are you going to come with me?"

"I'll be along in a minute."

"I'll send First Mate Debrek along to make sure this room is locked. I'll have him give you the key, if you want it that way."

"I do want it that way."

"I thought you would. You know, Mr. Demarkian, you really ought to be careful. I made a mistake having you here when you refused to take my money. I don't like the kind of leverage you have when you're not in my employ. You can make a few mistakes yourself, if you're not careful."

"But I'm always careful," Gregor said.

Jon Baird stepped out into the passage and shook his head. In the darkness there, he looked like an evil spirit, with the power to disappear. Seconds later, he was gone.

Gregor went back to the bunk and looked down at the face of Charlie Shay. He would stay here and wait for the first mate to lock up. He thought it was crucial. He had expected disbelief when he announced his judgment on the cause of Charlie Shay's death. It was a judgment hard to credit, in view of Charlie Shay's life. What he hadn't expected was this—this meretricious horse manure.

Gregor Demarkian knew that Charlie Shay had died from taking strychnine because he had seen enough of death from strychnine to know what he was talking about. He didn't expect to be believed. The problem was, he had been believed, instantaneously, by both Tony Baird and Tony's father. Their protests were not based on doubt but on plausibility, like the protests of a man who has committed the crime he has been accused of but knows it cannot be proved against him. That led to a couple of interesting conclusions, including the one that said that in that case, either Tony or Jon or the two of them together had murdered Charlie Shay. And the problem with that was—

Gregor went to the door of the cabin, looked out, and sighed. He wished the first mate were already on the premises. He wished there were electric lights on this boat. He wished he didn't have to go up and spend the rest of his night questioning people who were going to think, quite rightly, that he had no business asking them anything at all.

He also wished he knew what was going on. He couldn't shake the feeling that the situation was still lethal.

Two

1

It took nearly half an hour for First Mate Debrek to arrive at the cabin where Gregor Demarkian was keeping watch over Charlie Shay's corpse, and when he did Gregor had to give up his last hope that some sort of sensible procedure could be established for this crime. Gregor had never really believed in the legends of men so powerful that no one around them was willing to risk their wrath for any reason whatsoever. There might have been men like that in the small Communist bloc countries before the fall of the Soviet Union, but this was America. Even J. Edgar Hoover, with his paranoia and his illegal files, had been able to go only so far, and then only against men willing to be black-mailed to keep their careers. Quite a few other men had simply told him where to put it—and got away with it, too, because if The Boss had ever tipped his hand about those files, he would have been politically dead meat. Surely Jon Baird's crew wouldn't be willing to sail up the Atlantic coast with the body of a possible murder victim locked into a cabin on their own deck, arousing the wrath of police departments in four or five states *and* the FBI *and* the Coast Guard just to keep the old man happy. Gregor wasn't sure who had jurisdiction here—and, he had noticed, neither was Jon Baird—but somebody did, and a few other somebodies were going to want it. It had to be simple to convince the crew that it would be in their own best interests to ignore their orders and head immediately for land.

It might have been simple indeed, but Gregor never got the chance to find out. He waited patiently until the small, spare man came down with his candle. He stood in the passageway while the door was locked and the key handed over. Then he said a perfectly pleasant "Good evening," and was met by a blank stare.

"Damn," Gregor said. "Don't you speak English?"

Debrek said something that sounded like *"Betzhitzi dem bournidin"* and turned his back. Gregor winced. He knew Armenian when he heard it—he couldn't help it—and French and German as well, but this was something convoluted and obscure. He had a terrible feeling that Jon Baird had taken on a few refugees of his own. Estonia, Latvia, Lithuania, the Ukraine—over the last six months, Baird could have picked up a few men from any of those places, and they would be perfectly safe from the importunings of friends and enemies alike. Gregor knew more than most people about refugees. He knew that if Debrek knew that what his employer was asking him to do might jeopardize his chances for a green card or a set of naturalization papers, he would abandon it as soon as he possibly could. The only problem was in getting Debrek to understand that what he was engaged in was illegal. Gregor gave it a second try. "I would like to talk to you," he said, in a very hopeful voice. It did no good. At the sound of talking, Debrek turned and waited politely. It was the attentiveness of manners, not comprehension. When the talking was done, Debrek turned again and hurried off, toward the narrow staircase to the deck above. Gregor followed him. There didn't seem to be anything else to do.

Reaching the passenger deck, Gregor stopped, listened to the murmur coming from behind the door to the mess, and stopped to look around. All day, this long, narrow passageway had been dark. There had never been much sun even at noon, and what light had filtered through had been weak. Then, near dinnertime, some of the candles had been lit, but not many of them. They'd thrown off shadows more than light. They'd made the passageway as spooky as a closet in a haunted house. Now there was a candle in every available holder and they were all lit. The passageway was still spooky, but it was at least spooky and bright.

Gregor walked carefully to the door of the mess and then back toward the stairs that led above and then back again, trying to remember how dark it had been and what Charlie Shay must have seen as he was making his way along here. Then he put his foot on the bottom step and began to push himself upwards even more carefully. He didn't remember hearing any sound from this passageway after Charlie Shay had had his attack of sickness and headed for the deck above. That didn't mean there hadn't been any sound to hear. Gregor tested the step, stepped up, stepped down again and looked around. He thought about the mess, almost barren of decorations, and of the little row of mason jars marked "*Pumpkin Rind Marmalade*" in a careful Farmington script. He thought about salads and salad dressings and ships in bottles.

"Ipecac," he said to himself, and thought that that reminded him of Thanksgivings at home. Somebody under the age of eight was always swallowing something they shouldn't and getting physicked up by the old ladies. He tried the step again. Then he heard a sound from farther down the corridor and turned in its direction. He had asked for everybody to sit together in the mess and wait for him, but he didn't expect cooperation from Jon or Tony Baird. He wondered which one this was.

As it turned out, it was neither. The figure coming toward him was Bennis Hannaford, and she had emerged from the cabin they were supposed to share. Her black hair was slipping out of its combs and her flannel shirt was unbuttoned over the turtleneck she always wore under it, but other than that she might as well have been on Cavanaugh Street. She cocked her head when she saw him and came as close as she could before she spoke, as if anything they had to say to each other ought to be secret. Gregor could only thank the good God that she didn't go in for whispers.

"There you are," she said. "Everybody's shoved together in that little room talking about you and driving themselves to distraction. Tony knows the details of all your cases and he keeps telling people about them and putting in a lot of blood. I keep telling them there hasn't really been any blood, the one exception being the one I don't talk about, of course, but it doesn't matter because nobody listens to me, anyway. Are you all right?"

"I'm fine. Tony is in there, too?"

"Everybody is," Bennis repeated, "except Jon Baird himself, and I didn't expect that. He doesn't seem to me to be the kind of man who's really fond of crowds. Are you going to come in now and tell us what's going on? We're all dying to know."

"What did Tony Baird say about what was going on?"

"He said Charlie Shay had some kind of fit and died of it. What kind of fit that was supposed to be, I don't know. I've seen grand mal epilepsy and the kind of convulsions people have when they've been taking speed and downers together, and that was neither of those. Anyway, it doesn't matter, because we all heard the fight you had with Tony and we know you think it was a murder. Strychnine."

"Strychnine," Gregor agreed. He looked at the stairs again. A fine mistlike rain was coming down through the hole above above his head, making Gregor feel as if his face had been painted with dew. He went a few steps upward and poked his head out into the air. Then he came down again.

"Listen," he told Bennis, "do me a favor. I'm going to go up on deck. I want you to go back to the mess hall door, make your way along the passage, climb these stairs, and meet me above. You're used to boats, aren't you?"

"Fairly used to. It's like horses, Gregor. It's one of those things I was brought up to, so I know about it, but I don't like it much. I like boats a lot better than I like subscription dances, if that's any help."

"It's not whether you like boats or not that I care about. It's how well you move around on one. I'm always unsteady and I'm always slow. Charlie Shay, I think, was more like you. He was used to it. He could get around without struggling."

Bennis bit her lip. "Are you trying to figure out how long it took Charlie to get from the dining hall to the deck? If you're going to do that, shouldn't I slow myself down? He was an old man. I'm a lot faster than he was to begin with, and he was all bent over sick—"

"He was also remarkably fast," Gregor pointed out. "He was in the bow by the time I got up to the main deck. I didn't waste much time leaving the mess hall, either."

"Maybe. But there was the storm. That probably slowed him down, too."

"Just do what I'm asking you to do, Bennis. It's not an exact time I need, just an approximation."

Bennis looked doubtful, but she finally shrugged her shoulders and went back to the mess hall door. Gregor climbed up to the main deck, stepped away from the hatch, and checked his watch. Then he called down, "Now. Go."

Bennis must have gone. Gregor didn't hear her in the passage, but he did hear her on the stairs, and he approved.

She wasn't running, but she was keeping up a good forced walk. Her head appeared through the hatch forty-five seconds after Gregor had given her the signal. The rest of her body came on deck less than ten seconds later. "Go to the bow," Gregor told her, and she went.

The bow was a longer and harder trek than the one from the dining room to the deck above, but even allowing for Charlie Shay's slower pace and the storm and all the rest of it, there was nothing to disturb the impression he'd had when he'd first come up to the passenger deck after seeing Charlie Shay's body locked away. If he hadn't been so caught up in chasing bodies and confronting hostile Bairds and otherwise behaving less like an Armenian-American Hercule Poirot than like an overaged Mannix, he would have seen it sooner.

Bennis came to a stop too close to the bow's low rail. Gregor shut his watch with a snap and motioned her away from the side.

"Two minutes and fifteen seconds," he told her. "Make allowances for Charlie Shay and call it three minutes."

"Three minutes for him to get from the mess hall to here."

"That's right."

"So what?"

Gregor smiled. "So," he said, "I don't know what you know about strychnine poisoning, but assuming you know absolutely nothing, I'll tell you this. Under no circumstances did Charlie Shay make it from the mess hall to here in three minutes flat in the middle of a storm while he was in the grip of strychnine convulsions."

Bennis stared at him suspiciously. "What are you talking about?" she demanded. "Do you mean he didn't die of strychnine poisoning? Do you mean he didn't die of poisoning at all?"

"Of course I don't mean that. Charlie Shay definitely

died from being fed strychnine. I saw him die. There's nothing else like it on earth. I'm just saying it wasn't strychnine that caused him to leave the mess hall when he did. Which, by the way, makes sense. It takes at least five minutes for strychnine to take effect in most people, sometimes longer. Assuming he was fed the strychnine at dinner tonight—"

"Can you assume that?"

"I think so," Gregor said, "yes. We'll have to ask, of course, but the only other alternatives leave us with a problem opposite to the one we've got now. I mean if somebody fed him strychnine before dinner then he should have begun convulsing at dinner long before he got up and walked out. By then he wouldn't have been able to get up and walk out."

"Meaning he must have taken the strychnine in the salad or in the salad dressing," Bennis said.

"Exactly." Gregor nodded. "Only Jon Baird handled the salad, but everybody handled the salad dressing, and it was bitter enough to hide anything. What that man thinks he's doing—"

Bennis sighed. "To tell you the truth, it reminded me of my father. It comes from belonging to Cod House. It's a men's cooking club in Philadelphia. Only very old families need apply. They have a positive mania for making things with bitter herbs."

"I'll take Lida's positive mania for making things with chocolate any time you ask. Well. It still doesn't solve our problem here. Everybody seems to have known about the bitter salad dressing. Jon Baird could have used it to hide the taste of the strychnine, but so could anybody else at that table except you and me. Or maybe I should just say me. You knew all about this—Mackerel House."

"Cod House," Bennis said automatically. "Gregor, I don't understand. If he wasn't feeling the effects of strychnine, why did Charlie Shay leave the table? Was he just seasick?"

"He might have been. I don't think so, though. If you were going to kill someone with strychnine, would you really want to sit around and watch him die all over your dinner table?"

"I wouldn't want to kill anyone with strychnine."

"Good point." Gregor sighed. "*My* point is that I think Charlie Shay's seasickness got a little help from whoever murdered him. Do you know what ipecac is?"

"Sure. It's the stuff your mother gives you when you've just eaten every last one of a new bottle of St. Joseph's children's medicine because they're flavored with orange and you think they're candy. It makes you throw up."

"Perfect. The times are right, too, you know. Put the ipecac and the strychnine together. The ipecac would work first—"

"Wait, wouldn't it make you throw up and get rid of all the strychnine?"

"Depends on how much was used. If you gave a small enough dose of ipecac and a large enough dose of strychnine, your victim would be just as dead as if he'd had strychnine alone."

"And you could do that because you didn't really want him to throw up," Bennis said, "you just wanted him to get out of the mess hall and do his dying somewhere else."

"Preferably on this deck just about where you're standing," Gregor said.

"You mean preferably where he'd be likely to fall overboard," Bennis said. She walked to the bow's low rail and looked out over the water, shivering. "This is really nasty, isn't it, Gregor? Really sly. Do you think you'll find out who did it?"

"Oh, I already know who did it," Gregor said. "That's

hardly the problem here. Don't you think it's about time we went back inside?"

"Below," Bennis said reflexively, and then she gave him a hard, long stare. Gregor grabbed her hand and pulled her toward the hatch. She'd given him that stare before. It was the one she used to let him know she thought he was keeping her out of something. He couldn't help it.

Besides, everything he'd told her was true.

He did know who did it.

He just had a few details he had to clear up.

2

Innocent bystanders in a murder case always become sightseers, unless they have actually witnessed a bloody and terrifying death. Gregor had never known a case of poisoning where the people on the edges hadn't been possessed more by curiosity than by horror. Since that was often true of the murderer, too, Gregor expected to have no trouble questioning most of the people he wanted to question. They wouldn't care if he was "official" or not. They had either heard of him before they ever came on this boat—Gregor was perpetually astounded these days by just how many people had heard of him—or they had been filled in by Tony Baird as Bennis had said they had. They'd have a hesitation or two at the very beginning, but in the end they would succumb. They'd think it was just as thrilling as if they'd landed in the middle of a novel by Ellery Queen.

Opening the door to the mess hall, Gregor was struck by how true these observations had become. He'd first made them when he was a very new agent and assigned to kidnapping detail, and they'd been true then, God only knew how many presidents ago. Lately they'd become even truer yet, as if people had moved off a mark someplace, away from action and into a firmly fixed spectator role. Maybe it was all the cop shows on television or the murder mysteries in the bookstores or something Terribly Significant and Part of the National Subconscious like the aftermath of the Vietnam War. That was the kind of explanations "professionals" gave, and that Gregor had no use for. More likely, it was just plain human nature, seen more clearly in the raw than it once had been. Whatever it was, it suited Gregor's purpose very well. Spectators were never mere spectators. They were always reviewers as well. They liked to talk.

Gregor looked in on them all arrayed before him around the table—a table that had been meticulously cleared of dinner things and wiped down, so that now it was empty of everything except Fritzie's line of mason jars filled with pumpkin rind marmalade. Bennis came up behind him, ducked under his arm, and went inside, but they hardly paid attention to her. They were too busy looking Gregor up and down and back and forth as if he were about to sprout antennae. He looked them over as well, counting. Jon Baird was gone, of course. Gregor hadn't expected to see him. Someone else was gone as well.

"My wife went back to our cabin," Mark Anderwahl said suddenly, and guiltily, as if he were reading Gregor's mind. "She was really very ill. Very ill. She was green."

"She was a hell of a lot greener than Charlie was when he went upstairs," Sheila Baird said. "Don't frown at me, Tony. I can say *hell* if I want to. I'm a grown woman."

"I wasn't frowning at you for saying *hell*," Tony Baird said. He was sitting all the way back against the wall, but on the other side of the table from where he had been during dinner. Instead of being wedged immobile into a corner, he had easy access to a passage out. He used it. He stood up, tucked his shirt more firmly into his jeans, and stared at Gregor. "If you're going to elaborate on your ridiculous and dangerous theories of Charlie Shay's death, I'm not going to sit here and listen." He turned to Bennis. "I'll see you later," he told her. "If you get tired of listening to this old windbag, come down to my cabin and I'll give you a drink."

"That old windbag has done a lot more with his life than you've done yet," Sheila Baird said.

Tony ignored her. He brushed by Gregor and hustled out.

"Well," Sheila said, as soon as he was gone. "That's that. Now we can get down to something interesting."

Whether or not the others wanted to "get down to something interesting" in quite that way was moot. They all seemed to be embarrassed by Sheila's directness. Mark Anderwahl stared at his hands. Calvin Baird stared at the ceiling. Fritzie Baird stared into space. Only Sheila Baird looked directly at Gregor, and her eyes were avid.

Gregor found a chair, pulled it out into the middle of the room, and sat down in it. He noted that Bennis had taken Tony's chair at the back and nodded to her.

"Well," he said to the assembled company, feeling a little like a brand-new school teacher on his first job. "I take it you all know what happened. Or what I think happened."

"I know Jon doesn't agree with you," Calvin said pointedly. "And I know you've got no jurisdiction here, either. I don't see why we should talk to you at all."

"You shouldn't, if you don't want to," Gregor said pleasantly.

"But I do want to," Fritzie Baird said. "It will be much better this way, Calvin, it really will. Mr. Demarkian will find out what happened and then when we get to land he'll tell the police and then that will be that. We won't have to be bothered."

"But we will be bothered," Calvin said. "The police won't take this man's word for anything. They'll just investigate all over again and they'll investigate him in the bargain."

"I don't see why they should," Sheila Baird said. "He's got a reputation, after all. It's not like he's some stranger in off the street."

"He might as well be," Calvin Baird said stiffly. "I don't know anything about him. I never even met him before today."

Gregor considered saying something very similar to Calvin Baird—that he had no reason to believe Calvin hadn't murdered Charlie Shay, since he'd never met Calvin before today—but that sort of tweaking was almost always counterproductive, and in this case would have to wait. Gregor coughed into his hand instead and tried to get their attention.

"If you don't mind," he said, "there are really a few things I would like to know, and someone in this room will probably be able to tell me. They really are little things. Would you mind?"

"Yes," Calvin said.

"Oh, go ahead," Sheila told him. "If you keep asking permission, you're just going to have this old goat fussing at you without end."

"Fine," Gregor said. "Do any of you people know where Charlie Shay was right before dinner? And I do mean right before."

"I know where he was a little time before dinner," Sheila said. "Maybe ten minutes or so before. He was in our cabin, Jon's and mine. With Calvin here. The three of them were talking."

"That was a private meeting," Calvin said coldly.

"It was the usual business crap," Sheila said. "They'd been in earlier for hours, and then they went off and then they came back and then they went off again and then there was dinner."

"All right," Gregor said. "Now, I saw Calvin Baird in the passage on this deck about five minutes before dinner. I take it you were coming from this meeting Mrs. Baird is talking about?"

"You've got to say Mrs. Sheila Baird," Fritzie said suddenly. "Otherwise, I don't know who you're talking about."

"He was coming from that meeting," Sheila Baird said, giving Fritzie a murderous look. "He left after Charlie did. Jon and Calvin always have a lot to talk about together."

"Fine. Now. What happened then. In those ten minutes just before dinner. Did any of you speak to Charlie Shay?"

"Julie and I saw him in the passage on our way to dinner," Mark Anderwahl said. "He was right ahead of us when he started, but then he stopped to talk to somebody—"

"To Tony," Bennis said. "I was there. He wanted to know what there was for dinner."

"A dinner we haven't gotten to eat yet," Sheila said.

Gregor turned to Bennis. "Did you or Tony give him anything to eat or drink? Anything at all? A can of soda? Even a glass of water?"

"No." Bennis was emphatic.

"What about the rest of you?" Gregor asked. "Did you see him take anything to eat or drink?"

They all stared solemnly back at him, negative.

"Fine," Gregor said again, even though he knew they wouldn't believe he meant it. "Let's get on to dinner, now. I was sitting on the outside bench on this end between Jon Baird and Mr. Mark Anderwahl. Charlie was sitting directly across the table on the end, opposite Jon Baird. Who was sitting at Charlie's side?"

"Julie was," Mark Anderwahl said. "She didn't sit down next to him, though. She sat down first. She wanted to be close against the wall like that because she thought it might help her not to feel so motion sick. You know, steadier."

"So she sat down and then Charlie Shay sat down next to her."

"Right," Mark said.

"She didn't ask him to sit down next to her."

"Of course not." Mark flushed. "What do you think you're doing? Julie wouldn't kill anyone. She certainly wouldn't kill Charlie Shay."

"I didn't say she would. I'm just trying to put this in order here." Gregor rubbed his hands over his face and thought. "Everybody sat down," he said slowly, "and Charlie sat down on the end on that side next to Julie Anderwahl and across from Jon Baird. Then the salad came in, and Jon served out from the bowl, except that if I remember right, he forgot Charlie until the last minute."

"That's right," Fritzie said. "It was very rude of him. I remember. He served everybody else and then he just sat down and started eating, and there was poor Charlie with an empty plate."

"But he got up again and served Charlie himself," Gregor said.

"Yes, he did," Mark Anderwahl said. "I saw him."

Gregor moved on. "Then there was the salad dressing. The first I remember about the salad dressing was Mark Anderwahl handing it to me. Where was it? Who had it first?"

"We did," Bennis said. "Tony and me. It was sitting down at our end of the table."

"And you used it and passed it on?" Gregor asked.

"That's right," Bennis said. "First I used it, then Tony used it, then he passed it up to Mrs.—Sheila Baird."

"I passed it across the table to Calvin," Sheila said. "Julie doesn't eat salad dressing."

"Calvin passed it to me," Mark said, "and I passed it to you, Mr. Demarkian."

"I used it and put it in the middle of the table. Did any of you see what happened to it then? Did any of you notice if it was picked up again? Did Charlie Shay use it?"

"I saw Charlie's plate with the salad dressing on it," Mark Anderwahl said. "We talked about it at the time. I didn't see Charlie pick up the cruet."

"He could have picked it up himself," Bennis said.

"I don't see where all this talk about salad dressing is supposed to get us," Calvin Baird erupted. He had turned a mottled red. "After all, Charlie couldn't have been poisoned by something in the salad dressing. If there was something in the salad dressing, we all would have been poisoned too. If there was something in the salad, we all would have been poisoned too. Charlie couldn't have been poisoned without poisoning the rest of us, so Jon and Tony are right. Charlie wasn't poisoned at all."

"Oh, God," Sheila Baird said. "How do I stand hanging around these people who've never seen a single episode of *Matlock* on TV?"

"I," Calvin Baird said, "don't have to watch *Matlock* on TV. I have a mind and I'm willing to use it. I'm certainly not going to allow it to go to rot around here any longer. Good night to you all."

With that, Calvin Baird stood up, knocked his chair to the floor, and tried to stride toward Gregor and the door. He tripped twice and got his belt loop caught on the back of a chair in the process. Still, his progress had a certain air of magnificence about it, and that air was intensified when Calvin finally got through the door and slammed it shut behind him. The slam made a sharp cracking noise that sounded like splintering wood.

This, Gregor thought, was going to be even more difficult than he had feared.

Three

1

Like many other women in her position, Sheila Baird had very little patience with sex. She knew how to use it, because she had to know how to use it. It was important in the care and feeding of important husbands, although not so important as the way she appeared to other important husbands in public or the prestige of the charity balls she got them invited to. Sheila could moan and groan and shudder and shake with the best of them. She wasn't above buying upscale how-to manuals and proposing forays into the sexually absurd. She had had love made to her while she was hanging by her knees from a gymnast's bar and while she was tied to the wall of a Pullman compartment on a train. It was one of the things she liked best about her marriage that Jon had no interest in that sort of thing and confined his sexual attentions to the ordinary and to bed. No matter how he confined them, however, he did display them. He had made love to her three times a week like clockwork from the day they were married. Then he had gone into jail and not made love to her at all. Now he was out, and Sheila thought she had every right to expect him to do *something*. Sheila was unshakably convinced that all that talk about female orgasm was bunk. Females didn't have orgasms, and that was a good thing for them, too. Males had orgasms, though, and for them that was a kind of addiction. There was always something wrong when the addiction seemed to have been cured. Sheila had been worried about it ever since Jon got out of jail. She had expected him to come back and leap on her. Instead, he had come back, walked into his study, and shut and locked the door. For hours after that, she had heard him tapping away at his computer terminal and talking on the phone. For all the weeks since, he had done practically nothing else. Sheila was beginning to get nervous, and not because she felt sexually deprived.

Husbands who weren't sleeping with trophy wives were on the way to divorcing trophy wives. That was the ticket. Husbands who were on the way to divorcing trophy wives had to be subjected to—shock treatment.

Sheila was a naturally curious woman, about some things, but under ordinary circumstances she would never have stayed in the mess hall to listen to Gregor Demarkian ask questions when Jon had gone back to their cabin. Tonight, she had wanted to think. She had let Jon go and sat with all the others, busy making plans while Mr. Demarkian was busy belaboring the obvious. Sheila had heard all about how Gregor Demarkian was supposed to be a great detective, but now that she'd met him she didn't believe it. Great detectives were either men like Sherlock Holmes— meaning the sort of men who not only knew everything, but made a point of displaying the fact—or fighter types like Starsky and Hutch. They weren't big fuzzy ethnic lumps like Gregor Demarkian, and they didn't ask silly questions about who had the salad dressing first. Sheila had sat through it all with her mind more than half on something else—meaning Jon—and then, when it was over, she'd said good night to everyone and been the first out of the room.

She went down the passage carefully, leaning to the left

to keep her hair out of the candle flames, and let herself into the cabin she shared with Jon. The outer room was empty, but the door to the inner room was open and a wash of light was coming through the door. The light was strong, which meant that Jon was using a great many candles, or that he'd found the flashlight she'd hidden away in the bottom of her make-up case. Sheila thought about going in just as she was, thought better of it, and opened the lid of the boxy looking thing Jon insisted on calling her "locker." The locker was full of lingerie. She took out a pair of green silk panties, a green silk nightgown, and a green robe so sheer it could have been a form of light and put them on.

"Are you coming to bed?" Jon called to her from the next room.

"Mmm," Sheila said. If there had been a little teasing in his tone, she would have been heartened, but there hadn't been. She found a mirror and a comb, combed out her hair, and wished she had the wall of mirrors she had in her dressing room back home. It was impossible to tell what you really looked like as long as you were on this boat.

"What was the gossip rodeo like?" Jon called out again. "Did Demarkian ask a lot of questions about the length of Charlie's big right toenail?"

Sheila went to the door that led to the inner room. Jon was lying in bed, surrounded by candles in holders, bent over a stack of computer papers. Business, business, business.

"He didn't ask about toenails at all," Sheila told him. "He asked a lot about the salad dressing and who had passed it. He asked a lot about the seating arrangements. He wanted to know who was where."

"I hope you told him where I was," Jon said, "right across from Charlie Shay and passing out the food and the salad dressing. Although he ought to have known that already. He was sitting right next to me."

"He mentioned that. I don't know if he got a lot of answers that mattered, anyway. Tony stormed right off practically as soon as Mr. Demarkian got there."

"Just Tony? Not Calvin?"

"Calvin was huffy," Sheila said. "Every time anybody asked a question, he gave a little lecture about how they had no right to ask him any questions. You know what Calvin's like."

"I do know that, yes."

"Is that important business you're working on? All those papers? It seems to me that ever since you got home from jail you've just been surrounded by papers."

Jon was sitting up on the bunk covered with blankets as well as papers, like a child in a sandbox who had started to bury his knees. Sheila had her own bunk on the other side of the cabin, but she didn't want to get into it. She didn't think she could sit still long enough to make a pretense of going to sleep. She went over to Jon's bunk and looked down at the computer printout, but it was like all the computer printouts. There were long columns of numbers. They meant nothing to her. She picked up a loose page, squinted at it, and put it down again. Jon chucked the papers off his knees and looked up at her.

"I'll take all this into the next room if you want to get to sleep," he said. "I've got a little more work to do before I can go to bed."

"That's all right. I'm not sleepy. I'm going to make myself a drink. Do you want one?"

"Yes. A Scotch. A straightforward Scotch. When you start making something for yourself, try to remember we don't have any ice on this boat. It won't keep."

"I know it won't keep." Sheila moved back to the outer room and went for the glasses and bottles they kept in a cupboard near the inner room door. Then she reached into the cupboard above and got down a bottle labeled, "*S. Baird. One before bedtime as needed.*"

"Jon?" she said. "Were you serious downstairs? Do you really think Charlie just had some sort of fit and wasn't murdered at all?"

"Of course I was serious."

"But why couldn't he have been murdered? All that jumping and twitching around. And Demarkian saying it was strychnine."

"So?"

"So Donald McAdam died from strychnine. Isn't that too much of a coincidence?"

"It would be if Charlie died from strychnine. But Charlie didn't die from strychnine. That's just Demarkian running his private nut."

"I've never known Charlie to have a fit before. And I asked Julie. She'd never known him to have a fit either. He wasn't an epileptic."

"What difference does that make?"

"I don't know. It's just like I was telling you. It's strange. And it makes me feel creepy."

"Well, don't feel creepy while you're still holding onto my drink. All this will be cleared up when we get the body to a competent medical authority. They'll do an autopsy and they won't find any strychnine and that will be that. Give me my Scotch."

"Right away."

Sheila put the bottles back in the cupboard, including the small one with her name on it, and closed up. Then she picked up a drink in each hand and walked back into the inner room. Jon was sitting up expectantly, no longer poring over papers, no longer oblivious to anything but numbers on a page. What did it mean, when a man became more eager for practically anything on earth except for sex?

"You ought to get yourself involved in a really good

book," he told her. "Read something exciting. That way you won't be worried too much by all this stupidity Demarkian's putting out."

"Mmmm," Sheila said, and handed over his Scotch. For a moment, the amber of the liquid was caught in the light from a dozen candles. It looked as clean and pure as the water pouring from a spring in an ad for Evian. It made Sheila feel much better, because there wasn't a trace left of the sleeping pills she'd put in there at all.

2

Julie Anderwahl had always thought that morning sickness was just that, a sickness that came in the morning. The only other time she'd had a chance to find out otherwise, she hadn't given herself a chance to find out otherwise. She'd been seventeen years old and scared to death. Because of the way the laws on parental consent were written in her state, she'd had to go over the state line to get a private abortion. Later she would wonder why she had wanted to go over the state line at all. She got along very well with her parents. They were both conservative and traditionalist, but they were not doctrinaire, and they weren't naive, either. What was she hiding from them for? She'd had no answer to that, and she'd had no answer to the other question that had come up almost as soon as the abortion was finished and her life was supposed to go back to normal: What exactly had she done? She had expected the answer to that one to be easy. She had thought it would be like the final disposition of the one that went: Is there life after death? You died. If there was life after death, you knew it. If there wasn't, you knew nothing. Surely, she'd thought, it would be the same way with abortion. You had one. Then, if the antiabortion people were right, you sank down under a crushing weight of guilt. If they weren't, you felt—nothing.

Julie Anderwahl had not felt nothing following her abortion. She had not felt a crushing weight of guilt, but she had not felt nothing. She had not told anyone she was going to have it, and she had not brought anyone with her when she had gone, so she had no one to discuss it with, but after a while she worked it out. Never again. That was it. She had girlfriends who had two and three and, in one case, even four abortions, but that was something she knew she couldn't do. She didn't care if it was a right. She didn't care if her life would go down the tubes and she'd have to give up her career for welfare. She didn't care about anything. Never again.

It was because of Never Again that she was lying here in this bunk, listening to Mark bouncing around their cabin and willing herself not to vomit, feeling depressed beyond all reason at this odd mutation of Thanksgiving. Back home, Thanksgivings were not like this, pretentious and self-conscious on the surface, pinched up and mean underneath. Thanksgivings were a time for everybody's children and eating too much food and forgetting about the fight you'd had with your cousin Andrea last spring. Julie wrapped her arms around her stomach and closed her eyes. The storm had nearly dissipated now, or they had sailed out of it, and the motion of the boat was once more gentle—but in some ways that was worse than the violent rocking and shaking had been. There was something insidious about it, oozing and sly, that got under her skin and into her throat and made her want to race for the upper deck. She restrained herself, because she knew there really wasn't any way to race for the upper deck. It was an obstacle course of beams and ladders and ropes and candles out there. She couldn't stand the thought of battling her way through it.

Mark was pacing back and forth at the side of her bunk, taking off his shirt, taking off his belt. He seemed more excited and happy than he had for months, and interested, too. Julie didn't think she'd ever seen him really interested in anything before. There were things she had thought he was interested in, like work. They'd never elicited a tenth of this response from him. What did that mean?

"It was really amazing to watch him work," Mark was saying. "It was just like an Agatha Christie novel, or Albert Finney in that movie of that Agatha Christie novel, you know, *Murder on the Orient Express.*"

"Don't say that," Julie said. "That's the one where everybody did it together, and they had a perfect plan and got found out anyway."

"If Charlie Shay really was murdered, I'm sure Demarkian will find whoever did it. I wasn't just throwing Agatha Christie around because it's a name even a moron would recognize, you know. I've read about Demarkian in the papers. They call him the Armenian-American Hercule Poirot."

"Yes," Julie said. "Yes, I know that."

"I thought he was going to haul out a piece of paper and start making a timetable right there. Tony had the salad dressing at four oh five and two seconds. Fritzie had the salad dressing at four oh five and seven seconds. It was wonderful."

"It was after six o'clock."

"You know what I mean. It was just a stunning performance. God, I wish I could do something like that with my life. It's so much more interesting than—business."

Business. Julie had been lying flat on her back, keeping her eyes open, trying not to feel the boat move. Now she eased herself up into a sitting position and arranged her pillows as props behind her back. She had to move slowly. Every sudden movement made her feel as if she were being stabbed. Mark had stripped down to his shorts and was standing in the middle of the cabin, lost in a daydream and looking sort of soft-boiled. Julie didn't think she'd ever noticed how unattractive his skin was.

"Mark?"

Mark came to with a start, looked around guiltily, and grabbed for his pajama top. It was navy blue and covered with little tiny dollar signs embroidered in gold thread.

"I'm sorry," he said. "I really am sorry. I seem to be— out of it tonight."

"I can see that. Did he say anything in particular? About anything besides salad dressing, I mean."

"He talked about the salad," Mark told her. "And, of course, who was sitting next to who and who was sitting next to Charlie and all that kind of thing. It's like I told you. It could have been right out of a—"

"Out of an Agatha Christie novel," Julie finished for him, a little impatiently. "That's not what I mean. I mean did he say anything about the other thing."

"Oh," Mark said.

"Well," Julie said, "you have to admit it's strange. Sick as I am, I can tell it's strange. Donald McAdam died from strychnine. And now Charlie Shay dies from strychnine—"

"Jon doesn't think it was strychnine at all," Mark put in. "He and Tony and Calvin, too. They've been going around staying Charlie took sick and had some kind of convulsions and all this talk about strychnine is just Demarkian promoting himself."

"What do you think?"

"I think Charlie Shay died from strychnine."

Julie nodded. It made her head hurt to do it, but she nodded. "That would have been too much of a coincidence, really. The two of them convulsing all over the place and with one of them it's strychnine and with the other it's not. That doesn't make any sense at all. Do you remember what we said when McAdam died?"

"We said we couldn't be sure."

"Oh, Mark, for God's sake, don't chicken out on me now. We said McAdam had enemies and it was likely. Do you remember that?"

"Yes."

"Good. I know we also said we couldn't be sure and it didn't make any sense to do anything with what we knew because McAdam was McAdam and who could tell, but now it's Charlie Shay we're talking about. I can't imagine anyone wanting to kill Charlie Shay. Can you?"

Mark looked confused. "That's what Jon and Tony and Calvin are saying. Charlie couldn't have been murdered because nobody would have wanted to murder Charlie."

Julie eased herself up a little farther on the pillows, shook her head out carefully—she felt full of fuzz, as if she'd been lined with felt—and rearranged her blankets. It was so hard to think, but she had to think, because she was the one who did the thinking in this marriage. Mark couldn't think his way through the moves in a game of Chinese checkers.

"Look," she said. "You're impressed with this man Demarkian, aren't you?"

"Yes, Julie. Of course I am."

"All right then. It's not like it was back in New York, back in August, when we weren't impressed with anybody and it was just McAdam who was dead and it wouldn't have mattered what we said to anybody or what we started because it was just going to come to nothing. Things have changed, don't you agree?"

"I don't know," Mark said truthfully. "Things have changed, but have they changed that much? Aren't you going a little overboard on this?"

"No."

"Julie—"

"No," Julie said again. "I'm not willing to spend the rest of my life looking across the dinner table at family parties and wondering if the person I'm talking to is a double

murderer. We have to tell somebody. I say we tell Demarkian."

"Now?"

"In the morning."

"You might change your mind in the morning."

"If I do, I'll tell you about it. I won't."

"I don't know. You've been acting really strangely on
this trip, Julie, you really have."

Had she been? Julie supposed she had, and it wasn't just
because that old woman on the street yesterday had told her
what she already knew, or at least suspected. She was
beginning to wonder if pregnancy caused some kind of
fundamental biochemical change in the brain. It probably
did.

Mark had his pajama bottoms on now, more navy background, more gold dollar signs. Julie eased herself back
down on her mattress, turning her attention again to the
ceiling above her head, turning her attention away from
Mark. The motion of the boat was a little more pronounced
now but not so effective. The steady pressure of sickness
she'd been feeling since the start of dinner had begun to
recede.

"Mark?" she said. "Promise me something. When it's
time for us to talk to Demarkian tomorrow, don't chicken
out."

"I won't chicken out," Mark said. "I never chicken out."

Julie closed her eyes. Mark chickened out. Mark chickened out all the time. He called it "prudence," but chick-
ening out was what it was and what it always would be.

Lying here in the middle of the Atlantic Ocean on a boat
without a motor or a radio, with a murderer on board and a
baby on the way in the bargain, didn't seem the right time to
tell him so.

3

There was a great iron bell hooked into a bell lever on the main deck near the wheelhouse, and every hour someone from the crew was supposed to go up and ring it. The crew was a very good crew, but this was too much for them. They got distracted by serious work and forgot about the bell for hours at a time. Tonight, they forget at ten and eleven and remembered again at midnight. Tony Baird heard the gonging as he was coming out of the kitchen below. He'd gone to the kitchen for the obvious reason. He was starving. He'd eaten less than half a salad, run around like a maniac chasing a convulsing Charlie Shay all over the main deck, and then forgotten all about his dinner. Everybody had forgotten about dinner. When he finally made his way to the kitchen to see what there was to eat, he found an entire crown roast of pork with the little paper crowns still stuck onto its bones hiding under the lid of a silver serving tray. He was willing to bet they hadn't had silver serving trays on the *Mayflower*, but he wasn't willing to bet with his father. His father was a dyed-in-the-wool eccentric. Tony had accepted that long ago.

He got himself a huge, heaping plate of pork and a half loaf of hard brown bread that came from Zabar's and that he had always liked very much. He said a prayer of thanksgiving that his father's peripatetic passion for authenticity didn't extend to salt pork and hard cod. Then he climbed back up the stairs and down the passage to his own cabin with the plate in his hand, moving as easily in the darkness as he did in the light. The crew might forget about the bell for hours at a time, but they didn't forget about the candles. The candles were authentic. They were also dangerous. One forgetful hour and the whole ship could burn itself straight into the sea. The crew came down every half hour or so and checked them out, and at eleven when everybody was supposed to be asleep they put the candles out.

Tony went to his cabin door, balanced the plate in one hand, and unlocked to let himself in. Here, as back in New York, he was always careful to lock up behind him. He didn't like the idea of someone being able to get in and look at his things. Especially not now. Especially not with that man Demarkian on board. Tony propped open the door with his foot and felt along the wall just inside for the empty space of table. He found it and put his plate down there. Then he got his matches out of his pocket and lit the candle in the holder next to the door.

Farther along the passage, another door opened and a head stuck out into the hall.

"Tony?" Sheila said. "Is that you?"

"It's me."

"I came down looking for you before, but you were out."

There was a doorstop made out of a polished rock on the table where he had put his food. Tony dropped it to the floor and kicked it across to hold the door open, letting the dim light of the single candle glow into the passage. Sheila came out into the passage with no light of her own and closed the door to her cabin behind her.

"For a while there I thought you were with that Hannaford woman," she said. "You've been with her all day."

"She's an interesting woman. She's led an interesting life."

"I stopped worrying when I remembered she had a cabin together with Mr. Demarkian."

Sheila came up to Tony's door, looked at the plate of food on the table and made a face.

"I couldn't face food if you paid me," she said. "Not after all that terrible stuff about Charlie Shay. I think you're very callous to be able to eat."

"I think you're a dyed-in-the-wool bitch to be pulling this now. I am hungry, you know, Sheila."

"Mmm."

"What about my father?"

"Your father took a sleeping pill."

"Dad never takes sleeping pills."

"He does when I want him to."

"Are you trying to tell me you drugged him?"

Sheila walked around the table, poking at the food as she went. Tony watched her move with fascination. He'd always thought of Sheila as something not exactly human, almost as something feline. The more he saw of her the more convinced he was that that description was true.

Tony bent over, picked up the doorstop, and stood while the door swung shut on its own. It had an old-fashioned hasp and wouldn't close by itself. He leaned over and closed it and then threw the bolt.

"Good," Sheila told him. "No sensible person would want to eat anything right now."

Actually, Tony wanted to eat everything right now, what he had on the plate and what he had left back in the kitchen. He was ravenous and obsessed. He was also very conscious of the rules of the game here. He knew what he had to do as long as he wanted to go on having an affair with his father's wife.

Sheila came around to the front of him and wrapped her arms around his neck. He put his hand on her back and pulled her toward him. He still felt more hunger than he did anything else, but he knew the moves of this dance as well as he knew how to chew.

He could have done it in his sleep.

Four

1

Gregor Demarkian had brought along the FBI report on the death of Donald McAdam because the very young man from the Bureau had asked him to read it. He had even intended to read it, in spite of the fact that he thought the exercise was silly. It didn't matter if the death of Donald McAdam was murder or suicide or accident or the will of an angry God. Nobody was going to prove it one way or the other now. If it was murder, nobody was going to jail the murderer. Gregor had never been the sort of investigator who gave up on his cases forty-eight hours after they had started. He'd known agents and cops like that and never had much use for them. Still, there was a point at which you had to accept the inevitable. To bring a case to court you needed either one or two pieces of hard physical evidence, or the very best kind of story. Gregor had seen story-cases brought and won. The Woodchipper Murderer had been jailed on a story. So had Frances Schreuder, who had manipulated her teenage sons into killing her father. To make it stick, you had to have a veritable epic, a large-scale morality tale with background music. There was nothing like that in Donald McAdam's fall. Gregor had listened to the very young man from the Bureau and then thought the problem through himself. The lack of strychnine in the apartment was suggestive—it might even be definitive—but it couldn't quite dispel the dispirited limpness of it all. Donald McAdam had been a fool. Donald McAdam had behaved foolishly. Donald McAdam was dead. A marginally intelligent public defender just two days out of the South Podunk Community College Law School could establish reasonable doubt with the likes of that.

Once Charlie Shay was dead—once Gregor had seen him die, and gone through the motions necessary to secure the body and bring some kind of order to the resulting situation—Gregor had thought he would go back to the file for other reasons. Gregor had lived too long a life not to believe in coincidence. He knew that if a man intent on cheating on his wife runs into that wife in the lobby of the very hotel where he has established his rendevous, the chances are that the wife has a meeting of her Sunday school teachers' support group in that very place at that very time and isn't following her husband at all. There was, however, a limit. Two men connected to the same enterprise, both poisoned with strychnine, both falling off things—or almost falling off them, in Charlie Shay's case. That had to be too much for anybody. Gregor wanted to get down to the file and see if he could clear up a few of the points that had been bothering him when he'd talked to the very young man from the Bureau. He wanted to read through the whole thing with a felt-tipped highlighter in his hand. He wanted to really concentrate. He did not, however, want to do any of those things now. Now was very late on their first night on board, only hours after Charlie Shay had died. Gregor was tired and cold and wet. His body ached from the battering it had taken making sure Charlie's body didn't disappear into the sea. His head ached from the stuffy closeness of the cabins and the unending need to compensate for the rocking of the boat. His stomach was empty. Dinner had disappeared in the confusion. They had been just about to sit down to it when Charlie had gotten sick and gone up to the main deck. They had never sat down to it again after Charlie's body was stowed below. Excitement had carried Gregor through all of that without allowing him to feel hungry, but excitement had come to an end. He was now hungry enough to eat wood.

He used the forked throne that hung over the sea that was all that was provided for a toilet and then made his way back to the cabin he shared with Bennis. He came in to find her sitting in the one chair, dressed for bed, her legs folded under her Turkish-fashion. Gregor had never seen Bennis dressed for bed before, although he'd been with her on one or two occasions when he should have. For some reason, at those times she'd gone to sleep in her jeans or drifted away from him to rest in private. Gregor didn't know what he'd expected of her in the way of nightwear. He didn't know if he'd ever thought about what to expect of her in the way of nightwear. He was still a little surprised by what he found. Bennis was dressed in what looked like a pair of men's pajamas, except that they were made of silk and vertically striped in white and candy cane pink. Over them she had a wrap robe that was also vertically striped in white and candy cane pink. Gregor didn't know why, but he got the idea that both these articles were very expensive. Bennis looked about fourteen in them, even with the grey in her hair.

Bennis looked up when Gregor came through the door. Gregor shut the door and latched it and went over to sit on the side of the bunk. It was not a comfortable position. The bunk's side was really just a polished slat of wood, less than an inch thick. Sitting on it was like sitting on the pickets of a fence.

"So," he said, "what have you got there? I take it it's mine."

"It's the FBI report on Donald McAdam," Bennis said. "You can't chew me out about this, Gregor. You showed it to me yourself."

"I'm not chewing you out. I was just thinking about it myself. Thinking I ought to read it, I mean. But not now. I'm tired."

"I'll bet you're hungry." Bennis waved her hand toward the narrow, stern-side end of the cabin, where an odd arrangement of slats served as a luggage holder, holding their suitcases against the motion of the sea. "Look in the zipper compartment under the top flap of my bag. You know, open it up and look right under what you're holding. Donna packed us some food."

"Donna?"

"On orders from Lida and Hannah Krekorian. They were busy doing something or other with the Society for the Support of an Independent Armenia."

Gregor got up and went to the suitcase, opened it up, and found the "zipper compartment" just where Bennis said it would be. He unzipped it and looked inside. With that blissful disregard for practicality that characterized every resident of Cavanaugh Street on the subject of food, Donna had packed not only honey cakes and breads, which made sense, but stuffed grape leaves and eggplant salad, which needed refrigeration to stay fresh. Gregor took these out and added a whole small loaf of what looked like Lida's best four grain and went back to the side of the bunk. It still hurt to sit down, but he accepted it better because it was in such a good cause. It was the only place he could go to eat.

Over in the chair, Bennis was sucking on her fingers, a sure sign that she had just finished a honey cake. He waited until she looked up and said, "Has all that reading gotten you anywhere? Have you come to any conclusions about the death of Donald McAdam?"

"I hope I've come to the same conclusions you have," Bennis said. "You have to think it's murder, now."

"I always did think it was murder," Gregor said. "That wasn't my point. My point was that it was a murder that was never going to be proved, and for which no one was ever going to go to jail."

"Fine. Let me ask you this. Do you think Charlie Shay and Donald McAdam were killed by the same person?"

"I think it would be a very strange world if they were not." Gregor scooped up eggplant salad with a chunk of bread and ate it. "Let's look at it this way," he said. "There are a great many people on this boat who would dearly have liked to see Donald McAdam dead. Donald McAdam is dead, and so is another man, who has died in a way very similar to the one in which we suppose McAdam died. It would be a one in a billion chance if these two things were not connected; therefore we must assume they were connected."

"All right."

"All right," Gregor repeated. "What does that tell you?"

Bennis looked puzzled. "It doesn't tell me anything," she said, "except that there's a murderer on this boat, and I already know that. It doesn't tell me who the murderer is. Oh. It means whoever it is has to be the same person who murdered McAdam, so that lets out Jon Baird."

"Excuse me?"

"Jon Baird was in jail at the time, so he couldn't have murdered Donald McAdam. Of if he had, McAdam would have died before he did because strychnine works fast. Actually, if you believe this report, it lets out everybody. I've been paying careful attention to where everybody said they were ten minutes or so before McAdam died, and they were all halfway across town."

Gregor looked down at his lap and saw that he was out of

food. He got up, went back to the suitcase, and got some more.

"Let's change the subject for a minute." He gave up on taking pieces of food and simply acquired the entire brown paper bag. There were some things in there he hadn't seen before, including a little pile of meatballs in crust. What had Donna been thinking of? He sat down on the slat again and put the bag on the bunk's mattress. Then he began to unpack it. "Did you talk to Calvin Baird today?" he asked Bennis.

Bennis made a face. "Of course I did. Everybody's talked to Calvin Baird today. He's been wandering up and down the boat, behaving like the ancient mariner of certified accounting."

"He was talking to you about a discrepancy in some numbers?"

"He certainly was."

"Did you understand what it was about?"

"Of course I did."

"Explain it to me."

Bennis looked nonplussed, the way she always did when Gregor asked for financial information. After all, didn't Gregor have a degree in accounting—a master's degree, from the Harvard Business School? Gregor never seemed to be able to explain to her that he had taken that degree a long time ago, and only because in those days a man had to have a degree in accounting or law to get taken on at the Bureau. Once he had been taken on at the Bureau, he had volunteered for kidnapping detail and forgotten all about numbers. Bennis rearranged herself on her chair and said, "The discrepancy is in the list of figures that are supposed to be reporting the cash Baird Financial had on hand about eight months or a year ago when they made their formal offer for Europabanc. You understand what I mean by a formal offer? Baird and Europabanc had been talking to each other for years, I think. The first article I ever read about Jon Baird, I think it was in *Forbes*, went on at length about how he'd always wanted to found a great international banking house like Rothschild and how he'd had his eye on Europabanc and a possible method of doing that. You can have your eye on anything, though, if you know what I mean. They only made the formal offer this past year, or maybe it was last."

"While Jon Baird was in jail."

"I don't know," Bennis said slowly. "It might have been before that—I'm sorry to be so fuzzy, Gregor, you ought to ask Calvin or Jon Baird about the exact timing—but you know, if it wasn't after Jon Baird had gone to jail, then it was probably after they knew he was going to. If you see what I mean."

"I see what you mean. This cash on hand. How important was it?"

"At the time? Very important. Now? Not important at all." Bennis shrugged. "When they made the offer, they would have had to have come up with proof that they could make the deal. If they hadn't, Europabanc wouldn't have bit, and neither would the governments they had to deal with, one of which I'm pretty sure was Switzerland. The Swiss like guarantees. Then they would have signed a set of preliminary agreements, and after that their cash could have all turned out to be counterfeit and it wouldn't have mattered."

"Why not?"

"Because," Bennis said patiently, "if there was a problem like that, Jon Baird is smart enough to make sure it was covered in the prelims. He'd put himself in a position where all that mattered was that he had the cash when he showed up to close. And he'll certainly have the cash."

Gregor turned this over in his mind. "That would be

because of Donald McAdam's junk bonds," he said. "I seem to remember something about a sale."

Bennis grinned. "I'm glad Mark Anderwahl wasn't around to hear you say it like that. It wasn't just a 'sale,' Gregor. It was hundreds of millions of dollars. Which just goes to show. There are junk bonds and junk bonds."

"What's that supposed to mean?"

"That's supposed to mean that there are some bonds that are junk because the companies behind them are insolvent, and there are some bonds that are junk because the companies behind them are new and unknown. It's like junk stock in the old days. My father bought some of that once, in a small company nobody had ever heard of. American Halographic. Paid sixteen dollars a share, spent a hundred and sixty thousand dollars, his banker tried to have him committed. A couple of years later, the company came out with a new product and changed its name to Xerox."

"Good God."

"You just have to know what you're doing," Bennis said complacently. "Are you going to eat all of that? I could use some bread and butter."

"Here." Gregor passed the bread and butter across. "Can I see the file for a moment? There's something I want to look up."

"You can keep the file as far as I'm concerned." Bennis passed it over and concentrated on buttering her bread. "I'm going to go to sleep as soon as I stuff enough into myself to feel tired. Don't you think we ought to do something about this? About where we sleep, I mean."

"Do what?"

"Well," Bennis said slowly, "I've been thinking about it. You really can't take the other bunk, Gregor, and neither can I. No adult human being would fit. So I thought, you know, that maybe what we ought to do is bundle."

"What do you mean, bundle?"

"It was a form of courting in Colonial New England," Bennis said, "which seems entirely appropriate to me. Not the courting part, Gregor, the part about Colonial New England. Anyway, what you do is, the woman—it would have been a girl then, seventeen or younger probably— anyway, she gets in bed and gets wrapped up in the sheets like a mummy so she can't move, and then the man does the same thing, and then they sleep together. No hanky panky. Lots of conversation. It was supposed to be a great way for two people to get to know each other."

"Get to know each other," Gregor repeated stupefied. "Bennis, are you out of your mind?"

"According to you, yes."

"Bennis, listen to me. Do you realize what would happen, if we do what you're suggesting and it got out on Cavanaugh Street?"

"How would it get out on Cavanaugh Street?"

"You'd tell Donna Moradanyan. Donna Moradanyan would tell her mother. Marie would tell Lida Arkmanian— how do you think it would get out on Cavanaugh Street?"

"Now, Gregor—"

"And you think you've got problems now with them trying to match make us together," Gregor said. "I'd come home from the library one day and find the church decked out with flowers and old George all ready to give you away. They'd probably have you chained to the church door so you couldn't bolt. What's the matter with you?"

"Gregor—"

"Never mind," Gregor said.

He hopped down off the slat, clutching the bag of food to his chest in one arm and the FBI file on Donald McAdam to his side with the other. Then he headed for the cabin door with the sort of determination he usually brought only to making complaints to the heads of government departments.

"Don't worry about me," he said. "I know where I can sleep."

"You can't sleep on the floor," Bennis warned him. "You'll roll."

"I won't sleep on the floor."

Gregor wedged the cabin door open, stuck his head out into the dark hall, and decided that the coast was clear. For the moment, at any rate, the passengers on the *Pilgrimage Green* seemed to be minding their own business.

"I'll see you in the morning," Gregor told Bennis.

And then he left.

2

Where he went was on deck below, where the crew slept in two bunk rooms that were less like cabins than old-fashioned dormitories and Charlie Shay rattled grandly around in a room of his own. He opened that room up, went inside, and locked up again behind himself. Charlie's corpse was invisible between the slats of its bunk. The other bunk was empty. Gregor stared at it for a moment, trying to decide if he was really capable of doing what he'd come here to do. God only knew it was gruesome, sleeping in the same small room with a corpse and with the door locked besides, but it had its advantages. Gregor had noticed the bunks in this cabin when they'd first brought Charlie in. They were much larger than the ones on the deck above, maybe because on the original ship they'd been meant to sleep more than one. For whatever reason, Gregor was more likely to fit in the empty one here than he was in either of the ones in the cabin he was supposed to share with Bennis, whether Bennis was also in residence or not. Being in here, Gregor would also be able to keep his eye on the corpse. He wasn't feeling very easy about the corpse. If everything he suspected was true, Charlie Shay's murderer would have to get rid of Charlie Shay's body sooner or later—and preferably sooner, because they could only wander around the coastal waters of the northeastern United States so long. Eventually, they would have to either make landfall or head out to sea, and heading out to sea might very well kill them all. Gregor didn't think the murderer was much interested in a venture that might kill them all. This was a murderer who took risks, but only calculated risks.

Gregor got a couple of candles lit and went over to look at Charlie Shay's body. It was completely covered with blankets and barely recognizable beneath them. Gregor lifted them up to make sure. He needn't have worried. Charlie Shay lay there calmly, looking better than he ever had in life. Gregor covered him up again and retreated to the chair near the door. He put his bag of food on the floor and wished he hadn't brought it. He wasn't going to eat it here at the side of a dead man. He picked up the FBI file and rifled through its pages. Less than an hour ago, he was so tired he could have fallen asleep in his tracks. Now he didn't think he'd ever fall asleep again. Either just talking about the murder, or being presented with its victim, had charged all his batteries again.

Gregor opened the FBI file and thumbed through it. Since it was a file presented to a confidential source—which is what he'd be considered for the purposes of satisfying the Bureau bureaucracy—it wasn't inked over the way files released under the Freedom of Information Act were. It was simply straightforward Bureauese, which made it difficult to understand and often unintentionally funny, but at least something he was used to. He stopped for a moment at some agent's thumbnail description of Charlie Shay— "considered to be more of a gopher than a fully trusted partner of Baird Financial, Shay's principal function over the past year seems to have been to run errands for

Jonathan Baird while Baird was serving time in the Federal Correctional Institution at Danbury"—and then went on to what had bothered him back on Cavanaugh Street. Actually, it had bothered him even when it had only been the very young agent telling him about it. Gregor found it impossible to understand why it hadn't bothered the very young agent's superior officer, Gregor's old friend Steve Hartigan. There was only one way it made any sense, but nobody seemed to have noticed. It was at times like these that Gregor wished he could see the real police reports. He thought an everyday working cop would be much better at this sort of thing than most Bureau agents were.

He found the first of the two pages in question and reread it.

". . . *some five minutes after going upstairs,*" it read, "*the subject was reported by doorman J. Gonzalez to have returned to the lobby to mail a letter. He passed through the lobby proper and greeted J. Gonzalez. Then he turned down a hall that leads to the mail room. In the mail room at that time was a resident of the building, one Mrs. Gail Creasey. Mrs. Creasey was not acquainted with the subject but knew him on sight. According to her statement, the subject entered the mail room and went directly to the slot into which all mail was to be posted in the building. He deposited a letter there, which Mrs. Creasey described as being a thickly packed legal-size envelope. He then turned, bumped into Mrs. Creasey as she was trying to make her way to the door from her own mailbox, and said good evening. It was at that point, according to Mrs. Creasey, that Mrs. Creasey noticed a very strange thing. The subject was a familiar sight to other residents of the building. He was usually very nattily*

*dressed and very careful with his clothes. On this
occasion, however, his tie was pulled a little off-
center and one of the snaps on his suspenders, the
one on the right in the front, had become undone.
According to Mrs. Creasey, the subject kept pulling
at the suspender snap in an absentedminded and
irritated way, but without bothering to refasten it.
Mrs. Creasey found this behavior so out of character
that she asked the subject if he was feeling well, in
spite of the fact that, according to her statement, she
had never spoken to him before. He told her he was
feeling 'better than he had in years' and passed on.
Mrs. Creasey was left with the distinct feeling that
the subject was behaving oddly and was possibly on
the verge of some sort of psychological trouble.'*

Some sort of psychological trouble. Gregor sighed. He
had met witnesses like Gail Creasey. They drove him to
distraction. They could make a Freudian epic out of a man's
preference for coffee over tea. He had met report writers
like the one who had put this together, too. He thought they
all ought to be sent back to school. He flipped to the back of
the report and found the lists. At least, with the lists, he
didn't have to suffer through anyone's awful prose.

As in any FBI report, there were lists of many things,
some of them so arbitrary you had to wonder why the list
maker had bothered. Gregor always imagined them being
put together by a little man with an eyeshade who lived in a
vault deep in Bureau headquarters, and who wrote lists for
secular sources, like *The Book of Lists*, in his spare time.
The list that Gregor wanted now, though, could have been
put together by any decent detective, federal, state, or local.
It was the list of things that had been found on Donald
McAdam's foyer table after Donald McAdam had died.

"Crystal paperweight in the shape of a swan, Steuben glass," the list began and then:

> *copy of book,* Collecting Antique Brass, *by*
>   *Devonbarr. Paperback*
> *sterling silver cocaine spoon, unused*
> *roll of stamps, 29 cent*
> *sterling silver letter opener*
> *manila envelope, used, addressed to Donald*
>   *McAdam, letterhead Baird Financial Services*
> *copy of contract, agreement Donald McAdam and*
>   *Baird Financial Services, dated day of death,*
>   *signed Donald McAdam and Jonathan Edgewick*
>   *Baird*
> *three brass suspender clips*
> *mason jar, preserves marked "Melon Rind*
>   *Marmalade"*
> *one silk rep tie*
> *one gold tie tack, shape of musical note*
> *three number 2 pencils*
> *one gold Mark Cross pen*
> *one paging device, made by Sony*

Gregor shook his head. A "paging device" would be a beeper, but other than that the list was simple enough. Taken together with the testimony of the doorman and Mrs. Creasey, it could mean only one thing. Gregor thought that had to be significant. In fact, it had to be more than significant. It struck out at him like a snake. He just couldn't figure out what it meant.

He tossed the FBI file into the bag with the food Donna Moradanyan had sent and stood up. He could hear people moving above his head, shuffling steps that reminded him of the dead walking in a terrible movie Donna and Bennis had made him take them to because they wanted to see it and it was playing in an uncertain part of town. He wondered what it really was, members of the crew or passengers. He had a sudden vision of the passengers getting up to go into each others' cabins in the dead of night, engaging in hanky-panky of every possible description—and then the hanky-panky he was imagining was between Bennis Hannaford and Tony Baird, and he knew he had to give it up.

What he did instead was to blow out the candles, climb into the empty bunk, say good night to Charlie Shay in a loud voice, and fall asleep.

When the door was opened two hours later and a head stuck through, listened to his snoring, and withdrew again, Gregor Demarkian knew nothing about it.

Five

1

For Gregor, the worst thing about being a passenger on a boat like the *Pilgrimage Green* was the utter unending sameness of it all. If he had been crewing on a smaller boat—God forbid—he would at least have had work to do. If he had been a passenger on a large modern liner, he would have been forced into voluntary paralysis by some social director with a whistle around her neck. On this boat, he had nothing to distract him but the weather, and that had calmed significantly while he slept. Gregor Demarkian didn't count murder as a distraction. That was something he had to think about. He wanted something to *do*.

He came awake in the spare bunk in Charlie Shay's cabin tomb with no idea what time it was, or even if it was morning. There were no portholes in the cabins down here, because these cabins were at the waterline or below it. Gregor unwound himself and climbed out onto the center of the room. It had taken a great deal of winding to fit himself into that small high-sided bunk, so much that the very idea of trying to wind himself into one of the smaller ones on the deck above appalled him. His back ached and his muscles were throbbing. His head felt like a helium

balloon. He looked into Charlie Shay's bunk, found the
body lying there undisturbed, and felt around in his clothes
for the cabin key. It was a heavy iron old-fashioned thing
and hard to lose. He put his hand right on it, because it was
sitting in his hip pocket and making a dent in the top of his
thigh. His only problem was to get it untangled from the
cotton there. He got the FBI file on the death of Donald
McAdam and tucked it under his belt. Then he let himself
out, locked the door behind him, and headed for the decks
above.

The deck immediately above seemed to be deserted.
Gregor went to the cabin he was supposed to be sharing
with Bennis and looked in, but she wasn't in the one useful
bunk and she wasn't sitting in the chair and her pajamas had
been neatly folded and left on top of her pillow. Gregor
looked through the porthole and saw grey air and what
looked like a calm sea. The boat didn't seem to be rocking
much. He poured water into the basin, washed himself off,
and found some clean clothes. He also found a mason jar
just like the ones that had been on the mess hall table last
night, marked "Pumpkin Rind Marmalade" in that same
Farmington script. The label was a little different from
the ones that had been on the jars last night. It had a line
drawing of a grinning turkey on it and and little orange-
colored collection of generic vegetables that could have
been meant to be decorative gourds and could have been
meant to be corn. Gregor decided it didn't put him any
more into the Thanksgiving spirit than anything else on this
godforsaken boat and put it aside. He picked up a red cotton
sweater with a teddy bear on it that Bennis had given him
for his "birthday," meaning a day she and Donna had
decided to call his birthday and give him a party on. In
Gregor's opinion, if letting Bennis know when his birthday
was was going to result in ridiculously expensive sweaters

with pictures of stuffed animals on them, he would just as soon be assumed to be coexistent with eternity.

Gregor stowed the FBI report in his suitcase and got the pair of deck shoes Bennis had also bought for him, but that he had refused to wear yesterday because he thought they were silly. They were the kind of thing people wore yachting in Southhampton, assuming that the people who went yachting would have called it yachting, which they wouldn't have. The linguistic convolutions of rich people made him dizzy. He tied the deck shoes tightly onto his feet and headed up again. If there was no one on this deck they had to be above. Just to be sure he stopped at the dining hall and looked in, but it was empty.

Actually, the main deck was empty, too, which was a surprise. Gregor supposed there was more of the boat beneath where he had been with Charlie Shay's body—wouldn't it have been called the hold?—but he couldn't imagine his fellow passengers trooping down there en masse for any reason whatsoever. They didn't like to troop en masse into dinner. He looked at the broad flat expanse of the stern and then into the wheelhouse. The stern was deserted and the wheelhouse was full of small dark men talking whatever language the man had talked to Gregor the night before. Gregor smiled and waved and went forward without trying to get a conversation started. The bow was deserted too, but for some reason Gregor found it more restful than he had the rest of the boat, and decided to stay there for a while. It was odd to think that this had been the scene of Charlie Shay's death only hours before. It was odd to think that this had been the scene of anything violent. The wind, the rain, the body slashing back and forth against the deck—everything was perfectly calm now, the sails flat, the sea like glass. Gregor kept away from the low bow rail and went into the point of the bow itself, which was high. He looked out over the water and wondered how close they were to land. From what he could see, they could have been drifting off the edge of the world.

He had just about decided that this was an exercise in futility—and spooky, too; he was reminded of those boats found drifting and uninhabited in the Sargasso Sea—when he heard the clatter of someone coming up from the deck below, and the low polite murmur of a woman's voice thanking someone for helping her up. Gregor turned and looked expectantly at what was still the single narrow passage in and out of the bow. He had noticed that passengers who came on deck almost always came forward. He was not disappointed this time. There was a faint squeaking of rubber soles against wet wood, and Julie Anderwahl made her way slowly into the bow.

Gregor Demarkian had, of course, seen Julie Anderwahl before. He had even spoken to her. He had never really paid attention to her. Now, while she was busy staring at her feet and trying to contain her unrelenting nausea, he examined her. She was prettier than he had realized at first, in that take-charge, faintly glamorous, New York career woman way, and she was also younger. She was not, however, as pretty as Bennis. Bennis had a sharply defined face, full of lines and angles, uncompromising. Julie Anderwahl had the sort of face that graces America's Junior Miss year after year and shows up with regularity on prom queens from Lewiston to Tulsa. She was blond. She was blue-eyed. Her features were very regular. It was the steel in her spine and the determination in her gaze that set her apart, not the originality of her body. Bennis had originality of body. Of course, she also had steel and determination. In Gregor Demarkian's opinion, Bennis Hannaford was altogether a woman and a half.

Julie Anderwahl was having difficulty making it across the deck to him. She really was very sick, unbelievably sick considering the state of the sea. Either she was a woman who got seasick in the bathtub, or something else was going on. Gregor had no trouble guessing what.

"Would you like me to help you?" he called out. "You seem to be having some trouble."

"I'm fine." There was an edge of irritation in Julie's voice, and Gregor didn't blame her. "I came up because I was feeling sick downstairs and I thought the fresh air would help, but the fresh air smells like salt and now that's making me sick, and you don't know how glad I'm going to be when we make land."

"I'm going to be glad when we make land, too," Gregor said. "I don't like the idea of us floating around on the Atlantic Ocean with a dead body on board. There should have been some way to call the Coast Guard in an emergency."

"There probably is." Julie had made her way to the front now. There was a low, round line spool lying in the bow and she sat down on that, not seeming to care that it was a little wet. Up close she looked less attractive than she had from afar—but Gregor didn't think she would have, ordinarily. Her face was much too pale and tinged with green. Her hair hung limply against her head, in spite of the fact that it was stringently clean. Her eyes were dull. She leaned against the ridge of wood in the bow and sighed. "They're all down there trying out the *Green*'s idiosyncratic version of a shower. It's not authentic, but Jon had to do something to keep people on the boat for three days running. I gave it up after a short try and just washed myself down in my cabin. How about you?"

"I didn't even know there was a shower. Where is this down there?"

"Down there," Julie said vaguely, waving toward nothing in particular. "You go down past where we put Charlie Shay last night. We were all wondering where you were."

"I was with Charlie Shay."

Julie Anderwahl shuddered. "I wouldn't have liked that. I don't like any of this. I keep thinking of the Puritans, coming all the way over from England on a little boat like this, having babies at sea, eating God only knows what, and then instead of landing in Virginia the way they thought they were going to they end up in Massachusetts and all the land they have to farm is full of rocks. No wonder they held a Thanksgiving. As soon as we get to Candle Island, I'm going to hold a Thanksgiving. I'm going to kiss the ground."

"My mother said she kissed the ground on the day she arrived in America," Gregor said. "Of course, she also said she kicked a man who tried to examine her ears, so I don't know what to believe."

"Was your mother born in Armenia?"

"In Alexandria, in Egypt. It was my grandmother who was born in Armenia, but she left with her family after the Turks came."

"My family came over in 1707," Julie said. "They settled in New York State. Mark's father never came over at all. He was European and very starchy about it, from everything I've heard. I wonder why Americans do that, marry Europeans."

"I suppose for the same reasons they marry anybody else."

"Maybe. But I don't like Europeans, if you want to know the truth. I spend a lot of my time dealing with them. One of our soon-to-be partners from Europabanc took Jon aside once and said that he ought to get a man in to supervise me. I had much too important a position for it to be entrusted to a woman."

"Oh, dear."

"People think it's the Japanese who don't think like us," Julie said. "They ought to meet the Swiss. What about you? Mark says you're sure Charlie Shay was murdered. He says he agrees with you."

"Do you?"

"I didn't see much," Julie said. "I was in the back of the crowd up here when all that was going on. And I was too sick to be in the mess hall last night, of course. I was a little surprised that you didn't come rapping on my door demanding to interrogate me."

"I don't think we're in that kind of a hurry," Gregor said drily. "I did want to ask you a few questions, though."

"Did you?" Julie held herself very still. Gregor got the distinct impression she was trying to make up her mind about something. The decision she came to seemed to be negative. She shook her head sharply and looked away. "So ask me," she said. "I'd be interested to know how your mind was working."

"And you think my questions will tell you that?"

"Well, they should, shouldn't they?"

Gregor agreed they should. In his experience, they rarely did. He said, "Tell me something about Baird Financial. You run their public relations department, is that right?"

"That's right. I'm vice president for, in fact."

"Do you know anything at all about the housekeeping functions in your department? How things are filed? How correspondence is dealt with?"

"Some." Julie bristled. "I'm not a secretary, though, Mr. Demarkian. I never was a secretary."

"I know that. It's policy I'm interested in here. In my experience, firms file their correspondence in one of two ways—with the envelope it came in or without. Do you know which Baird Financial does?"

"Oh." Julie looked confused. "Well, I think it depends. In Public Relations we always throw away the envelopes. There's no point to keeping them. I have heard that Financial keeps them, though. For tax purposes."

"What about whatever department handles general firm business? Like the Europabanc deal."

Julie laughed. "They've kept absolutely everything about the Europabanc deal," she said. "The joke in the typing pool is that after one of our conferences with the Europeans, the secretaries are required to go around and preserve the ashes in the ashtrays. We have an entire separate office suite in the Trade Center that does nothing but hold papers relating to Europabanc. Trust me, we keep envelopes with the correspondence."

"Would you do that in any other case?"

"I told you. Financial does it. I don't see why you're making such a big fuss over this. A lot of firms operate this way. A postmark is very good evidence in the event of a lawsuit where time is an important factor. It's very good evidence when you have a little trouble with the tax people, too. As far as I know, we keep envelopes of any correspondence having to do with money and we keep them for at least five years. After that, I don't know what we do with them."

"Mmm," Gregor said. "That's what I thought. About the envelopes."

"What do envelopes have to do with the death of Charlie Shay?"

"I'm not sure yet." Gregor looked up into the rigging over his head. The sails were still flat. He wondered how long the ocean could remain untouched by wind. He was worried the answer might be "weeks." He turned back to Julie. "You said something before I wish you would clarify. I said there ought to be some way to call the Coast Guard in an emergency, and you said there probably is. Do you mean Jon Baird has flares somewhere and isn't telling us about them?"

"No. I meant everything on this boat is done with fires. I didn't realize Jon had refused to call the Coast Guard."

"He made out that it was impossible."

"I don't see how it could be. We have fires to cook with and candles and matches. I'm sure somebody must have a cigarette lighter. Your friend Bennis smokes. Tony smokes sometimes, too—"

"I don't think Tony would be much help."

"Taking his father's side?" Julie was sympathetic. "Tony is nearly a fanatic on the subject of his father. It's upset the hell out of Fritzie since the divorce. I think after Jon married Sheila, Fritzie just expected Tony to take her side. Instead, he behaved like a man."

"That must have been disturbing."

"It was worse than disturbing, it was insulting." Julie eased herself up from the spool she'd been sitting on, gripping the ridge along the inside of the bow, and took a deep breath. "Let's go downstairs and find Mark," she said. "I wanted you to talk to him anyway. And he knows all about this kind of thing. He used to go to wilderness camps when he was in high school."

"What in the name of God is a wilderness camp?"

"It's a place where you go to rough it in a national forest for a couple of weeks. The most famous one is Outward Bound. They take people out and let them live off rattle-snakes in the desert or roots and berries in the forest with no modern conveniences or ways of getting them. They have guides, of course."

"Of course," Gregor said. "And I thought Jon Baird was an isolated eccentric."

"He's eccentric enough, all right." Julie straightened her back, took a deep breath, and seemed to get better hold of herself. Her face lost a shade or two of its green tint and her smile was genuine and unforced. "Let's go find Mark. He'll know a way to rig up a flare that won't blow us up when we use it. Maybe we can rig up a couple and get the Coast Guard to rescue us."

What Gregor thought he needed the Coast Guard to rescue was the body of Charlie Shay, but he didn't say that. Julie was beginning to look green again. He gripped her firmly by the elbow and guided her carefully into the narrow passage leading out of the bow. She put her hand out and steadied herself against the side of the boat. She almost missed. The low bow rail was like a cutout in the boat's side. At one point there was nothing at shoulder height but air, and at the next there was a thick polished wall. Julie's hand came down on the dividing line between the two and she stumbled.

"Careful," Gregor said.

"I am being careful," Julie said, "I—oh, there's Mark."

"Where's Mark?" Gregor looked up as soon as he spoke, and when he did there was no avoiding Mark. He was standing at the back, beyond the wheelhouse and the stairs to the deck below, on the way to the stern. He had his back to them, but he looked tense.

"Mark?" Julie called tentatively.

Mark didn't hear her. He jerked his arms above his head, brought them down again in fists, and yelled, "Tony Baird you son of a *bitch*."

Then he launched himself into nothingness.

2

Gregor would have moved faster if he hadn't had Julie Anderwahl at his side. His instinct told him to get her away from his side as quickly as possible—and it wasn't sexism, either. He'd seen women agents at the Bureau who had been taught to fight. He'd also seen women like Julie, who had been taught not to fight, get messed up in a fight. He helped her forward anyway, at least far enough so that she had another spool to sit on. Then he left her and went running into the stern.

Coming up behind Mark Anderwahl, Gregor had not been able to see Tony Baird or anything else in the stern. He didn't know what to expect. Everything else that had happened on the *Pilgrimage Green* had happened in a crowd, as far as he could tell. Maybe that was why he was half-convinced he would find a crowd when he got to the stern. He didn't. Tony Baird was there, flat on the deck with Mark Anderwahl on top of him. Both of them were fighting like men who had never been in a fight before. That was what happened when you did away with the peacetime draft. Men didn't learn how to punch each other out. They probably didn't learn how to punch each other out at Groton, or wherever these two had gone, either.

Tony's face was turning blue. Gregor thought Mark Anderwahl was strangling him. From the way Mark was lying on Tony, it was hard to tell. Mark Anderwahl was kicking his feet into the deck, pounding them like a child having a tantrum. The tips of his shoes were splintering against the wood. Gregor looked them both over and went for Mark Anderwahl's ankles. That seemed to Gregor to be his mission on this trip: to go for people's ankles.

Gregor Demarkian was fifty-six years old, tall and broad but twenty pounds overweight and out of shape. Mark Anderwahl was a well-muscled young man in his thirties with a membership in a fashionable gym. It didn't matter. Mark was an amateur and at a positional disadvantage. Gregor jerked him loose with no trouble at all and hauled him across the deck. The action brought back to Gregor one of the primary truths of his life. He was not a physical man. He was not supposed to do things like this. He was supposed to think.

He dropped Mark Anderwahl against the inside curve of the stern and turned back to Tony Baird. Tony was sitting up and rubbing his hand against the side of his throat, still angry.

"Don't even think about it," Gregor told him. "*After* you two tell me what's going on, you can go back to killing each other. *Before* you do you can just sit right where you are. Both of you."

"He threw it overboard," Mark Anderwahl said. "He had a walkie-talkie or a radio or something and he threw it overboard."

"He's out of his mind," Tony Baird said.

"I saw him," Mark Anderwahl insisted.

The two young men were now both standing again, and instinctively squaring off. Gregor tried to interpose himself between them without letting it become too obvious that that was what he was doing. The last thing he wanted was to end up in the middle of this fight.

"You had something on you the day we arrived," Gregor said to Tony Baird. "You dropped it on the pier when Bennis Hannaford and I were coming through the fog to come on board. At the time I thought it looked like a child's walkie-talkie."

"It was probably a cigarette lighter."

"I know what a cigarette lighter looks like, Mr. Baird."

"Cigarette lighters look like anything. I've got one in the shape of a football."

"You wouldn't have tossed a cigarette lighter out to sea," Mark Anderwahl said. He turned to Gregor, appealing. "I came up on deck to look for Julie. I was just wandering around when I came back here, and there he was, standing at the side, holding his arm back like he was going to pitch a baseball. And then at the last moment I saw it. A radio."

"There was no radio," Tony said.

Mark brushed this aside. "It was like he said when I was talking to him last night before we went to bed. About how he doesn't believe Charlie Shay was really murdered and about how you only want to cause trouble. And then he said it would all be much better if the investigation took place in Massachusetts, because the Bairds had ways of protecting themselves in Massachusetts that they don't in places like Virginia and New Jersey and Delaware. We were right there in that room next to the mess hall with all the ship models in it—"

"Ship models?" Gregor was bewildered.

"Ships in bottles," Tony said. "He's very good at it."

Gregor thought of that great elaborate thing in the mess hall. "Did he do the clipper ship with the flags—"

"In the mess hall?" Tony said. "Yes, he did. He did all the ships in bottles on this boat."

"What do ships in bottles matter?" Mark Anderwahl said. "The radio, that's what matters. It doesn't matter if we've got a murder or not. We've got a dead man on this boat and my wife's sick. We've got to get help."

"You've got to get help," Tony Baird said coldly. "You need a psychiatrist, Anderwahl. And a pair of glasses."

"Why you son of a—"

Gregor thrust out his arms and pushed hard against Mark Anderwahl's chest. Then, fractions of a second before it would have been too late, he whirled around and pushed against Tony's. Tony went stumbling backward. Mark Anderwahl sat down abruptly, like a man who had been sent into shock.

"Oh, for goodness' sake," Julie said. It was the first sound she had made since all this started. "You've got to stop this, both of you. What good is it going to do to cause another death on this boat?"

The three men turned to look at her. Gregor felt vaguely surprised. He had forgotten she was here. Tony and Mark both looked astonished and ashamed of themselves, like small boys caught fighting by their mothers. They also looked distinctly resentful. *Here we are again*, their faces seemed to say, *with women coming around and spoiling all the fun.*

It was the impression of a moment. A moment later, Gregor might have imagined it. That was when Mark broke away from their circle and hurried to his wife, holding out his arms to her as if she were a child he needed to comfort.

"Julie," Gregor and Tony heard him saying. "Julie, I'm sorry."

"He probably is sorry," Tony muttered, and then, seeing that Gregor had heard him, shrugged. "I don't understand how he lives. I don't understand what he wants out of life. I don't understand what you want out of life, either. I'm going below now."

"Did you throw a radio or some kind of communicating device overboard?"

"Some kind of communicating device?" Tony smiled. "You mean like a spy phone or a laser satellite contact pencil or whatever it is James Bond is carrying around these days?"

"I mean like an emergency beeper."

Tony shrugged again. "I don't see that it matters anyway. If I did it's gone and you'll never be able to prove I had it. If I didn't, this is just a lot of fuss about nothing. I *am* going below now."

"So go."

"Maybe I'll stop in and see how Bennis is doing. At least there's one person on this boat who appreciates what I'm up against."

"If you mean Bennis, I don't believe you."

"Actually, I meant my father, but you weren't supposed to notice."

Tony turned away and nearly jogged down the deck, past the embracing Julie and Mark, toward the ladderlike staircase that led below. Gregor watched him until he disappeared, and then turned his attention to the other two.

Love and marriage were all well and good, in Gregor's

opinion. In fact, they were even better than that. The problem was, you could only indulge them so far under emergency conditions.

These, Gregor was sure, were emergency conditions. Murder always made the part of the world it touched spin a little out of control. It was that much harder when the people connected with that murder wanted to make the spin go faster and faster by the minute.

Besides, all this nonsense between Mark Anderwahl and Tony Baird made Gregor think of something.

Six

1

Mark Anderwahl was very conscious of the fact that his wife wanted him to talk to Gregor Demarkian about the things they had seen and heard around the time Donald McAdam died. Once he was well away from Tony Baird and calmed down to the point where he could think again, he remembered that. He rarely remembered much when he and Tony got into fights—and down through the years, he and Tony had gotten into many fights, although most of them hadn't been physical. There was something about the idea of Tony as Heir Apparent that made Mark hot. Tony was brilliant and Tony was good-looking and Tony was brave—but Tony was also lazy as hell and spoiled rotten. Mark would never have allowed himself, or been allowed by the people around him, to indulge in Soho art galleries. He'd gone to prep school and he'd gone to college and then he'd gone to work. If he'd ever suggested he needed "time off" to "find himself," he'd have been shown the back of his mother's hand and ended up flipping burgers at the Home of the Whopper. That, his mother had told him, was the old-fashioned way. When she was growing up, rich young men were not indulged in their whimsies. They were trained to take up their responsibilities. Of course, Mark had never been a rich young man. His mother hadn't had that much and his uncles weren't the kind to pass out cash without a reason. Unlike Tony, he'd never found himself wandering around Paris at four o'clock in the morning, scared to death that the two thousand dollars in his pocket were going to get him mugged.

He smelled Julie's warm, soft skin, caught himself wondering what it would be like to make love to a girl with a spike in her ear, and stopped himself. He straightened up and looked at Demarkian, who was hanging back and half-concentrating on the state of the ocean. The state of the ocean was flat. Mark coughed.

"Mr. Demarkian?"

"Mr. Demarkian wants us to make a flare to call the Coast Guard with," Julie said.

Mark leaned closer to Julie's ear and whispered. "Aren't we going to tell him about the other thing?" he asked her. "Isn't this the perfect time?"

"I don't know."

They both looked over at Gregor Demarkian, who was looking more distracted by the second. Mark was sure Demarkian hadn't heard a word they'd said, even though they were close and they hadn't been whispering all that softly. Mark drew in his breath and coughed again.

"Mr. Demarkian?"

"Excuse me," Gregor Demarkian said, shaking his head. He gazed back at the water again and then seemed to force himself to look their way. He smiled, but the smile seemed surreal. "I'm sorry. I've got to go downstairs."

"Below," Julie said automatically.

"You can go below in a minute," Mark said, "Julie and I—"

Gregor Demarkian cut him off. "There's one thing I've been meaning to ask somebody," he said. "I don't know if you two are necessarily the ones to ask, but we'll see. This deal that Baird Financial is doing with Europabanc. It was in gear before Jon Baird was indicted on insider trading charges? Not just before he went to jail, mind you, but before he was indicted?"

"Oh, yes," Mark said. "Well before. A couple of years at least."

"A couple of years in negotiation?"

"We went into serious negotiation with Europabanc for the first time about three months before Uncle Jon was indicted."

Gregor nodded. "And Europabanc didn't mind. They didn't care they were going to get a jailbird as head of the firm."

"Of course Europabanc didn't mind," Mark said. "The charges weren't all that serious anyway—they weren't even really a felony. The only reason Jon was in jail for over a year is that the judge got exasperated and made him serve his sentences consecutively. And what he went to jail for isn't even illegal in Switzerland and France and the other places Europabanc operates. Even not paying your income taxes isn't illegal in Switzerland. They just think we're nuts."

"And when the indictment came down, there was never any suggestion that someone else at the firm might be implicated? Your Uncle Calvin, for instance?"

"If there had been, I'd have known the charges were bogus," Mark snorted. "Uncle Calvin, for God's sake. Uncle Calvin is such a tight-assed old maid, he wouldn't—"

"Mark," Julie said.

"Well, he is," Mark said stubbornly. "Mr. Demarkian only wants to know. What he should know is that the SEC and the people from Morgenthau's office came in and investigated us to death over the course of three months and didn't find a thing."

"Except for what they discovered about your Uncle Jon," Gregor pointed out.

Mark Anderwahl shook his head vigorously. "They didn't discover a thing about Uncle Jon," he insisted. "All they had on Uncle Jon was the records of four transactions through a blind account in the Cayman Islands and those were handed to them. I mean they showed up at Morgenthau's office in the mail."

"Recent transactions?" Gregor asked.

Mark shrugged. "I think so. I think they were maybe four or five months old when the investigators got hold of them. But there was no corroboration at the office, Mr. Demarkian, and there was no evidence of anybody else having been pulling any junk. We run a pretty tight ship at Baird Financial."

"Ah," Gregor Demarkian said.

Julie leaned forward. "Now we want to talk to you," she told him, and Mark nodded behind her approvingly. "We discussed it between ourselves last night and we think—"

"Excuse me," Gregor Demarkian said.

"Where are you going?" Mark Anderwahl said.

"Julie will tell you all about the flare," Gregor called back to them over his shoulder.

Mark stared after him, nonplussed. "What was that all about?" he demanded of Julie. "I thought we were going to talk to him. Didn't you tell him we had something important to say?"

"I wanted to leave it until we could tell him together," Julie said. Then she went to the rail by herself and looked out over it. It was high back here and perfectly safe. Mark found himself feeling a little relieved to see that she wasn't looking as sick as she had been.

He went up to the rail, leaned against it as close to her as he could get without actually touching her, and said, "I'm glad to see you're feeling better. If I'd known how seasick you got, I'd never have insisted we come along on this trip."

Julie blew an exasperated raspberry. "Oh, for God's sake," she said. "What's the matter with you?"

"What do you mean, what's the matter with me?" Mark was bewildered. Julie had always bewildered him, but lately she had gone past enigmatic to inscrutable. "What could possibly be the matter with me? I'm only concerned about your health."

"Mark," Julie said, "how much debt are we in?"

"No more than we can handle."

"That's not what I asked."

"I don't know," Mark told her. "A lot. There's the mortgage on the co-op for one thing, that's a pile, and then we have run up the cards a little—why are you worried about what kind of debt we're in?"

"What would happen if I quit work?" Julie demanded.

"Why would you want to quit work? Julie, you're not making any sense."

"Oh, yes, I am."

"If you quit work, we'll go bankrupt."

Julie took a deep breath. "Well," she said, "then get ready, because I'm going to quit work and I'm going to do it soon and I'm going to tell you why."

"Good," Mark said a little desperately.

"*A*," Julie held up a finger, "I have come to the conclusion that public relations is the silliest endeavor ever invented by human beings. *B*," another finger went up, "I am sick of it. And *C*—pay attention to this one here, Mark, it's the clincher—I am four and a half months pregnant and I have every damn intention of having the baby. Put all that where it'll do the most good and learn to live with it."

"Right!" Mark said in the kind of voice cheerleaders use to celebrate touchdowns. His head was spinning, his stomach was raw, and he figured he was going to be seasick himself in a minute, but he figured all that could wait until he got a hold on just what was going on here.

For some reason, he couldn't seem to make his mind think any more kind thoughts about girls with spikes in their ears.

2

From the beginning—from the very minute when she had received the invitation to spend Thanksgiving on this trip with these people—Fritzie Baird had been worried about one thing, and that was that Thanksgiving wouldn't really get celebrated at all. Of course, Jon had always had a positive obsession about the *Mayflower* and the fact that his ancestors had come over on it. Fritzie had known a lot of people who had that obsession in their lives. In Jon's case, it didn't translate into what you might expect. Jon was so cold, really, so out of touch with the emotional side of life. He wanted to spend all his time concentrating on the "deep" things. He never understood why the things he considered superficial—like pleasantry and decoration— were so important to other people. In the normal course of events, Sheila would have been expected to take care of all that. Sheila was, after all, Jon's wife. Sheila was also, after all, Sheila. That was why Fritzie had brought what she'd brought in her small suitcase—not the jewelry she would have been expected to bring (and that Sheila had undoubt- edly brought) but the makings of a real Thanksgiving holi- day. In Fritzie's mind, the makings of a real Thanksgiving holiday had nothing to do with food, except in the sense that everything in Fritzie's life had to do with food. What Fritzie wanted here and now was decoration. Her small suitcase was full of multicolored corn and ribbons and even candles.

The candles made her feel a little foolish, because there were so many candles already on the boat. The other things gave her a great sense of peace. As soon as she'd taken her turn in the makeshift shower, she went back to her cabin and got them all out. Sheila had breakfast in bed. Fritzie didn't have to worry about her. Jon was somebody Fritzie actually liked to talk to. As for the rest of them . . . Fritzie didn't care about the rest of them. They came and went. They wouldn't bother her.

She put the multicolored corn and the ribbons and the two packages of pipe cleaners in a brown paper bag and headed for the mess hall, which was the only room on the boat with a table big enough to accommodate what she wanted to do. She looked inside and found the room deserted, but the table set with food. She went in and shut the door behind her. The anachronistic, battery-operated toast warmers and samovars from the day before had not been resurrected here. There were only good china plates and sturdy wooden baskets lined with colored cloths. Still, the food was not "authentic" in any sense of the term. No one would have eaten it if it had been. The Puritans were very big on meat dried rock hard and lard. They drank a lot of liquor and fried almost everything they put into their mouths. What had been put out on the mess hall table were corn muffins and blueberry muffins and bran muffins and scones, each plate or basket flanked by a crock of butter and a crock of cheese and a small silver butter knife. It was just the kind of breakfast Jon had preferred when he was still living at home with her. It made Fritzie warm and soft inside, just to look at it.

Actually, it made Fritzie hot and pained inside just to look at it. She didn't eat butter and she didn't eat cheese— too many calories in both—and she'd given up on bread around the time that Robert Kennedy was shot. What she had for breakfast when she had breakfast was a half a grapefruit, untouched by sugar. It was good for her and it should have tasted good to her, but she had never gotten over hating it. For a while it had made her wonder if she was crazy. Then all the research about eating disorders had come out, and Fritzie had been able to relax. She was just one of those people whose psychological needs overwhelmed their physical ones entirely. She couldn't love the foods that were good for her the way normal people did because there was something wrong with her brain. If she hadn't hated therapy almost as much as she hated grapefruit, she would have gone in for it. Instead, she found herself wishing she could have a different kind of eating disorder than the one she had. She wished she could be an anorexic.

It won't hurt me if I have just one blueberry muffin, she thought to herself. I promise not to put any butter on it.

She moved tentatively away from the door, realized she was still carrying her brown paper bag full of corn, and put it down on the floor. Over the last few seconds, she had become so tense she could barely move. Every muscle in her body seemed to have been stretched out into a wire. She edged toward the table, slowly, slowly, dragging herself against some invisible undertow. She thought if she moved any faster she would leap at the plates and eat them along with anything that was on them.

She had made it halfway across the floor, inch by inch, millimeter by millimeter, when she heard the latch on the door jiggle. Fritzie froze in place, unable to breathe. The latch jiggled again and then the door opened. Fritzie looked at the plate piled high with blueberry muffins and bit her lip. Then she turned around to see who had come in behind her.

Who had come in behind her was Gregor Demarkian,

and that made Fritzie confused. Gregor Demarkian didn't know anything about her. He didn't know what a terrible pig she could be about food or how hard it was for her to have any control over her eating. If she ate the entire plate of blueberry muffins in front of him, he would think she was an ordinary person with a larger than usual appetite this morning. He wouldn't jump to condemn her. Fritzie looked back to the blueberry muffins again. Rationalizations aside, there wasn't anything she could do about the blueberry muffins. As long as Mr. Demarkian was there to watch, she couldn't allow herself to eat them.

"Well," she said, "if it isn't Mr. Demarkian. I was just going to have a cup of tea. Will you join me?"

"I take coffee," Demarkian said. "And I'm going to have a lot more than that. Would you like me to pass you a muffin of some kind?"

"No, thank you. I don't eat breakfast, as a rule." Fritzie walked determinedly to the hot water kettle, poured now tepid water into a cup over a teaball she had found beside the spoons, and sat down. Where she was was as far from the food as it was possible to get and still sit at the table, but that wasn't very far. Fritzie felt dizzy.

"Well," she said again, "I suppose you've been detecting. Trying to find out what really happened to poor old Charlie Shay."

Gregor picked up a plate, put a blueberry muffin and a bran muffin and a scone on it, then added a huge slab of butter to the mix. Then he looked around for a chair and sat down.

"I'd forgotten all about breakfast," he said. "Forgetting about food happens a lot on this boat. I say it's a terrible way to celebrate Thanksgiving."

"That's what I was doing here, trying to find a way to make the boat more festive for Thanksgiving." Fritzie waved at the brown paper bag, abandoned now in the middle of the floor. "It's full of the makings for decorations. I thought I'd put up some multicolored corn and make a cornucopia. Jon was never much for decorations. If it were up to him, all he'd have adorning his life would be things like this."

Fritzie gestured dramatically at the ship in the bottle that reposed in a niche in the wall at the back end of the table. It had been there all along, of course, but the food had driven it away from her attention. Besides, she had lived for years with Jon and his ships in bottles. Mr. Demarkian was looking at it curiously, though.

"It's very elaborate, isn't it?" Fritzie said. "Jon started doing them when he was a boy, and as far as I know it's his only form of relaxation. And practice makes perfect, you know, and he is in the way of being nearly perfect. Even the people who do this for a living admire Jon's work. I've heard them say so."

"It fits him," Gregor Demarkian said. "He didn't seem to me to be the kind of man who could have a real hobby, something he didn't mind doing half-well because it made him relax."

"He certainly wouldn't like doing anything half-well," Fritzie said. "I don't think Jon could tolerate doing anything even ninety-nine percent well. He's not like that."

Mr. Demarkian slathered his scone with butter. "I suppose that made him very different from Charlie Shay," he said. "The general consensus I get, asking around on the boat, is that Mr. Shay wasn't exactly a high performer."

The butter on Gregor Demarkian's scone was at least an inch thick. Fritzie was sure of it. It was so yellow and thick and strong, she thought she could smell it, even though she knew you couldn't smell butter unless it was cooking or until it went bad. It smelled like salt.

"Well," Fritzie said again, turning her head away. "Charlie Shay."

"Mmmm."

"Charlie Shay was sad, really. I'd known him all my married life, of course. He was a friend of Jon's from college or prep school or somewhere. And there are people who say he was better in those days, when everything first started, but he wasn't. He was always—sad."

"By sad do you mean ineffectual?"

"I don't know." Fritzie couldn't seem to remember what "ineffectual" meant. The definition had got caught up in a river of butter. "I mean he was always a gopher, as they put it these days," she said. "He was always the someone who ran errands. It wasn't as bad as it got after Jon went to prison, of course, but it was always true."

"Why 'of course'?" Gregor asked curiously. "Why should Charlie Shay have turned into more of a gopher just because Jon Baird went to jail?"

"Because Jon wasn't at the office to protect him, for one thing," Fritzie said. "But the real reason was Jon himself and the way Charlie felt about him. Charlie always idolized Jon. And once Jon went to jail, he needed a lot of help. He was stuck in that cell and he couldn't just jump up and do things by himself. So he asked Charlie to do them."

"And Charlie didn't mind," Gregor Demarkian said.

"Charlie thought the mere fact that Jon Baird asked him to do something made that something important." Fritzie smiled wanly. "Aren't you wondering how I know all this? After all, Jon and I have been divorced for a while. He's married to that woman now, although I must say I don't know for how long. Doesn't it seem odd to you that I know all this?"

"Should it?"

"It shouldn't if you really knew Charlie Shay, but you

didn't." Fritzie got up, walked slowly and deliberately to the kettle, and made herself more tea. Then she walked just as slowly and deliberately back to her chair again and sat down. "Charlie would call me up and tell me all about it. All the things Jon had asked him to do. All the errands he had run. He was so proud of it all, and so much of it was humiliating."

"What was humiliating?"

"Well," Fritzie said, "for instance, Jon made one of those ships in bottles in prison. Charlie trotted back and forth getting him all the things he needed, the glue, the string, the bottle."

"That could have been affection," Gregor pointed out. "Here was Charlie Shay's friend, in prison. Here was Charlie Shay, in a position to make that prison time pass a little more easily. After all, everything Charlie Shay was asked to do wasn't humiliating. I've been told by half a dozen people that it was Shay who delivered the final McAdam contracts to Jon Baird so that Baird could give them to Donald McAdam."

"Three copies of the contract and a stamped, self-addressed envelope to bring it all home to Baird Financial," Fritzie recited. "Yes, I know. I've heard all about how it worked. But you know, even when Charlie brought the contracts in, Jon didn't let him get any ideas about his place. It was the same day Charlie brought the contracts in that Jon made him bring in the bridge."

"The bridge?"

"Jon has this bridge for the lower left-hand side of his jaw," Fritzie said. "Because of the way it's made it's very delicate and it breaks. Jon was very worried about that when he was going into prison, so he had a spare made. And sure enough, right around the time McAdam was supposed to sign his contracts, Jon broke his bridge. So he sent Charlie Shay to get the spare and to deliver it, and Charlie never once thought what an awful thing that was for Jon to do."

"Why was it so awful?"

"Because you don't ask for that sort of thing from a business partner," Fritzie said. "That isn't how the world works. That's the kind of thing you ask from a wife."

"Was this spare bridge somewhere where his wife could have gotten hold of it? Did Jon Baird keep it in his apartment?"

"I don't know."

"I think maybe you're making too much out of Charlie Shay's feelings," Gregor said. "It's been one of the hardest things I've had to learn, but I have learned that not everybody takes offense at the same things I do. There are things I care about desperately that many people don't care about at all."

"Do you think it could have been like that?" Fritzie asked. "I don't. I don't think there's a man on earth—and I mean man, not human—who doesn't think of his pride first, even if he tries not to. I think Charlie must have been only inches away from striking Jon dead."

"Maybe so," Gregor said, "but it isn't Jon Baird who's dead. Do you think anyone would mind if I brought a couple of these back to my cabin?"

"I don't think anyone would mind at all."

Gregor Demarkian picked up a bran muffin and a corn muffin, slathered them both with butter, and gripped them both firmly in one large hand. "Well," he said, "I think I'll go off and try to find Bennis Hannaford. I haven't seen her around today."

"I'm sure she's somewhere," Fritzie said.

"I'm sure she is."

Gregor left the mess, shutting the door firmly behind him as he went, not bothering to look back to her. As soon as he was gone, Fritzie expelled a great gust of breath and stood bolt upright.

The blueberry muffins were less than a step away from where she stood. She took that step, snatched up a muffin as big as a fist, and stuffed the thing into her mouth, whole.

Then she reached for the knife and the crock of butter.

3

A few doors down the hall, in the dim light cast by the single candle lit at that end of the passage, Bennis Hannaford was returning to her cabin from her "shower." She was cold and damp and generally disgruntled. In her view it was possible to take authenticity too far, and that shower had been too far. She wanted to wrap her head in a towel and change into something made of flannel. Then she wanted to get something to eat and tell Jon Baird what she thought of him for putting them through all this nonsense. It would have been bad enough if he had really been a nut about authenticity, but he was so haphazard about it. If he had to break his own rules at every turn, he might as well install decent seagoing plumbing.

She had left the cabin door unlocked, so she let herself in without difficulty. She saw Gregor's dirty clothes lying in a heap on the chair and decided he'd been back to change. Then she went to her suitcase, found a honey cake neither she nor Gregor had devoured the night before, stuffed it into her mouth, and started rooting around for her best Campbell plaid robe. She was just unwinding it from a tangle of shoes and silk blouses when she saw what she thought was the FBI file on the death of Donald McAdam lying in the middle of her bunk. What made her go for it, she would never know. She had read it thoroughly the night before. She had no interest in reading it again. She just walked over to the bunk and picked it up.

She had been holding it in her hands for quite some time when she realized what was wrong. The top page of it was the title page, just as it was supposed to be, but instead of reading "AGENT REPORT: MCADAM, DONALD" as it was supposed to do, it said something Bennis could barely comprehend at all.

It said, "AGENT REPORT: FEDERAL BUREAU OF INVESTIGATION, BACKGROUND. "GREGOR DEMARKIAN."

Seven

1

During the long course of his career, Gregor Demarkian had known many men who broke the rules and reveled in it. There had been Jack Hartnell in the San Francisco office, who had had about as much use for the exclusionary rule as Santa Claus had for the Grinch who stole Christmas. Jack was always sneaking into hotel rooms and picking people's pockets—although what good it had done him, Gregor never knew. Jack investigated organized crime and didn't seem to get very far with it. Then there was Michael DeVere in the Tulsa office, who felt that a talent for cat burglary was necessary for the investigation of interstate fraud. Michael didn't seem to get very far, either, but Gregor had once seen him go six stories up the side of a building on suction cups. Best of all, there was good old J. Edgar Hoover himself—a man about whom, Gregor was sure, the less said the better. The point was that Gregor had never been like any of these people. He had always followed the rules, and been glad of it. He knew the fine points of evidentiary discovery as well as any lawyer, and he was glad of that, too. The problem was, right at this moment, he would like to shuck the habits and convictions of a lifetime and do the one thing he really wanted to do: search Jon Baird's cabin whether he had a warrant or not.

Since he had retired from the Bureau and moved to Cavanaugh Street, Gregor had been a player in five murder investigations. In each one of these he had had the confidence of the local police and the kind of help only police could provide. Crime labs, blood tests, fingerprint identification—all that was very nice, but what you really needed a police force for was to keep the suspects in line. Stuck out here in the middle of the ocean like this, wherever the hell they were, there was no incentive for any of these people to cooperate.

Gregor came out of the dining hall, pounding along almost as steadily as if he were on land. He was still not moving as quickly, but that had more to do with the low ceiling of the passage than it did with the motion of the sea. He passed the door to his own cabin without giving it a glance, noted that the door to Tony Baird's was open and that the cabin beyond was empty, and stopped in front of Jon Baird's door. He really was exasperated beyond all measure. What he wanted to do was kick the door in and shout, "This is a raid!" at the top of his lungs. He'd never in his life done anything even remotely like that. He'd never sprung into firing position and shouted "Freeze!" either. He thought it would be good for his soul. He thought there had to be some way of getting around the fact that if he kicked at Jon Baird's door, all he'd get for it was a broken foot.

He took a deep breath, counted to ten, and waited for himself to calm down. It took less time than he'd expected, and he raised his hand to knock at the door. Just as he did, the door opened from inside and Calvin Baird came tumbling into him, looking annoyed.

"What are you doing here?" Calvin demanded, stepping

back a little. "I'd have thought you'd be off investigating something."

"I am investigating something," Gregor said.

"Oh, for God's sake."

Calvin dodged around Gregor and into the passage, leaving Gregor staring through the open door at a perfectly composed Jon Baird sitting in a wood chair. He had a robe on over what looked like silk pajamas and a towel around his neck. Gregor stepped into the cabin and shut the door behind him.

"I want to talk to you," he said.

"I don't want to talk to you," Jon Baird said pleasantly. "Why don't you give it up?"

"I'm not going to give it up. I may have to ask somebody else—your present wife, for instance—but I'm not going to give it up. I want to see your bridge."

"My *bridge*?"

There was a ship in a bottle fastened to a small occasional table at Jon Baird's side. Gregor stared at it for a moment—the things were all over the boat, it was true—and then looked away. "I want to see your bridge," he said again. "The one you're always breaking."

"Do you want to see a broken one or an intact one?"

"Do you have both?"

"Of course." Jon Baird got up and went into the inner room. When he came back he was holding what looked like a wad of tissue in his hand. He held the wad out to Gregor and smiled.

"Take a look for yourself. I broke that the first day we were aboard. I had a spare, of course."

"Do you always have a spare?"

"I make a point of it."

"Who provides you with the spares?"

"If you mean who makes them up for me—well then, my dentist, of course. If you mean who brings them to me

when I need them—" Jon Baird shrugged. "I think everybody in the family has brought me one at one point or the
other. It's a very fragile bridge. Too many teeth in too
strange an arrangement to fit the peculiarities of my jaw."

Gregor unwrapped the tissue paper and looked at the
bridge. It did look as if it would be fragile—Jon Baird must
be very vain to put up with this instead of putting up with a
set of false teeth—but other than that it was a perfectly
ordinary bridge. There was a plastic and metal understruc-
ture. There was the small row over very white teeth that
looked perfectly real. There was the small tooth that had
broken in half when the bridge had broken, looking like the
hollow shell of a fake pearl. Gregor passed the bridge back.

"Is that always where it breaks?" he asked. "Right in the
middle of that tooth?"

"No. Sometimes it breaks in the tooth to the back of that
one. Do you really think this makes a difference?"

Gregor put his hands in his pockets. "When Donald
McAdam came to see you at Danbury on the day he died,
did you see him alone?"

"No. Calvin was there every minute, at least, and the
lawyers. I wouldn't have been allowed to see him alone in
any case. Danbury is a cakewalk, but it's not that much of a
cakewalk."

"Did you give him the contracts yourself?"

"No. The lawyers gave them to each of us. Then when it
was over we passed them all down to McAdam and he took
them home."

"They were signed?"

"Oh, yes. By me, of course."

"But not by McAdam."

"No. I decided to go in for a little insurance. It's almost
impossible to sue on the basis of undue influence if you've
been allowed to take a set of contracts home to look them
over. That's what I made him do."

"But you'd had the contracts yourself, on your own, for at least overnight?"

"Oh, yes. I'd had the whole package. Charlie Shay brought it to me."

"And what was in that package?"

Jon Baird cocked his head. "Why bother to ask me? Why not ask Mark or Julie or one of the secretaries—one of the secretaries especially. It's the kind of thing they know. And it's hardly a secret. The package consisted of three copies of the contract, a stamped envelope addressed to Baird Financial, the descriptive sheets outlining the exact nature and extent of the McAdam corporation holdings as of the previous Friday, a standard set of currency conversion tables, also valid as of the previous Friday, for anyone who had to work through the foreign holdings and didn't know how to do that, a set of legal waivers for everything on earth, and a check for twelve million five hundred thousand dollars, as per agreement."

"You gave Donald McAdam the check before he had even signed the contracts?"

"Of course we didn't give him the check. It went into the file. For exactly the same reason and in exactly the same way that your binder check goes into a file when you make an offer for some real estate."

Gregor considered. "What happened to that check after Donald McAdam died?"

"Absolutely nothing. It stayed in the file. It's still in the file. If we ever come across an heir, we'll hand it over. If we don't and the time limit runs out, we'll hand it over to the state of New York."

"Mmm," Gregor said.

"This is idiotic," Jon Baird told him. "You must know these questions make no sense. If you weren't so insistent on turning poor Charlie's death into something it isn't, you wouldn't get caught up in this sort of foolishness."

"Maybe I wouldn't," Gregor said pleasantly.

Jon Baird looked at him suspiciously, but Gregor wasn't worried about that. He knew there was nothing to see. He backed toward the door again, opened it up, and stepped into the passage. The passage was still narrow and the ceiling was still low, but all of a sudden he felt much less claustrophobic than he had been feeling. The boat, in fact, no longer felt like a prison at all. It was just a very small place.

Jon Baird looked like he was about to say something, and then changed his mind. He came to the door and shut it firmly in Gregor's face. Gregor looked at the polished wood and then turned away, heading for the staircase and the deck above. Claustrophobic or not, he did feel like a bad-minton birdie on the *Pilgrimage Green*. First bounce this way. Then bounce that way. Never a third way to bounce. It was maddening.

Halfway down the hall, right in Gregor's path, a cabin door opened. If Gregor had been paying attention, he would have noticed that it was his own cabin. Instead, the first thing he noticed was a hand on his wrist and Bennis's voice hissing loudly into the silent air. "Gregor, quick, get in here. I have something to show you."

If Bennis Hannaford's life ever depended on her calling not even the slightest bit of attention to herself, she would be dead.

2

The FBI report was lying on the seat of the chair where Gregor had found Bennis when he came in the night be-fore. When he first saw it, Gregor made the same mistake Bennis had made when she first saw it lying on the bunk. He thought it was the FBI file on the death of Donald McAdam.

His eyes went over it without pausing and then surveyed the rest of the room. He noticed that Bennis had made up the bunk and neatly folded their clothes into piles. Then Bennis tugged at his wrist again, and waved the file in his face.

"Will you look at this?" she demanded. "I found it in here when I came back from my shower. It isn't what you think it is."

"What is it?"

"Here."

Gregor took the file, read the title—"AGENT REPORT: FEDERAL BUREAU OF INVESTIGATION, BACKGROUND. GREGOR DEMARKIAN"—and flushed. Then he turned quickly to the second page, found what he'd been hoping for, and relaxed. He handed the file back to Bennis.

"Don't lose that," he said. "There's a little string of numbers on the back of the title page that tell anyone who can read them where that came from. When we finally get off this boat, we can get somebody fired."

"Get somebody fired," Bennis repeated. "Gregor, for God's sake, doesn't it bother you? Doesn't it bother you that somebody had this? Don't you wonder how it got here?"

"No to both questions," Gregor said. "In the first place, I know who had it. Jon Baird had it. He's the only one who could have gotten hold of it and getting hold of it fits his personality. In the second place, I know who put it here, and that's Sheila Baird. Tony, Jon, and Calvin wouldn't have put it here at all. Julie, Mark, and Fritzie would have knocked on my door and handed it over in person. What else would you like to know?"

Bennis sat down in the chair. "I'd like to know what's going on around here," she demanded. "I mean, this thing shows up in our cabin, all marked over with yellow highlighter—"

"Is it?" Gregor took the file back again and flipped through it. It was definitely marked over with yellow highlighter. He read, "'*Demarkian's strengths are in determining complex series of transactions over short periods of time*'—that's Bureauese for I'm good at figuring out what happened when and in what order when the times are tight. That's true enough. Here we go again. '*He has particular expertise in the uses and effects of common poisons.*' Well, I can do what I do with a lot more than common poisons. This is a second-tier evaluation report. I had no idea I was so well thought of in the Bureau. Would you like this back?"

"What's a second-tier evaluation report?"

"It's what you get when you ask the Bureau what one of its agents is best capable of doing. You get it for former agents, too, if you have a good reason for asking. One of the police forces I've been of aid to over the last two years must have put in a request and got this. Or an excerpt from this. The Bureau wouldn't have handed over the whole file. Jon Baird must have very good connections. I wonder if he knows someone in the White House."

"Your birthday isn't in it," Bennis said. She took the report back, turned it over in her hands, and put it down on the floor. "You look different somehow. Calmer. I've been driving myself crazy with all this business of being becalmed."

"I was driving myself crazy yesterday," Gregor said, "but I finally got it worked out this morning. Remember how I told you last night that I knew who had killed Charlie Shay?"

"I remember."

"Well, now I know I can prove it—or if I can't prove it in the case of Charlie Shay, I can at least prove it in the case of Donald McAdam, which will do just as well."

"Are you serious?"

"Of course."

"The same person who killed Charlie Shay killed Donald McAdam?"

Gregor was impatient. "What did you expect?" he demanded. "That the New York financial community is awash in homicidal maniacs? Of course the same person killed both those men. It was even done in the same way."

"With strychnine."

"With sleight of hand," Gregor told her. "Think about what happened to Charlie Shay. He must have been fed that strychnine at dinner last night, in the salad and not the salad dressing—"

"But—"

"But I said he must have been fed ipecac, too. And he was. Also in the salad, not the salad dressing, because the salad dressing was being passed back and forth across the table in no particular order. On the other hand, there were at least three people capable of doctoring the salad— Julie Anderwahl, who was sitting beside him, Jon Baird, who was sitting across from him, and me."

"Julie Anderwahl saw Donald McAdam on the day he died," Bennis said slowly. "He was in her office. It's in that report we were reading. But that was earlier in the day. The times don't make sense."

"They make even less sense for Jon Baird," Gregor said. "After all, the man not only saw McAdam in the morning, he saw him in jail—and I don't care how lax Danbury is, they wouldn't have allowed a vial of strychnine to get into a prisoner's cell if they'd known anything at all about it."

"You mean neither of the people who could have killed Charlie Shay could have killed Donald McAdam?"

"No," Gregor said, "I mean you shouldn't give up on the obvious so easily. What has Baird Financial just done?"

"Made a deal with Europabanc," Bennis said dutifully.

"No. That's what it's about to do. What has it just *done*?"

"Oh. Well, I guess the last big thing was selling off those junk bonds that belonged to McAdam's investment company."

"That's right," Gregor said. "And they made a few hundred million, and the firm is now awash in cash. What have we been hearing from Calvin Baird ever since we got on the boat?"

Bennis was sitting up a little straighter. "I see," she said. "He's been talking about discrepancies in the cash flow reports for the time of the original Europabanc offer—but Gregor, that doesn't make any sense."

"Of course it does," Gregor said. "Baird Financial wanted to merge with Europabanc, which in this case meant that they wanted to buy it. Unfortunately, they didn't actually have the money to buy it. Everybody has told me that. Mark Anderwahl came right out and said it to me at dinner last night, before all the mess started. Baird Financial didn't have the money, so somebody faked the cash-on-hand reports to make it look like they did. That didn't matter once the formal preagreements were signed, but at that point what would matter was actually having the cash. Where do you think they were going to get it?"

"From selling the junk bond portfolio McAdam had put together?"

"Exactly," Gregor said. "It was a good portfolio, right?"

"It was a great portfolio," Bennis said. "A least four emerging companies that look like first-class winners in the next decade and all for issues with stock conversion provisions—good Lord, everybody wanted those things."

"Not exactly," Gregor said. "They didn't want them if they would benefit McAdam."

Bennis protested. "They would have eventually, Gregor. Money is money."

"Eventually wasn't good enough," Gregor pointed out. "They're going to close on the Europabanc deal—when? Right after we get back from this trip?"

"Around Christmas or just after."

"Fine. So Baird Financial had to have the cash on hand

by then. Before it could do that it had to get rid of McAdam. It had managed to get rid of him to the extent of paying him off, but from what I've heard that hadn't made people happy, either. If McAdam hadn't died—"

"It might have taken months to put that auction together," Bennis said. "I see what you mean. You might be right."

"I might be wrong, but I'll bet you this. Nobody at Baird Financial was going to take the risk that a Donald McAdam with an executed golden parachute was going to be looked on any more kindly by his enemies than a Donald McAdam without one."

"So, in order to make sure that the money was in place to do the Europabanc deal, someone at Baird Financial murdered Donald McAdam."

"Right. Now, think about this. If you knew you were going to kill Donald McAdam, why would it be necessary to execute the gold parachute agreement? Why bother with that part of it at all? Why not just kill the man and get it over with?"

Bennis looked confused. "I don't know. I—maybe it wasn't the same person. Maybe Jon Baird wanted to give McAdam the golden parachute, and somebody else, Calvin Baird maybe, wanted to kill him, only Calvin couldn't come right out and tell Jon that he was going to off McAdam—"

"Why not just kill him before the contracts were handed over? Why wait until the last minute?"

"I don't know." Bennis looked dispirited.

Gregor moved away from where he had been standing, leaning up against the side of the bunk. There seemed to be a little more motion under them now than there had been. Over their heads, men were calling to each other in tight and urgent voices. Other men—it might have been women, too, it was hard to tell—were running. Gregor heard a pounding of footsteps that sounded like large hailstones hitting against a roof.

"I think we're about to stop being becalmed," he said. "Is that what all this activity sounds like to you?"

"I don't know," Bennis told him. She walked past him, climbed into the bunk, and looked out the porthole there. She pulled back, shaking her head. "There's a little more motion to the sea," she reported, "but I don't see it's all that much different than it has been. I don't know what's going on up above. Maybe we ought to go and see."

"Maybe we should."

"Maybe if I think about this a little longer, I'll get it all straightened out in my head." She climbed all the way out of the bunk, fixed her clothes, and went back to her chair. Instead of sitting down in it, she brushed off the seat in that unconsciously neat way she had and then walked over to the locker to get her jacket. Her hair no longer seemed as wet as it had when Gregor had first come into the cabin, but it still looked slick. Gregor found himself wondering why he always liked it best when Bennis looked a mess. Bennis looking perfect made him uncomfortable.

"Ready?" he asked her.

"Absolutely," she said.

"Put something on your head," he told her. "Your hair's wet. You're going to give yourself a sore throat."

"I never get a sore throat," Bennis said.

She brushed past him, out into the passage. He came out behind her just as a pair of legs disappeared up the staircase to the deck above. He made a mental note that they looked like Sheila Baird's legs and then ushered Bennis formally down the passage. It was the sort of thing he had no idea if she liked but that he was too used to doing to give up.

Bennis had her foot on the bottom step of the staircase when the shouting started—and the screaming, too, because after the first startled "Hey! What are you doing!" the next thing they heard was definitely a woman's shriek. Bennis spun around to him in alarm and grabbed him by the lapels.

"Come on," she said. "It's sounds like someone else is getting murdered."

"They're not," Gregor said calmly.

"How can you possibly know? Can't you hear that screaming? We've got to hurry."

"I've been hurrying ever since I got here. I'm through. The screaming is only Fritzie Baird, having hysterics."

"But Gregor—"

"But Gregor nothing," Gregor said. Bennis was still blocking his way on the stairs. He lifted her out of the way and started up himself. "Do you know what that is you hear? That's the—wait. Listen to the splash."

There was a splash. There was a very loud splash. Somebody above them yelled, "Man overboard!"

"Corpse overboard," Gregor said wearily. "That's Charlie Shay, being tossed to the sharks by Jon or Tony Baird, it doesn't matter which. And don't tell me I ought to go up there and dive in after it, because I can't swim very well and Charlie Shay's pockets are probably stuffed full of rocks. Let's go upstairs and get hold of our murderer."

Bennis grabbed his calf, firmly and painfully. "Gregor," she said, "just last night you went to no end of trouble to make sure that corpse stayed on this boat."

"I know."

"Now you're telling me the corpse is no longer on the boat and you don't care?"

"I think it's too bad for Charlie Shay. It doesn't matter."

"But Gregor—"

"Besides," Gregor said, "I've been chasing that thing from one end of this ship to the other, and I'm sick of it."

Part Three

Finis

One

1

Calvin Baird had never been under any delusions that he was a respected man. As a child he had been something of a joke—Jon Baird's not so bright, not so sharp younger brother—and as an adult he had survived mainly through protective coloration. Fortunately, he was equipped with all the necessary acoutrements of camouflage. He could have had a body that matched what he imagined his soul to be. Instead, to people he didn't know, he appeared positively aristocratic, the epitome of the Eastern seaboard Brahmin, the ultimate representative of WASP superiority. It was an impression he used to good effect when he was among strangers. He could go into a charity ball or a White House task force on the problem of the moment and be reported out as a paragon. It was only among people he did know that he had trouble—and now, of course, he was definitely among people he knew. He couldn't get away from them. Calvin Baird hated a great many things about boat trips like this one, whether provided with decent plumbing or not, but what he hated most was his forced proximity to all the people who knew him too well. He couldn't even fall back on his position in the firm. Here, he didn't have a position in the firm. He was supposed to be family. He had only one thing to be thankful for in this situation. He had just asked his latest wife for a divorce, and because of that he hadn't had to put up with her presence on this boat. Since the younger of his two stepdaughters was coming out this year at the Grosvenor, which took place on the day after Thanksgiving, he wouldn't have had to put up with her in any case.

Since what he did have to put up with was intolerable, Calvin had decided, this morning, not to fight with the "shower." He knew all about that "shower," and he didn't think it was worth it. They were supposed to have an "authentic" Thanksgiving when they got to Candle Island, but Calvin knew all about that, too. There was indeed an authentic Puritan cabin there, taken apart stick by stick from its place at the center of a small town in Massachusetts and reassembled where Jon thought it would do the most good. It had roughly planed log walls and a big black stove for heat and an outhouse in the trees out back. Jon always told his guests it was the only building on the island. It wasn't. On the other side, where the coast was too rocky to allow for any approach by sea, there was another cabin. It was also log, but it had come from Rocky Mountain Log Homes and been assembled by a first-class builder. It had six bathrooms, including one with a Jacuzzi for four. Calvin thought he could wait to get there before he cleaned up, especially since he knew that getting there wouldn't take them long.

What he couldn't wait for was to clean up these numbers. In spite of the fact that nobody else seemed to care, Calvin could not force himself to abandon the effort. He had the papers he had been going over with Jon stacked up in his cabin. He'd gotten up once or twice in the night to look them over again. Now, with sunlight streaming thinly through his porthole, he picked them up again and looked at the sheet at the top of the stack. It wasn't a particularly important sheet, no more important than the sheets underneath it. It offended him anyway.

Calvin had a brass carriage clock sitting in a hollow on the table next to the chair next to his door. It was the same brass carriage clock he had on his desk in his office in New York. He had bought it through the Tiffany's catalog nearly a dozen years ago and took it everywhere. It said nine forty-five—nearly an hour since the expedition to the showers had started—and Calvin found that satisfactory. By now, those who had been at the head of the line ought to be back upstairs. That included Bennis Hannaford, whom Calvin did not want to see, and probably Jon, whom he did. It was hard to tell, with Jon. He might have been excruciatingly polite, which would mean he would still be at the "showers," waiting his turn, determined to go last. He might have taken charge and insisted on his own priorities, which meant he would have been the first one through. Given the way Jon had been behaving on this trip, Calvin picked the prize behind door number two.

He tucked the papers under his arm and let himself out into the passageway. He saw Tony Baird come storming down from the main deck and go on storming to the deck below. He saw Bennis Hannaford come up a moment later and let herself into her own cabin. Everything looked normal. Calvin went down the passage to the door to Jon's cabin and knocked. He was disappointed when his knock was answered by Sheila, who looked bleary-eyed and resentful.

"I don't know where he is," she told him, without waiting for him to speak. "He's not here."

Then she slammed the door in his face.

Calvin looked down at the papers in his hand and frowned. A door opened back along the passage and Fritzie Baird came out of the mess hall. The mess hall seemed like a good idea. Even Jon had to eat. Calvin decided to go there.

He walked up to the mess hall door, opened it, and looked inside. It was empty, but there was a pile of corn muffins on the table. There was also a scattered collection of plates, covered with crumbs, as if almost everybody else on the boat had been in and had breakfast before him. Then there were the mason jars, three or four of them, nestled now in a pile of not-so-artfully arranged corn husks. None of the mason jars was open, and Calvin wasn't surprised. Like most of the people connected in one way or another with Jon Baird during Jon's long marriage to Fritzie, Calvin had received his share of Fritzie's special gift marmalades. He'd eaten his share, too. He wasn't likely to volunteer for an assignment like that again.

Calvin went into the mess hall, leaving the door swinging open behind him—a really bad idea on a boat, he knew that, he could just never make himself remember—and approached the food. It wasn't Thanksgiving breakfast food, if there was such a thing, but then Calvin could never keep the details of holidays straight. He looked over the table and saw that the butter was almost entirely gone. What was left of it looked strangely arranged in the crocks. If he hadn't known it was insane, he would have said that someone had been eating the stuff with a spoon.

Calvin put his papers down, picked up a corn muffin, and used one of the clean knives to put what little butter there was left on it. He had finished just about half of it when he heard footsteps in the passage that seemed to be coming his way. He looked up, hoping to see Jon, and saw Mark Anderwahl instead. Mark was moving much too fast to be intending to stop, but once he saw Calvin he seemed to change his mind. He had gone a little past the mess hall door. He stopped, backed up, and stuck his head inside.

"Do you know where I could find some baking soda?" he asked Calvin.

Calvin blinked. He hadn't expected anyone else to have

spent a sleepless night over the discrepancies in the cash-on-hand reports for better than a year ago, but—baking soda? Mark Anderwahl looked flushed and upset.

"I suppose they have baking soda in the kitchen," Calvin said. "What do you need baking soda for?"

"I have to make flares."

"Flares?"

"Flares," Mark Anderwahl repeated. "We've got to call the Coast Guard some way. We can't go along the way we have been."

Calvin Baird frowned. He hadn't been paying much attention to what had been going on. He hadn't been close to Charlie Shay, and he hadn't needed to be convinced that Jon's theory was absolutely right. Charlie had had a fit of apoplexy, an aneurism, or a respiratory convulsion. Gregor Demarkian was just being annoying by insisting on calling it death by strychnine, which was something that would turn out not to be true. Calvin had never put too much stock in detectives, even in famous ones. What was a detective but a glorified police officer, and what was a police officer but a man who with worse luck would have ended up working the line at Ford? In Calvin's mind, the most important thing now was to stand behind Jon and not contradict him.

"We're not going along," he told Mark Anderwahl. "We're going to Candle Island. We can get hold of the Coast Guard or the police or whoever from there."

"It'll be hours before we get to Candle Island at least," Mark said stubbornly. "It may be a day or more. We haven't had any wind for hours. We hardly have any now."

"But it doesn't matter," Calvin insisted. "Charlie's dead. It isn't as though we had to rush him to a hospital. There's nothing to get all worked up about."

"There's Julie," Mark said.

"Julie?"

"Julie's pregnant."

"I don't understand."

Mark looked exasperated. "How can you not understand what it means to be pregnant?" he demanded. Then he turned around and began walking down the passage again, calling back over his shoulder, "I'm going to find the kitchen and get some baking soda. We need flares." He reached the stairs to the deck below, started down them, and was gone.

Calvin Baird had a very straightforward mind. He believed in doing what you were supposed to do when you were supposed to do it, which was not the same thing as believing in staying within the law. First and foremost there was loyalty to family. In this family, loyalty meant loyalty to Jon. Calvin Baird didn't believe that any of this nonsense should have a claim on his valuable attention. Charlie Shay and Mark Anderwahl and strychnine and flares were no more serious to him than the midnight creature feature shows the theaters held on Halloween. He wanted to go back to his cabin and work over his numbers one more time. He felt constrained by what he was sure he owed to the family enterprise. He did go back to his cabin—after eating a corn muffin and wishing he'd got to the food before all the other kinds were gone—but all he did there was put his papers back on the table and lock up behind himself after he left.

Then he went where he should have gone to begin with, which was straight downstairs. He should have realized. No matter how much Jon wanted to be the first one in and out of the showers, the first one cleaned and ready to take up the business of the day, he much less wanted to leave these people alone with Charlie Shay's dead body.

2

Actually, Jon Baird was not particularly worried about leaving these people alone with Charlie Shay's body. As far as he could tell, the only person who wanted to be left alone with it was Gregor Demarkian, and Gregor Demarkian was up and about, wandering around the boat somewhere. Jon had seen him leave the cabin where the corpse was kept much earlier. It was possible to see the door to that cabin from where Jon was standing only if you bent over and leaned sideways. Unlike the deck above, the passage down here was not straight. Jon spent a fair amount of his time scrunched into that position. He wanted to know what was going on. The answer turned out to be simple enough. Nothing was going on. By the time it was his turn under the water, everyone else had gone upstairs and the coast was clear.

Most of the rest of the people who had taken showers this morning had taken very short showers. The position they had to stand in and the temperature of the water were both uncomfortable. Jon almost enjoyed himself. He'd noticed as soon as he'd taken the first sip of the drink Sheila had handed him last night that the drink was drugged—with Sheila's sleeping pills, naturally, the woman had no imagination—but he'd tossed off about a third of it anyway, before he'd "lost" the rest in the cabinet drawer beside his bed. He'd thought he could use the relaxation. He'd never taken a sleeping pill before. He thought now that they were probably a mistake, at least for him. He woke up with a fuzzier head than any he'd ever gotten from a hangover.

He was just coming out of the shower when Tony came downstairs, and he wrapped the towel around his waist and waited while his son came up to him. A lot of the men he knew reveled in the fact that their sons looked exactly like them. Jon Baird didn't understand that at all. To him, Tony was an idealized form of Baird, the happiest kind of accident. Bairds were usually either tall and beautiful and stupid or short and ugly and smart. God only knew, both Calvin and their sister, Mark Anderwahl's mother, fit the "tall and beautiful and stupid" description to perfection. Tony was tall and beautiful enough for anybody, but he was also smart. He came down the passage, looked blankly at the door to the cabin where Charlie Shay's body lay, and came the rest of the way to his father.

"Look at this," he said. "He knocked a tooth loose."

"Who?" Jon asked him. "Demarkian?"

"Of course not." Tony was contemptuous. "Mark. He caught me tossing the damned radio overboard. I thought you were going to keep them down here while I got done what I had to do upstairs."

"I didn't count on your taking three quarters of an hour to find the radio. Did it work?"

"It did when we were closer to shore. I don't think it would have this far out. Better safe than sorry."

"Exactly," Jon Baird said.

Tony looked up the passage, but not all the way up. He didn't scrunch around or twist his back to get a better view. He let his line of sight be stopped by the wall. "What about the other thing?" he said. "Can I do it now? They're all wandering around in knots, muttering at each other and getting in the way."

"I've been thinking about that." Jon Baird nodded. "There are other ways between decks than just those staircases. There are the trap doors, for one thing."

"Trap doors?"

"Not really. Convenience openings to stuff food through and lines and other things you might need that would be kept in the hold and hard to get to in an emergency. I've been wondering if they'd been too small for you to fit through."

"They sound like they'd be too much of a problem if I didn't have any help. Don't things like that usually require one person below and one person above to work right?"

"Yes, they do."

"Well, then."

"Don't get upset." Jon pulled the towel more tightly around his waist. He hated talking to people when he was undressed, even women in bed. It made him feel off balance. "I was just thinking these things through," he said. "I suppose you will have to go up the stairs. Do you think you can do it without being stopped?"

"I'd like to do it without being seen."

"And make a big mystery about it?" Jon said. "No, I don't think so. We have too many mysteries around here as it is. Let it be perfectly straightforward with a perfectly straightforward explanation."

"I could get arrested."

"For what?"

Tony rocked back on his heels. He was so tall, it was difficult for Jon to see his eyes. That gave Jon an anxious moment, but only a moment. It was soon clear enough that Tony was not angry or worried, but amused. Why had he never really gotten to know this boy before? He'd thought Tony would turn out to be like his mother. Instead, he was nothing like his mother at all. Jon leaned over and checked the rest of the passage again.

"All clear," he said.

"I've got an idea," Tony said.

"What?"

Tony shook his head and went back down the passage, to the door of the cabin where Charlie Baird's body lay. He took out a skeleton key and let himself in. It was one of four skeleton keys on the boat, any one of which would have opened every door except the one to Jon Baird's private safe. That was new, not "authentic" at all, and had a combination lock. That, Jon thought, was the problem with bush league celebrities like Gregor Demarkian. They never could teach themselves to think one step ahead.

He had gone down the passage himself, past the door behind which Tony was still contemplating his "idea," and had started up the staircase to the deck above when he met Calvin coming down. Calvin was flushed and indignant and a little breathless, the way he got when someone in the office suggested he was much too fussy about where his pens were kept. It took Calvin time to work himself into a state like that. Jon wondered what had happened to upset him now.

The staircase was too narrow for two people to pass each other on it. Calvin and Jon ended up stuck facing each other and immobile. It did not seem to occur to Calvin that he had no other purpose in coming down the stairs than to find Jon.

"Go back up," Jon urged him. "I want to get into my clothes."

"You've got to hurry," Calvin said. "Mark Anderwahl is making homemade flares, and he's going to call the Coast Guard."

Jon pushed at Calvin's side, gently at first, and then harder, pressing until he got Calvin to move up the stairs. Jon followed without haste, shivering in the cool draft but not otherwise in a hurry.

"It'll take hours for Mark to make a flare," he said. "There's time for me to get into my pants."

"He was looking for baking powder," Calvin said ominously. "Or maybe it was baking soda. I don't remember. But I think he knows how to do this thing."

"I'm sure he does. I paid his way to Outward Bound myself, and it wasn't cheap." Jon had now managed to get Calvin all the way up onto the deck above. He pushed Calvin back along the passage—that was Gregor Demarkian going into his own cabin—and then climbed up into the passage himself. "It's all right," he insisted. "I really do have time to get dressed."

"I don't think you're taking this seriously," Calvin said, his face working himself up into a monumental pout. "I don't think you're even beginning to take this seriously. You haven't been the same since you came back from jail."

"No?"

"It changed you," Calvin said piously.

Jon Baird sighed. "I don't see why it should have," he said. "It was my idea to go in the first place. This is my cabin along here, Calvin, and I want to get into something warm."

Calvin blinked, offended, but Jon ignored him. He just forced his way into his own cabin and shut the door. Then he looked around and wondered where Sheila had gone and if she intended to come back.

He also wondered how Sheila had done the night before, with Tony on the agenda, but he didn't think it would ever be polite to ask either one of them. If that had been the kind of thing fathers and sons confided in each other, Jon would have told Tony not to bother.

3

Tony Baird didn't need to confide anything to anyone. Sex had never been important to him. It was more like the giant roller coaster at Palisades Park: fun to do but not really necessary to life. Secrecy wasn't important to him, either. He was firmly embedded in that generation that had shifted the focus from what it was they did to what it was they got caught doing. Since he knew that there was nothing terrible that could happen to him because of what he was about to do, he wasn't worried about doing it. It didn't even bother him that he had a fairly good idea, now, why it had to be done. He had learned it first at prep school and had it hammered home to him in college. There were no absolute standards of morality, no objective norms of behavior, no real way to tell an unchanging "right" from an unchanging "wrong." Everything was relative and connected inexorably to gender, race, and class. Since he'd hit the jackpot on all three, he had every right on earth to do what he had to do to get where he was going. One of the reasons he liked his father was that his father wasn't old-fashioned at all. His father had figured out all this stuff long before the professor who taught Tony had ever been born.

Charlie Shay's body was lying on its side under a pile of blankets. It would have been much better for everybody if he could have gotten to it the night before, but Demarkian had been asleep in the other bunk. There had to be something wrong with a man who preferred sleeping with a corpse to sleeping in the same cabin with Bennis Hannaford.

Tony got the weights he'd been carrying out of his pockets. They were lead weight sinkers for buoys, left in the hold after a less determinedly Puritan voyage God only knew how many years ago. He put the sinkers into Charlie Shay's pockets and the cuffs of his pants and his shoes. There were fewer of them than Tony wished there were, but he thought there were enough. Bodies sank, after all. They didn't float to the surface until they were puffed full of gas and rot. It would take weeks before Charlie got like that. Tony turned Charlie on his back, considered picking him up just the way he was, and decided against it. He didn't really want to touch any more dead skin than he had to. He wasn't sure he could carry Charlie around loose like that without making the sinkers fall out to the floor.

Down at the end of the passage where the makeshift showers were, there was a storage bin full of canvas and lines. Tony left Charlie where he was, went down there, and got a little of both. The passage was empty. The whole deck was empty, as far as Tony could tell. The crew must be occupied above, trying to get them moving in this awful calm. Tony didn't care about the calm. If it hadn't come up naturally, they would have had to devise something else to take its place.

He got the canvas and the line back to the cabin, went in and laid it on the floor. Then, after a little deliberation, he unfolded the canvas until it made a kind of rug on the wood deck and rolled Charlie off the bunk onto it. Charlie's body landed with a thud that was much too soft and squishy for Tony's taste. He swallowed his discomfort and wrapped Charlie firmly up in canvas, the way hospitals wrap babies and patrons in Chinese restaurants wrap moo shu pork.

When the wrapping was done, Tony took a long length of line and tied the package together. He had to wind the line around a half dozen times and was still left with something that looked like a kindergarten child had done it, but he didn't care. All that mattered was that he get the body up on the main deck without losing any of the sinkers or brushing against the skin of that face. All that mattered was that he get this over with and get it over with quickly.

He threw Charlie Shay over his shoulder like a sack of sand and made his way out into the passage. It was a tight fit but not an impossible one, and the passage was still empty. He went to the staircase and climbed to the deck above. The passage there was empty, too, and so was the final staircase up. If he had been able to do this last night he wouldn't have been so tense. The rest of them would all have been asleep and he wouldn't have had to rehearse in his head what he would say when someone came up and found him in the middle of this.

He got the corpse up to the main deck without incident, and then into the bow. He came to rest for a second against a spool of line that had been pushed into the center of the triangle by someone who should have known better. Even if you've never been on a boat before, it had to be obvious that it was dangerous to leave a spool like that where it could smash back and forth in the first rough sea. Then Tony stood up again, and flexed his legs, and wondered how Charlie Shay had ever gotten so heavy. There was still not a single person around.

"Am I going to get away with this?" he asked himself.

The answer was no. There was already activity on the deck. He would have picked it up if he hadn't been so tired. Instead, just as he lifted Charlie Shay's body into the air, someone behind him shouted, "Hey! What are you doing?" and someone else started to scream. The screaming was definitely coming from his mother, who could scream longer and louder than anyone else on earth. Tony shut all the sounds out and pitched the body as far into the sea as he could. It landed much too close to the boat with a large splash.

"Man overboard," Julie Anderwahl yelled.

Out in the water, Charlie Baird's body sank, quickly and inexorably. It took only seconds before it was completely out of sight.

"There," Tony said to the assembled company. "House-keeping completed. No need to get all worked up about wandering all over the ocean with a corpse."

It was a stupid thing to say, of course. He hadn't expected applause. He hadn't expected anything. He knew when he went to work on this project that if he completed it this morning he'd get caught, and there he was, caught, and so what? So what?

What he hadn't expected was Sheila, marching out of the crowd at him, so furious she could hardly breathe.

"You asshole," she screamed into his face. "I can't believe you let him do this to you."

Two

1

There was a warm thick wind blowing up from the south, creating a steady pressure against the masts and the lines and the little pennant that was Jon Baird's version of an official flag for the *Pilgrimage Green*. The crew was up in the rigging unfurling the sails. Gregor Demarkian stepped out onto the main deck and looked up to watch them, heedless of the fact that Bennis was behind him and in a hurry. He wasn't holding her up, exactly. She could have gone by him at any time. He knew she didn't want to go by him, because she wanted to be on the spot when whatever he did got done. Gregor went on looking at the crew in the rigging anyway. He didn't know enough about boats to know if they had truly been becalmed over the last few hours. He'd always had the impression that it was the sort of thing that happened only in deep water. Truly becalmed or manipulated into immobility, it didn't matter. It was over now. As soon as the crew got the sails into place, the *Pilgrimage Green* would be on her way to Candle Island and the state of Massachusetts.

Bennis tapped him on the shoulder.

"Are we going to go do something?" she demanded. "Or

are you going to stand here watching the sails go up all day?"

"At least one of the sails is coming down," Gregor said, because it was true. The sail on the mast in the middle—he was going to have to learn what to call these things someday; not knowing got to be frustrating—unfurled from the top like a kitchen shade. Bennis made a face at it.

"If you turn just a little to your left," she said, "you can see Calvin Baird's back. I wish I understood you, Gregor."

"You understood me fine. I just wanted—there we go."

"What?"

"The last of the sails are unraveled."

"So?"

"So there will no be no plausible way to get this boat to stop moving without saying that what you're doing is stopping this boat from moving. Mr. Jonathan Edgewick Baird can keep us here in the middle of nothing and on our way to nowhere, but he can't do it without letting us know he's doing it. Do you see what I mean?"

"No."

"Come on."

Gregor took Bennis by the wrist and began to lead her gently toward the bow. With the sails up, the boat had begun to rock again, although without the force or eccentricity of the night before. He rolled easily into it, as if he'd been walking on boats all his life. It was incredible how fast it had begun to seem natural. On the other hand, he was glad he didn't have to test it against something really violent, like a storm. The bow was only a little way up from where they had been standing, although not in the direction Bennis had indicated when she'd pointed out the body of Calvin Baird. Calvin was standing next to the piled up tables and chairs and equipment that blocked passage from the rest of the deck to the bow on the port side. They had to go through the narrow space on the starboard side, as they had been since that first morning.

Bennis came up behind him and whispered in his ear, "I was just thinking of something. *The Murder on the Orient Express.*"

"What about it?"

"Well, I just hope this isn't like that. I mean, that's the one where everybody did it, do you remember? Except they were on a train, not a boat. Well, if I'd been those people and I were on a boat and not a train, what I'd do is take Hercule Poirot and just throw him overboard."

"What would you do with Hercule Poirot's favorite sidekick?"

"Throw me over, too, I guess," Bennis said.

Gregor sighed. "Then you'd have three deaths to account for instead of one, and with the confusion about jurisdiction you'd have at least three separate law enforcement agencies looking into it, and then one of your coconspirators would break down under questioning—"

"All right," Bennis said peevishly. "For God's sake, Gregor, it was only a suggestion."

"Limit your suggestions to new magic powers for unicorns. And while you're not suggesting things, do me a favor. Block this passage."

"Why?"

"So that nobody can get out, why do you think?"

"Gregor—"

Gregor sighed again. "I am going to go in there," he said, "and behave just like your Hercule Poirot. I am going to give a presentation, and I am going to name a murderer—and I daresay the name won't come as a surprise to at least half the assembled company. Doing that sort of thing in real life has a few unfortunate side effects, one of which is that key parts of your audience have a tendency to bolt. I want you to block this little passage up so that that's nearly impossible, or at least a lot of work. Can you do that?"

"If you give me time. Do you really think Jon Baird is going to try to run off somewhere? Where would he run?"

"It's not Jon Baird who's going to try to run off somewhere," Gregor said, and then, because he really didn't have any more time, he turned away from her astonishment. If Bennis wasn't so damn convinced that she would make a wonderful amateur detective, right along the lines of one of those new hard-boiled female private eyes, she wouldn't spend so much of her time astonished.

Gregor left her standing where she was, gaping after him and not moving at all, never mind with the speed he wanted of her, and headed into the bow with a determined step. The boat was tiny. He didn't have far to go. It was just that with the way things were situated on the deck, it was hard to see into the bow until you were practically there. It might have been easier to see on the port side, but nobody ever went that way. Maybe that was why it had been blocked up. Gregor made himself go a little faster. There was no urgency at the moment, but he was ready to be finished with all of this.

He got through the passage just as Bennis got into gear, running toward the stern in search of God only knew what. Gregor trusted her. Bennis would come up with something. Gregor came up behind Julie Anderwahl, tapped her politely on the shoulder, and nodded to ask her permission to pass. She said "Oh!" and got out of his way.

Julie Anderwahl's "Oh!" attracted attention. The rest of them were strung out across the bow in a rough semicircle, facing away from him. Only Tony Baird was facing in Gregor's direction, and he wasn't looking at Gregor. He was looking at his father, a smug, self-satisfied smirk spread across his face that made Gregor feel faintly nauseated. Jon Baird was smirking back, leaning against an empty spool with his arms crossed in front of his chest. The rest of them seemed paralyzed. Even Fritzie Baird didn't look as distracted as she usually did. She was staring from her former husband to her son and back again, appalled.

It was Sheila Baird who decided to recognize Gregor's presence for real, instead of just spying on him out of the corner of her eye. She was standing very close to Tony Baird. She spun around on her heel and marched up to Gregor in a huff, not so much as glancing at her husband on the way.

"He put him up to it," Sheila said spitefully. "Don't you dare believe anything else. He put him up to it."

"He didn't put me up to anything," Tony Baird said.

Sheila ignored him. "He would never have killed Charlie otherwise. I know. I know them both. He would never—"

"But Tony didn't kill Charlie," Fritzie said, confused. "He couldn't have. He was—"

"He was sitting much too far away at dinner and you had his attention most of the time before Charlie got ill anyway," Gregor said pleasantly. "That's right, Mrs. Baird. It was Jon Baird who killed Charlie Shay. Jon Baird was the only person who could have killed Charlie Shay. Julie Anderwahl was much too sick to put both strychnine and ipecac into Charlie's salad without being noticed. That took skill. And I'd have had no reason to."

"Someone might have hired you to," Tony Baird said.

Gregor pivoted, so that he was facing Jon Baird. Jon Baird was still leaning against the spool, keeping his arms crossed on his chest. Now he looked amused.

"I could sue you for this," he said happily. "You've got no proof. You couldn't have any proof. You don't even have a body. The body just went—"

"I heard the body go," Gregor said. "It doesn't matter. You're right. I can't prove you killed Charlie Shay."

"Well, then," Jon Baird said.

"What I can do," Gregor Demarkian told him, "is prove

you killed Donald McAdam, and how, and tell any police official who might be concerned where to lay hands on the physical evidence. How about that?"

Jon Baird didn't look in the least bit worried. "When Donald McAdam died, I was in jail," he said. "Nobody knows that that was a murder anyway. And there is no physical evidence."

"Would you like to hear what I have to say?"

2

Whether Jon Baird or anyone else wanted to hear what Gregor Demarkian had to say was moot. They were going to hear it no matter how they felt about it. They were incapable of moving out of its way. Gregor had seen reactions like this before. That was why he'd never been as harsh on the people who stopped to look at accidents as some of his colleagues inevitably were. He knew the paralysis of fascination. He thought it was normal.

He moved into the middle of the group, taking over Jon Baird's place at the center of the bow's small triangle and Tony Baird's place as the center of attention. The two men yielded without protest.

"It all starts," Gregor told them, "a few years ago, at least two, when Jon Baird decided that the time had come to rival the Rothschilds. He wanted to buy a European banking conglomerate called Europabanc. He still wants that. On purely objective grounds, he could even afford it. Baird Financial had stepped in during the last serious market slump and bought a controlling interest in Donald McAdam's McAdam Investments. Part of what came along with that acquisition was a large portfolio of junk bonds that weren't really junk. Maybe I should say they were the right kind of junk. The problem was, Jon Baird could only sell those junk bonds and use the proceeds for the Europabanc deal if he either had Donald McAdam's permission—which wasn't going to happen—or if he bought McAdam out of his employment contract. Between the time Baird Financial had bought its interest in McAdam Investments and the time Jon Baird wanted to use McAdam assets for his pursuit of Europabanc, McAdam himself had become a pariah in the American financial community. He had turned state's evidence in a number of highly publicized insider trading investigations. He had tattled on his friends and caused a great many people to go to jail who would have been safe from the law otherwise. He had stirred up a great deal of enmity. According to the terms under which Baird Financial bought McAdam Investments, with Donald McAdam installed as head and virtually unfirable, McAdam Investments was no use to Jon Baird in the Europabanc deal at all. Junk bonds aren't cash. He couldn't use them in figuring his cash on hand for the initial round of mutual guarantees that started the merger. McAdam junk bonds were truly junk. Jon Baird couldn't sell them at their true value as long as Donald McAdam was still in the picture. Even if McAdam himself was willing to sell, almost nobody would be willing to buy as long as the sale benefited McAdam himself. That meant either selling the bonds at a discount—and I don't think Mr. Baird could have done that; I think he needed all the money he could get—or getting rid of McAdam. Since I've started paying attention to the facts in the McAdam case, I've heard one thing over and over again. Nobody at Baird Financial, people said, had any reason to kill Donald McAdam except pure spite or good old-fashioned hatred, because the contracts terminating McAdam's employment had been signed. McAdam was no longer a thorn in the side of the new owners of the company he himself had founded. I came to realize that that wasn't exactly true. In order to get rid of McAdam, Baird

Financial had to fork over twelve and a half million dollars, and nobody was happy about it. On several occasions people have told me that various members of the financial community were almost as upset at that twelve and a half million dollar payoff as they were about McAdam. In order to get a full field for an auction of those junk bonds, with no residual anger damping down the prices, it was much better for Donald McAdam to be dead. Not necessary, mind you, but better. And Jon Baird has always been a man who insists on perfection.

"Now we come to a difficulty. We are back a couple of years ago still, and we have a situation where Jon Baird wants Donald McAdam dead, but where of course he wants him safely dead. Safely for Jon Baird himself, that is. The problem here is the obvious one. The first thing any police department asks in a case of suspicious death is, who benefits? The facts in this case were going to be somewhat arcane, but the police would have picked up on them eventually. Who benefits most is most definitely Baird Financial. The auction from the sale of those junk bonds went off a little while ago, and I've heard it was the biggest in history. It was, therefore, a very good idea, in the first place, to make it look as if Baird Financial didn't benefit, and then that the man most likely to have the nerve and imagination to commit such a murder was definitely out of the possible run of murderers. That, I think, was vanity on the part of Jon Baird. He liked to think of himself as the only true genius of Baird Financial, and in a financial sense that might be true. In the business of day-to-day life, however, I think he has a few employees who can rival him, even ones on this boat. Never mind. The important point here is that he wanted to make sure he could not be suspected of this murder."

Jon Baird was no longer leaning against the spool. He was sitting down, with his arms still crossed on his chest and his legs stretched out in front of him. He looked awkwardly like someone not used to relaxing, but trying to.

"All this is very interesting," he said, "but I still don't see how you're going to prove it. And if you can't prove it, I still don't see why anybody ought to listen to it."

"I can't prove this part of it," Gregor admitted, "but it wouldn't be necessary to in a court of law. It's just good to get the background in, don't you think? The important point here is that you set out to commit a murder you could not be charged with—or that you thought you could not be charged with—and how you went about it was this. You got yourself arrested."

"What?" Sheila Baird said.

"He got himself arrested," Gregor repeated. "The more I heard about the case that sent Jon Baird to Danbury for fourteen months, the phonier it seemed. In the first place, it was the wrong kind of charge. The kind of insider trading Jon Baird was accused of participating in is unnecessary for anyone like Jon Baird. He can go to Paris and trade that way perfectly legally if he wants to. In the second place, it's very hard to detect and almost impossible to prove. Well, the authorities didn't detect it. They were tipped off to it, anonymously. And they didn't have to prove it, either. Jon Baird pleaded guilty with no fuss at all. The more I looked at it, the more I had to conclude that the only reason Jon Baird went to jail was because Jon Baird wanted to go to jail.

"I also noted something else. Men who go into jail do a hundred things in preparation—or at least, they do if they're middle-class, white-collar criminals with responsibilities they can't ignore even if they have just got their hands caught in the cookie jar. Jon Baird had a business to run, a wife, a son, an ex-wife, partners—and yet, in the middle of all that, what did he do? He made advance preparations in case his dental bridge should break, going so far as to have a spare made and put aside should he need to call for it. And in spite of everything else he had on his mind, when he got to jail he went to work on a very elaborate ship model in a bottle, one that took him most of his term to complete."

"But Dad's bridge does break," Tony Baird said, "and he's always made ship models. They cool him out."

"I know," Gregor agreed. "But now look at this. Jon Baird is sitting in jail with only two months to go before his release. He suddenly—and a dozen people have told me it was suddenly—decides to buy off Donald McAdam's employment contract, right now, right this minute, won't wait. Of course, he did have the Europabanc deal in the offing. He needed the cash for that. He faked his records for the preliminaries, but when the sale came he was going to have to have the cash. But look what happened with that. The auction didn't go off until well after Jon Baird had been released from prison. There was no reason on earth why the McAdam signing shouldn't have waited until Jon was back in his office. Except, of course, that he didn't want it to wait. He didn't want to be in a position to be suspected of hastening McAdam's death. After all, we were going to have to have death by strychnine here. McAdam was notorious for putting strychnine in cocaine to give himself an extra kick—courting suicide in the process—and although that was likely to be what the police believe in this case, there was no way to be sure. And as it turned out, the police didn't believe, although when they were talking for public consumption they said they did. As a matter of fact, there was no strychnine in the cocaine McAdam used the night after he saw Jon Baird in Danbury, and there wasn't any in the apartment, either."

"Ah," Jon Baird said, "I didn't know that."

This was a piece of information Gregor had gotten from the FBI report on Donald McAdam's death. He nodded at Jon Baird and said, "It's not something very many people know. I want to back up a minute now. On top of the strange timing of the McAdam signing, there was something else that was strange. That was the way the signing was set up to take place. On the night before McAdam was to come to Danbury to pick up the contracts, Charlie Shay brought Jon Baird—at Jon Baird's request—three things. One of those things was that spare bridge. Jon Baird had broken the one he'd been using. The next thing was the McAdam contracts, all three copies. That was understandable enough. Jon Baird wanted to read the contracts—and to check them against some research which had also been provided—and it might be considered safer to have all the contracts together in one place. The third thing, though, made no sense at all. The third thing Jon Baird wanted was the stamped, preaddressed envelope Donald McAdam was supposed to use to send back those contracts after he'd signed them."

Gregor shifted on his feet, wishing he could sit down. "If you look at it carefully," he told the assembled company, "everything in any way connected to that envelope comes out nonsense. Why have Donald McAdam take those contracts home and mail them in to Baird Financial? Why not have him sign them right there in the conference room at the prison or later in the day in the Baird Financial offices? When I asked Jon Baird about that, he said he was protecting himself from later being sued by McAdam on grounds of undue influence or coersion, but that's nonsense on the face of it. This wasn't a back-room meeting where fifteen men from one side and a single representative from the other are holding secret negotiations. This is a very public, highly structured process where McAdam would have been allowed to bring his own lawyers and assistants in at any time, and probably did, if we check. Why send him home with those three copies of the contract and that envelope?

"It took me a while, but it finally came to me, and then I checked the reports I had heard and the things people had said to me. Jon Baird went over a year at Danbury without breaking his bridge. He broke it the day before he was to meet with McAdam. Charlie Shay brought him the spare he had had made up before he went to prison, and the next day that one was broken as well. It's true that that particular bridge breaks easily. It broke on this boat. It's not usual, however, for a spare to break the day after an original has. In fact, if we check that out, I'll bet we'll find it's damn near unheard of."

Jon Baird chuckled. "So now what?" he said. "I was supposed to have strychnine concealed in my teeth."

"Yes," Gregor said, "that's exactly what you had. The teeth are hollow. I saw that this morning when you showed me a broken set. What you did was to tap a small hole into one of those teeth very near the gum line, fill the cavity with strychnine, and repair the hole the way you'd build a ship model, but working with wires from the inside out. It wouldn't be noticeable. It wouldn't be dangerous, either. You could wear the bridge at least for a short period of time, and a short period of time was all you needed, without having to worry about being poisoned. That inside-out method is the same one they use to repair water mains. Its the best possible way of sealing a cavity against leaks. You broke the new bridge Charlie Shay had brought for you, which was, of course, already full of strychnine. You then applied ship modeling glue to the flap of the envelope, right over the glue provided, and into this new glue you sprinkled the strychnine. You were perfectly safe. Nobody looks at the flaps of envelopes, not even when they're licking them. All you had to do was sit back and wait for Donald McAdam to lick this one. Which he did."

"How can you know he did?" Tony Baird demanded. "You're making all kinds of crazy assumptions."

"I know Donald McAdam sent that envelope and two of the three contracts back to Baird Financial on the night he died because it's the only possible explanation for the series of events immediately preceeding his death," Gregor said. "He went down to mail something. He was seen by two people. And when the police searched his apartment the next day, they found one copy of the executed contract, but not the other two, and not the envelope." Gregor swung to Jon Baird, looking him full in the face now. "That's how I can prove it, you see. Like a lot of other companies, Baird Financial keeps the envelopes with letters that deal with matters that might have a bearing on a future IRS audit. Any high-level financial payout would qualify under that definition. I think if we go into the files at Baird, we'll find Donald McAdam's contracts and that envelope, and if we analyze the glue on the envelope, we'll find traces of strychnine."

"Maybe," Jon Baird said easily. "If you find the envelope. Of course, Baird Financial is a very large company for the kind of company it is, and we have the usual high rate of turnover in support staff. Things get lost."

"This didn't get lost," Julie Anderwahl said suddenly.

The rest of them swung toward her in a body, making her blush. Mark stood just behind her, holding her by the shoulder. For the first time since all this had started, Jon Baird looked wary.

Julie grabbed Mark's hand and squeezed it tightly. "It didn't even occur to me to think about the envelope," she said, half-apologetically, half-mechanically. "Mark and I were going to tell you all about it because it was so strange. Especially after Charlie—after Charlie. It doesn't matter. When you asked about envelopes this morning, I didn't even think."

"If this isn't about the envelope, what is it about?" Jon Baird demanded. "I thought the question on the table here was whether Gregor Demarkian could send me to jail on the strength of an envelope."

"If there really is strychnine on it, he can," Mark Ander-wahl said. "Except we thought it was the contracts he was trying to get rid of. We never even considered the envelope."

"Who was trying to get rid of them?" Sheila Baird said.

"Why, Charlie Shay, of course," Julie told them. It was right after McAdam died. You know what Charlie's like— what he was like. He never stayed late at the office. Never. But maybe three or four days after McAdam died, there he was, when there wasn't anybody there but me, and he was putting something in the pile for the shredder for the next morning. But he wasn't putting something on the pile, on top of it, the way you normally would. He was lifting up a whole raft of papers and putting whatever he had under it. It was so strange. So I waited for him to leave and then I went down there myself and looked. And there were our two copies of the McAdam contracts and the envelope, and if I hadn't taken them out myself they would have been confetti in the morning."

"You took them *out?*" Jon Baird said.

"Oh, Jesus Christ," Tony Baird said.

"I didn't understand what was going on," Julie Ander-wahl said, sounding frightened. "I thought Charlie was— that he was sick or having a breakdown or something—and I took what I'd found to Mark and we talked about it and then I put them away in my safe, just in case. Just in case anybody ever needed them again, if you see what I mean. And if it turned out that it was just that nobody wanted to remember that we'd actually done a deal with McAdam now that he was dead, well, they'd be gone. I mean, after all, McAdam's estate would have had to have a copy. It wasn't as if shredding ours would be obliterating the deal."

"Damn," Jon Baird said.

"Damn nothing," Tony Baird exploded. "It's just a question of who gets to a radio first."

With that, he launched himself toward the narrow passageway out of the bow, where Bennis Hannaford had been busily piling up lines and spools and stray boxes all through Gregor's talk. That slowed him down, but it didn't stop him. What did stop him was Mark Anderwahl's flare.

"Don't you dare move another millimeter," Mark Anderwahl shouted, in his best swashbuckler-wanna-be fashion. "I'll blow you right off this boat."

He did not, of course, blow Tony Baird off this boat. He simply lit the very short fuse on his homemade flare, tossed it in Tony's direction, and stood back.

It turned out he had used a great deal more baking soda than he should have.

Epilogue

The Life of Gregor Demarkian

1

On Thanksgiving morning, there was a little old Armenian grandmother sleeping on the floor in Gregor Demarkian's living room on Cavanaugh Street, and a plump Armenian mother of three sleeping in his bathtub. The three children were in Gregor's bed, where he had not slept since coming back from the *Pilgrimage Green* four nights before, after one of the clumsiest rescues at sea he'd ever had the bad luck to witness. Maybe it was clumsy because the Coast Guard didn't really believe they needed to be rescued, merely torn away from each other's throats. The Coast Guard might even have been right. Gregor didn't know. What he did know was that Julie and Mark Anderwahl had sailed triumphantly off in a police cruiser, on their way to what a colleague of Gregor's from the Federal Bureau of Investigation called a "voluntary discovery." Gregor didn't know if that was the jargon these days or not. He just knew that the FBI man had been able to commandeer a police cruiser, and since they had come to rest in Connecticut instead of Massachusetts, had been perfectly willing to drive straight west to New York. In the old days, Gregor would have made himself sit down and figure it all out: who had jurisdiction over what, who was allowed to investigate whom. Now it seemed like a lot of peripheral nonsense. He was tired and he wanted to get home. He had forgotten all about Lida Arkmanian and Hannah Krekorian and the Society for the Support of an Independent Armenia. He had also forgotten about the refugees. If he lived to be a hundred and one, he'd never understand where the good ladies of Cavanaugh Street had found so many of them.

Getting up on Thanksgiving morning, he washed his face and brushed his teeth very quietly, so as not to wake the woman sleeping in his bathtub. Then he tiptoed through the living room, also very quietly, so as not to wake the grandmother sleeping on the floor. Then he went out to the kitchen and looked around. In at least two ways, living with all these refugees was definitely better than living alone. For one thing, his apartment was always clean. Gregor never saw the women cleaning, but they must have been at it constantly whenever he was out of sight. The world's pickiest medical doctor could have performed neurosurgery on his kitchen floor. For another thing, he was never out of food. Lida and Hannah had introduced his refugees to the American supermarket, and they had taken it to their hearts. Or their stomachs. Or somewhere. His refrigerator was crammed full of casserole dishes. His tiny pantry looked as if he'd just got the news that nuclear Armageddon was on the way. Even his kitchen table was loaded down with pastries and breads and odd fruit concoctions deemed hearty enough not to need refrigeration. It was enough to make him lose his appetite, except that he couldn't seem to stop eating.

He went into his kitchen, took a piece of halvah from a platter on the stove, and looked around. His uncomplicated jars of instant coffee had been replaced with coffee beans and a grinder—God only knew where this group got that—and they intimidated him. He'd tried for years to learn how to make decent coffee and never been able to make much more than mud. He opened the refrigerator and took out a grape leaf stuffed with rice. Then, because it was morning and breakfast is the most important part of a balanced diet, he took two large bulgar-encrusted meatballs, a chicken breast cooked in lemon and oregano, a lamb chop stuffed with dill and mint, a small sandwich with a filling made of ground chick-peas and garlic, and a bacon meat pastry made with phyllo dough. Then he sat down at the table and ate it all, thinking as he did that Elizabeth would brain him if she saw him. Elizabeth had always been very careful about what he ate. She'd known a lot about cholesterol, too, while the refugees seemed never to have heard of it.

Finishing off the food, he stood up, cleaned off in the kitchen sink, and looked around again. He needed a shower, but he couldn't have one with the lady sleeping in his bathtub. He needed a good night's sleep, too, but he wasn't going to get one as long as he had children in his bed. What was he supposed to do? He thought about staying around long enough for everybody to wake up, but decided against it. The refugees awake weren't much less disconcerting than the refugees asleep. The women flirted with him, which was all right, but the men wanted to talk politics—and Gregor didn't know anything about politics.

Gregor got hold of another piece of halvah, tiptoed back through his living room again, went a little more quickly and more noisily through his foyer, and let himself out into the hall. From far below him he could hear a clattering and a humming that could belong to only one person. He leaned over the banister and tried to catch her coming home. A second later, he did. Bennis Hannaford was bouncing jauntily up the steps, a load of newspapers in her arms. She seemed well-rested, energetic, and unruffled, just as if her apartment weren't just as full of refugees as Gregor's was. Gregor wondered if she had more nerve than he did and insisted on sleeping in her own bed while the refugees slept on the floor. Actually, knowing Bennis, that was unlikely. She had probably just gone out and bought a few extra beds.

She reached the second-floor landing and stopped in front of her own door. Then she put the newspapers down at her feet and began fumbling in her pockets for the keys. She got the key out, tried it in the door, realized the door wasn't locked in the first place—was it ever?—and blew a cheerful little raspberry. Gregor leaned over the banister a little farther and whistled.

"Bennis," he said. "Can I use your shower?"

Bennis backed up and threw back her head. "You've got to use Donna Moradanyan's shower except you can't now because Tommy is still sleeping. Mine has a teenager from Yekevan in it who insists on wearing his cowboy boots when he sleeps. Come down and visit me anyway. I've got the papers."

"I can see you have the papers."

"No, Gregor," Bennis said patiently. "I've got *the* papers. We're finally news. They've got the most god-awful picture of you coming off the *Pilgrimage Green* in Essex, looking sick and about two hundred and forty years old, but they're all calling you a genius from what I can see. Are you going to come down?"

"I guess I'd better."

"You're right you'd better," Bennis said. "Hannah and Lida and Tibor and all the rest of them will have read every word by the time we get across the street for dinner, and you're going to have to perform for a spot quiz. I'll put some coffee on."

She picked up the papers again and disappeared

through her door, leaving it just a little bit open. Gregor sighed and started down the stairs.

He didn't mind being mixed up in extracurricular murders. He even liked it, in a way. He didn't mind having a decent reputation for solving the things, either. That was part of the reward for work well done. What he did mind was the papers, and everything they represented. The Armenian-American Hercule Poirot.

He went down the stairs as quickly as he could, devising arguments against calling him an Armenian-American anything as he went.

2

From the day that she moved in, Bennis Hannaford had had more decoration in her apartment than Gregor had had in his. She had paintings from her book covers and posters from the publicity campaigns for her books and papier mâché models of all kinds of unidentifiable things that had something to do with the nonexistent world in which she spent most of her working life. Gregor found a life-size model of Devonerra, Queen of Zedalia—in full royal Zedalia ceremonial regalia, complete with blue and gold robes and a crown that seemed to be made of gold-leaf chipmunks flattened into stamps—standing in her foyer, and a small-scale model of a castle with a dragon in the moat next to her kitchen door. He also, of course, found refugees, but they were more decorously placed than the ones in his own apartment. Bennis had not gone out and bought extra beds. She had bought cots.

Bennis's refugees were sleeping just as soundly as Gregor's were. Gregor shut Bennis's door very carefully and tiptoed through the back of the living room until he could let himself into the kitchen. He found Bennis at the kitchen table with the newspapers spread out before her. For a moment, he thought she had been shortchanged on food. Her refugees didn't seem to have cooked at all. Then he looked at the floor and saw the plates of pastries stacked up there, and realized that Bennis had just cleared the decks to read.

Bennis looked up as he came in and raised a newspaper for his inspection. It was the *Philadelphia Inquirer*, and the headline on its front page just below the fold said:

"PHILADELPHIA'S MASTER DETECTIVE DOES IT AGAIN."

Below the headline was the worst picture of himself Gregor had ever seen. His eyes were drowned in bags. His cheeks looked collapsed into his gums. His shoulders were stooped. The only one in the picture who looked worse was Jon Baird, and that was because he was fighting mad. Bennis, standing on the other side of Gregor from Jon Baird, looked wonderful. Gregor took the newspaper out of her hands, folded it back up again, and put it on the table.

"I take it it's a slow news day," he said.

Bennis shrugged. "It is Thanksgiving, after all. The vice president is in the Middle East talking to the Israelis and the Arabs, but someone's always in the Middle East talking to the Israelis and the Arabs. So there you are. And you can't really complain, Gregor. You only look that tired because it took you so long to convince the police to do what you wanted them to do, and you won and you were right."

"I was right," Gregor said grudgingly. "I got a call from Steve Hartigan last night. They did find the contracts. They did find the envelope. And they did find strychnine in the glue."

"So are they going to arrest Jon Baird now, for real?"

"I don't know."

"Couldn't they at least get him for killing Charlie Shay?

I mean, that was so obvious. And Tony ought to be an accessory after the fact for tossing the body into the sea."

"But Tony did toss the body into the sea," Gregor pointed out. "So what would the police have? My statement that what I saw was strychnine poisoning? Anyone could talk a jury out of that one. There's no other available evidence. I should have thought of preserving the salad plates, because the strychnine had to have been delivered to Charlie Shay in the salad, but in all the excitement I didn't think of it—"

"You'd have had to have been fast," Bennis said drily. "By the time we got downstairs again, it had all been cleaned up."

"Had it? Well, that could be suspicious or it could not. There's no real way to tell." Gregor looked meaningfully at Bennis's coffeepot, perking away merrily on the counter, and Bennis got up to pour him a cup.

"What I can't figure out," she said, "is how you knew so soon. Right after Charlie Shay died you said you knew who killed him. Did you know?"

"You mean, did I change my mind later? No, I didn't. I thought it was Jon Baird in the beginning. I thought it was Jon Baird in the end."

"Why?"

"For a couple of reasons. In the first place, there was the problem of just what I was doing on that boat. The investigate-the-leaks explanation disintegrated in a hurry, because no one was asking me to investigate anything. It did occur to me, however, that I was observing a lot. Do you remember when we were pulling out of port and Tony Baird fell into the sea and I told you that Jon Baird had pushed him?"

"I remember," Bennis said, "I'd forgotten about that."

"I hadn't. That was when I decided that Tony Baird was willing to do anything his father wanted without waiting for an explanation, and when I began wondering what was going on, too. What was this little scene supposed to establish, after all? It was supposed to show us how easy it was for someone to fall overboard from the bow. I was Jon Baird's insurance, you see?"

"No," Bennis said.

Gregor smiled. "Think of that FBI report and the things that were outlined in it. That I was good at poisons. That I was good at unraveling situations where the times were tight or the circumstances weren't right. I was Jon Baird's best possible witness. If I said Charlie Shay fell overboard and that was it, nobody would ever bother Jon Baird about that death again. But, of course, there were other reasons."

"Like what?"

"Like the fact that, once I saw Charlie Shay die from strychnine, it wasn't very plausible to believe I was looking at a coincidence. McAdam died of strychnine. Charlie Shay died of strychnine. One person was most likely responsible for both. But if that were the case, then the one person had to be sitting on that boat with us. And that meant that that same person had not only killed Donald McAdam, but killed him after the contracts were signed. Didn't that bother you?"

"No. Why should it?"

"Because there was no point to it," Gregor insisted. "Why go to all the trouble of getting the contracts signed before you kill Donald McAdam if you are, for instance, Calvin Baird? If you're Calvin Baird, you can kill Donald McAdam any time."

"Oh, I see. But Jon Baird needed an excuse to see Donald McAdam, because he and McAdam weren't friends, and McAdam wouldn't have visited him in prison."

"Exactly. As it turned out, of course, Jon Baird had better reasons than that for setting it up the way he did, but that didn't matter. I was onto it anyway. I did have a wild idea that the bridge Jon Baird broke on the *Pilgrimage Green* might contain strychnine, too, but I should have known better. Why go to all that trouble? I got Steve Hartigan to get the police to run a check on it anyway, but there was nothing. It was clean."

"And Tony?"

Gregor shrugged. "I don't like that young man," he said. "I don't trust him, and if you ask me he's the next best thing to a psychopath. But the fact is, he didn't really do enough of anything to get caught out this time. They can't charge him with being an accessory after the fact in the murder of Charlie Shay unless they can prove there was a murder of Charlie Shay, which they can't. They could prosecute him for getting rid of the corpse, but in the long run that would turn out to be a misdemeanor. They won't bother him."

"That's too bad," Bennis said. "I didn't like him either."

Gregor raised his eyebrows. "You didn't?"

"He gave me the creeps, if you want to know the truth," Bennis said. "He was one of those men—you and Father Tibor think I'm doing dangerous stuff going out with the people I do, but at least I always pick ones who are— beneficent. Or something."

"For a while, I thought you had something of a crush on Tony Baird."

"On Tony *Baird*? Tony Baird was sleeping with his own stepmother, for God's sake, what do you take me for?"

"I take you as someone who accepts the idea that Jon Baird murdered Charlie Shay without asking why Jon Baird would want to," Gregor said, hastily changing the subject.

"Jon Baird murdered Charlie Shay because Charlie Shay did all that stuff for him around the killing of Donald McAdam and especially trying to shred the envelope and the contracts and Tony didn't do any of it because he wasn't that close to his father before this trip and he wouldn't have looked right wandering around the offices of Baird Financial. Anyone with half a brain can figure that out for himself. I want to get back to the subject. What do you mean you thought I had a crush on *Tony Baird*?"

"Bennis—"

"Sometimes, Gregor, I swear, you're so exasperating I want to kill you myself and why I shouldn't—"

"That's the doorbell," Gregor said desperately. Then he bolted out of his chair and headed for the foyer at a run.

3

In the end, Gregor Demarkian never made it to Bennis Hannaford's foyer at all, at least not then. After all, this was Cavanaugh Street. Nobody locked their doors. Nobody thought the least thing of coming right in before they'd ever been asked. Gregor was just coming through the kitchen door when Bennis's front door opened and Father Tibor Kasparian stepped in. Behind him, a seemingly endless crowd of bright refugee faces beamed beatifically. The refugees on the cots in Bennis's living room woke up and peered about. The teenage boy who had taken up residence in Bennis's bathroom came stumbling out, his cowboy boots polished to a high black and red shine. Tibor looked around at them all and threw out his arms.

"Krekor! Bennis! Just who I was hoping to see. I have a surprise for you I have been working all night to make perfect."

"Watch out," Bennis said, hissing in Gregor's ear. "This has got to be a pip."

"Do you know what it is?"

"No."

All the refugees seemed to. They sat up expectantly, as they looked from Father Tibor to Bennis and Gregor and back again. Then Father Tibor brought his hands down to his sides, raised them up again, and hummed a distinctly off-key note. It had to be an off-key note, because Father Tibor Kasparian was as tone deaf as a brass coat stand.

"Now," he said. "Listen. We have here, entertainment for after the dinner at Lida's townhouse this afternoon." Then he said a few words in Armenian, and his charges straightened up.

A very little girl in jeans and a sweatshirt stepped forward, opened her mouth and sang,

> *We gather together to ask the Lord's blessing*
> *He chastens and hastens his will to make known—*

The rest of the crowd took deep breaths simultaneously and belted out,

> *The wicked oppressing*
> *Shall cease from distressing*
> *Sing praises to His name*
> *He forgets not his own.*

"What is that?" Gregor hissed into Bennis's ear, as the crowd launched into what was apparently the second verse. "What are they singing?"

"It's the 'Plymouth Song Book Hymn,'" Bennis hissed back, "except they seem to be chanting it."

"This is supposed to be a traditional WASP something for Thanksgiving?"

"Yes."

"Good God."

"They mean well, Gregor."

"I mean to go up and use Donna Moradanyan's shower," Gregor said, "and I mean to do it right now."

That was what he did do, too, smiling his way through

the crowd, practically running up the stairs until he got to the fourth floor and Donna Moradanyan's door.

Later that day, though, when all the refugees got together and sang that song at Lida's—followed, as he should have suspected, by "America the Beautiful"—Gregor stayed put to listen.

about the author

JANE HADDAM is the author of twelve Gregor Demarkian holiday mysteries. *Not a Creature Was Stirring*, the first in the series, was nominated for both an Anthony and the Mystery Writers of America's Edgar awards. *A Stillness in Bethlehem, Precious Blood, Act of Darkness, Quoth the Raven, A Great Day for the Deadly, Feast of Murder, Murder Superior, Festival of Deaths, Dear Old Dead, Bleeding Hearts*, and *Fountain of Death* are her other books. She lives in Litchfield County, Connecticut, with her husband, her son, and her cat, where she is at work on a birthday mystery, *And One to Die On*.

If you enjoyed
Feast of Murder,
you will want to read
the latest Jane Haddam hardcover,
AND ONE TO DIE ON.

Here is a special preview of
AND ONE TO DIE ON,
available at your local
booksellers in March 1996.

And One to Die On
A BIRTHDAY MYSTERY
by Jane Haddam

Sometimes, she would stand in front of the mirror and stare at the lines in her face, the deep ravines spreading across her forehead, the fine webs spinning out from the corners of her eyes, the two deep gashes, like ragged cliffs, on either side of her mouth. Sometimes she would see, superimposed on this, a picture of herself at seventeen, her great dark liquid eyes staring out from under thick lashes, her mouth painted into a bow and parted, the way they all did it, then. That was a poster she was remembering, the first poster for the first movie she ever starred in. It was somewhere in this house, with a few hundred other posters, locked away from sight. She had changed a lot in this house, since she came to live here, permanently, in 1938. She had changed the curtains in the living room and the rugs in the bedroom and all the wall decorations except the ones in the foyer. She had even changed the kind of food there was in the pantry and how it was brought there. She had felt imprisoned here, those first years, but she didn't any longer. It felt perfectly natural to be living here, in a house built into the rock, hanging over the sea. It even felt safe. Lately she had been worried, as she hadn't been in decades, that her defenses had been breached.

Now it was nearly midnight on a cold day in late October, and she was coming down the broad, angled stairs to the foyer. She was moving very carefully, because at the age of ninety-nine that was the best she could do. On the wall of the stairwell, posters hung in a graduated rank, showing the exaggerated makeup and the overexpressive emotionalism of all American silent movies. TASHEBA KENT and CONRAD DARCAN in BETRAYED. TASHEBA KENT and RUDOLPH VALENTINO in DESERT NIGHTS. TASHEBA KENT and HAROLD HOLLIS in JACARANDA. There were no posters advertising a movie with Tasheba Kent and Cavender Marsh, because by the time Cavender began to star in movies, Tasheba Kent had been retired for a decade.

There was a narrow balcony to the front of the house through the French windows in the living room, and Tasheba went there, stepping out into the wind without worrying about her health. They were always warning her—Cavender, the doctors, her secretary, Miss Dart—that she could catch pneumonia at any time, but she wouldn't live like that, locked up, clutching at every additonal second of breath. She pulled one of the lighter chairs out onto the balcony and sat down on it. The house was on an island, separated by only a narrow strip of water from the coast of central Maine. She could see choppy black ocean tipped with white and the black rocks of the shore, looking sharp on the edges and entirely inhospitable.

Years ago, when she and Cav had first come here, there was no dock on the Maine side. She had bought the house in 1917 and never lived in it. She and Cav had had to build the dock and buy the boat the first of the grocery men used. They had had to make arrangements for the *Los Angeles Times* to be flown in and for their favorite foods, like caviar and pâté, to be shipped up from New York. They had caused a lot of fuss, then, when they were supposed to want to hide, and Tash knew that subconsciously they had done it all on purpose.

Tash put her small feet up on the railing and felt the wind in her face. It was cold and wet out here and she liked it. She could hear footsteps in the foyer now, coming through the living room door, on their way to find her, but she had expected those. Cavender woke up frequently in the night. He didn't like it when he found the other side of the bed empty. He'd never liked that. That was how they had gotten into this mess to begin with. Tash wondered sometimes how their lives would have turned out if Cavender hadn't been born into a family so poor that there was only one bed for all six of the boy children.

The approaching footsteps were firm and hard-stepped. Cav had been educated in parochial schools. The nuns had taught him to pick his feet up when he walked.

"Tash?" he asked.

"There's no need to whisper," Tash said. "Geraldine Dart's fast asleep on the third floor, and there's nobody else here but us."

Cav came out on the balcony and looked around. The weather was bad, there was no question about it. The wind was sharp and cold. Any minute now, it was going to start to rain. Cav retreated a little.

"You ought to come in," he said. "It's awful out."

"I don't want to come in. I've been thinking."

"That was silly. I would think you were old enough to know better."

"I was thinking about the party. Are you sure all those people are going to come?"

"Oh, yes."

"Are you sure it's going to be all right? We haven't seen anyone for so long. We've always been so careful."

Cav came out on the balcony again. He reminded Tash of one of those Swiss story clocks, where carved wooden characters came out of swinging wooden doors, over and over again, like jacks-in-the-box in perpetual motion.

"It's been fifty years now since it all happened," Cav said seriously. "I don't think anybody cares anymore."

"I'd still feel safer if we didn't have to go through with it. Are you sure we have to go through with it?"

"Well, Tash, there are other ways of making money than selling all your memorabilia at auction, but I never learned how to go about doing them and I'm too old to start. And so are you."

"I suppose."

"Besides," Cav said. "I'll be glad to get it all out of here. It spooks me sometimes, running into my past the way I do around here. Doesn't it spook you?"

"No," Tash said thoughtfully. "I think I rather like it. In some ways, in this house, it's as if I never got old."

"You got old," Cav told her. "And so did I. And the roof needs a twenty-five-thousand-dollar repair job. And I've already had one heart attack. We need to hire a full-time nurse and you know it, just in case."

"I don't think I'll wait for 'just in case.' I think that on my hundred and third birthday, I will climb up to the widow's walk on this house, and dive off into the sea."

"Come to bed," Cav said. "We have a lot of people coming very soon. If you're not rested, you won't be able to visit with them."

Cav was right, of course. No matter how good she felt most of the time—how clear in her mind, how strong in her muscles—she was going to be one hundred years old at the end of the week, and she tired easily. She took the arm he held out to her and stood up. She looked back at the sea one more time. It wouldn't be a bad way to go, Tash thought, diving off the widow's walk. People would say it was just like her.

"Tell me something," she said. "Are you sorry we did what we did, way back then? Do you ever wish it could have turned out differently?"

"No."

"Never? Not even once?"

"Not even once. Sometimes I still find myself surprised that it worked out the way it did, that it didn't turn out worse. But I never regret it."

"And you don't think anybody cares anymore. You don't think anybody out there is still angry at us."

"There isn't anyone out there left to be angry, Tash. We've outlasted them all."

Tash let herself be helped across the living room to the foyer, across the foyer to the small cubicle elevator at the back. She came down the stairs on foot, but she never went up anymore. When she tried she just collapsed.

She sat down on the little seat in the corner of the elevator car. Cav's children. Her own sister. Aunts and uncles and nieces and nephews. Lawyers and accountants and agents and movie executives. Once everybody in the world had been angry at them. When they had first come out to the island, they'd had to keep the phone off the hook. But Cav was probably right. That was fifty years ago. Almost nobody remembered—and the people who did, like the reporter who was coming for the weekend from *Personality* magazine, thought it was romantic.

Good lord, the kind of trouble you could get yourself into, over nothing more significant than a little light adultery.

The elevator came to a bumping stop.

"Here we are," Cav said. "Let me help you up."

Tash let him help her. Cav was always desperate for proof that he was necessary to her. Tash thought the least she could do was give it to him.

Hannah Kent Graham should have let the maid pack for her. She knew that. She should have written a list of all the clothes she wanted to take, left her suitcases open on her bed, and come out into the living room to do some serious drinking. Hannah Graham almost never did any serious drinking. She almost never did any serious eating, either. What she did do was a lot of very serious surgery. Face-lifts, tummy tucks, liposuction, breast augmentation, rhinoplasty: Hannah had had them all, and some of them more than once.

She was fifty-seven years old and only five foot three, but she weighed less than ninety pounds and wore clothes more fashionable than half the starlets she saw window-shopping on Rodeo Drive. Anyplace else in the world except here in Beverly Hills, Hannah would have looked decidedly peculiar—reconstructed, not quite biological, made of cellophane skin stretched across plastic bone—but she didn't live anyplace else in the world. She didn't care what hicks in Austin, Texas, thought of her, either. She was the single most successful real estate agent in Los Angeles, and she looked it.

So far, in forty-five minutes, she had managed to pack two silk day dresses, two evening suits, and a dozen pairs of Christian Dior underwear. She was sucking on her Perrier and ice as if it were an opium teat. In a chair in a corner of the room, her latest husband—number six—was sipping a brandy and soda and trying not to laugh.

If this husband had been like the three that came before him—beach boys all, picked up in Malibu, notable only for the size of the bulges in their pants—Hannah would have been ready to brain him, but John Graham was actually a serious person. He was almost as old as Hannah herself, at least fifty, and he was a very successful lawyer. He was not, however, a divorce lawyer. Hannah was not that stupid. John handled contract negotiations and long-term development deals for movie stars who really wanted to direct.

Hannah threw a jade green evening dress into the suitbag and backed up to look it over.

"What I don't understand about all this," she said, "is why I'm going out there to attend a one hundredth birthday party for that poisonous old bitch. I mean, why do I want to bother?"

"Personally, I think you want to confront your father. Isn't that what your therapist said?"

"My therapist is a jerk. I don't even know my father. He disappeared into the sunset with that bitch when I was three months old."

"That's my point."

"She murdered my mother," Hannah said. "There isn't any other way to put it."

"Sure there is," John told her. "Especially since she was in Paris or someplace at the exact moment your mother was being killed on the Côte d'Azur. It was your father the police thought killed your mother."

"It comes to the same thing, John. That bitch drove him to it. He went away with her afterwards. He left me to be brought up by dear old Aunt Bessie, the world paradigm for the dysfunctional personality."

"There's your father again. That's it exactly. What you really want to do, whether you realize it or not, is brain your old man. I hope you aren't taking a gun along on this weekend."

"I'm thinking of taking cyanide. I also think I'm sick of therapy-speak. You know what all this is going to mean, don't you? The auction and all the rest of it? It's all going to come out again. The magazines are going to have a field day. *People. Us. Personality.* Isn't *that* going to be fun?"

"You're going to find it very good for business," John said placidly. "People are going to see you as a very romantic figure. It'll do you nothing but good, Hannah. You just watch."

The really disgusting thing, Hannah thought, was that John was probably right. The really important people wouldn't be impressed—they probably wouldn't even notice—but the second stringers would be all hot to trot. The agency would be inundated with people looking for *anything at all* in Beverly Hills for under a million dollars, who really only wanted to see her close up. If this was the kind of thing I wanted to do with my life, Hannah thought, I would have become an actress.

The jade green evening dress was much too much for a weekend on an island off the coast of Maine. Even if they dressed for dinner there, they wouldn't go in for washed silk and rhinestones. What would they go in for? Hannah put the jade green evening dress back in the closet and took out a plainer one in dark blue. Then she put that one back, too. It made her look like she weighed at least a hundred and five.

"What do you think they have to auction off?" she asked John. "Do you think they have anything of my mother's?"

"I don't know. They might."

"Aunt Bessie always said there wasn't anything of hers left after it was all over, that everything she had was in their house in France and it was never shipped back here for me to have. Maybe he kept it."

"Maybe he did."

"Would you let him, if you were her? Reminders of the murdered wife all around your house?"

"You make a lot of assumptions, Hannah. You assume she's the dominant partner in the relationship. You assume that if he has your mother's things, they must be lying around in his house."

"*Her* house. It was always her house. She bought it before she ever met him."

"Her house. Whatever. Maybe he put those things in an attic somewhere, or a basement. Maybe he keeps them locked up in a hope chest in a closet. They don't have to be where your aunt is tripping over them all the time."

"Don't remind me that she's my aunt, John. It makes me ill."

"I think you better forget about all this packing and go have something to drink. Just leave it all here for the maid to finish with in the morning, and we can sleep in the guest room."

"You only like to sleep in the guest room because there's a mirror on the ceiling."

"Sure. I like to see your bony little ass bopping up and down like a Mexican jumping bean."

Hannah made a face at him and headed out of the bedroom toward the living room. She had to go down a hall carpeted in pale grey and across an entryway of polished fieldstone. Like most houses costing over five million dollars in Beverly Hills, hers looked like the set for a TV miniseries of a Jackie Collins novel. The living room had a conversation pit with its own fireplace. It also had a twenty-two-foot-long wet bar made of teak with a brass footrail. Hannah went around to the back of this and found a bottle of Smirnoff vodka and a glass. Vodka was supposed to be better for your skin than darker liquors.

Hannah poured vodka into her glass straight and drank it down straight. It burned her throat, but it made her feel instantly better.

"You know," she said to John, who had followed her out to get a refill for himself, "maybe this won't be so terrible after all. Maybe I'll be able to create an enormous scene, big enough to cause major headlines, and then maybe I'll threaten to sue."

"Sue?"

"To stop the auction. You're good at lawsuits, John, help me think. Maybe I can claim that everything they have really belongs to my mother. Or maybe I can claim that the whole auction is a way of trading in on the name of my mother. Think about it, John. There must be something."

John filled his glass with ice and poured a double shot of brandy in it. This time, he didn't seem any more interested in mixers than Hannah was.

"Hannah," he said. "Give it up. Go to Maine. Scream and yell at your father. Tell your aunt she deserves to rot in hell. Then come home. Trust me. If you try to do anything else, you'll only get yourself in trouble."

Hannah poured herself another glass of vodka and swigged it down, the way she had the first.

"Crap," she said miserably. "You're probably right."

For Carlton Ji, journalism was not so much a career as it was a new kind of computer game, except without the computer, which suited Carlton just fine. Two of his older brothers had gone into computer work, and a third—Winston the Medical Doctor, as Carlton's mother always put it—did a lot of programming on the side. For Carlton, however, keyboards and memory banks and microchips were all a lot of fuss and nonsense. If he tried to work one of the "simple" programs his brothers were always bringing him, he ended up doing something odd to the machine, so that it shut down and wouldn't work anymore. If he tried to write his first drafts on the word processor at work, he found he couldn't get them to print out on the printer or even to come back onto the screen. They disappeared, that was all, and Carlton had learned to write his articles out in longhand instead. It was frustrating. Computers made life easier, if you knew how to use them. Carlton could see that. Besides, there wasn't a human being of any sex or color in the United States today who really believed there was any such thing as an Asian-American man who was computer illiterate.

Fortunately for Carlton Ji, his computer at *Personality* magazine had a mouse, which just needed to be picked up in the hand and moved around. It was by using the mouse that he had found out what he had found out about the death of Lilith Brayne. He didn't have anything conclusive, of course. If there had been anything definitive lying around, somebody else would have picked it up years ago. What he had was what one of his brothers called "a computer coincidence." The coincidence had been there all along, of course, but it had remained unnoticed until a computer program threw all the elements up on a screen. The trick was that the elements might never have appeared together if there hadn't been a program to force them together, because they weren't the kind of elements a human brain would ordinarily think of combining. Computers were stupid. They did exactly what you told them to do, even if it made no sense.

Carlton Ji wasn't sure what he had done to make the computer do what it did, but one day there he was, staring at a list of seemingly unrelated items on the terminal screen, and it hit him.

"FOUND AT THE SCENE," the screen flashed at him, and then:

GOLD COMPACT
GOLD KEY RING
GOLD CIGARETTE CASE
EBONY AND IVORY CIGARETTE HOLDER
BLACK FEATHER BOA
DIAMOND AND SAPPHIRE DINNER RING

Then the screen wiped itself clean and started, "TA-SHEBA KENT IN PARIS." This list was even longer than the previous one, because the researcher had keyed in everything she could find, no matter how unimportant. These included:

SILVER GREY ROLLS ROYCE WITH SILVER-PLATED TRIM
DIAMOND AND RUBY DINNER RING
BLACK BEADED EVENING DRESS
AMBER AND EBONY HOOKAH
BLACK FEATHER BOA
VIVIENNE CRI SHOES WITH RHINESTONE BUCKLES

If the black feather boa hadn't been in the same position each time—second from the bottom—Carlton might not have noticed it. But he did notice it, and when he went to the paper files to check it out, the point became downright peculiar.

"It was either the same black feather boa or an identical one," Carlton told Jasper Fein, the editor from Duluth House he was hoping to interest in a new book on the death of Lilith Brayne. Like a lot of other reporters from *Personality* magazine, and reporters from *Time* and *Newsweek* and *People*, too, Carlton's dream was to get a really spectacular book into print. The kind of thing that sold a million copies in hardcover. The kind of thing that would get his face on the cover of the *Sunday Times Magazine,* or maybe even into *Vanity Fair.* Other reporters had done it, and reporters with a lot less going for them than Carlton Ji.

"You've got to look at the pictures," Carlton told Jasper Fein, "and then you have to read the reports in order. The police in Cap d'Antibes found a black feather boa among Lilith Brayne's things just after she died. That was on Tuesday night—early Wednesday morning, really, around two-thirty or three o'clock. Then later on Wednesday morning, around ten, they interviewed Tasheba Kent in Paris, and *she* was wearing a black feather boa."

Jasper Fein shook his head. "You've lost me, Carlton. So there were two feather boas. So what?"

"So what happened to the first feather boa?"

"What *happened* to it?"

"That's right," Carlton said triumphantly. "Because after the black feather boa was seen around Tasheba Kent's neck at ten o'clock on Wednesday morning, no black feather boa was ever found in Lilith Brayne's things in the South of France again. That feather boa just disappeared without a trace."

Jasper Fein frowned. "Maybe the police just didn't consider it important. Maybe it's not listed because they didn't see any reason to list it."

"They listed a lipstick brush," Carlton objected. "They listed a pair of tweezers."

"Twice?"

"That's right, twice. Once at the scene and once again for the magistrate at the inquest."

"And the only thing that was missing was this black feather boa."

"That's right."

Jasper Fein drummed his fingers against the table-cloth. They were having lunch in the Pool Room at the

Four Seasons—not the best room in the restaurant, not the room where Jasper would have taken one of his authors who had already been on the bestseller lists, but the Four Seasons nonetheless. Carlton had no idea what lunch was going to cost, because his copy of the menu hadn't had any prices on it.

"Okay," Jasper conceded. "This is beginning to sound interesting."

Carlton Ji beamed. "It certainly sounds interesting to me," he said, "and I'm in a unique position to do something about it. I'm supposed to go up to Maine and spend four days on that godforsaken island where they live now, doing a story for the magazine."

"Love among the geriatric set?"

"I can take any angle I want, actually. My editor just thinks it's a great idea to have Tasheba Kent in the magazine. Hollywood glamour. Silent movies. Love and death. It's a natural."

"Did you say those feather boas were identical?"

"They were as far as I could tell from the photographs, and there are a lot of photographs, and most of them are pretty good. The descriptions in the police reports are identical, too."

"Hmm. It's odd, isn't it? I wonder what it's all about."

"Maybe I'll have a chance to find out when I go to Maine. Maybe I can get someone up there to talk to me."

"Maybe you can," Jasper said, "but don't be worried if you don't. They're old people now. Tasheba Kent must be, my God—"

"One hundred," Carlton said.

"Really?"

"Among the other things that are going on during this weekend I'm supposed to attend is a hundreth birthday party for Tasheba Kent."

"There's the angle for *Personality* magazine. That's the kind of thing you want to play up over there. Not all this stuff about the death of Lilith Brayne."

"To tell you the truth," Carlton said, "I'm going to have to play up the death of Lilith Brayne. My editor's going to insist on it."

Jasper Fein looked ready to ask Carlton how that could, in fact, be the truth, when Carlton had said only a few moments before that his editor would take any angle he wanted to give her. Jasper took a sip of his chablis instead, and Carlton relaxed a little. At least they understood each other. At least Jasper realized that Carlton was going to hang onto his ownership of this idea. Now they could start to talk business for real, and Carlton had a chance of ending up with what he wanted.

Carlton wasn't going to talk money now, though. He wasn't going to talk details. He was going to wait until he got back from Maine. Then he'd have more to bargain with.

BANTAM MYSTERY COLLECTION

____57258-X **THE LAST SUPPERS** Davidson • • • • • • • • • • $5.50

____56859-0 **A FAR AND DEADLY CRY** Peitso • • • • • • • • $4.99

____57235-0 **MURDER AT MONTICELLO** Brown • • • • • • • • $5.99

____29484-9 **RUFFLY SPEAKING** Conant • • • • • • • • • $4.99

____29684-1 **FEMMES FATAL** Cannell • • • • • • • • • • $4.99

____56936-8 **BLEEDING HEARTS** Haddam • • • • • • • • • $5.50

____56532-X **MORTAL MEMORY** Cook • • • • • • • • • • $5.99

____56020-4 **THE LESSON OF HER DEATH** Deaver • • • • • $5.99

____56239-8 **REST IN PIECES** Brown • • • • • • • • • • $5.50

____56537-0 **SCANDAL IN FAIR HAVEN** Hart • • • • • • • $4.99

____56272-X **ONE LAST KISS** Kelman • • • • • • • • • • $5.99

____57399-3 **A GRAVE TALENT** King • • • • • • • • • • $5.50

____57251-2 **PLAYING FOR THE ASHES** George • • • • • • • $6.50

____57172-9 **THE RED SCREAM** Walker • • • • • • • • • $5.50

____56954-6 **FAMILY STALKER** Katz • • • • • • • • • • $4.99

____56805-1 **THE CURIOUS EAT THEMSELVES** Straley • • • • • $5.50

____56840-X **THE SEDUCTION** Wallace • • • • • • • • • $5.50

____56877-9 **WILD KAT** Kijewski • • • • • • • • • • • $5.99

____56931-7 **DEATH IN THE COUNTRY** Green • • • • • • • $4.99

____56172-3 **BURNING TIME** Glass • • • • • • • • • • • $3.99

- -

Ask for these books at your local bookstore or use this page to order.

Please send me the books I have checked above. I am enclosing $_____ (add $2.50 to cover postage and handling). Send check or money order, no cash or C.O.D.'s, please.

Name _____

Address _____

City/State/Zip _____

Send order to: Bantam Books, Dept. MC, 2451 S. Wolf Rd., Des Plaines, IL 60018
Allow four to six weeks for delivery.
Prices and availability subject to change without notice.   MC 2/96

AN UNSTOPPABLE SERIAL KILLER HUNTED BY A
DETECTIVE YOU'LL NEVER FORGET...
BY AN AUTHOR YOU WON'T WANT TO FORGET...

LESLIE GLASS

BURNING TIME

A savage killer is on the loose in New York City. His calling card is a
tattoo of flames; his trail of victims leads from the scorched sands of
California to the blistering heart of Manhattan.

Only Detective April Woo can block this vicious madman's next
move. And with the help of psychiatrist Jason Frank, this NYPD
policewoman will prove that the predator she's hunting is no ordinary
killer -- but then, April Woo is no ordinary cop.

____ 56172-3 $3.99/4.99 in Canada

HANGING TIME

Amid the upscale elegance and random violence of New York's
Upper West Side, a saleswoman hangs from the chandelier of a trendy
boutique.

Once again April Woo, of the NYPD together with Dr. Jason Frank
pit themselves against a vicious killer driven by fury -- and a passion for
revenge.

____ 09712-1 $19.95/$27.95 in Canada

*Watch for the next April Woo novel, LOVING TIME, coming soon in
hardcover.*

Ask for these books at your local bookstore or use this page to order.

Please send me the books I have checked above. I am enclosing $____ (add $2.50 to
cover postage and handling). Send check or money order, no cash or C.O.D.'s, please.

Name _____

Address _____

City/State/Zip _____

Send order to: Bantam Books, Dept. MC 9, 2451 S. Wolf Rd., Des Plaines, IL 60018
Allow four to six weeks for delivery.

Prices and availability subject to change without notice.   MC 9 10/95

Enthralling tales of deception, detection, and murder from

DOROTHY CANNELL

THE WIDOWS CLUB
___27794-4 $5.50/$7.50 Canada

MUM'S THE WORD
___28686-2 $4.99/$5.99 Canada

THE THIN WOMAN
___29195-5 $4.99/$5.99 Canada

HOW TO MURDER
YOUR MOTHER-IN-LAW
___56951-1 $4.99/$6.50 Canada

HOW TO MURDER
THE MAN OF YOUR DREAMS
___07494-6 $19.95/$27.95 Canada

FEMMES FATAL
___29684-1 $4.99/$5.99 Canada
